"My toe is stuck in the faucet."

"Seriously? How is that even possible?" Gabe asked through the closed bathroom door.

"I don't know. I guess I have a fat toe. I was trying to push up the lever to let the water out, and my foot slipped and my toe went up the spout, and it won't come out," Mallory said.

"Try turning the water on high and see if the pressure causes it to release your toe."

There was the sound of splashing, grunting, and then groaning. "I think it's making it worse."

"Okay, turn off the water. Do you have any butter or oil?"

"Ah, Gabe, you're not coming in here."

"Unless you have a better idea, it looks like I am." He hoped she did have a better idea. He might've fantasized about Mallory Maitland naked but the last thing he needed right now was to have his fantasies about her come true.

PRAISE FOR DEBBIE MASON

"Debbie Mason writes romance like none other."
—FreshFiction.com

"I've never met a Debbie Mason story that I didn't enjoy."
—KeeperBookshelf.com

"I'm telling you right now, if you haven't yet read a book by Debbie Mason, you don't know what you're missing."
—RomancingtheReaders.blogspot.com

"It's not just romance. It's grief and mourning, guilt and truth, second chances and revelations."
—WrittenLoveReviews.blogspot.com

"Mason always makes me smile and touches my heart in the most unexpected and wonderful ways."
—HerdingCats-BurningSoup.com

"No one writes heartful small-town romance like Debbie Mason, and I always count the days until the next book!"
—TheManyFacesofRomance.blogspot.com

"Wow, do these books bring the feels. Deep emotion, heart-tugging romance, and a touch of suspense make them hard to put down…"
—TheRomanceDish.com

Christmas on Reindeer Road

DEBBIE MASON

A Highland Falls Novel

FOREVER
New York   Boston

Copyright © 2020 by Debbie Mazzuca
Cover design and illustration by Elizabeth Turner Stokes. Cover copyright © 2020 by Hachette Book Group, Inc.

Hachette Book Group supports the right to free expression and the value of copyright. The purpose of copyright is to encourage writers and artists to produce the creative works that enrich our culture.

The scanning, uploading, and distribution of this book without permission is a theft of the author's intellectual property. If you would like permission to use material from the book (other than for review purposes), please contact permissions@hbgusa.com. Thank you for your support of the author's rights.

Forever
Hachette Book Group
1290 Avenue of the Americas, New York, NY 10104
read-forever.com
twitter.com/readforeverpub

First Edition: September 2020

Forever is an imprint of Grand Central Publishing. The Forever name and logo are trademarks of Hachette Book Group, Inc.

The publisher is not responsible for websites (or their content) that are not owned by the publisher.

The Hachette Speakers Bureau provides a wide range of authors for speaking events. To find out more, go to www.hachettespeakersbureau.com or call (866) 376-6591.

ISBNs: 978-1-5387-1696-0 (mass market), 978-1-5387-1695-3 (ebook)

Printed in the United States of America

OPM

10 9 8 7 6 5 4 3 2 1

To my granddaughters Lilianna and Gabriella, who love Christmas as much as I do. Thank you for providing the inspiration for Teddy and for helping our family to see and to believe in the magic of the holidays. Love you to the moon and back.

Christmas on Reindeer Road

Chapter One

Mallory Maitland hummed along with the Christmas carols playing on the car's radio as she took the long way from Atlanta to Highland Falls, North Carolina, the day after Thanksgiving. Despite her best friend living there, she wasn't anxious to return to her hometown. For years, she'd done her best to avoid Highland Falls. Except now she no longer had just herself to think about.

She glanced in her rearview mirror at the sons of her late husband, Harry—Oliver and Brooks—who were no doubt silently plotting how to get back at her for ruining their lives. If they knew how difficult it had been for her to accept the job offer from Highland Falls' mayor, they might take some pleasure in today's move from the big city to the small mountain town.

Instead of blaming her and burning holes into the back of her skull with their resentful glares, they might want to take a good, long look at themselves in the rearview mirror. They were the reason she'd lost six of her seven clients at Aging Awesomely, her newly formed senior care company. They were also the reason her landlord had presented her with an eviction notice two weeks ago.

But did she tell them they were to blame? Remind them how often she'd warned them what could happen if she kept leaving her clients to meet with their overbearing principal? Or how often she'd told them that the next time they invited half the school to their apartment when she wasn't home, the building's manager would kick them out and good luck finding another one without a reference?

No. She didn't blame them or give them an I-told-you-so lecture. She wanted to but she couldn't bring herself to do it. And the reason she couldn't was because, no matter how difficult they'd made her life these past two months, she understood why they hated her and acted out. They'd needed a scapegoat for the crummy hand life had dealt them, and she was it.

Their mother, Harry's second wife, had given up her parental rights in exchange for half of Harry's fortune when Brooks was born. Mallory hadn't been around then. She'd been fifteen at the time. Harry wouldn't make the fateful decision that forever cast Mallory in the role of stepmonster until the lead-up to their wedding. He'd sent his sons to boarding school a month before the big day.

Oliver and Brooks had no idea how hard she—a woman who hated conflict—had fought to change their father's mind, and she'd never tell them. She wouldn't do anything to diminish Harry in their eyes. She'd gladly shoulder the blame to protect them. She knew what it was like to grow up feeling unwanted and unloved.

Yet despite her understanding and empathy for her teenage stepsons and the many weeks she'd spent applying every piece of parenting advice she'd gathered from podcasts, books, and friends, she'd come to the depressing conclusion that establishing a loving relationship with Oliver and Brooks was a lost cause. They'd never be a family, no matter how hard she tried or how much she wanted them to be.

Abby Everhart, her best friend, had told her not to lose hope, that love was the answer. But Mallory knew better. Love wasn't enough to guarantee a happily-ever-after. Her own experiences had proven that to her time and again. Except, deep down, beneath all the hurt and pain, beat the heart of an eternal optimist. She couldn't seem to help herself. She always looked for the bright side of life, the light at the end of the tunnel, the good in the bad.

And thinking of finding the good in the bad, she forced a smile in the rearview mirror while trying to make eye contact with Oliver and Brooks in the backseat.

Her stepsons could pass for British royals William and Harry. Almost-sixteen-year-old Oliver, with his sandy blond hair providing a curtain for his eyes, looked like William. While Brooks, with his curly ginger hair and freckles, looked like Harry—the prince, not his father.

The boys also had British accents to go along with their royal good looks, which only served to make Oliver's superior attitude sound even more superior. He had a way of making Mallory feel like a downstairs maid in an episode of *Downton Abbey*. Why on earth Harry had thought it a good idea to send the boys to boarding school in England, she'd never know.

When smiling and staring at Oliver and Brooks in the rearview mirror failed to get their attention, she cleared her throat. "Only ten minutes until we arrive in Highland Falls!" she said with fake cheer. She continued in the over-the-top upbeat voice despite the boys' chilly blue stares. "Abby checked out the house on Reindeer Road, and she says we'll love it." She actually said the house needed some TLC but the backyard was a nature lover's paradise. Since Oliver and Brooks weren't exactly fans of the great outdoors, Mallory didn't think that would help her cause.

The boys shared a mutinous glance, which made her nervous. Sometimes it felt like they could communicate telepathically, and whatever they mentally shared never boded well for her.

"Okay. I get that you guys are unhappy about the move. You've made your feelings perfectly clear. But let's be honest: you haven't exactly been happy in Atlanta either. It'll probably be easier for you to make friends in Highland Falls."

At the insulted expressions on their faces, she realized she shouldn't have implied that they didn't have friends. But it was true. They didn't. Not real friends. "I mean better friends."

They shared another look before Oliver said, "We need to use the loo."

"We're not far from...okay." She folded like an

accordion at Oliver's pointed stare. "There's a truck stop up the road."

She reached for her Christmas-spiced latte and took a restorative sip as she continued on Highway 64 with Mariah Carey singing "All I Want for Christmas Is You" on the radio. All Mallory wanted for Christmas was for Oliver and Brooks to give her a chance. To give *them* a chance.

And right then, with the smell of Christmas in her nose, the taste on her tongue, and the sound in her ears, the answer came to her. She knew exactly how to solve her stepparenting dilemma.

Love wasn't the answer; Christmas was.

She need look no further for evidence than two of her favorite childhood holiday reads: *A Christmas Carol* and *How the Grinch Stole Christmas*. The holiday changed Ebenezer Scrooge into a kind and generous man, and the Grinch's tiny heart grew three times its size that day.

But proof of the holiday's power was found not only in fiction. During World War I, soldiers on the Western Front called a cease-fire to celebrate the holiday. Surely if Christmas could change the hearts and minds of sworn enemies, it could change her stepsons' minds about her.

Her optimistic heart beat a little stronger as she turned off the highway and into the truck stop's parking lot. "Do you need me to come in with you?" she asked as she parked the car.

Oliver rolled his eyes. "I think we know how to go on our own."

"That's not what I meant. I just thought—" He shut

the passenger door on her explanation. Some days—okay, most—she wished Harry had had daughters instead of sons.

Brooks scrunched his nose as he watched his brother walk toward the red clapboard diner. "Me and Ollie are starved. Can you give us some money for crisps?" he asked, referring to potato chips.

"I gave you guys your allowance last week. Surely you haven't spent it already." The move had taken a chunk out of her nest egg, and she had to watch her pennies. But while she knew the value of a dollar and was fiscally responsible, her stepsons didn't and weren't.

"Ollie's mates needed a loan."

Needed a loan, my eye. It was probably a shakedown. As much as she wasn't thrilled to be moving back to Highland Falls, she was relieved Oliver and Brooks would be away from the influence of the juvenile delinquents they called friends. *Mates*, she corrected herself.

"All right, but this has to last until next week." She reached for her oversized brown leather satchel on the passenger seat and withdrew a ten-dollar bill for each of them from her wallet. "I'll order pizza for dinner so just buy a bag of chips. Crisps."

"Thanks." Brooks pocketed the money and took off to join Oliver, who waited for him outside the diner. When he reached his brother's side, Oliver opened the door, and both boys glanced her way. She lifted her hand to wave. Oliver shoved his brother inside.

With a sigh that came straight from her exhausted soul, Mallory picked up her latte and settled back in the driver's seat to wait for the boys. As the minutes ticked by, she glanced around the packed parking lot and decided she had time to indulge in her guilty pleasure. Nothing relaxed her more than a good love story. She credited romance novels for getting her through the past few difficult years.

She pulled up the audiobooks app on her phone and connected it to her Bluetooth. She was already three-quarters of the way through the book. She'd left off at the part where the hero was trying to sweet-talk the heroine into his bed.

Mallory couldn't believe the woman was playing hard to get. She wouldn't have to be asked twice. She'd be dragging the handsome small-town sheriff into bed. Then again, the heroine wasn't a twenty-nine-year-old widow who couldn't remember the last time she'd had sex. Sadly, now that she'd inherited two teenage boys, she didn't see any sexy times in her future. Unless she counted living vicariously through the heroines in her romance novels.

She leaned back and let the story take her away, smiling at the heroine's attempts to deny that she'd fallen in love with the hero. Mallory knew it was only a matter of time before the woman realized he was perfect for her in every way. They were meant to be. She was silently cheering the hero on when she happened to glance at her phone and was shocked to discover that Oliver and Brooks had been gone for twenty minutes.

She glanced at the diner's window but a giant blow-up Santa swaying in the breeze made it difficult to see inside. She powered down her window to stick her head out. The crisp mountain air smelled of wet leaves and wood smoke and brought back childhood memories of the holidays.

She didn't let her mind take a trip down memory lane. Like her life, it never ended happily. Instead, she focused on her stepsons. They were either making her wait on purpose or had decided to have a burger and fries at the lunch counter. She figured it was the former. Still, she couldn't see them being much longer and went to turn off her book.

All she'd need was for Oliver and Brooks to catch her unawares and overhear the story couple in the throes of passion. Besides, it wasn't like she could get caught up in the fantasy while worrying the boys would suddenly appear.

A flash of white light in her side mirror caught her eye. Midafternoon sunshine glinted off the shiny chrome grille of an SUV pulling into the truck stop. She caught sight of the blue Highland Falls police logo on the side of the vehicle as it drove by, and her shoulders tensed.

Please don't let it be him, she prayed and slid down in her seat. Only she forgot she had her latte in her hand as she did so, and her elbow hit the console, spilling Christmas-spiced coffee down the front of her white shirt.

"Son of a nutcracker!" She grimaced as the words came out of her mouth. It was a favorite made-up curse word of one of her clients. He said it so often to Mallory as she tried to help him age awesomely that she wasn't surprised it stuck.

She returned the latte to the cup holder and then reached once more for her bag, pulling out a stack of neatly cut paper towels and a purse-sized stain remover. In her job, she could never be too prepared—aging wasn't always awesome. As she dabbed at the stain with the paper towel, she looked to where the SUV had parked. This prayer, just like all the others, had gone unanswered.

The tall, dark-haired man coming around the front of the SUV wore a pair of aviators that hid the gray eyes that had mesmerized her, the hint of scruff on his chiseled jaw hiding the shallow dent in his chin that had fascinated her. But no matter the distance between them, it was obvious he filled out the navy uniform under his open brown leather jacket as magnificently as she remembered.

For one brief and shining moment last July, she'd thought the Highland Falls chief of police, Gabriel Buchanan, could be the man of her dreams. Until he became the man of her nightmares.

She pulled out her cell phone to text Brooks. He didn't seem to hate her quite as much as his older brother did.

Hey, sweetie, what's taking you guys so long?

Waiting for a response, she cast a nervous glance at the door. The last thing she wanted to do was go inside and risk Chief Buchanan seeing her. But as the minutes ticked by, she didn't have a choice. Something could've happened to the boys. At the thought, every horrible thing she'd ever heard about truck-stop restrooms came to mind, and she practically leaped from the car.

Her heart fluttered against her rib cage like a trapped canary. As the past two months had proven, she wasn't equipped to deal with teenage boys. Seniors, she could handle. Being married to a man decades older had left her well equipped to deal with golden-agers.

As she approached the diner's door, she zipped up her burgundy leather jacket to hide her stained white shirt and then reached for the knob.

She stepped back when a barrel-chested man opened the door, offering him a smile when he stepped outside. "Do you know where the restrooms are?" she asked.

"To your right and down the hall on your left. Word to the wise: buy gas or some food else Dot, the owner, will tear a strip off you."

"I will, thank you."

He touched the brim of his ball cap and headed for a big silver rig.

The smells of hamburgers and fries, coffee and apple pie, greeted Mallory when she walked inside, and her stomach rumbled. She couldn't remember when she'd last eaten. The air was warm and filled with the sounds of people talking and the clang of pots and pans. She did a quick scan of the diner, which was filled with seniors— not a teenager in sight. To her left, a man called *hello* to the chief.

"How's it going, Walter?"

Gabriel Buchanan's voice was even deeper and sexier than she remembered. It was also close, like he was sitting at the lunch counter. And she was standing there, mooning over his voice, drawing the curious attention of the customers lined up to pay at the cash register.

Afraid he would see her, she bent at the waist to brush a piece of imaginary lint off her jeans while following the truck driver's directions down a wood-paneled corridor. To her left, she spotted a sign for the men's restroom midway down the hall and hurried for the door.

She knocked. "Oliver, Brooks, we have to go."

Thinking her stepsons might not have heard her over the gravelly-voiced waitress yelling out orders for hamburgers and fries, she tried again.

When there was no response to her second attempt, she said, "Guys, this isn't funny anymore. Come on." Pressing her ear to the door, she jiggled the knob. It was locked.

Someone cleared their throat. She looked down the hall to see an older man watching her with a bushy white eyebrow raised.

"It's not what it looks like," she said with an awkward laugh. "My stepsons are in there."

Pressing her lips close to the door, she knocked again. "Do you hear that, boys? There's a nice gentleman who'd like to use the restroom."

The way the man was looking at her made her as nervous as the absolute silence coming from the other side of the door. "I'm really sorry," she apologized while attempting to force the knob to turn. She used both hands. It wouldn't budge. "I'm sure they won't be…" She went to tell the older man they wouldn't be much longer, but he wasn't there.

She bent down to look under the door but couldn't see anything from that vantage point. With a quick glance up and down the hall to ensure no one was around, she got down on her hands and knees. Her cheek touched the tile as she tried to get a look under the door. She grimaced at the gritty feel beneath her face, imagining how many pairs of boots and shoes had walked over the floor today.

"Oliver, Brooks, I'm not fooling around anymore. If you don't get out here this second, I'm going to..." *What? What was she going to do?* "I'm going to break down the door?"

She sighed. She hadn't meant for it to come out as a question.

"Or you could simply ask for the key," a deep and familiar male voice suggested from behind her.

Chapter Two

The blonde on her hands and knees looking under the men's restroom door didn't acknowledge Gabriel Buchanan's presence or his suggestion about the key. Since it took a concerted effort to drag his admiring gaze from her heart-shaped backside to what he could see of her face through her hair, he decided it was probably a good thing she hadn't looked up.

When his interest in the profile he could barely make out beneath the long, blond locks seemed equally intense, he wondered what was behind his odd reaction.

He frowned. There was something familiar about her. Even if his reaction to her was decidedly unfamiliar. Or so he thought until she lifted her cheek from the floor to offer him a weak smile over her shoulder.

Mallory Maitland. He should've known.

He'd had a similar reaction to her last summer. When his eyes had met hers in the crowded bar, everything had faded away until it was just the two of them. He'd stared at her with his heart racing and a smile he couldn't wipe from his face. He hadn't felt that instant attraction to a woman for more than a decade. It was how he'd felt when he first met Lauren, his late wife and the love of his life.

"I know it looks bad," Mallory said, using the door handle to pull herself to her feet. "But my stepsons are in there and...they're kind of mad at me. About moving. Here. To Highland Falls."

Despite Mallory being a widow without children when they'd first met, he wasn't surprised to learn of her recently acquired stepsons. For some reason he'd yet to discover, Abby Everhart, her best friend, had decided Gabe needed to be kept apprised of whatever was going on in Mallory's life.

He probably would've attributed Abby's need to keep him informed to her tendency to overshare—about anything and everything—but lately she wasn't the only one who'd decided he needed regular updates on Mallory. So did Winter Johnson, the town's mayor and his boss.

Which meant he already knew that Mallory had accepted the job to implement a new seniors program at the community center. Better her than him, he'd thought at the time. Except that wasn't all he'd thought or felt upon learning she was moving to town, he reminded himself and nudged her carefully out of the way.

The last thing he needed living in tempting proximity was a woman who made him feel things he hadn't felt in a very long time. His life was complicated enough.

"How long have they been in there?" he asked as he inserted the key into the lock while trying to ignore the warmth of her body so close to him and her spicy, sweet fragrance. She smelled like Christmas.

"Twenty minutes."

He glanced at her.

She averted her gaze, raising a hand to smooth strands of honey-colored hair away from her face. "I was on a call with a client. It took longer than expected."

Her flushed cheeks and her unwillingness to meet his eyes told another story—she was lying.

As though she picked up on his silent suspicion, she looked him in the eyes and lifted her chin. "They're teenagers. Oliver is almost sixteen, and Brooks is fourteen."

She had the bluest eyes he'd ever seen. They were mesmerizing, making it difficult to look away. He wanted to look away. No, he reminded himself, he had to. As he dragged his gaze from hers, he noticed a speck of dirt on her face.

"You, ah, have something on your cheek." He touched his own face to keep from touching hers.

She made a face and rubbed her cheek. "Better?"

No, not better at all. "About an inch below your finger."

Before he did something stupid like touch her, he turned to give the door another try. "Did you check the diner?" he asked when he couldn't get the lock to budge.

"I looked around when I walked in. I didn't see them."

Neither had he. They weren't among the many seniors who congregated at the diner on a daily basis. If Dot, the owner, didn't make the best beef burgers in town,

Gabe would've headed to Highland Brew. Housed in an old mill on the water, the pub-slash-coffeehouse had a younger clientele. It was where he'd met Mallory.

But besides the burgers, eating at the diner—as was the former chief of police's habit—was part of Gabe's plan to win over the seniors of Highland Falls. They'd been playing with him like cats with a cornered rat since he'd taken the job as chief of police five months before.

His officers assured him they were just putting him through his paces—Gabe being an outsider and all—and would soon tire of their fun and games. They'd better because, if he didn't win them over soon, he'd most likely throw them all in jail and get fired. For his sons' sakes, he had to keep this job no matter how much he didn't want it.

Mallory searched his face. "Why? What's wrong?"

"The boys aren't in there."

"How do you know? You haven't even opened the door."

"The door's been jammed." Plus, it was too quiet.

She clutched her leather jacket at her throat. "You don't think someone took them, do you?"

"Relax, Mallory. We'll find them." As a father of three boys, he empathized with her fear but he knew better than to make her a promise like that. Still, he was ninety-nine-point-nine-percent certain of the outcome. He'd also say just about anything to wipe the fear from her eyes.

Apparently, his reassurance didn't work. As though seeking comfort, she moved closer. He gave her shoulder an encouraging squeeze and then asked her to give him some room.

"Of course. Sorry." She backed away, wincing when his shoulder hit the door. The moment it burst open, the coins her stepsons had wrapped together to jam the door flew across the tiled floor. Beneath the window sat a garbage can.

The boys had gone AWOL.

As Gabe moved into the empty restroom, his adrenaline spiked at the opportunity to do some actual police work. It wasn't as if he wanted any harm to come to Mallory's stepsons but, other than the seniors of Highland Falls sending him on wild-goose chases, there were days when he thought he'd lose his mind from boredom.

He missed his old job as a homicide detective in New York. There'd been nothing he enjoyed more than tracking down the bad guys and putting them behind bars.

"Dadgummit, Chief, what are you doing busting down my bathroom door?"

He turned to the sturdy woman with the steel-gray spiked hair staring in at him with her hands on her hips. "Sorry about that, Dot. Couldn't be helped. We've got a couple of missing boys."

"If I'd gotten to you a few seconds sooner, might've saved my door," she grumbled, surveying the damage before lifting her gaze to Gabe. "Jimmy just called. He found a couple stowaways in his rig. He's bringing them on back here."

"Two teenage boys?" he asked. Beside him Mallory held her breath.

Dot nodded, turning her hard gaze on Mallory. "They

say their stepmother keeps them locked in their rooms and doesn't feed them for weeks at a time."

"No." Mallory laughed, then pressed two clear-polished fingers to her lips, her gaze darting from Dot to him. "Sorry. I didn't mean to laugh. The boys' accusations aren't funny. Far from it. But they're also not true." Her eyes were pleading as she held his gaze. "Please, you have to believe me. You have to know that I'd never harm a child or anyone else for that..."

Her shoulders slumped. "You don't really know me though, do you? All you know are the lies—"

"There had to be a reason your late husband left his first wife his fortune and his sons." The look Dot aimed at Gabe seemed to indicate she wanted him to arrest Mallory right then and there.

"My husband didn't leave Marsha his fortune. She contested the will." Mallory briefly closed her eyes as if mad at herself for letting Dot draw her in. "But none of that's important right now. I have legal cust—"

Dot cut her off. "Mrs. Maitland the First contested the will and won. Court awarded her the money, the mansion, and the boys. Must've had a good reason. Maybe they knew you weren't fit to raise them. Guess it's true what they say. The apple doesn't fall—"

Gabe didn't know why he was surprised the older woman went there. He should've cut her off sooner. "That's enough, Dot. How about you get back to your job and let me do mine?"

"Don't see your cuffs out so not sure I trust you to do your job. I'd feel a darn sight more confident justice would be served if Owen was back wearing the badge."

Like the rest of the seniors in town, Dot believed that the former and beloved chief of police, Owen Campbell, had been forced to retire to make way for Gabe. There was also some resentment among the younger generation, who felt the position should've been awarded to one of their own. The one thing both factions agreed upon: Gabe had gotten the job because palms had been greased.

He suspected their suspicions might be true. Although he'd never confronted his in-laws, who had the means and the motive. That was one boat he didn't rock. He was too afraid of what they'd say if he did.

Mallory looked from Dot to him, her eyes wide.

Yeah, welcome to my world, Gabe thought before saying to Dot, "Where I'm from, we don't arrest someone without evidence, and right now all we have is the word of a couple of teenage boys who aren't happy about moving to Highland Falls." He understood how they felt. He wished his boys felt the same.

"Is that right? So you didn't arrest her on hearsay once before?"

Dammit. He'd walked into that. "I had evidence," he said, then winced when Mallory crossed her arms. "Planted evidence that was false, of course, but I did have reason to suspect—" He cut himself off. This wasn't an argument he could win. "We might as well head out front. Jimmy will be pulling in with your stepsons anytime now."

Mallory opened her mouth and then glanced from him to Dot and closed it. He suspected she'd been going to ask if he believed her but thought better about asking in front of Dot. Good call.

As he followed Mallory to the front of the diner, from behind him the older woman muttered, "Should've known he'd be taken in by a pretty face."

Gabe stopped, about to turn around and defend himself and Mallory, but then he thought better of it and kept walking. No matter what he said, Dot wouldn't believe him. As he'd learned, once the senior citizens of Highland Falls formed an opinion, good luck trying to change their minds. They were as stubborn as they were judgmental.

All conversation in the diner died as they made their way to the front door. Mallory bowed her head and quickened her pace, tripping on the mat. Gabe reached out and took her by the arm.

The whispers started then, the volume ratcheting up when several seniors called, "What's that you said, Hamish?"

"I said it's no surprise she can't take care of them boys. Her daddy couldn't take care of her."

"Who's her daddy?"

Mallory made a low, distressed sound, and Gabe moved in front of her to open the door, casting a *shut-it* stare at the seniors in the diner.

He imagined that the negative attention brought back memories of what Mallory had endured during the court fight with her late husband's ex. The press had eviscerated her. Their attacks were unwarranted as far as he knew. Her youth, beauty, and wealth at the time had played against her.

"You okay?" he asked as they stepped outside, the door closing behind them.

She wrapped her arms around herself and gave her head a small, negative shake. "I don't know what I was thinking accepting the job."

"Why did you?" He stuffed his hands in the pockets of his leather jacket as he scanned the highway for Jimmy's rig. Gabe wasn't a touchy-feely kind of guy, yet with Mallory, that was all he seemed to want to do—reach out and offer her comfort. "Sorry, none of my business," he said when the silence between them lengthened.

"No, it's fine. I have to tell you anyway. If only so you'll understand why Oliver and Brooks are accusing me of being an abusive parent." She looked across at the tree-covered mountains, blinking back what he imagined were tears. "I can't believe they said those things about me. I mean, I knew they were mad about the move but what they said..." She trailed off.

"Look, they probably thought if they made you out to be bad enough, Jimmy would sympathize with them and take them wherever they wanted to go. What they didn't know is driving truck is a side-hustle for Jimmy. He's one of my officers." And Gabe didn't have the budget to give him full-time hours. Another strike against him in the eyes of Highland Falls' seniors.

"I know exactly where they wanted to go—the thirty-four-thousand-square-foot mansion in Atlanta. I don't blame them. Some days I wouldn't mind going back there myself. But Marsha got the estate along with the money and the boys. Only two months ago she decided she didn't want them." Staring straight ahead, she flicked an impatient finger under her lashes.

"So why would the boys want to go back to her if

she doesn't want them?" She cast him a *you can't be serious* glance. "Aside from the fact they'd be living in a mansion the size of my street."

"They don't know she doesn't want them." She lifted a shoulder at his incredulous stare. "I told them I fought for custody and won. Marsha went along with it."

No wonder the boys were mad at her. From what Abby had told him, Mallory's living arrangements were several steps down from how she used to live. "Why would you do that?"

"They lost their father last year, but even if they hadn't, I'm not going to tell them that a woman they looked to as a grandmother doesn't want them."

After what Marsha Maitland had put Mallory through, he was surprised she didn't tell her stepsons the truth. "So what did you tell them?"

"That she was too old." There was a glint of amusement in her eyes before it dimmed, and she made a face. "That came back to bite me pretty quick."

He imagined it had, since her late husband, the boys' father, was several years older than his first wife. Gabe decided to keep that observation to himself.

She glanced at the diner over her shoulder. "Looks like my decision to move back here is doing the same."

"Don't let them get to you. They're annoying but harmless." What the hell was he thinking? He should be encouraging her to leave, not encouraging her to stay.

"Easy for you to say. I have to work with them, and now they think I'm an unfit parent. Not to mention having to live down my father's reputation."

She was handing him the perfect ammunition to get her to reconsider the mayor's job offer, only he couldn't bring himself to use it. Sometimes the overprotective side of him was as big a pain in his ass as the senior citizens of Highland Falls. "I haven't had any trouble with your father since I took over from Owen, so you can put that worry aside."

Her father, Boyd Carlisle, lived in a shack in the mountains and, according to multiple charges filed against him over the years, made moonshine without a license. Gabe had also heard him referred to as the town drunk. Since he hadn't met the man or seen him in town, he couldn't say if the rumors were true. But the part about Boyd not taking care of his daughter was.

From what Gabe had been able to piece together, Mallory had been removed from her father's care when she was twelve, remaining in foster care until she'd aged out at eighteen. He suspected her past played into why she'd assumed custody of her stepsons, and damned if the thought didn't fill him with both admiration and sympathy and an urge to give her a hug.

"We'll clear up your stepsons' accusations as soon as they get back, and that'll be the end of it."

"I hope so," she said, then gave him a small smile. "Thank you, you know, for not arresting me."

"I guess I deserve that. But honestly, I was left with very little choice last summer, Mallory."

"I know. Really, I do. I understand how convincing—"

His cell phone's insistent ring interrupted her. "Give me a sec," he said, then took the call. "What's up, Ruby?" he asked the older woman who handled just about everything at the station, including dispatch when they were in a bind.

"The gal from social services is here. I set her up in your office. How long before you get here with those poor boys?"

Gabe turned. Dot stood at the door to the diner with her arms crossed and her eyebrows raised in challenge. Or was it victory?

As he tried to figure out how to break the news to Mallory that things had just gotten a whole lot worse for her, Ruby continued talking. "I've ordered them up a pizza. They must be starved. And I'm having Sam clear out a cell for that woman who calls herself a mother." Ruby breathed out what sounded like a sigh of relief, then said to Gabe, "I'll see you when you get here." She hung up but, as was the case practically every time she did, the call hadn't completely disconnected.

"Ruby, hang up the damn phone," he ground out as he stared down Dot, letting her know she wasn't getting away with stirring the pot this time. He waited for the phone to disconnect but instead heard Ruby say, "Chief, I'm so glad you dropped by. We've got a big case, and I don't think our boy is up for it."

Chapter Three

At the chief's muttered curse, Mallory's gaze shot from the cars speeding along the highway to him. His display of anger surprised her. It seemed out of character. Granted, she didn't know him all that well.

But last summer she'd gotten the distinct impression that Highland Falls' new chief of police remained calm, cool, and collected in any situation. Now it appeared that a volcano of passionate intensity roiled beneath his calm and cool demeanor. A volcano of passionate intensity? Where had that even come from? And why on earth the evidence that Gabriel Buchanan's emotions ran hot and passionate on occasion caused her stomach muscles to clench with desire, she had no idea.

She grimaced, remembering the last time her stomach muscles had clenched like that—about forty minutes ago when she'd been listening to her audiobook in the car. She supposed it made sense in an embarrassing sort of way. Ever since meeting Gabriel last summer, despite how their last encounter had ended, the hero in every book she read reminded her of him.

It didn't matter if they had brown hair, red hair, or blond; brown eyes, green eyes, or blue; in her mind they all looked and sounded like Highland Falls' dark-haired, gray-eyed, handsome chief of police.

Handsome? The man was beyond handsome—he was off-the-charts gorgeous. And still angry, she decided when the muscle in his chiseled jaw throbbed. Throbbed? Jaws clenched; they didn't throb. No, no, no, she silently cried when images of clenching and throbbing body parts filled her mind.

Gabriel glanced at her with a disproportionate level of concern, and she wondered if she'd made the panicked sound out loud. Worse, were her lustful thoughts visible on her face?

Of course he couldn't read anything on her face, she assured herself. It was his job to be concerned about people. Protective too, she thought, remembering how he'd stood up to Dot and stared down the seniors in the diner on her behalf.

He was strong and kind, a man you could depend on, a man whose reassuring presence and gentle squeeze of her shoulder had made her wish that she could turn back time, that none of what happened last summer had happened, that her stepsons weren't missing, and she could, they could...

All right, enough was enough. This was getting completely out of hand. If simply looking at Gabriel Buchanan had her thinking of happily-ever-after, she needed to deal with her addiction to romance novels once and for all. A wave of panic swamped her at the idea of going cold turkey. She needed them. They alleviated her stress far better and far faster than anything else she'd tried.

That was it—stress. She didn't have to stop reading her love stories after all. It was stress over the situation with Oliver and Brooks making her fantasize about Gabriel, envisioning him as her hero. She didn't need to read or listen to less romance; she needed to read and listen to more!

But as soon as she had that sorted in her head, another equally disturbing thought popped into her brain. From what she'd overheard of his one-sided conversation with Ruby, Mallory had the distinct impression something was wrong. So maybe the concern she'd seen on his face seconds ago had nothing to do with her emitting a panicked squeak or him deducing the reason for her heated cheeks.

"Is everything all right, Chief Buchanan?" she asked, praying that whatever was wrong had nothing to do with her. She'd had enough go wrong today.

"It's Gabe, and everything's fine," he said without looking at her. "Or it will be once I talk to your stepsons." He lifted his chin at the silver truck barreling down the highway and started making his way across the parking lot.

She didn't believe him. His earlier anger indicated that something was wrong. And if he wouldn't look her in the eyes, she surmised that something had to do with her and the boys.

There'd been a time in her life when she would've

given anything to have someone look out for her, to protect and shelter her. Apart from Harry's Sean Connery good looks, his charm, and his kindness, those were the very reasons she'd married him—a man older than her own father.

She hadn't known or admitted it to herself then, but she'd had lots of time to ruminate over her choices this past year. She wouldn't make the same mistake again. She didn't need someone to protect her or to make decisions they believed were in her best interest. She could take care of herself…and her stepsons. Although she was doing a lousy job of that to date. But, clinging to the hope that Christmas was the answer, she truly believed that was about to change.

As if to encourage her, the blow-up Santa waved. It was probably a gust of wind but it felt like a sign she was on the right track, and she really needed a positive sign right then.

She hurried after Gabe. He turned just before she reached him. His eyes hidden behind his aviators, he held up a hand. She might not be able to read his expression but she sensed his tension.

"What is it? What's wrong? Other than Oliver and Brooks's accusations against me, I mean," she said as she tracked the silver truck now pulling into the lot. She went up on her toes to see if the boys were in the cab.

"I need to talk to your stepsons without you around, Mallory. It might take a few minutes. Why don't you wait in your car?"

"I thought you believed me. You told Dot—"

He rested his big hand on her shoulder, giving it

another gentle squeeze. "This has nothing to do with whether I believe you. It's standard procedure. The boys made an accusation against you, and it's my job to investigate their complaint. For them to speak freely when I question them, they have to feel safe."

Her pulse raced. "Do I need a lawyer?" She blinked when he hesitated. Nerves had made her blurt out the question. She hadn't actually thought a lawyer would be necessary.

"Let's just take this one step at a time. I'm sure it'll be fine. Just relax, okay?" He glanced over his shoulder when the barrel-chested man Mallory had almost bumped into earlier opened the truck's door and climbed out.

"Five minutes ago, I thought it would be fine too. But ever since you took that call, you've been acting different. Toward me. What happened between then and now?"

He rubbed a palm over his jaw, the dark stubble making a scratchy sound. "You don't miss much, do you?"

"Apparently I do, or I would've seen the boys climbing out of the bathroom window, crossing the parking lot, and sneaking into your officer's truck."

"Trust me, I'm trained to be observant, and you wouldn't believe what my boys have gotten away with."

"You—" Her voice cracked, and she cleared her throat. "You have sons?" The smile she offered him was strained; any romantic fantasies she might've entertained featuring her and Highland Falls' chief of police in the leading roles went out the window. She could barely manage having two boys in her life. There was no way she'd get involved with a man who had two of his own.

She might consider it if he had a daughter, a newborn, or even a toddler.

"I do." He smiled. "I have three sons. The twins, Cody and Dylan, are ten, and Teddy is almost six."

"Oh, how lovely," she said, and any desire she might've felt for Gabriel Buchanan went out the same window as her fantasies.

"Yeah? Then how come you look like you're going to throw up?" He laughed, and it was such a warm, sexy sound that she almost questioned her newly formed rule of never dating a man with children, especially male children.

"Chief." His officer waved him over, so Mallory didn't get a chance to answer. Which she decided was a good thing, because what was she supposed to say?

She definitely had something to say to her best friend, Abby Everhart, who'd failed to mention in their twice-weekly conversations that Gabriel Buchanan had three sons. Despite sharing that he was a widower in nearly every one of those phone calls, something Abby had decided made them perfect for each other, no matter how often Mallory told her she wasn't interested.

Gabe lowered his shades. "Mallory?"

"Yes?"

"You were going to wait in your car?"

"Oh right, I'll—" She glanced to where his officer helped the boys jump down from the truck. "I really think I should be there when you talk to them. They don't realize how serious this is."

"I'm sorry, but you can't be, Mallory. I'll make sure Oliver and Brooks understand exactly what the consequences of bringing the charges against you are, and that there are serious repercussions if I discover they're lying."

"They're not bad boys. They're really not. They've been through a lot." She glanced at Oliver, who appeared to be comforting his brother, and her heart squeezed. "I should've tried harder to convince Marsha to keep them or even to get Harry's brother to take them. At least they'd be living a life they're accustomed to."

"Why didn't you fight harder to get them to take the boys?"

"Because they didn't want them, and no child should ever feel unwanted. Sorry," she apologized for the forceful way she'd spoken. "I'll wait in my car. Tell the boys I'm sorry for taking them from their friends and uprooting them again. I just...I didn't have any other options available to me." She turned away before the tears welling in her eyes could fall. She didn't want Gabe or the boys to see her cry.

At the continuous tinkle of bells, she glanced at the diner. There seemed to be a mass exodus underway. She doubted it was a coincidence. Bowing her head, she fast-walked to her car, blocking out the looks being cast her way and the whispered speculation.

She was something of an expert at hiding her feelings. It was how she'd survived all those years in foster care. No one knew how scared and lonely she'd been. No one knew the hurt she'd carried inside. But today wasn't just about her. It was about Oliver and Brooks too.

She glanced over her shoulder, relieved to see that Gabe was shielding her stepsons from the curious onlookers.

Though it meant she couldn't see them to gauge if they were telling the truth or continuing to lie.

From the way Gabe nodded every so often, she knew the boys were at least talking. Gabe appeared to be entering some of their comments into his phone. Oliver's comments, she imagined, knowing from experience that he spoke for the two of them. Even if he wanted to, Brooks wouldn't go against his big brother. She'd seen the power dynamics play out before.

Although it made her life difficult, she envied their closeness. In foster care, she'd learned the hard way that to grow close to someone only ended in heartache so she'd rarely let anyone in. She would've done well to remember that in college. Except if she hadn't gotten close to Harry's niece, Blair, Mallory never would've met him.

And you wouldn't have gone through years of heartache and pain. She gasped at the disloyal thought. It was nerves and exhaustion. She loved Harry. She did. He'd been good to her. No one had ever treated her as well or given her so much. Far more than she'd deserved.

She slowed as she approached her car, digging in her purse for her keys. She found them and beeped the lock, anxious to hide away in her car. But just as she was about to open the driver's-side door, Oliver's voice stopped her cold.

"You're lying! Marsha does so want us. Tell him. Tell him the truth," Oliver yelled as he ran across the parking lot, dodging a car pulling out, to confront her.

Mallory's jaw dropped as she looked from Oliver—his cheeks flushed, his eyes angry and tear-filled—to

Gabe, who was following close behind with Brooks. "How could you? I told you that in confidence."

Gabe blew out a breath and rubbed the back of his neck. "I know. I'm sorry. But you don't understand what's at stake, Mallory. The boys needed to know how serious this was for—"

Oliver scrubbed viciously at his eyes while shaking his head. "It's not true, it's not. She's lying."

"I'm not. I wish I was for your and Brooks's sake, Oliver. I truly do. But Marsha..." She trailed off, at a loss as to what to say without hurting them further. "You're right about one thing: I did lie about fighting for custody of you. I would've though. If you take nothing else away from this, know that I wanted you guys. I still do. But Marsha, she's...she hasn't been well, and she's getting old...er. You'd recently lost your father. She didn't want you to face another loss so soon." For goodness' sakes, she was basically killing off the woman. "Not that she's going to die in the near future. But you know Marsha. She's a hypochondriac." That at least was true.

As Brooks moved to his brother's side, Gabe looked around the parking lot. "We should probably head to the station. We can get everything sorted—"

Mallory's hand went to her throat. "Police station? I don't understand. Why would we have to go to the police station?"

"Because you've been starving these poor children to death, that's why." The diner's owner, wearing an oversized winter jacket, pushed past Gabe to hold out takeaway bags for each of the boys. At the smell of burgers and fries emitting from the bags, Mallory's stomach gurgled loudly enough for everyone to hear. Self-consciously, she placed a hand on her stomach.

"Thank you," Oliver and Brooks said as they accepted the bags. Then they shared one of their silent conversations. After which Oliver gave his brother a nod, and Brooks, looking from Gabe to Dot, said, "Mallory doesn't starve us, and she doesn't lock us in our rooms." He cast a sheepish glance at Mallory and lifted a shoulder. "We didn't want to leave our mates. We thought we could live with Marsha. We didn't know she didn't want us. You should've told us."

"You're right. I should have. I'm—"

"Now, now, don't let her intimidate you, boys. I'm sure the lady from social services will find a nice home and family for you to live with."

Mallory stared at Gabe. "Social services? You called social services on me?"

"I didn't call them, but there is a caseworker at the station. Don't worry, we'll get this straightened out right away."

"I'm supposed to believe that? I should've known better than to trust you." After having been arrested by him last summer, she certainly should have. But she'd let herself get taken in by a pretty face, by his kindness and protective concern. She was such an idiot, falling into the same pattern. Hoping that the big, strong, handsome man would rescue her. She'd learned the hard way she needed to be her own hero, and she'd be the boys' too. Whether they wanted her to be or not.

But judging from the panicked expression on Oliver's face as he wrapped an arm around his brother's shoulders, they'd be okay with her stepping in on their behalf.

As Oliver's plea a second later proved. "You can't let them take us, Mallory. They'll separate me and Brooks."

She put a hand on his shoulder and one on Brooks. "No one is taking you away from me. You got that? No one." She opened the car door. "Get in, boys."

"What are you doing? Stop her! She's going to drive off with those boys," Dot said to Gabe.

"I'm not driving off with them. I'm going to the station." She opened the driver's-side door and slid behind the wheel before Gabe could stop her.

"Mallory, wait." He held the door open. "For your sake, you shouldn't—"

"You can talk to my lawyer." She went to close the car door with one hand while pressing the ignition button with the other. At the same time the engine started up, so did her audiobook.

At the sounds of lovemaking filling the car, she released a horrified squeak and tried clicking off the audiobook while simultaneously pressing the radio button on the steering wheel to lower the volume. Instead, she raised it. It wasn't until that moment that she realized how much the narrator sounded like her.

Chapter Four

Gabe held open the door to the station for Mallory and her stepsons. Her head was bowed, the boys trailing behind her. "It wasn't me on the tape. It was an audiobook," she said.

"I didn't think it was you." Half the crowd gathered outside the diner had, but not him. Did he maybe fantasize that it was on his drive back to the station? *Probably not a good idea to let your mind go there right now,* he told himself. Especially with Mallory looking up at him with her windblown hair and flushed face.

He wondered if she had any idea how incredibly beautiful she was. He didn't get the impression that she did. She was unassuming and soft-spoken. *Unless you threatened her stepsons,* he thought with an inward smile.

Even if he hadn't appreciated her taking off with the boys in her sweet-looking black Jag, he'd admired the fire in her eyes when she'd gone all protective mama bear on him. Except she'd put him in a difficult situation.

And the difficult part of the situation was sauntering toward them with a bowlegged gait.

"There you are, son. Wondered when you'd finally show your face," former chief of police Owen Campbell said, looking like a villain in an old Western. All he needed to do to make the image complete was twirl the end of his silver handlebar mustache.

If someone were to have told Gabe that the former chief of police came with the job, he would've refused to take it. He'd liked the older man well enough when they first met, but that was before he became his shadow at work.

"Now, I'm not a man to tell someone how to do their job"—he told him every single day—"but just so you know for next time, it's kinda frowned upon to let the suspect drive her and her victims to the station. Don't worry though; I covered your behind with the gal from social services."

"Mrs. Maitland's not a suspect, and her boys aren't victims, Owen. That was cleared up before I allowed her to drive the boys to the station." An out-and-out lie, but the man was ticking him off. Besides that, Ruby was practically falling off her chair trying to hear what was said. No doubt to pass along to Dot, who Gabe was positive was on the other end of the phone Ruby had pressed to her ear.

Owen frowned and leaned to the right to get a look behind Gabe. It was then that Gabe realized he'd blocked the older man's view of Mallory and her stepsons. As her gasp seconds before had indicated, she'd been able to hear what Owen said.

The older man paled, then tipped the brim of his cowboy hat at Mallory. "No one told me it was you they were bringing in." He shot Ruby a glare over his shoulder and the woman shrugged, pointing to the phone still pressed to her ear. It seemed Dot had kept that bit of intel to herself.

Gabe stepped aside to usher Mallory and her stepsons into the station. His overly quiet station. He glanced to where several of his officers sat at their desks pretending to be working and not listening. Given the smell of pumpkin and apple pie permeating the air, they hadn't been working much before he'd arrived. He couldn't say he blamed them. Like him, they'd worked through Thanksgiving.

His in-laws, Karl and Diane, had his sons at their home in Atlanta. The closer proximity to Highland Falls, near where they'd once had a vacation home, was one of the reasons they'd pushed Gabe to put his name forward for chief of police. That and they hated New York. They blamed the city for the death of their beloved only child.

"Why don't you boys come with me? I'll take you on a tour of the station. Ruby there"—Owen hitched his thumb at the older woman hefting herself up from behind the desk—"she brought in pies and cookies from the bakery, and I might just know where they tried to hide them from me."

If Gabe didn't know better, he'd think Owen was trying to suck up to...

How could he have forgotten? Of course Owen was sucking up to Mallory. He'd been the one to call social services on Boyd Carlisle all those years before, a man who'd been his best friend. So, indirectly, some might say Owen was responsible for Mallory being put in foster care, and it was obvious the decision haunted him to this day.

Owen had relayed some of his history with the Carlisles to Gabe last summer when he'd tried to convince him to ignore Blair Maitland's accusation of kidnapping against Mallory. There was a part of Gabe that wished he'd listened to him. But the problem was that Owen hadn't been asking him to look the other way because he believed Mallory was innocent.

Oliver and Brooks looked at Mallory, and she looked at him. "It's fine by me. The caseworker will want to talk with you separately anyway."

Her full lips flattened at the reminder of why they were there. But she wasn't just angry, he thought when he saw her rub her earlobe between her thumb and forefinger—he'd become familiar with her nervous habit last summer. Despite what other parts of his body seemed to think, it was probably a good thing he didn't want to pursue a relationship with her. There was no way she'd want anything to do with him after today.

"I'll take good care of your boys, Mallory. You have my word. And I'll put in a good word for you too." With his thumbs hitched in the belt loops of his jeans, Owen rocked on the heels of his cowboy boots and shot Gabe a sidelong glance. "Don't know what he was thinking arresting you."

Three pairs of blue eyes blinked up at Gabe, and he blew out a frustrated breath instead of the curse word that was on the tip of his tongue. "Does she look like she's under arrest, Owen?" At the whispers coming from his officers, he raised his voice. "She's not under arrest, and you can all share that with the rest of the town. If I arrest anyone, it'll be Dot and her pals at the diner."

"Easy now, son. You don't want to mess with the senior citizens of Highland Falls. Trust me, they can make your life a living hell." He grimaced and apologized to Mallory and the boys for his language.

"Oliver and Brooks, you can go with Mr. Campbell, if you'd like." Mallory looked around. "I'll be right here if—"

"If you need her, Mallory will be in my office," Gabe informed the boys, who appeared torn between going and staying. He lifted his chin at the takeaway bags in their hands. "Owen will heat up your burgers and fries for you."

"No, *she* won't be in your office," Mallory said once the boys walked off with Owen. "*She's* waiting for her attorney."

"Okay, look, Mallory, I get it. But this isn't a big deal. It's just a formality. The boys recanted their accusations. Besides, the woman has been waiting in my office for almost an hour. By the time your lawyer arrives from Atlanta—"

"My lawyer isn't coming from Atlanta." She nodded at the door. "And she's here now."

Gabe groaned when a pregnant blonde with a briefcase and a petite redhead with a dog in her purse walked into the station. Eden Mackenzie and her soon-to-be sister-in-law Abby Everhart gave him the evil eyes before rushing over to pull Mallory in for a hug.

Great. Now not only were the seniors of Highland Falls ticked at him, so were two prominent members of the Sisterhood. The *Sisterhood* that had been creating problems for him since his first day on the job. He rubbed the heel of his palm against his chest. It wasn't Dot's burger giving him heartburn; it was this town.

Mallory's eyes narrowed on his hand, and he dropped it to his side while addressing the three women, who looked at him with less-than-impressed expressions on their faces. "Ladies, I don't know what Mallory has told you but we're all good here. We should be able to clear things up in the next twenty minutes or so. If you'd like, you can wait—"

"Oh no, Chief Buchanan," said Abby, the redhead with the dog. "You are not getting rid of us that easily. My best friend doesn't stand up for herself very well.... You know it's true, Mal. You let everyone walk all over you, including those boys." She waved off Mallory's objections. "Yes, yes, I know they've been through a lot, and I sympathize with them, too, but that doesn't mean they're allowed to treat you like crap. Honestly, Mal, what if someone actually believed their accusation?"

"Obviously someone did. Several someones," Mallory said, studiously avoiding his gaze.

"You're right. But it's okay. You've got Eden to take care of the legal end of things, and I'll look after your reputation. Sorry, Bella Boo, Mommy needs her cell phone," she said to the Yorkshire terrier as she dug around in a purse the size of a suitcase.

When she held up her phone, he said, "No way. You're not filming any of this, Abby. And no disrespect intended, Eden. I know you're a good lawyer, but you don't practice family law so—"

Abby cut him off. "Eden's an amazing lawyer, and because she is, as soon as she got off the phone with Mal, she called one of the best family attorneys in North Carolina, who just happens to be her bestie. They met—"

The woman could talk for hours. He had to get rid of her before she turned a simple situation into a Greek tragedy. As he racked his brain for a reason for her to leave, he remembered something his youngest had said when he'd called Gabe at the butt-crack of dawn that morning. "Aren't you supposed to be filming behind-the-scenes footage of the Christmas parade for your YouTube channel?"

Teddy was a big fan of *Abby Does Highland Falls* and kept up a running commentary whenever he watched. Teddy was also a big fan of Highland Falls and Christmas, and he couldn't wait to celebrate their first holiday here. Just the thought of which had Gabe rubbing his chest again.

They'd lost Lauren ten days before the holidays and hadn't done much in the way of celebrating for the past three years. Teddy seemed determined to up the ante on their barely remembered traditions. About as determined as Gabe, Dylan, and Cody were to keep things status quo.

"Why, yes, I am, Chief Buchanan. Are you keeping tabs on me?" Abby grinned up at him.

"I'll leave that to Hunter." At his mention of her fiancé, Abby lit up like a Christmas tree, and Gabe decided to take advantage of the fact that she was head over heels. He'd feel guilty about it later. If she managed to talk her way into the meeting (and he knew from personal experience she was very good at talking her way into anything and everything), he'd be lucky to get home in time for his boys' and in-laws' arrival.

The last thing Gabe needed was to be late. In his mother-in-law's eyes, it would be further proof that he was failing as a father. Diane had hinted on more than one occasion that the boys would be better off living permanently with her and Karl in Atlanta. After all, they had all the time in the world to devote to his sons. Money too, although she was too polite to point that out. Sometimes her hints sounded a lot like threats.

He glanced at his watch. "Speaking of Hunter, have you gotten him a Christmas present yet?"

Mallory and Eden shared a raised-eyebrow glance.

"Why? Did he drop a hint?" She made prayer-hands. "Please tell me he did, because I haven't got a clue what to get him. You wouldn't believe how difficult the man is to buy for. I've—"

Gabe cut her off before she went on for another five minutes. "Hunter didn't mention anything to me, but Ed at the hardware store, he was showing this guy a carving knife he had on display the other day, and I immediately thought of Hunter." That at least was true. Abby's fiancé was a gifted wood-carver. His work was highly sought after. "It's a beauty. If you want it, I'd head over there now seeing as it's Black Friday."

"You're right, but I can't leave Mal." She chewed on her thumbnail. "You couldn't wait to start the meeting, could you?"

"It's okay, Abby. I'm good. Eden's with me," Mallory assured her best friend.

"Okay, if you're positive you don't mind. I'll see you at your place in an hour. You're going to fall in love with your new neighborhood." She gave Mallory a hug, shooting Gabe a smile that made him nervous.

"That better not have just been a story to get rid of Abby, Gabe, or you'll find yourself featured on her YouTube channel. Again," Eden said as they walked to the back of the station.

"Don't remind me." He held open the door to his office. "I'm sorry to keep you waiting...." *Oh hell.* "Hey, Kayla." He walked in and shook the woman's hand. She was attractive, with long dark hair and voluptuous red lips. He'd gone out on one coffee date with her and had spent the past month avoiding her and her phone calls. "Ruby didn't mention you were the caseworker social services sent."

"I didn't give my name. I didn't want to make her uncomfortable. You know, since she's the one who's been helping you avoid me."

This was going to be worse than he'd anticipated. He glanced at Mallory and Eden as he shrugged out of his jacket to take a seat behind his desk. From where they now sat across from him, they looked intrigued as well as slightly concerned. They had reason to be.

The last thing Mallory needed was to plead her case to a woman who already appeared to have an ax to grind, even if that ax was with him. He rubbed his chest as the ache expanded. He blamed his mother-in-law for the mess he now found himself in.

To counter his fear of a custody battle with his in-laws, he'd stuck his toe in the dating pool. Now that he'd gotten a job closer to them and in a small town, he'd expected things to settle down. But he hadn't been in Highland Falls three months when Diane began hinting that the boys needed a woman in their lives.

She'd probably meant herself, because God knew no one would ever be able to meet her exacting standards. But he couldn't lay the blame entirely on his mother-in-law. His youngest had been hinting the same, and he was pretty sure Teddy had shared that with his grandma.

But as soon as Gabe had sat across from Kayla at Highland Brew, he'd known it was a mistake. There'd been no sparks, no instant attraction like he'd felt with Mallory. But worse than his lack of attraction to the woman was that every minute he'd been in her company he'd felt like he was betraying his wife.

Kayla looked at him with a thin black eyebrow raised, clearly expecting a response. Mallory distracted him by leaning over to place two tablets on his desk.

"For your indigestion," she said at his questioning glance. "They're just an over-the-counter antacid."

"I didn't think you were trying to poison me." He smiled, then, remembering why they were there, cleared his throat. "It was a joke."

Kayla looked from him to Mallory, and her lips pursed. "In light of the reason for this meeting, perhaps you should refrain from any further attempts at humor," she said, implying she didn't find him the least bit funny. That was something else he hadn't enjoyed about his coffee date with Kayla: the woman didn't have a sense of humor.

"You're right. Sorry." He had to fix this before Mallory paid the price. "And I'm glad it was you who social services sent so I have the opportunity to apologize in person for not returning your calls, Kayla. My plate's been full these past few weeks, and I was waiting until I cleared off a couple things before giving you a call to set up another date."

Yeah, yeah, I know it's totally inappropriate, he thought in response to Mallory and Eden's wide-eyed stares. He wasn't any happier about it than they appeared to be. Thankfully, he hadn't just trashed his professional credibility for nothing, because Kayla's entire demeanor changed.

Pushing her long hair over her shoulder, she smiled. "We can talk about a time that works for both of us after we're done here."

"Sounds good," Gabe said and made the introductions before bringing Kayla up to speed.

"I see." She tapped a manicured finger against her lips. "So your opinion is that the boys made up the accusations of abuse simply to return to Atlanta and their stepmother's care. Obviously, I'm referring to their father's wife."

"Mallory was their father's wife. Just, ah, not the first one," Gabe said.

"Actually, that's not true, is it"—she swiped her finger across the iPad's screen several times—"Ms. Carlisle?"

Chapter Five

It may have been petty, but Mallory had already formed an unfavorable opinion of the attractive, dark-haired woman simply on principle when she'd walked into Gabe's office. So learning that the woman had dated him and was going to date him again had only added to the case she was making against Kayla McPherson in her head. But this, to bring up something so personal and private, was inexcusable. The caseworker wasn't a nice person at all.

Mallory avoided looking at Gabe and Eden, but mostly at Gabe. She thought about asking him to leave. It was one thing to talk about her sex life in front of two women, but in front of a man she was attracted to—and there was no denying she was, no matter how much she didn't want to be—was embarrassing to say the least.

She cleared her throat. "I'm not sure how you obtained that information, Ms. McPherson. Both my and Marsha's attorneys agreed to keep it private and out of the public record."

"Mrs. Maitland was the one who informed me—"

Gabe raised his hand. "Hold up here. Is what Kayla's saying true? You weren't married to Maitland?"

Mallory's cheeks grew uncomfortably warm, but she lifted her chin. She'd done nothing wrong, and she wasn't about to let anyone make her feel like she had. "Harry and I were married, but because of his health issues, our marriage wasn't consummated. Marsha's attorneys used that information to corroborate evidence that led to our marriage being ruled invalid." It wasn't the most damning evidence, just the one piece of evidence that was true. The rest were lies that Marsha and her lawyers concocted to win. Lies they'd promised to bury if Mallory walked away without a fight.

Marsha had gotten what she'd wanted since the day Harry had told her he was marrying Mallory instead of remarrying her as she'd always hoped, as he'd supposedly led her to believe. It didn't matter that Harry was gone. She'd ensured that Mallory was no longer his wife in the eyes of the law and, Marsha seemed to think, God.

Mallory glanced at Gabe from under her lashes. If he had an opinion on her admission, she couldn't tell. His handsome face was an expressionless mask.

Then he scoffed. "Come on, this isn't the nineteen hundreds," and it was obvious he thought it was a joke. She had, too, at the time. So had her lawyer. "If nothing else, your marriage should've been recognized as a common-law union."

"I agree with Gabe, Mallory. I wish you would've talked to me before you waived your rights to your husband's estate."

Mallory lifted a shoulder. "It's over now." There was nothing she could do to change the outcome. Marsha's attorneys had drafted an ironclad agreement, and Mallory's lawyer had encouraged her to sign. All he'd seen ahead of them was a protracted court battle and even more embarrassing headlines for Mallory if Marsha and her attorneys went to the press as they'd threatened.

But the real reason Mallory had given up was that she'd been too tired and heartsick to continue fighting. It had never been about Harry's estate for her. It had been about ensuring his last wishes were honored. And at that point, she'd begun to wonder if the lies Marsha and her lawyers spun were really lies at all.

"As I understand it, common-law marriages aren't recognized in Georgia," Kayla said.

If that was all she came back with, Marsha hadn't aired all her dirty secrets. She'd just shared the most titillating.

"What I'm more concerned about at the moment, Ms. McPherson, is that a legal document was in place to ensure this information remained confidential. I object to its use today. I also insist that you sign a nondisclosure agreement once we wrap this up," Eden said.

"Your objection is noted, but the information was given freely by Mrs. Maitland, so I'm not sure what you're objecting to. Unless it's to the fact that it proves Ms. Carlisle has no legal claim to the boys."

Eden put a hand on Mallory's arm when she opened her mouth to protest. "Besides Marsha Maitland signing over custody to my client, you mean?" Eden withdrew a printed copy of the agreement Mallory had emailed to her before she'd committed to taking the job in Highland Falls. Eden had wanted to make sure Mallory was within her legal right to leave the state with the boys.

"As you can see for yourself, the document is notarized, legal, and binding. Mrs. Maitland felt it was in the best interest of Oliver and Brooks to grant my client full custody. But what she didn't grant my client was oversight of the boys' trust funds. And when Mallory asked that the funds be managed by an outside party to ensure the money would be there when Oliver and Brooks were legally able to access the funds at twenty-one, Marsha refused."

"Is there a point to all of this, Mrs. Mackenzie?"

"Yes. I'm surprised you haven't picked up on it already, Ms. McPherson." She gave the other woman a pointed look. Clearly, Kayla McPherson wasn't Eden's favorite person. "The point is my client had nothing to gain by assuming custody of Oliver and Brooks. However, some people might say she had plenty to lose. And if you've dug deep enough, you'll discover that it was because of her stepsons' behavior that Mallory lost several clients and her apartment."

Mallory cringed. At the speed the caseworker was inputting the information on her iPad, it would seem Eden hadn't proved her point; she'd proved Kayla's. Mallory glanced at Gabe, who was leaning back in his chair, rubbing his hand over his chin. He caught her eye and nudged his head in Kayla's direction.

Mallory pointed at her chest and he smiled, giving her an encouraging nod. He was right. She had to speak for herself. "Ms. McPherson, I'm not going to deny that Brooks and Oliver have had, are having, trouble adjusting. But my hope is that, once we get settled here, things will turn around. I want the boys. I want us to be a family, and I believe that's what their father would've wanted."

"Yet, he sent the boys to boarding school a month before you were married."

Marsha must have given the caseworker an earful. And just like with the journalists, it was clear whose side the woman was on.

"He did," Mallory admitted. "And I'm sure the boys blame me for that, but I had nothing to do with my husband's decision. I wanted Oliver and Brooks to live with us."

"If that's true, why would your husband send them away? Is it possible he didn't think you were up to mothering two boys? After all, you were only twenty-three at the time."

Mallory briefly closed her eyes. She heard the judgment in Kayla's voice. You'd think she'd be used to it by now.

Gabe's chair squeaked as he straightened. "I don't know what purpose this line of questioning serves, Kayla. Mallory didn't starve the boys or lock them in their rooms. She has legal guardianship. She wants the boys, and I, for one, think they're damn lucky she does."

"Thank you, but I don't mind answering Ms. McPherson's question, Ga—Chief Buchanan." Mallory smiled. She appreciated him standing up for her. She'd been mad at him for sharing her confidence with the boys but as she'd sat there, she'd had to face the truth.

It wasn't his fault she was in this situation. Like Brooks said, she should've been honest with them from the start. If they'd known Marsha had given up custody, they wouldn't have tried to run away. She had a feeling that was why Gabe felt he had no choice but to tell the boys.

And now she had to make Kayla understand something Mallory herself hadn't been able to understand at the time. "Harry never told me why he wanted to send the boys away, and there was no convincing him otherwise. When my husband made a decision, he wasn't easily swayed. And he was adamant that Oliver and Brooks attend boarding school in England. He went to the same school at their age, and he attributed his success to the education he'd received there as well as the contacts he'd made. But over this past year, I've begun to wonder if, even back then, he knew he wouldn't survive his latest battle with cancer, and he didn't want his sons to watch their father waste away."

And if that were the case, she had to wonder if Harry had simply married her because he'd needed a caregiver and she'd checked all the boxes. It was what Marsha believed. In her mind, the only reason he'd chosen Mallory over her was because he knew he was sick, and he thought Mallory might be able to save him. But the argument that seemed to play the best with the judge— a man Mallory would later learn had been burned by a much younger wife—was that Mallory had coerced Harry, using his illness to manipulate him, to have him pay for her school loans, and to give her a life that the former foster child could only have dreamed of.

"I appreciate you sharing that with me. Despite what Chief Buchanan seems to be implying, I don't have a vendetta against you. My job is to ensure the boys are in a safe, loving environment. As you yourself mentioned, they're having issues settling in. So, at this point, my recommendation would be that—"

A knock on the door cut her off, and Ruby popped her head into the office. "Sorry to interrupt, Chief. But I thought the ladies might like some refreshments." The older woman's breathing was labored as she made her way around the outside of the room to deposit a tray loaded down with two urns, four cups, and a plate of pumpkin-spice cookies on Gabe's desk. Then Ruby turned, brushing the damp white curls back from her forehead. "How's it going in here?" she asked.

Mallory might've sighed at the evidence that the older woman was more interested in getting the inside scoop—probably at Dot's directive—than she was in being hospitable if not for the gray cast to her brown skin and the beads of perspiration on her upper lip.

"Just about to wrap it up, so if you don't mind?" Gabe lifted his chin at the door.

"Actually, I think Ruby should sit down. Here, please, take my seat," Mallory said as she came to her feet.

"I think I'll stay right where I am, if you don't mind. I'm feeling a little woozy. Tray was heavier than I thought."

Mallory moved to her side and wrapped her fingers around Ruby's wrist, checking her pulse. "Do you have dizzy spells often? Any pain to speak of?"

"I'm only dizzy when I get up too fast. Pain in my back is more annoying."

"Chief, would you please bring your chair around and help Ruby to sit down?" It had wheels, and they could easily move her to the front of the station. Gabe, like Eden and Kayla, frowned at Mallory. "Now, please," she said.

"You mind telling me what's going on, Mallory?" Gabe asked as he stood to move his chair behind Ruby.

"A lot of fuss for nothing, if you ask me," Ruby said as Gabe helped her into the chair.

Mallory went to retrieve her bag, keeping an eye on Ruby as she dug inside for a bottle of aspirin. She noted the older woman's wince of discomfort and shook a pill into the palm of her hand. "Is the pain in your back getting worse?"

Ruby winced again and then nodded. If possible, she looked paler than she had moments before. Mallory gave Ruby the tablet. "Chew this. Gabe, please call nine-one-one."

"And why am I calling nine-one-one?"

"Ruby's having a heart attack," she said, once the older woman had done as she asked. Mallory placed a comforting hand on Ruby's shoulder. "Everything will be all right. I just want you to relax, and we'll wheel you to the front of the station."

"I'm not having a heart attack. I can't be. I don't have any pain in my chest," Ruby argued while Gabe radioed for an ambulance.

"It's not uncommon for women to have pain in their

back when they're having a heart attack." And just as common that they'll deny they're having one.

"How do you know? Did you have one? You seem awful young."

"No, I haven't, but I am a doctor." She didn't think it was necessary to add that she'd only completed her first year of residency before leaving to marry Harry. Right now, she needed Ruby to trust her and to remain calm.

"Is there anything we can do?" Eden asked.

"If you could have the officers clear a path to the front door of the station, that would be a big help. Thanks." Mallory moved behind Ruby.

As both women got up from their chairs, Kayla said, "I'd still like to wrap this up today. I'm not comfortable leaving it as is."

"Agreed, but at the moment Mallory is a little busy. Once we've done as she asked, you and I can discuss next steps," Eden said.

Kayla glanced at Gabe, who was on the radio with his back to them, and then nodded her agreement.

Gabe disconnected and walked over to where Mallory was unsuccessfully trying to move the chair. He nudged her out of the way and took over, pushing the chair without a problem. "How are you doing, Ruby?"

"The doctor here says I'm having a heart attack so I guess not so well, Chief."

He glanced at Mallory and murmured, "You're full of surprises, aren't you?"

"Some I would've preferred to keep to myself," she murmured back.

"I bet." He offered her a warm and sympathetic smile.

"I'm sorry it came up today. You have my word, it won't go any further than my office."

"Thank you," she said, walking ahead so Gabe could get the chair out the door.

"I'm all right. You all just get back to work," Ruby told the officers, who milled around, looking on in concern. They called out their well wishes, promising to stop by the hospital after their shift. "Would you mind giving Charlie a call, Chief? He'll be wondering where I'm at if I'm late getting home."

"Already done. He'll meet us at the hospital."

"Oh now, you don't have to come, Chief. You have to get home on time to meet the boys."

"Don't worry about me. It's about time you start thinking about yourself instead of everyone else, Ruby."

A door to what Mallory knew from her overnight stay last year was the holding cells opened, and Owen and the boys walked into the station's waiting area. Catching sight of them, Owen rushed over while Oliver and Brooks hung back. "What's going on?" Owen asked.

"I'm having a heart attack, and Mallory here saved me. What do you think of that? Boyd Carlisle's daughter is a doctor."

"Thank you for saving her, Mallory. We wouldn't know what to do without Ruby running things around here, would we, son?" Owen said to Gabe.

Before Mallory could correct Owen, Oliver's eyes narrowed at her, his hands balling into fists at his side. "You saved her?"

Brooks shot his brother a nervous glance.

Mallory understood why her medical intervention

would make the boys angry. She hadn't been able to save their father after all. But the last place she wanted to defend herself to Oliver was in the middle of a police station, in front of a woman who wanted to take the boys away. Mallory glanced to where Kayla and Eden leaned against Ruby's desk, talking. Definitely within earshot if Oliver raised his voice.

"No. I didn't save Ruby," Mallory said as she walked toward the boys, herding them several more feet from Ruby's desk. "I simply identified her symptoms."

But not far enough away that Ruby didn't hear her. "Now don't you go playing down your role in saving me. If not for you, I probably would've gone home and died in my sleep."

Gabe frowned, looking from Mallory to Oliver. She wasn't surprised he'd picked up on the tension between them. Oliver wasn't exactly adept at hiding his feelings. His cheeks red, he looked seconds away from blurting out an accusation that had been leveled at Mallory immediately after Harry's funeral.

"Ollie, no," Brooks pleaded. Then, glancing at Kayla and Eden, he added in a whisper, "They'll take us from her. They'll split us up. Don't do it."

Worse than Oliver accusing Mallory of killing his father in a police station with a caseworker for social services looking on was realizing that the boys truly believed she was responsible for Harry's death.

She didn't know if it was Brooks's plea that stopped Oliver from talking or the swirl of lights and the siren of the approaching ambulance. Whatever it was, she was grateful. Though it was clear she couldn't put off this conversation with the boys any longer.

"Once we leave here, I'll tell you whatever you want to know about the night your father died, and I'll tell you the truth."

Without looking at her, Oliver nodded.

"She's not taking us away, is she? Ollie and I get to stay together?" Brooks asked, and Mallory fought the urge to give him a hug. Any show of affection from her had always been rebuffed.

Instead she looked over her shoulder at Eden, who happened to glance her way at the same time. Eden smiled and gave her an almost imperceptible nod that Mallory took to mean they were good.

"No one's going anywhere. Well, other than to our new home. We can—"

"Mallory." Gabe waved her over.

"I won't be long," she told the boys and hurried to Gabe's side.

As he helped the paramedics load Ruby onto the stretcher, Mallory relayed the symptoms that informed her diagnosis and the amount of aspirin Ruby had taken, and then Mallory followed Gabe and the paramedics out the glass doors and onto the sidewalk.

In a state of near panic when she'd driven up Main Street earlier, Mallory hadn't noticed that Highland Falls was decked out for the holidays. Wreaths with big red bows hung from the street lamps, and the trees that lined the sidewalks were wrapped in white lights. A cheery Santa sign announced the holiday parade. It was tomorrow.

The perfect opportunity to put her Christmas plan into action, Mallory thought, and felt the heavy weight lift ever so slightly from her shoulders.

"What's going on? Is that Ruby? Is she going to be okay?" two older women with shopping bags stopped to ask. Soon a small crowd of shoppers and shopkeepers had gathered on the sidewalk. Gabe patiently answered their questions, and a moment later, the EKG monitor they'd hooked to Ruby confirmed Mallory's suspicions.

"You okay?" Gabe asked as the ambulance drove away and the crowd dispersed.

"I've had better days," Mallory admitted.

"I bet you have." He held the door open for her. "I know this was the last place you wanted to be today, but I've gotta tell you, I'm glad you were here. Ruby's right, you know. You undoubtedly saved her life. I'm grateful."

"You're both giving me too much credit. But I'm glad I was here to help."

"I owe you one."

"It looks like I might need to call in that favor sooner rather than later," she said, noting what appeared to be a tense exchange between Kayla and Eden. Mallory's gaze shot to the boys, who were now sitting behind Ruby's desk. "Kayla must've spoken to Oliver and Brooks."

Gabe stopped her with a hand on her arm. "Is there anything I should know? I can't help you if you don't tell me the truth, Mallory. I saw Oliver's face when Owen said you saved Ruby."

She briefly closed her eyes and put a hand on her churning stomach. "I . . ." She trailed off as Eden walked their way.

"Good news," Eden said when she reached them. "Kayla and I have worked out a compromise that I think you'll be able to live with, Mal."

"That doesn't exactly sound like the news I was hoping for." But it did sound like Oliver had at least kept his suspicions to himself. Otherwise Mallory imagined she would've been dragged back into Gabe's office. Either that or into a holding cell.

"Ms. McPherson insists that, given the boys' *precarious* situation, your progress is closely monitored. For the next three months, she expects you to provide detailed progress reports on a weekly basis, and there will be periodic at-home drop-ins."

"And where exactly is the good news in that?" Mallory asked, because to her it felt like a nightmare. For the next three months, her and the boys' every movement, every interaction, would be put under a microscope and judged. If she didn't live up to Kayla's expectations, she would lose Harry's sons. It had been patently clear during the meeting that the caseworker already had a bias toward Mallory, questioning her character and judgment.

"I'm sorry. I wish you didn't have to do any of this, but let's try to look at this from a different perspective. The boys are having problems adjusting—you said so yourself. This is all new for you. You've never had children or siblings, and you're only thirteen years older than Oliver. Gabe is a single parent raising three boys on his own. I'm sure he'll have plenty of great advice on how to turn this around. Better than you having to report to Kayla on a weekly basis, right?"

"Pardon me?" Mallory said.

"Excuse me?" Gabe said at almost the same time.

Mallory recovered faster. "So I'm supposed to report to Gabe once a week for three months." Which admittedly would be easier—in some ways—than reporting to Kayla, but did it also mean that he held her and the boys' fates in his hands? "And then what? Does he get to decide if I'm a fit parent? Is it his decision whether or not the boys remain in my care?"

"I guess his opinion would hold weight. But I'm sure it won't come to that, Mal. You'll see, moving back to Highland Falls will turn out to be the absolute best thing for you and the boys."

Chapter Six

"You said you'd tell us about the night our dad died," Oliver reminded Mallory as she drove through the red wooden covered bridge on the way to their new home.

So much for her reprieve. She'd hoped to put off this moment for as long as possible. She'd stopped at the grocery store right after they'd left the station in an attempt to distract them. Buying bags of their favorite foods and snacks hadn't worked nearly as well as the ridiculously overpriced headphones they'd convinced her to buy at the electronics shop on Main Street. You'd think by now she'd have learned that bribery rarely worked for long. All it did was take another bite out of her nest egg.

She glanced in the rearview mirror, gauging if she could push off her confession a few minutes longer. Taking in Oliver's dogged expression, she didn't think so. In the end, it was probably best to have the conversation in the privacy of her car. Abby and the movers were at the house.

Mallory drove out from under the covered bridge onto

a road lit up with a canopy of white lights. Had her hands not been perspiring and her stomach not jittering with nerves, she might've taken a moment to marvel at the holiday display. As it was, she pulled to the side of the road.

Drawing in a steadying breath, she undid her seat belt and turned to face them. "For the last year of your father's life, he'd spent the majority of it confined to his bed."

Oliver's eyes narrowed. "He didn't look that sick when we talked to him on Skype."

"Only because we took extraordinary measures to ensure that he didn't. But like I told you at the funeral, I should've gone against his wishes and told you the truth. It wasn't fair." It wasn't fair to her either. Because they'd gone to such efforts to keep the progression of the disease private, people were shocked to learn of Harry's death. And sometimes that shock turned to suspicion.

But Harry wouldn't have thought that far ahead. Or maybe he had and he didn't care. By then, he wasn't the same man she'd married. In some ways, it was probably best for the boys that they hadn't seen him. The cancer had gone to his brain. There was no telling what he would've said to Oliver and Brooks when he was in one of his rages. Midmorning had been his best time of day, so they'd Skyped with the boys then, and she'd kept their conversations brief.

"But you could've saved him just like you saved Ruby," Oliver objected. Beside him Brooks sat quiet and pale.

"Your father was very weak from the cancer and the treatments; so was his heart. A few weeks before he died, he made me promise not to take any extraordinary measures to save him. He wanted to die, and he wanted

to die at home." At that point, it had been too late to
have him sign a DNR—do not resuscitate order. Because
the cancer had gone to his brain, it could legitimately be
claimed he was not of sound mind.

"When I first suspected he was having a heart attack, I
gave him an aspirin just like I gave Ruby. He spat it out,
Oliver. He wouldn't let me near him until I promised I
wouldn't try to save him or call nine-one-one. You have
to believe me—the hardest thing I have ever done is
stand by and not try to save him."

Tears streaked their cheeks, and she worked to contain her own. "He didn't die alone. He died in my arms,"
she said, hoping that would make them feel a little
better, praying that they didn't share her confession with
Marsha. "He looked at peace for the first time in more
than a year."

The boys shared a look as they rubbed the evidence
of their tears from their faces. It was a look she hadn't
seen before, so she wasn't sure what it meant. Did they
blame her or forgive her? She was too afraid to ask the
question out loud and turned to fasten her seat belt, her
gaze meeting Brooks's in the rearview mirror. He looked
like he wanted to say something but instead followed his
brother's lead and put on his headphones.

* * *

Gabe drove slowly over the bridge on his way home from
the hospital. He'd learned the hard way when he'd gone
house hunting last summer that the deer around here
considered the red covered bridge their own personal

pathway across the rapids. He didn't kill the doe that morning last July but the bill from the veterinarian had nearly given him a heart attack.

Huh. He seemed to have heart attacks on his brain. They were lucky Mallory had recognized the signs that Ruby was having one, or Gabe and everyone else in town would've been heartbroken. Mallory didn't realize it yet but her public image no longer needed a ratings boost from Abby's YouTube channel. Whether she saw it that way or not, Mallory had saved Ruby, one of Highland Falls' most popular senior citizens. Gabe figured that alone should buy her enough goodwill to overcome her reputation as a bad parent.

It looked like he was the backup plan in case it didn't. Though he didn't have a clue why Eden had volunteered him for the job or how big a help he'd be. Half the time, he felt like he was floundering with his own sons. Single parenting wasn't easy, as Mallory had no doubt discovered. But as much as he didn't want the job, he couldn't very well foist her off on Kayla. He wasn't sure if Kayla sensed his attraction to Mallory or not, but it was obvious she wasn't exactly Mallory's number-one fan. It seemed to go both ways.

Mallory wasn't exactly his number-one fan either. He couldn't say he blamed her. In her mind he'd now become the enemy. The guy who got to decide whether she kept the kids. She wanted them, that much was obvious. But the boys, especially the older one, didn't appear to feel the same way about her.

Typically, Gabe was a good judge of character but he had to face the facts even if he didn't want to. He didn't

really know Mallory so it was possible she wasn't the
warm, genuine, caring woman he perceived her to be.
The one thing he did know: she was hiding something.
And while he couldn't be sure, if he was a betting man
he'd wager ten grand that something had to do with her
husband's death.

Blair Maitland had hinted as much to Gabe last
summer, and, as with all the other lies she'd told him,
he'd been obligated to follow up. So he'd quietly nosed
around and pulled some strings. The last thing he'd
wanted was to raise the alarm and create more problems
for Mallory. But despite Blair's attempts to lay the blame
at Mallory's feet, the coroner had ruled Harry had died
of natural causes. His cancer treatments had weakened
his heart, and he'd had a heart attack.

In light of what took place today and how Oliver
had reacted, Gabe figured he had his answer. Mallory,
a medical doctor who was trained to save lives, hadn't
saved their father's. Maybe she couldn't or maybe Harry
had signed a DNR. Gabe hoped that was the case. Otherwise, Mallory's problems could get a whole lot worse
if word got out she'd stood by while her husband died.
Which meant so would his. Either way he looked at it, it
seemed his boring job wasn't going to be quite so boring
anymore thanks to Mallory and her stepsons.

He could almost hear Lauren's voice in his head:
Careful what you wish for, honey, followed by her laugh.
She'd had a great laugh. But, like her voice, her laughter
was harder to hear these days.

In the months right after they'd lost her, it was
like she was walking beside him, whispering words of

encouragement, wisdom, and love in his ear. She'd visit him in his dreams. Sometimes they were so vivid and real he didn't want to wake up. Sometimes he didn't want to get out of bed. She got him through that first year. Her and the boys.

"If you've got any advice, I'm all ears, babe," he said as he drove out from under the bridge and onto Holly Road. The leafless trees on either side of the road that met to form a verdant canopy overhead in summer and fall were now decorated with white lights courtesy of the town council. There was a lot Gabe didn't like about Highland Falls, but he loved the natural beauty of the place. It was like living in the woods only with the amenities of town close by.

"So I guess I'm on my own," he murmured when his wife's voice remained silent in his head. He ignored the ache in his chest. It was heartburn. He wasn't lonely. He was content with his life just the way it was. If he couldn't have Lauren, he didn't want anyone else but his boys. A voice in his head called him a liar and it wasn't his late wife's. It was his own.

His headlights bounced off a car at the side of the road. His heart pumped an uneasy beat, and he leaned forward to get a better look. Sure enough, it was a black Jag. "If this is your advice, I'm not taking it," he muttered as he pulled up beside Mallory's idling car.

He powered down the passenger-side window. "You lost?" he asked when she lowered hers. She had a phone in her hand.

"My GPS isn't working, and Abby isn't picking up her cell phone."

He frowned. She looked like she'd been crying. "Have you been driving around all this time?" He'd left the station for the hospital almost an hour ago. As far as he knew, she'd left at the same time.

"No, I, ah, we stopped at the grocery store."

He glanced at the boys in the backseat. They had a couple grocery bags in their laps, iPads in their hands, and earphones on their heads. The expensive kind.

"Where are you headed?" He hoped to the other side of town.

She looked at her phone. "Twenty-five Reindeer Road." She searched his face. "Is everything all right? Is it a bad part of town? Abby said—"

"Abby found you the house?" So that was the reason for her *I've got you* grin earlier at the station.

She nodded. "Why?"

"Nothing. You can follow me."

"Thank you, but I don't want to put you out. I'll just wait to hear back from Abby."

Now that he was effectively serving as what Mallory no doubt considered her parole officer, she most likely didn't want anything to do with him other than her mandated weekly meetings.

"You're not putting me out. I live on Reindeer Road." He waited a minute for that to sink in. "Twenty-three Reindeer Road." And in case she thought he lived across the street, he added, "Right beside you."

She swallowed. "Oh, that's nice."

He snorted a laugh. "Look on the bright side. You won't have to go far for our weekly check-ins, and surprise home inspections will be easy enough for me to do." He'd been joking, trying to lighten the mood, but as she'd just lost what little color she had left in her face, it was obvious that she appreciated his attempt at humor as much as Kayla had earlier.

He had to straighten this out, and he had to straighten it out now. Whether they liked it or not, they were going to be neighbors. He glanced at the boys, who seemed oblivious to his presence. Either that or they were ignoring him. "I'm not the bad guy, okay? I'm not out to get you or to take the boys. I'll do whatever I can to support you."

"Thank you. That's very kind, considering how I acted earlier. You didn't deserve to be treated like the bad guy in all of this. I thought, once the boys told the truth, that would be the end of it. I didn't expect to be treated like a criminal."

"You're not, so stop looking at it that way. Sounds to me like you've been dealing with this on your own, and now you won't be. You have a support system here to lean on so take advantage of it, of us. Anyway, you've had a rough day. Take the weekend to get settled, and we'll figure out a game plan that works for the both of us on Monday."

"I start work at the center Monday morning."

"Station's only a couple blocks away. We'll grab a cup of coffee."

"Okay. Thank you." She glanced in her rearview mirror. "We better go. You're blocking traffic."

A Lincoln Aviator pulled up beside him, and a tinted window lowered to reveal his mother-in-law. She wore an air of disapproval like a second skin. "Gabriel, is there a problem?"

"No, just helping out a new neighbor who got lost."
The back passenger-side window went down and his
boys leaned over to wave at him. "Hey, Dad!" The three
of them yelled at almost the same time.

"Hey, guys. Welcome home."

"We brought you—" his youngest began before Diane
cut him off.

"Get your head out of the window, Theodore. It's
dangerous. We'll see you at the house, Gabriel." Diane's
window went up but not before Gabe heard her say,
"Karl, how many times have I told you to use the child
safety locks on both the windows and the doors?"

Gabe felt sorry for his father-in-law. Diane had never
been a particularly easy woman, but up until Lauren's
death, Gabe hadn't minded having her around. Not anymore. He made nice for the sake of his boys and his late
wife. Karl too. His father-in-law was a great guy.

He glanced at Mallory to make sure she was ready to
follow him, but at the look on her face, he said, "What's
wrong?"

"Was that Diane and Karl Rollins?"

"Yeah. You know them?" Of course she knew them.
She wouldn't ask if she didn't. But it wasn't something
he'd even considered. He supposed he should have.
Diane and Karl were rich and well connected. They probably hung out in the same social circle as Mallory's late
husband. After all, they were around the same age.

"We were members of the same country club." She
glanced at him. "You were married to their daughter,
Lauren?"

"I was."

"I remember hearing that they lost her. They were devastated. I'm sure you all were. I'm so sorry."

"Thanks," he said, instead of asking how well she knew Diane and Karl.

His in-laws had only started socializing again in the past eighteen months. Whereas Harry Maitland had been rumored to have been housebound the last few years of his life. Which meant there was a fifty-fifty chance Diane wouldn't have run into the Maitlands for years. And that meant there was a fifty-fifty chance she wouldn't say anything derogatory about his new neighbor in front of the boys.

The only problem with basing his conclusion on the premise that Diane hadn't seen Mallory at the country club in more than three years was that Mallory didn't have a forgettable face. And her face had graced the Atlanta papers quite a bit this past year.

He was debating warning Mallory to avoid interacting with his mother-in-law—who would no doubt have been firmly in Marsha Maitland's corner—when lights from an oncoming vehicle filled his SUV. "We should probably get going. Just follow me." If he drove slowly enough, maybe he'd get lucky and his in-laws and the boys would be inside.

"Should've known better than to think my luck would change," he said as he turned onto Reindeer Road. Karl, Diane, and his boys stood at the front of the moving van backed into the brick bungalow's driveway, talking to an animated Abby and her dog.

Gabe pulled alongside the curb in front of the sage-green Craftsman he now called home. He'd barely set his foot on the road when Dylan and Cody bounded up to him. The twins might have Lauren's chestnut-brown hair and hazel eyes, but, according to Gabe's mother, they were carbon copies of him growing up. The middle son in a family of five boys, Gabe had made his brothers look good. If he didn't find trouble, it found him.

The first thing his parents wanted to know on their weekly FaceTime calls was what Dylan and Cody had gotten up to. Gabe made sure to relay the news of his sons' latest exploits before the boys were around because his parents never failed to have a good laugh at his expense.

He pulled Dylan and Cody in for a hug, kissing the tops of their heads.

"Dad," they grumbled, shooting embarrassed glances around the neighborhood.

"You're never too old for your dad to hug. Pop Pop still hugs me, doesn't he?"

"Pop Pop hugs everyone, Dad," Dylan, the oldest by fifteen minutes, said.

Gabe laughed. It was true. "You guys have fun at Grandma and Grandpa's?" he asked as he shut the driver's-side door.

"Yeah, it was okay. Grandma got kinda sad at Thanksgiving dinner." Cody tried to shrug it off, but Gabe knew it bothered him. As rough and tumble and mischievous as the twins could be, they were also empathetic and kindhearted. And while Gabe knew better than anyone how difficult the holidays could be, he wished Diane would hold it together when his sons were around.

"Grandma wanted us to stay the weekend, but Teddy

didn't want to miss the parade. He wants to give Santa his letter in person," Dylan said and rolled his eyes.

"Okay, we had a talk about this, remember? No teasing your brother, and—"

"No telling him Santa is dead," Cody said as they rounded the back of the SUV. "We know, we know."

"Hey, look, Cody. The new neighbor has kids," Dylan said.

Gabe did his best not to grimace. He didn't know Mallory's stepsons well, but from what he'd seen so far, he had some reservations about them hanging around his boys. "They're quite a bit older than you two. So you might—"

"Whoa, is that their sister? She's really pretty," Cody said when Mallory got out of the car.

"Yeah and so is that car. What kind is it, Dad?"

They were his sons, all right. "A Jag, and it's a great-looking car." So was the woman but he'd keep that to himself. "Mallory isn't the boys' sister. She's their stepmother."

"Their dad must be even older than you," Cody said, and Gabe caught the twinkle in his eyes.

"Har har, you're as funny as your old man." They went to cross the yard, and he grabbed a fistful of their jackets to reel them back in. "Here's the deal. You say hello, welcome them to the neighborhood, and then we'll leave them alone to get settled."

"Aw, Dad," they both said at almost the same time.

"Come on, guys. It's movie night. We're going to binge the second season of *Lost in Space*, remember?"

"Yeah, right. Teddy says it's his turn to pick, and he'll want to watch a stupid Christmas movie."

"Cody," Gabe said as they closed the distance to his youngest and in-laws gathered at the front of the moving van. When Mallory and her stepsons reluctantly joined the group from the other side, Diane angled her head as if trying to place her.

Gabe needed a distraction, and he knew the perfect person to provide it. Teddy. Gabe smiled as he made his way to his youngest, who was holding court with Abby. He scooped him into his arms, angling his body to block Diane's view of Mallory. Teddy wrapped his arms around Gabe's neck and kissed him. Unlike his brothers, his youngest wasn't afraid of PDA.

In the end, Mallory didn't need his help. "Ma'am, where do you want the beds to go?" one of the movers called out.

"Just tell me, and I'll direct them. That way you can get better acquainted with your new neighbors." Abby shot Gabe a grin.

He gave her an I-know-what-you're-up-to-and-it's-not-going-to-happen stare. Her grin only widened. He shouldn't be surprised. Her fiancé was ex–Delta Force and left people quaking in their boots with just one look, but not Abby.

"Thank you, but you've done more than enough," Mallory said, and if he wasn't mistaken, there was an I-know-what-you're-trying-to-do-and-it's-not-going-to-work in her voice. Except she apparently couldn't hold a grudge, because she hugged Abby. Then she apologized to him and his family. "Sorry. We've kept the movers waiting so we better get in there. I'm Mallory, and these are my stepsons Oliver and Brooks." She offered Dylan and Cody a warm smile when they introduced themselves and offered their hands. "It's very nice to meet you too."

Her stepsons' smiles weren't warm, but they were polite, and they shook the boys' hands in return.

"Hi, I'm Teddy, and I'm going to be six soon." He pulled off his mittens and stuck them in his pocket before holding up six fingers. "You can come to my birthday party if you want."

"Thank you, Teddy." Mallory smiled, and for the first time today, her smile reached her eyes. He shouldn't be surprised. Teddy had a way with women. A way with everybody, actually. She took the hand his son offered and clasped it warmly between hers. "It was very nice to meet you."

"I liked meeting you too. You're really pretty, you know." He leaned forward, and Gabe had to adjust his hold on him. "Your eyes are all sparkly and so is your hair."

Mallory laughed, and Gabe liked the sound of it. Apparently his son did, too, because he beamed. Either that or he'd just fallen in love with their next-door neighbor. And if Gabe wasn't mistaken, the feeling was mutual, because Mallory leaned in as if to give Teddy a hug. Then she hesitated and went to pull back. But Teddy, like Gabe's dad, wasn't about to miss out on a hug and opened his arms.

"You are a very sweet boy, Teddy. And I needed a little sweetness today. Thank you."

Chapter Seven

Gabe's youngest stared after Mallory as she headed to the door of the red-brick bungalow with her stepsons and Abby. After hugging Teddy, she'd said a brief and polite hello to his in-laws before excusing herself to deal with the movers.

"Do you think Mallory wants to meet Santa with me tomorrow? Abby knows him, and she promised I could be at the front of the line."

"Hey, what am I, chopped liver? You've been gone two nights. I missed you, you know."

Teddy leaned back in Gabe's arms as they headed home, his in-laws trailing behind. "I brought home a really big container of all your favorites, Dad." He cupped his hand over the side of his mouth and whispered into Gabe's ear. "I snuck a whole pecan pie off the counter. I had to put it at the bottom of the bag so Grandma wouldn't know. It might be a little squished but it'll still be good."

Gabe looked into Teddy's earnest little face, and his

heart squeezed. His youngest was his mini-me in looks, but he'd inherited his mother's goodness and light. Gabe wasn't exactly sure when it had happened, maybe around the time Teddy turned four, but his youngest had appointed himself his family's caretaker. And while Gabe might not be able to pinpoint exactly when Teddy had assumed the role, he knew why. Lauren's death had devastated Gabe, Dylan, and Cody but Teddy had been too young to understand what was going on.

Gabe worried about the weight his little boy had taken onto his narrow shoulders, and it must have shown on his face. Except Teddy assumed that he was concerned about him taking the pie without asking. "It'd just go to waste, Dad. Grandma doesn't eat sweets, and she kept telling Grandpa he has to watch his waistline. So really, I'm saving Grandpa from the wrath of Grandma."

Gabe had to work to keep the laughter from his voice. "Wrath? Is that your word of the week?" Since he'd started kindergarten in the fall, Teddy had decided to learn a new word a week. But not an easy word like the ones his teacher gave to the class. Teddy had been reading since he was three. He read more than Gabe and his brothers combined. The kid was off-the-charts smart, which made him a little bit scary.

Teddy giggled and Gabe caught the sound of an underlying wheeze. His stomach clenched. Teddy's asthma scared him far more than his brainpower did. Gabe, Dylan, and Cody were as healthy as horses; Teddy wasn't and had never been.

"Theodore, it's impolite to tell secrets," Diane said, coming up the front door steps behind them.

Gabe swallowed a sharp rejoinder. She was right, but he didn't like her shaming his son. And shame was the only emotion anyone could feel when Diane corrected them in that condescending tone of voice. He winked at his youngest. "Good word."

Teddy grinned. "It's not my word of the week."

"No? What's your word of the week, then?" he asked as he unlocked the front door. Setting Teddy down, Gabe walked in and turned off the alarm.

"I'm going to have a theme for the rest of this month and next, and my theme is Christmas." His brothers' voices joined in on *Christmas* but with a groan in their voices instead of Teddy's smile.

Her lips pressed together in disapproval as she took off her coat, Diane obviously felt the same as Dylan and Cody. So did Gabe, but he wasn't about to put a damper on Teddy's excitement, no matter how much he wanted to. "Good idea, buddy."

Teddy smiled up at him as he sat on the hardwood floor to take off his boots. "This week's word is *Santa*, and I'm going to come up with more for every day of the week. I've got *Father Christmas* for Tuesday. Maybe Santa will be able to give me some other ones."

"*Père Noel*," Karl, who'd been a diplomat in France years before, suggested.

"Thanks, Grandpa. But it's kinda the same just in French."

"You got me there, partner," Karl said as he hung up his jacket and Diane's coat while his wife fussed over the mess the boys' boots had made on the floor.

"Don't worry about it, Diane. I'll clean it up later,"

Gabe said, frustrated that his in-laws had decided to hang around.

"Might as well save your breath, son," Karl said.

He was right, of course. Diane headed for the kitchen. As she did, she called out instructions to his sons: "Put your boots on the mat, boys. And Dylan and Cody, you both need to have a shower before you get ready for bed."

"Dad, do we have to?"

"Yes, you most certainly do," their grandmother answered for him. As though she sensed Gabe might go against her directive, she said for his benefit, "Despite being told not to leave the yard, after searching for them for over an hour, we found Cody and Dylan at the park behaving like two hooligans with a group of boys."

"Now, Diane, they were just having—" Karl tried to intervene on the boys' behalf.

"Do not undermine me in front of the children, Karl," she said, returning with a mop and a bucket. "My grandsons are running wild, and if their father won't put a stop to it, I will."

"Diane," Karl murmured, casting Gabe an apologetic glance.

"Hey, guys, do your old man a favor and take your overnight bags into your rooms. And don't just leave them on the floor. Unpack and put your stuff away. You too, buddy," he said to Teddy, who'd sidled up next to his leg.

His youngest reached into the front pocket of his jeans and pulled out his blue inhaler. It was his security blanket. He carried it wherever he went. Except school, where it was against the rules. If Teddy hadn't wanted to go to kindergarten so badly, Gabe imagined he would've had a hard time getting him to go. It helped that his teacher, an asthmatic herself, had shown Teddy where she locked up his inhaler in the classroom in case he needed it. Gabe patted his son on the butt to get him moving.

"Dylan and Cody, do me a favor and run a bath for Teddy." The boys looked ready to protest until Gabe gestured to his chest. The last thing any of them wanted was Teddy to have an asthma attack. They'd nearly lost him last January.

"But, Dad, I had a bath last night, and Grandma didn't let me out to play," Teddy said, casting a look at Diane from under his long lashes.

"I'll have a shower," Dylan offered. "Come on, Teddy. I'll let you play with my boats in the bathroom sink."

"Me too," Cody said.

His sons were the best. They knew that the steam from the shower helped their baby brother breathe easier.

Gabe waited until the boys were out of earshot to say to his mother-in-law, "Probably best if we continue this conversation in the kitchen."

"I agree. A conversation about the boys' behavior is long overdue. That's why Karl and I are here. We're concerned, Gabriel. Very concerned about our grandsons."

"Now, Diane, you're making it sound like..." Karl trailed off as she pushed the bucket and mop toward the kitchen as if he hadn't said anything.

"I'm sorry, son. It's the same thing every year around

this time. Holidays get the best of her. Just let her talk
and don't pay any mind to what she says. I'll have a
word with her when she's in a better frame of mind."
He handed Gabe the bag filled with Tupperware as if
it were a peace offering. "I think Teddy was afraid you
were wasting away up here without him looking after
you. Little bugger took my pecan pie." He chuckled and
patted his rounded stomach. "Not that I need it."

"They're good kids, Karl. And I don't like Diane
making them feel like they aren't."

"I know they are, son. It's just Diane's not used to
raising boys."

"Then it's a good thing she's not raising them, isn't
it?" he snapped. He briefly closed his eyes. It was fear
that put the bite in his voice. "I'm sorry. It's been a
long day."

"No need to apologize. Diane's not an easy woman,
but her heart is in the right place. She just wants the best
for the boys. We all do."

"If this were the first time, I might be able to let it go.
But I can't. If this doesn't stop, I won't allow the boys to
spend weekends with you and Diane. I don't want to do
it, Karl. But she's forcing my hand."

"Don't go there, son. I'm only saying this for your
own good. You try to keep those boys from her, and
there will be hell to pay. She'll fight you with everything
she has. And she always wins."

There it was. The threat was out in the open. He
hadn't been wrong. She'd go after custody of his boys,
and even his father-in-law believed she'd win. "And
you'd support that, Karl? You'd support her taking my

sons from me?" he said, his jaw so tight it felt like it would pop.

His father-in-law put his hands on Gabe's shoulders. "Gabriel, please. It doesn't have to be this way. Just let me smooth things over."

Diane rounded the corner, seemingly surprised to see them there. "What's going on? I've put the tea on."

"Hey, Dad! Can you come here for a second?" It was Dylan, and there was something in his voice that made Gabe wonder if they'd gone to their bedrooms as he'd asked. Or had they sensed something was up and stood huddled in the hall together?

He handed his father-in-law the bag of leftovers. "Give me a few minutes." He needed to go to his boys, but more than that, he needed time to calm down and weigh out the consequences of going up against Diane.

His sons' bedrooms were empty and so was the bathroom. "In here, Dad," Dylan whispered, waving him into the master bedroom. Teddy, with his inhaler clutched in his hand, sat beside Cody on the end of Gabe's bed. One look at their worried faces told him he was right. They'd been listening in on his conversation with Karl.

He scooched in between them. "Get over here," he said to Dylan and then wrapped his arms around the three of them. "This is why kids aren't supposed to listen to grown-ups' conversations. They get all worked up because they don't hear the whole—"

"We did so, Dad. Grandma thinks we're bad. She thinks we're out of control, and we're going to end up in jail, and that it'll be all your fault for letting us run wild."

"Cody, she doesn't think—" Gabe began, only to be cut off by Dylan, who was close to tears.

"She does. She said it right to our faces." He knuckled his eyes. "But we never meant to get you in trouble, Dad. We were just hanging out with some guys in the park and trying out their skateboards. It's so boring at Grandma's and Grandpa's house. She's always telling us to be careful that we don't break anything and how we need to start behaving like gentlemen."

They'd already heard him talking to Karl, so he couldn't pretend everything was fine. He'd never wanted to put them in the middle of this or force them to take sides. Somehow, he had to walk a fine line of being truthful without hurting their relationship with their grandparents, while at the same time alleviating their fears.

"You guys know better than to go off without telling someone. I'm sure half of what Grandma said to you came from fear that they'd lost you." He should know. It was fear that had him snapping at Karl. But they were impressionable kids, not adults.

Dylan shook his head, and Cody said, "Nuh-uh. She says stuff like that to us all the time."

Anger stirred inside him when they bowed their heads and their shoulders slumped. "Not anymore. I'm going to talk to Grandma right now and get this straightened out." He kissed the top of Dylan's and Cody's heads and went to kiss Teddy's before heading out to confront his mother-in-law.

But his youngest slid off the bed. "You can't, Dad. You can't make Grandma mad."

The worry on Teddy's face made Gabe as angry as the sense of defeat he was picking up from Cody and Dylan. "I promise, I'll do my best not to upset your Grandma, Teddy. But we have to stand up for the people we love. And right now, Grandma's making your brothers feel bad, and that's not okay."

"Teddy's right, Dad. We don't want..." Dylan glanced at his brothers. "Me and Cody will just ignore her when she says mean stuff."

They were as worried she'd go after custody of them as he was. And apparently just as worried she'd win. He didn't know what to do. Confront Diane and maybe lose his sons? Or go on as they had been and pray she didn't permanently damage the boys' self-esteem? If he went with the second option, there was still the threat that he'd do something she didn't approve of and she'd sue him for custody anyway.

"At school, when kids aren't being nice to each other, Mrs. Moore puts them in a time-out. Ben couldn't play with Sammy for a whole week at recess, and now they're best friends again. We just have to put Grandma in a time-out," Teddy said.

"Yeah, but you heard Grandpa. If Dad doesn't let us visit..." Dylan trailed off.

"Dad doesn't have to say anything. There's only three more weekends until Christmas, and Grandma and Grandpa are going to their friends' in Florida for the holidays."

Gabe hadn't realized how much he'd dreaded the thought of spending the holidays with his in-laws until that moment. He leaned over to grab Teddy, pulling him in for a hug. "Anyone ever tell you you're pretty smart for a five-year-old?"

"Yeah, you. And I'm almost six."

Dylan, who tended to be the more pessimistic of his sons, said, "But if Grandma and Grandpa are going away for Christmas, they'll want us to spend the weekend before with them."

"We can't go. I made my calendar already. We have Christmas stuff to do every weekend, and Grandma hates the holidays so she won't want to come here and join in the fun."

Dylan and Cody fell back on the bed and groaned. Clearly his sons were torn over which was worse, taking part in Teddy's Christmas fun or going to Grandma's house. All Gabe knew was it gave him some time. As today had proven, he needed to talk to a lawyer.

"And that'll give us lots of time to find you a new wife," Teddy said.

Gabe groaned and fell back on his bed with Dylan and Cody.

After sharing a father-and-sons wrestle on his bed, Gabe oversaw the boys' unpacking and showers. As they got into their pjs, Gabe headed for the kitchen. His hope that his in-laws would tire of waiting and head back to Atlanta didn't pan out. He'd barely stepped into the kitchen when his mother-in-law began complaining about the noise. He'd opened his mouth to defend his boys when he realized she wasn't talking about the noise in his house. The sound was coming from Mallory's. The bass was so loud it practically shook the house.

"What did I tell you, Karl? I knew that family would be

trouble the moment I laid eyes on them." She looked up from where she sat at the kitchen table with her husband. "There you are, Gabriel. I was going to send Karl over to tell your neighbors to turn down the music but it's probably best if you do. I've read too many stories about confrontations with neighbors ending in violence."

"That's not a problem we have in Highland Falls, but I'll go." He went to the pantry and pulled out the treats he'd bought the boys for movie night. At Diane's sharp intake of breath, he braced himself for a lecture on healthy eating and what sugar does to a child's brain. He'd heard it before. But his father-in-law covered her hand with his, and instead Gabe's mother-in-law simply pursed her lips.

"Guys, I'm just going over to the Mai—Mallory's," he corrected himself. "I won't be long but go ahead and start the first episode without me." Otherwise they'd be stuck making conversation with their grandmother, and who knew what she'd say.

He went out the side door. The moving van was gone, and so was Abby's truck, but Mallory's car was in the driveway. A definite concern given that the music was eardrum-shatteringly loud. He'd never tell his mother-in-law, but at that moment, he shared her concern that the Maitlands were trouble. Gabe banged on the door. After the third time with no response, he tried the knob. It turned, and he eased open the door.

"Anybody home?" he yelled into the house. It was dark except for a gleam of light from the back hall so he couldn't make out much else than that they still had some major unpacking to do. Getting concerned now, he walked into the house. "Mallory, boys, are you home?"

The music shut off, and then, seconds later, Brooks and Oliver appeared in the living room.

"Where's Mallory?" Gabe asked, shutting the door.

They shared a nervous glance, then Brooks pointed down the hall on his left. "In the loo."

"Is she sick?" Gabe asked as he walked around piles of boxes to reach the boys. In his mind, she had to be at death's door to have allowed her stepsons to play the music that loud.

"No. She said she was taking a bath."

With a bottle of wine? he wondered. Not that he really blamed her but it certainly wouldn't help her case if he were to find her passed out drunk in the bathtub. He nudged the boys out of the way and knocked on the closed door with light pooling beneath it. "Mallory?"

"She won't be able to hear you," Oliver said, and Gabe's concern kicked up a notch.

"Why's that?" he asked, fighting the urge to bust down the door.

"She has on her headphones."

He didn't know if it was Oliver's British accent that made it sound like the kid thought Gabe was an idiot, but either way he was not a happy man. "They must be damn good ones for you to be playing your music that loud and for her not to shut you down."

"Why would she? It's still early."

"Well, around here it's just as much about considera-tion for your neighbors as it is time of day. You broke a noise ordinance. Next time you do, I'm throwing you in jail," he said, because Diane had put him in a foul mood and this kid was testing more than his patience with his attitude.

Oliver looked like he was going to spout some smart-ass remark, but his brother tugged on his arm, then said, "I'm sorry, sir. We didn't realize our music was that loud. We won't do it again." He held up his phone. "I'll text Mallory. She has the phone with her in case we need her. She's very responsible."

Brooks reminded him of an older version of Teddy. They were the peacemakers in their families. And to a certain degree, like his boys, the threat that someone could come in and tear their family apart also hung over Oliver's and Brooks's heads. In their case, he was that someone.

"Thanks, Brooks. I appreciate it." Sounds of water sloshing and then the thud of something hitting the floor came from the other side of the door. "Mallory, are you okay?"

"Yes. I'll be right with you. I . . . ow. Ow, ow. Oh crap. No, no, no."

"Mallory, what is it?" he asked through the door.

"I'm stuck."

"What do you mean, you're stuck?"

"My toe is stuck in the faucet."

"Seriously? How is that even possible?"

"I don't know. I guess I have a fat toe. I was trying to push up the lever to let the water out, and my foot slipped and my toe went up the spout and it won't come out."

"Try turning the water on high and see if the pressure causes it to release your toe."

There was the sound of splashing, grunting, and then groaning. "I think it's making it worse."

"Okay, turn off the water. Do you have any butter or oil?"

"Yes, but I don't know how that's going to do me any good. I'm in here, and it's out there."

"Boys, do me a favor and find me some butter or oil in the kitchen."

Brooks nodded and took off, while Oliver gave Gabe a narrow-eyed look before following his brother.

"Ah, Gabe, you're not coming in here."

"Unless you have a better idea, it looks like I am." He hoped she did have a better idea. He might've fantasized about Mallory Maitland naked but the last thing he needed right now was having his fantasies about her come true. "Just cover yourself with a towel or something."

His suggestion was met with more grunting and groaning, a couple of *ow*s, and a *son of a nutcracker*.

He fought back a laugh. "Don't hurt yourself trying to get your toe out. I promise I won't look." He bent over the lock. The boys arrived with a container of margarine just as Gabe got the door unlocked. "Are you decent? I'm coming in now," he warned as the boys shared a look and then headed for their rooms.

"As decent as you can be lying naked in a bathtub."

He paused with his hand on the knob. "Maybe I should get my mother-in-law."

"Are you crazy?"

"Right." The last thing they wanted was to give Diane the time and opportunity to figure out who Mallory was.

Gabe braced himself as he walked into the bathroom,

closing the door behind him. The small space was warm and filled with the scent of lavender. He spared a glance for the woman in the tub. She was gorgeous, breathtakingly so. Her hair was piled on top of her head, and her skin was flushed and glowing. All of her skin except what was covered by a white towel was flushed and glowing. The towel was molded to her body, showing off her feminine curves and...

Face, look at her face. No, look at her legs. Not her legs, dumbass, her toes.

He dragged his forearm across his sweaty brow. "It's warm in here, isn't it?"

"Not really. I'm actually cold."

He knew that already. The white towel wasn't only molded to her incredible curves. It was practically see-through. He sat on the side of the tub with his back to her and removed the lid of the container he held.

Scooping out a glob of margarine, he placed the container on the floor. "So what were you listening to?" he asked as a way to distract himself from her shapely long leg and delicate foot with the sexy, siren-red painted toes.

"My book."

He glanced at the bamboo bath tray on the tiled floor. There was a glass of red wine with a lipstick stain near the rim and her phone. No book. She must've been listening to one on her phone. If it was the same one she'd been listening to earlier today—the one they'd all gotten a preview of when she started up her car at the diner—maybe she was flushed for an entirely different reason. The thought had him shifting uncomfortably on the edge of the tub, and he nearly fell in.

"I'm sorry about the boys playing their music so loud. They won't do it again, I promise. I know how bad me locking myself in the bathroom with a glass of wine and my book looks, especially when the house is in shambles. I can't even promise it won't happen again. Sometimes I just need a few minutes to decompress. And a glass of wine, a steamy bath, and a book help me unwind."

So he'd been right about the book. Do not think about the book, he told himself when he began feeling a little flushed himself. Naturally, the book was all he could think about now. The book and the fact that Mallory had been married to a man she'd never had sex with. He swore at himself in his head for letting his mind go there and bent over her foot.

"We all need to de-stress once in a while," he said in an attempt to alleviate her guilt and distract himself from thinking about the fact that he was slathering margarine on her feet and toes. Why the hell was he spreading it on her feet and toes? It was her big toe he had to unstick. Her big, fat toe, he thought in an effort to make himself stop admiring her sexy toes.

"What do you do to alleviate your stress?" she asked, sounding breathless.

Not surprisingly, the first thing that popped into his head was *Have sex.* It used to be how he relieved stress. His favorite way to relieve stress, actually. But he hadn't had sex in three years. Almost as long as Mallory. Except, maybe she had. "Go for a run. Work on my car. Play football with the boys or binge-watch Netflix."

She squirmed and released a tiny gasp. He looked down at his hands. He was massaging her calf. "I just, uh, thought that might help relax your foot."

"That was a good idea. A very, very good idea," she said with an audible swallow. He glanced at her, and she gave him a weak smile and fanned her face. "You're right. It's getting really warm in here."

Their eyes met and held like they had that day last July when he first saw her in Highland Brew. His pulse began to race and the sound of his heartbeat pounded in his ears. And then he thought he heard one of his sons calling for him from a long way away.

Before he realized his son actually was calling for him, Teddy burst into the bathroom, and his eyes went wide. Mallory gave a panicked squeak, and Gabe let go of her leg like he was a vegan who'd been caught with a rack of BBQ ribs in his hands. Twisting at the waist, he made a grab for the shower curtain to yank it closed, but it slipped through his fingers like a greased pig, and he fell backward into the tub.

"I found him, Grandma!" Teddy dragged in a puff of his inhaler. Then he yelled, "He's in the bathtub with Mallory."

Chapter Eight

It was perfectly natural to glance out one's kitchen window at eight in the morning but it didn't feel perfectly natural to Mallory. She was trying to avoid a face-to-face with her hunky next-door neighbor when she made her garbage run. Conveniently, or inconveniently—it depended on your point of view—her kitchen window faced his. At the moment, she was leaning toward it being convenient.

After his youngest son announced to his grandmother, not to mention Mallory's stepsons, that Gabe was in the bathtub with her last night, she wasn't particularly eager to see Gabe this morning. Teddy either, despite him being a sweetheart. The little boy had no idea how his innocent words could be misconstrued.

Anyway, she hoped Gabe was able to explain what had happened to his mother-in-law better than Mallory had been able to explain it to Oliver and Brooks. She'd stammered and stuttered through her explanation as to how Gabe had accidently fallen on top of her in the bathtub, only to discover they had zero interest in what she was saying. They still weren't speaking to her.

Not that they were ever overly chatty to begin with, but they were less so now that she'd told them the truth about the night their father died.

A jaw-cracking yawn overcame her. She'd been up since three in the morning. In the past few years, she'd developed insomnia. She'd believed the sleep disorder was a consequence of getting up at all hours of the night to care for Harry. After he'd died, she'd expected to return to her old sleeping habits, but it hadn't worked out that way. No doubt the stress of dealing with Marsha and Blair was a contributing factor.

But last night it was Gabe who had her tossing and turning in her bed, and in her dreams. Which were brief but explicit. She knew why, of course. Just as she knew why Gabe trying to free her big toe from the faucet had turned into a sexually charged moment.

Okay, the margarine part wasn't sexy at all; it was just gross. But having Gabe's big hands on her was completely fantasy-inducing and sort of dreams-coming-true, too, she supposed. After all, he'd been playing a starring role in her book fantasies since last summer.

They'd even had another one of those eyes-meeting, breath-stealing, sweep-you-off-your-feet moments like they'd had the day they'd first met at Highland Brew. And honestly, if things were different. If Gabe wasn't the person who would decide the fate of her and the family she hoped to make with the boys. If he wasn't the father of three boys, even if they seemed like very sweet boys, she'd want to explore just what those breath-stealing moments were all about.

They felt special, like a once-in-a-lifetime kind of thing. Then again, special didn't always turn out the way you'd think. Harry had made her feel special. So had her mom and her dad. She didn't really trust special anymore.

She yawned again, then worked on knotting the overstuffed garbage bag. Instead of tossing and turning for a few more hours, she'd decided to do something constructive and had gotten up to unpack the rest of the boxes and tidy the house. Abby had been right: the brick bungalow on Reindeer Road needed some TLC. But Mallory liked the feel of the place. She didn't think it would take much effort or, more importantly, much money, to make it feel like home.

Now that they were settled, and she'd gotten her confession out of the way, it was time to move forward with her plan. This was bigger than her weekly meetings with Gabe, bigger than the inconvenient feelings she had for the man, even bigger than the threat hanging over her head that she'd lose the boys. Because if she could change Brooks's and Oliver's minds about her before Christmas, she truly believed everything else would fall in place.

Humming "All I Want for Christmas Is You," she looked out the kitchen window to ensure the coast was still clear. It looked like the Buchanan family was still in bed so she was good to go. Garbage bag and car keys in hand, she headed for the side door.

As soon as she stepped outside, a brisk mountain

breeze swirled by, carrying with it the faded leaves that littered the backyard and the smell of pine. Shivering against the cold, she huddled deeper in the gray fleece sweatshirt she wore over her leggings and then fast-walked in her UGG slippers to the wooden garbage bin against the side of the house. After depositing the garbage bag inside, she rubbed her hands and took a quick look around.

Abby was right about something else. The area really was a nature lover's paradise. It was like they'd plopped the houses down in the middle of the forest. Mallory didn't remember the development being here. Then again, she didn't remember a lot about Highland Falls. For years she'd done her best to lock the memories away. It was easier to pretend that she'd never had a mother and father who loved her than to remember how much it hurt to be taken from everything she knew and for her father to abandon her.

Another gust of wind rattled the naked tree branches and the quaint yellow shutters that framed the windows, reminding her why she had her car keys in her hands. She'd been too tired to unload their winter gear from the trunk last night. She also needed her phone charger, she thought as she walked to the car. She opened the driver's-side door and leaned across the seat to unplug the cord. Then, remembering she'd left some homemade energy balls in the glove box, she slid into the driver's seat to open it.

"Where are you going?"

Mallory nearly jumped out of her skin. Pressing a hand to her chest, she turned to the little boy standing behind her. "Teddy, hi. Where did you come from?" He wore a navy winter jacket, knitted red hat and mittens, and a pair of snow boots with what looked to be red flannel pjs underneath.

He jerked his thumb at the back of his house. The Buchanans lived in a gorgeous Craftsman with a lovely porch at the front and an even lovelier screened-in deck at the back.

"I thought I saw one of Santa's reindeer in the woods, and then I saw you." He gave her a hopeful smile. "Did you see a reindeer too?"

"No, I didn't, but I wasn't looking. I was putting the garbage out. So maybe Rudolph or Dasher are in the woods. But it's probably best if you wait for your dad before checking it out." She looked around. "Does he know you're outside?"

"No, but it's okay. He was on the phone in his office." He lowered his voice in a conspirator's whisper. "My dad and brothers don't believe in Santa."

She widened her eyes in pretend horror. "Really? That can't be true. I bet they do. They're just trying to be cool. Oliver and Brooks are the same."

"Do you believe in Santa?"

"Of course I do." She smiled. He really was the cutest little boy she'd ever seen. She had a feeling he'd grow up to be a heartbreaker. He was the carbon copy of his father.

Teddy leaned in, peering at her as if he'd find the truth in her eyes. Whatever he saw must've convinced him she was a true believer because he rewarded her with a big smile. "I'm glad you moved here."

"Me too." This time, if he were to look closely enough, he'd be able to tell she was lying.

The last place she wanted to live was next door to a man who'd be watching her and the boys' every move. Last night was a perfect example of how detrimental their up-close-and-personal living arrangements could be. Which she'd shared with her matchmaking best friend as soon as Oliver and Brooks were out of earshot. Abby swore her choice of the house on Reindeer Road had nothing to do with matchmaking. The Highland Falls rental market was extremely tight, and Mallory's budget made it that much tighter. A quick search on her phone had proven that Abby was telling the truth.

"Where are you going?" Teddy repeated the question he'd first asked her.

"Nowhere." She held up her phone cord and the container of no-bake white-chocolate-and-cranberry energy balls. "I forgot I'd left these in the car, and I need to get our winter stuff out of the trunk."

"My brothers think your car is pretty. They think you are too. So does my dad."

Heat rose to her cheeks. This is exactly why she hadn't wanted to run into this adorable little boy. She smiled. "That's nice. I should probably—"

"Are you married?"

"I was, but my husband died."

"That's too bad. My mom died too. She was my dad's wife."

"I'm sorry your mommy died, sweetheart. Mine did too. It's hard, isn't it?" She didn't like to think about her mom. Mallory's life had imploded the day she died.

He shrugged. "It's harder for my dad and brothers. I don't really remember her. Just from pictures. She was really pretty too. And nice. My grandma misses her a lot. I think that's why she's an old battle-ax." He made a face. "That's what my brothers call her, but don't tell my dad. They only said it cuz she's kinda mean to them and that makes my dad mad. But he can't get mad at her or she'll take us away from him."

"I'm sure she wouldn't, Teddy. Adults say all kinds of things they don't mean."

"She meant it. She even talked to a lawyer. But don't tell my dad; he doesn't know. I heard her on the phone. She thinks just cuz I'm only five I don't understand stuff, but I do. But it's okay cuz I made a plan."

Mallory couldn't believe what she was hearing. She felt heartsick for Gabe and his boys. This was so much worse than her situation. It was obvious Gabe's sons adored him as much as he adored them. She was furious on their behalf, and concerned for Teddy. A five-year-old shouldn't be coming up with plans to save his family. He should be thinking of holiday parades and lists for Santa.

She took his hand and gave it a gentle squeeze. "Plans are always a good idea. But I'm almost positive you have absolutely nothing to worry about, Teddy. I don't know your dad all that well, but I'm sure he'll—"

"You know him pretty well. You were in the bathtub together, and you had no clothes on."

"Of course I had clothes on." She laughed, only nerves made her sound like a braying donkey. "It might not have looked that way, but I had on...a bathing suit!

A white one." She needed a distraction. "Here." She opened the container on her lap and offered it to him. "Have an energy ball."

She pulled the container back. "You don't have allergies, do you? On second thought, you should probably ask your dad if it's okay." She fitted the lid back on and handed him the container. "If it is, you can share with your brothers."

"Did you make them?"

"I did." She smiled, relieved that her plan had worked.

"Do you like to cook?"

"I love to cook."

"Just good food or do you make fun food too?"

"Are cookies and cakes considered fun food?" He nodded. "There you go, I never knew. I make fun food too."

"Do you mind if your sons play outside and get dirty?"

"To tell you the truth, I'd love if Oliver and Brooks played outside and got dirty once in a while, Teddy."

"Would you get mad at them if they were playing in the house and broke something?"

"Not if it was an accident. Did you break something when you were playing inside?"

"No, my brothers broke a doll at my grandmother's. They didn't mean to, but she got really mad at them and made them go to their room." He leaned in and whispered, "She made them stay in there until dinnertime. We didn't tell my dad though."

She'd only met Diane Rollins at the country club a couple of times, but she wasn't surprised by what Teddy shared. "Maybe you should tell your dad, sweetie."

"I can't, remember? I have a plan."

"Right, your plan. Well, I haven't known you for long, Teddy, but I have a feeling any plan you come up with will absolutely work." She also thought his father deserved to know what was going on with his mother-in-law but didn't feel it was her place to tell him.

"I wasn't sure it would work, but now I am."

"That's a great attitude, Teddy. You just stay positive," she said, thinking as much about her own plan as his. "And don't let anyone tell you that it won't work."

He high-fived her, and she high-fived him back with a smile as big as his.

"I'm going to tell my dad," he said, and from behind him came a voice Mallory had hoped not to hear until their Monday morning coffee meeting.

"Tell your dad what?" Gabe asked, coming to stand behind his son. He rested his big, bare hands on Teddy's shoulders, and heat spread from Mallory's chest to her cheeks as her mind rather inconveniently provided her with a slide show of images from last night.

"Mallory says my plan is going to work. So you don't have to worry anymore, Dad."

She dragged her gaze from Gabe's hands to his face, which did nothing to cool her heated cheeks. He looked like he'd just rolled out of bed. His thick, black hair was a gorgeous mess and the stubble on his jaw gave him a casually sexy air. The dark Henley he wore with his jeans and steel-toe boots gave off the same vibe while also highlighting his broad shoulders and wide chest. Just as the well-worn jeans showed off his long legs and muscular thighs.

"She did, did she?"

He didn't sound happy, and she glanced up. He held her gaze, a dark eyebrow raised.

She didn't know what to say. Sorry for ogling you? Or sorry for encouraging your little boy? The latter, no doubt. But he probably wasn't so worried about Teddy sharing his plan with her as he was that his son might have shared the reason why he needed one.

"Yep, so you should ask her now. We don't have a lot of time." He tipped his head to smile up at his unsmiling father and held up the container. "Mallory made them for us."

Oh my gosh, why did he say that? Now Gabe would think she was trying to bribe him or that she had a crush on him. "I, um, actually made them for—"

Apparently Teddy didn't hear her and kept talking. "She loves to cook, she loves to bake, and she doesn't mind kids getting dirty or breaking things, and she's really pretty, and you like her car."

She raised a finger. "Teddy, I think I might've missed something. What is your plan exactly?"

"We need a mom, and I pick you."

Chapter Nine

Mallory stared at the little boy smiling at her. She couldn't believe it. Teddy had actually been interviewing her to be his mother.

Now what was she supposed to do? Truthfully, she was touched he'd chosen her to be his mom. After spending the past two months feeling like a failure in the stepmom department, it was nice to be wanted.

Gabe saved her from having to respond. "Buddy, you can't go around auditioning women to be your mother."

"How come? We need a mom who doesn't mind if we get dirty or break things, Dad. Cody and Dylan do it all the time. And we need a mom who likes to cook because you don't. You interview people. That's how you know if they're good or bad, and I know Mallory is good."

Gabe's mouth twitched. "You make some excellent points, honey. You've obviously given this some serious thought, but you forgot one important thing."

"Yeah, what's that?"

"I have to marry the person you choose, and I'm kinda fussy. So if you don't mind, I'd like to pick my own wife."

"Don't you like Mallory?"

"I do, but we don't know each other—" At Mallory's squeak of dismay, he glanced at her. He was walking into the same trap she had, and it was embarrassing. "Very well."

"You do so, Dad. You were in the bathtub together and Mallory was nak—"

"Okay, I think we're done here. Your favorite You-Tuber called. Seems Abby arranged a special breakfast with you and Santa, so you better go and get dressed."

"No way!" Teddy looked like he might cry.

"Way." His father grinned at him. Then he took him by the shoulders and turned him toward the house. "Get your brothers out of bed."

"Aw, Dad, they won't want to go. They'll make a big fuss and ruin everything."

"I promise I won't let them ruin anything. It's a pancake breakfast, and you know how much they like pancakes."

"Can Mallory come? She likes Santa too."

Getting the distinct impression that Gabe didn't want her hanging out with them, she said, "Thanks for thinking of me, Teddy. Any other time I would've loved to go with you, but I have to finish unpacking. Maybe I'll see you at the parade though." It was the perfect opportunity to kick off her plan. Surely the parade would get her stepsons in the Christmas spirit.

"Okay. We'll be standing in front of the police station."

"Sounds great. Have fun at your breakfast with Santa." She would've loved to see his face when he met the man himself. Maybe she'd ask Abby to send her a picture. She inwardly rolled her eyes at herself. If she did that, her best friend would totally up her matchmaking game.

"Get going, buddy." Gabe patted his butt to get him moving.

Teddy glanced at his father over his shoulder. "Aren't you coming?"

"I'll be there in a minute. I just want to talk to Mallory for a sec." At his son's big, knowing, gap-toothed grin, Gabe sighed and grumbled, "Teddy."

Gabe waited until the back door closed behind his son to turn to her. "Scooch over. It's freezing out here."

She stared at him. "You want me to crawl over the console and get in the passenger seat?"

"Yeah." He smiled and waggled his eyebrows. "I've wanted to get behind the wheel of this baby from the moment I saw her."

"So Teddy wasn't lying. You really do like my car," she said as she awkwardly climbed into the passenger-side seat.

"Ah, yeah. She's a beauty. Don't you?" he asked as he slid into the driver's seat. He adjusted her seat to make room for his long legs and big frame. Then he turned on the car and closed the door.

"Harry was into cars. He loved the Jag but they all look the same to me. Put me in a parking lot, and I wouldn't be able to tell you which car was mine."

"Okay, that's just sacrilege." He looked sincerely

offended. "So what else did my precocious son say? Other than you were his choice for new mom."

She watched as he ran his long, blunt fingers over the interior of her car and debated whether or not to tell him about his mother-in-law's plans. Forewarned is forearmed, but she worried about breaking Teddy's confidence.

He stopped midstroke to cock his head. "What is it?"

"Teddy told me something that I think you should know. I mean, I'd want to know if I were you."

"Considering the position he was interviewing you for, I can take an educated guess." He twisted his hands on the steering wheel. "He's worried my mother-in-law is going after custody. It's my fault. They overheard me talking to Karl. I should've been more careful. But I've put up with Diane's veiled threats for the past couple years, and I guess they've worn me down."

"I'm so sorry, Gabe. That must be horrible for you and the boys."

"I used to be able to convince myself I was wrong. But last night, it was obvious I'd been right all along."

"What are you going to do?"

"Only thing I can do. Hire a lawyer."

"That's a good idea."

His eyes narrowed. "You're not telling me something. What is it?"

"Please don't tell Teddy I told you. I wouldn't want him to think he can't trust me. But I think it's important for you to know. Teddy overheard Diane speaking to a lawyer."

He slapped the heel of his palm against the steering wheel and grimaced. "Sorry."

She touched his arm. "Don't apologize. I can't imagine what this is like for you."

"Of course you can. Indirectly, I'm playing the role of Diane in your custody nightmare."

"It's not the same at all. The boys are yours, and they obviously adore you. They'd be devastated if your mother-in-law got custody, which, by the way, no judge in their right mind would grant."

"Except we both know that if someone has the money and connections and they're willing to do whatever it takes to win, there's a ninety-nine-point-nine-percent chance the verdict will go their way. Don't deny it," he said when she opened her mouth. "That's what happened to you."

"No, it's not, Gabe. I gave up. I didn't have the energy left to fight. Or the desire. The only reason I didn't walk away in the beginning was I wanted to honor Harry's last wishes. But as time passed and the court battle dragged on, I began to believe Marsha had a point. Maybe the only reason Harry married me was because he knew he was dying. I might not have completed my residency, but I had the qualifications to care for him. In the beginning, maybe he even clung to the hope that together we could beat it.

"Except when all was said and done, he had to settle for someone to simply care for him until he took his last breath." She looked down at her hands twisting in her lap. She no longer wore her wedding ring.

"You can't seriously believe that, Mallory. You're

gorgeous, smart, and sweet. Any man would count himself lucky if you agreed to be his wife."

She'd counted herself lucky that Harry had wanted to marry her. Everyone told her she was, including Marsha and Blair an hour before her wedding.

"You forgot that I can cook and don't mind kids getting dirty or breaking things," she teased. Gabe playing a starring role in her daydreams was one thing but contemplating anything more than that would only lead to heartache.

"My son's smart and has great taste." Gabe moved the steering wheel with his finger. "We're not kids, so I'm not going to play games or dance around the truth. I think it's pretty obvious that I'm attracted to you."

Her heart took a panicked leap. Why couldn't he be like other men and play games? Why did he have to be honest and good and someone she could only dream of having a happily-ever-after with? She wasn't as brave as him. What she felt for him was so much more than a simple attraction.

"Abby seemed to think so." It was all she'd allow herself to admit.

He shifted in the driver's seat to look at her. "You honestly couldn't tell I was attracted to you last summer? That I'm still attracted to you?"

"Maybe. But then you arrested me, and I preferred ignoring you and...and my attraction to you. Yesterday was more of the same. I seem to have a love-hate relationship with you, Chief Buchanan." Her cheeks flushed, and she shook her head. "I didn't mean...you know what I mean."

"Yeah, and in my defense, it's not like I had a lot of choice. And I didn't arrest you yesterday."

"From where I'm sitting, you might as well have."

"I'll talk to Kayla, see if we can't cut your probationary period down to a month."

"'Probationary period.' Do you see what I mean?"

"Nothing I can say will make you feel better about this, but could you withhold judgment for now? If we put our heads together, we might be able to come up with a strategy that'll actually work. It sometimes helps to have a fresh pair of eyes look at the situation."

"You're right. I'm sorry for overreacting. I didn't get much sleep last night." And his talk about how he felt about her was making her nervous.

"I didn't hurt you when I fell on top of you, did I?" He pushed his fingers through his dark, messy hair. Clearly, he'd been doing that a lot this morning. "I should've stuck around to make sure you were all right, but the last thing I wanted was my mother-in-law seeing us, seeing you—"

"Trust me, the last thing I wanted was for Diane Rollins to walk in on us like that. It was bad enough Teddy did." She made a face. "He thinks I was naked. I told him I was wearing a bathing suit."

His lips twitched. "That must've been an interesting conversation."

"One I'd rather not repeat, to tell you the truth."

"Yeah, that's kinda why I thought we should talk." His eyes moved over her face. "As much as I agree with everything Teddy said about you, it would probably be best if we avoid being in each other's company around him. I don't want him to get the wrong idea. The kid's tenacious. When he's got a plan, he doesn't give up. And right now, he has his eyes firmly set on you for his new mom."

"To thwart his grandma."

He moved his head from left to right. "Yes, and no. He just started kindergarten this year, and some of the moms volunteer. He's the only one in his class without one, so he's been hinting for a couple months now that I should get out there and start dating again. He offered to set up a Tinder account for me."

Mallory laughed. "That I would've liked to see. But it's a little scary how smart he is."

"You're telling me. His new plan is scary too. Not the part about you, although, yeah, that is kinda scary too. But it's his time line that concerns me most. He was adamant that I didn't have time to waste finding a new wife. I didn't pay much attention to it last night. I was more interested in calming their fears. But after what he heard, my gut says Diane's planning to serve me with a petition for custody at the beginning of the new year."

"Or maybe she's hoping that you'll deal with whatever concerns she's having about the boys?"

He scrubbed a hand over his jaw. "It's my parenting she's concerned about. Diane and Karl moved in with us when my wife died. My family's close, but my mom and dad still work and my brothers have busy lives of their own. At first, having Diane and Karl there was a godsend. I don't know how I would've gotten through those first months without them. Teddy was a toddler, but the twins were struggling, and I couldn't afford to take time off. My job——" He grimaced. "Sorry, I don't know why I'm telling you all of this."

"Don't apologize. I'm happy to listen. Like you said, sometimes it helps to talk things out with someone who isn't emotionally invested. Although, to be honest, I'm feeling pretty invested, and I hardly know you and your sons."

"I really wish things could be different, Mallory. But despite what Teddy thinks, the worst thing I could do right now is get involved with someone. No matter how much I want to." He smiled, reaching over to tuck a strand of hair behind her ear.

His fingers lingered on her cheek. She wanted to hold them there. Just for a few minutes. Because this was as close as she and Gabe Buchanan could ever be.

"Especially with someone like me. No, don't deny it," she said when he went to object. "Please, Gabe, let's be honest with each other. I would be the worst person for you to get involved with. Diane would crucify you in court. Her lawyer would present every lie the press printed about me last year. And after yesterday, she'd have the evidence to portray me as an unfit mother."

He stared out the windshield. "Over the last eighteen months, Diane has given me plenty to be angry about. I moved away from my family and a job I loved to make her happy. But I don't think I've ever been as angry at her as I am now." He turned his head to hold her gaze. "There's something about you, Mallory Maitland. And I'm afraid I'm making one of the biggest mistakes of my life not saying to hell with Diane to see where this might take us."

He was going to make her cry. She had to think of something to lighten the mood. "You never know—she may have done you a favor. I have a difficult time with two boys in my life. What would I do with five, six including you? Now if you would've had girls..." She trailed off, her teasing smile fading at the look in his eyes.

"My son isn't only smart. He's an excellent judge of character. So I don't doubt, given half a chance, that you'll make a wonderful mother."

Chapter Ten

Gabe stood behind Mallory and Teddy on the sidewalk outside the station, watching the Santa Claus parade. So much for keeping their distance from each other when his son was around.

Gabe didn't blame Mallory. She'd given it her best shot, huddling among a group of people half a block up the road and on the opposite side from the station. Teddy shouldn't have been able to see her but somehow his son had spotted her in the crowd. Then again, so had Gabe. Maybe Teddy had simply followed his father's long, lingering glances in Mallory's direction.

Teddy hadn't let up until Gabe had texted her to watch the parade with them, after he'd inappropriately accessed her cell phone number. At that point, it had seemed the lesser of two evils. All Teddy's talk about Mallory had garnered the curious attention of the people standing within earshot, including several of Gabe's officers.

As far as his plan for them to keep their distance, today was a wash anyway. He'd spotted his sons in the kitchen window looking out at them when he was opening the door to Mallory's car. Teddy had been beaming like his dreams had come true. Whereas Dylan and Cody looked like their dad getting cozy with the new neighbor veered into nightmare territory.

There was no way the twins would be onboard with their baby brother's plan to find them a new mom or their dad a new wife. They'd given a big thumbs-down to the idea when Teddy broached the subject in late September. Last night they'd been so focused on their baby brother's Christmas plans that they'd missed the part where Teddy had said that Gabe didn't have a lot of time left to find himself a wife.

He didn't think it was a good sign that, at the thought, Gabe's gaze went straight to Mallory. She'd twisted her hair into a messy knot on the top of her head, and the puffy blue ski jacket she wore matched her eyes. He supposed it was a good thing Teddy was too busy oohing and ahhing over the parade with Mallory to notice Gabe once again gazing longingly at the woman his son had chosen as his top choice for new mother.

Gabe couldn't seem to help himself. He'd told Mallory the truth earlier. Just put it all out there. It was so unlike him; he couldn't believe he had. He was a private person. He didn't trust easily. And the last thing he wanted to talk to anyone about was his feelings.

But Teddy had put him in an awkward position, and the news that Diane had gone so far as to hire a lawyer had thrown Gabe for a loop. He'd been off balance— still was, if he was being completely honest with himself. But that didn't explain why he'd spilled his guts to

Mallory, a woman he barely knew. And yet while that was true, on a soul-deep level, he felt like he'd known her forever.

There it was, the heart of the matter. He'd told her he was attracted to her. He'd even gone so far as to admit he was afraid he was making one of the biggest mistakes of his life, which was the God's honest truth. What he hadn't told her was that his late wife had been the love of his life. They'd had what he thought of as a once-in-a-lifetime love. And when you were lucky enough to find a love like that once, the odds you'd find another were stacked against you. That was the reason he'd never had the urge to get back in the game.

Until last summer when he'd first seen Mallory at Highland Brew. Only the price was too high. He wouldn't risk losing his sons.

His eyes found their way back to her. Her head was tipped back as she shared a laugh with his son. She looked like she was enjoying the Highland Falls Santa Claus Parade as much as Teddy. The way the two of them were carrying on, you'd think they were watching the Macy's Thanksgiving Day Parade, not a small-town parade.

He glanced at Cody and Dylan, who stood off to the right of him kicking a stone back and forth between them. At least they'd stopped complaining and sharing how bored they were while the citizens of Highland Falls listened in. Half of them already had an ax to grind with Gabe. He didn't need his sons to draw any more negative attention his way.

At least Mallory's stepsons were quiet about their

disdain for the parade. Other than him, he didn't think anyone else noticed the eye rolls or head shakes they directed at their stepmother whenever they looked up from their phones. He honestly didn't know how she'd managed to get them here. If not for Teddy, he would've happily given it a pass.

Mallory glanced at her stepsons over her shoulder. "Oliver and Brooks, look. It's the high school band and the cheerleaders."

Okay, so that answered that question. Still…Gabe stepped forward and leaned into her. "You seriously bribed your stepsons with the promise they'd get to check out a bunch of pretty teenage girls in cheerleading uniforms?"

She wrinkled her nose. "When you put it like that it sounds pretty bad."

His youngest frowned up at him. "Dad, don't make Mallory feel bad." Teddy glanced at her stepsons, who were now watching the parade with rapt attention, and whispered, "She had to get Oliver and Brooks to come. It's part of her plan."

Oh no, not someone else with a plan. "What exactly is this plan? Come on, you can share with me. I promise not to judge." She raised an eyebrow. "Okay, this time I won't judge."

"Christmas, Dad," Teddy said like he was surprised Gabe hadn't figured it out.

His youngest made no bones about his dad being the best detective alive. So Gabe didn't want to disappoint him, but he seriously didn't understand what Christmas had to do with Mallory's plan to win over her stepsons.

"Yeah, I get it. The parade is all about Christmas. I'm just not sure what—"

"Oliver and Brooks are grinches, Dad. Just like you, Cody, and Dylan are. Not really the same but kinda."

Gabe sighed. "I'm not a grinch, and neither are your brothers."

"It's okay, Dad. I understand why you guys don't like the holidays."

As Gabe had told Mallory, Teddy was smart, so there was no sense in denying what his youngest must've discerned even though Gabe had done his best to make the holidays special for him. Now that he knew, he'd do a better job of faking it. He'd get Cody and Dylan onboard too.

A group of pipers played "O Come, All Ye Faithful" and he waited for them to pass before asking, "I'm still not sure what any of this has to do with Oliver and Brooks."

"Dad, remember how the Grinch's heart grew three times its size in the story?"

"Yeah, so…"

Teddy made a disgusted sound and bowed his head. Probably feeling sorry for his son, Mallory explained, "Christmas is a time for family and forgiveness. If Christmas can touch the boys' hearts like it did the Grinch's, maybe they'd have some room for me." Her cheeks flushed. "I know it sounds silly, but I'm desperate."

It did, but that didn't stop him from wanting to give her a hug and then pulling her stepsons aside and giving them a piece of his mind.

"It doesn't sound silly at all, does it, Dad?" Teddy

said, sounding like a stern little old man, which meant Gabe hadn't done a good job hiding his skepticism.

"Teddy's right. It's a great idea. Maybe we should try it out on Grandma." He realized his mistake when his son and Mallory shared a look. "I was joking."

It didn't matter what he said—he could practically hear the wheels turning in their heads. Luckily, the local bakery's float rolled by, providing a distraction. The gingerbread house decorated for the holidays won cheers from the crowd, but it was Bliss, the bakery's owner, dressed as a gingerbread woman, who got the loudest applause. Probably because she was handing out gingerbread men and women to the kids lining either side of the street.

Teddy jumped up and down trying to get Bliss's attention. Instead of standing with the other kids on the edge of the sidewalk, he'd chosen to stick with Mallory.

"Go stand up front or you'll miss out on all the candy, Teddy. The clowns are handing out candy canes," Mallory said.

"It's okay." Teddy took her hand and smiled up at her. "I don't really like candy canes."

Gabe shook his head; the kid was addicted to candy. "Your nose is going to grow, you know?" he said to his son.

"Yeah, if I was made of wood," Teddy quipped, and then shot Mallory another adoring smile that tugged on Gabe's heartstrings.

He hadn't realized until that moment how much his son had been craving a woman's attention. And he couldn't help but wonder if his mother-in-law was right after all. Maybe his sons really did need a woman in their lives.

He glanced at the twins, who'd pushed their way to the edge of the sidewalk. The two of them grinned as they pocketed handfuls of candy canes. Just what Gabe needed. They were hyper enough without the added sugar.

Shouts of "Granny MacLeod! Over here, Granny MacLeod!" drew his attention from the boys. Granny MacLeod, who bore a striking resemblance to the actress Betty White, albeit with a Scottish accent, was riding down the street on a white horse sporting a sparkly gold unicorn horn. Granny MacLeod owned I Believe in Unicorns on Main Street, a gift shop that sold anything and everything unicorn.

Sitting on top of the horse wearing a long, white fur-trimmed cape with the name of her business on the back, Granny MacLeod gave the parade watchers a royal wave. The older woman considered herself the town's matriarch. Her family was said to have settled Highland Falls in the mid-eighteen hundreds. The Clearances in Scotland had sent many highland families to the Americas, and several, including the MacLeods, had chosen to settle in the Blue Ridge mountains of North Carolina.

"Mal! Teddy!" a familiar voice called out. It was Abby.

Dressed in a red jacket and a Santa's hat, she drove a tractor pulling a float with a log cabin, fake trees, a beehive, and a couple dressed in highland garb with a beautiful white wolf at their side. The white wolf was actually half-dog, half-wolf and belonged to Abby's fiancé, Hunter Mackenzie. No doubt Hunter was responsible for building the float, because it could have held its own in the Macy's Thanksgiving Day Parade. Gabe had a feeling that Hunter would be roped into building all of the floats for the town's parades from now on.

Hunter's cousin and a pregnant Sadie Gray, Granny MacLeod's granddaughter, were posing as popular literary couple Jamie and Claire Fraser. The couple of *Outlander* fame were rumored to have settled on the ridge outside of town in the eighteen hundreds.

The rumor had been started by none other than the town's famous YouTuber. Abby had exploited the myth to relaunch her career and Highland Falls' flagging tourism industry. It had been a success on both counts, but not without some drama. Gabe had learned the hard way last summer that things got out of hand quickly when Abby was involved.

Mallory and Teddy waved at Abby, laughing when she held up her dog, Bella, an eight-pound gold-and-black Yorkshire terrier that was dressed as one of Santa's reindeers. Bella and Wolf were almost as popular on Abby's YouTube channel as she was.

Then, as though Mallory had just recognized the woman on the float, she called out, "Sadie! I didn't know you were coming to town."

"Someone didn't give me a choice," Sadie yelled back, hitching her thumb at Abby. "See you at the community center after the parade?"

Mallory nodded enthusiastically, which was fine. What wasn't fine was Teddy was doing the same. Between the special breakfast with Santa and the parade, Gabe had thought his holiday duties were done for the day.

"Hey, buddy," Gabe began, thinking he'd lay the groundwork as to why going home would be way more fun than going to the community center. He was interrupted by a *Ho, ho, ho* coming through a bullhorn. Santa had lots of practice with the bullhorn because Santa was being played by none other than Owen Campbell. Whoever had taken on the task of turning the slender older man into a rotund Santa had done a masterful job.

Gabe had been avoiding Owen and his phone calls since he'd left the hospital last night. It had been harder to avoid him at the pancake breakfast this morning, but he'd managed. His predecessor and nemesis had offered to fill in for Ruby while she was off.

Santa rode in a gorgeous red antique sleigh on the back of a flatbed with the town's mayor, Winter Johnson, sitting beside him. Santa's helpers, a couple of teenage girls, including his sons' babysitter, sat on oversized, brightly wrapped Christmas presents tossing out candy to the kids. The mayor and Owen had asked Gabe to join them, but he'd politely declined. Now he wondered if he'd made a mistake. Owen now had plenty of time to convince the mayor to let him fill in for Ruby.

"Okay, guys. Show's over. Who's up for pizza and a game of foosball? Teddy, you can be on my team," Gabe said.

"We have to go to the community center, Dad. I have to tell Santa what I want for Christmas," Teddy said.

"I thought you gave him your letter at the breakfast."

"Santa was telling us about the North Pole and his reindeer, and I didn't want to interrupt him." Teddy glanced at Mallory, who was trying to convince her stepsons that the festivities at the community center wouldn't be as lame as they claimed they'd be. No doubt Cody and Dylan, who thought anything to do with Santa was lame, unless it involved candy, would agree with them. But the twins were busy searching the sidewalk for overlooked candy as the crowd began to disperse.

"I just think it would be a good opportunity for you to meet some kids around your own ages before you start school on Monday."

Teddy, who'd clearly taken a page from Mallory's playbook, said, "I can introduce you to Ainsley. She's our babysitter and one of Santa's helpers. She's really pretty, and she's sixteen too."

What his son conveniently left out was that Ainsley was dating the high school football team's star quarterback. Teddy didn't completely win over Mallory's stepsons, but they reluctantly agreed to go for twenty minutes. They conceded to thirty if Mallory agreed to order in pizza and download a game on their phones.

Cody and Dylan didn't complain as loudly about going as Gabe had expected them to, in part due to his boys' angling for a way to hang out with Mallory's stepsons. They thought their edgy attitudes and accents were cool but the real draw, Gabe knew, was their expensive tech toys.

On the short walk from the station to the community center, Gabe's sons regaled Oliver and Brooks with stories Ainsley had told them about high school life in Highland Falls.

"Not exactly what they're used to, is it?" Gabe said to Mallory, who walked beside him.

"No, but given the crowd they were running with in Atlanta, I consider that a positive. I just hope they'll give the school and the kids here a chance."

"It took Cody and Dylan a couple weeks to adjust, but now it's like they've been going there for years. They've got good friends, and they're doing well in class."

He'd been surprised at how easily they'd adjusted. Back home, they'd gone to the same school since kindergarten. He'd said as much to his parents on a call home in the early days. His mother hadn't been as surprised as he was. Other than not having them close by, she'd believed the move would be good for them. She'd felt they'd needed a fresh start.

"If Oliver and Brooks were given a choice, they wouldn't go back to the school in Atlanta. They'd go back to boarding school in England. They were happy there."

"I take it Marsha won't pay for them to go."

"No. As far as she's concerned, it's a complete waste of money. And I can't say I disagree with her. The yearly costs are exorbitant."

"If you had the money, would you send them?"

"On the one hand, I guess I'd want to. They lived there for years and think of the school as home. But on the other hand, I can't believe they're not better off having more of a normal childhood."

"Like attending small-town holiday parades and paying a visit to Santa?"

The way she smiled up at him, her cheeks pink from the cold and her eyes sparkling with humor, he was glad Teddy had insisted she join them.

"I doubt I'll get them to sit on Santa's knee, but I appreciate Teddy getting them to come at all. If they could meet a few kids before school, I'm sure they'd be less anxious."

So would she, he thought, so he didn't lecture her on letting the boys blackmail her. He had a feeling it was a ploy they used often with her. Probably because it worked. But now wasn't the time or the place. The boys walked inside the community center, and Gabe held the door for Mallory.

"I see you're taking your job seriously, Chief Buchanan," a feminine voice said from behind him. It was a voice he recognized. Kayla McPherson. Something else he recognized was the underlying sarcasm. Kayla wasn't happy to see him with Mallory.

Mallory cast him a nervous glance. He gave her a reassuring one in return. No matter how much he'd like to avoid another coffee date with Kayla, he had to take one for the team. The thought brought him up short. Since when did he think of himself and Mallory as a team?

He forced a smile, thinking it'd be safer to ignore her comment. "Hey, Kayla. Nice day for the parade. Did you enjoy yourself?"

"I did, and you and Ms. Carlisle seemed to be enjoying yourselves as well," Kayla said, referring to Mallory by her maiden name. No doubt in an attempt to put Mallory in her place.

By the way her shoulders inched up, Mallory was probably regretting accepting his invitation to stand with them and watch the parade. She wasn't the only one.

"Mallory and her boys—" Gabe began, about to give

a perfectly reasonable explanation for them being at the parade together, only to be cut off by Abby and her smartphone.

"For all of you who've been asking whatever happened to Mallory Maitland and Gabriel Buchanan, have I got an update for you!" Abby said into her smartphone, then turned the screen to face them.

"Abby, why don't we do this another time? I could really go for some hot chocolate right now." Mallory blocked the camera with her hand.

Gabe gave Mallory credit for trying, but Abby was as persistent as her purse-sized Yorkshire terrier. As Gabe had learned over the past months, nothing stopped Abby from getting the story for her YouTube followers. Except her husband. Gabe had a feeling this was one story he and Mallory didn't want out there and desperately searched the crowd for Hunter Mackenzie.

"I'm sorry, Mal, but my followers have been begging for an update about you and our hunky chief of police ever since he arrested you last July. And I always give my followers what they want—don't I, guys?" She ducked out of the way of Mallory's hand. "So breaking news from Highland Falls: our hunky chief of police and single father of three adorable boys is the next-door neighbor of our gorgeous senior care specialist and single stepmother to two handsome teenage boys! Sounds to me like Highland Falls just got their very own Christmas romance. Stay tuned for weekly updates!"

Chapter Eleven

"Come on, Kayla. You can't possibly be buying that. Abby is just trying to promote her channel. It's a gimmick, nothing more," Mallory heard Gabe say from behind her as they walked into Highland Falls Recreation and Civic Center. She couldn't hear the other woman's response, but the way Kayla walked past her with her head held high and her back stiff didn't bode well.

"You didn't do your best friend any favors," Gabe said to Abby. Then he gave Mallory's arm a brief, reassuring squeeze. "I'll talk to her and get it straightened out."

She nodded her thanks as he followed Kayla through the open double doors on the right. The center had several meeting rooms as well as a gym, an arena, and a pool.

Abby, who'd been standing with her mouth hanging open, recovered and called after Gabe, "I resent that. I wouldn't use my best friend to promote my channel."

That's exactly how it sounded to Mallory, but the one thing she didn't doubt was that Abby's heart was in the right place.

"So what was your plan?" Mallory asked as she and Abby walked through the double doors. At the front of the room, a mural of Highland Falls in winter filled the back wall. Two trees decorated with colorful lights stood in front of it, while Santa sat on a big red chair between the Christmas trees. She didn't have to search the crowd for the boys. Gabe's sons and hers stood to the right of Santa, talking to a couple of teenage girls dressed in green elf costumes.

"Other than pointing out the obvious that you and Gabe are perfect for each other? Although I'm kinda ticked at him right now."

Mallory filled Abby in on everything that had happened at the station yesterday. She hadn't been able to tell her last night with the boys around. "So now you understand why Gabe reacted like he did. The last thing we need is for Kayla to think we're involved or that Gabe's recommendations are biased."

"Yes, and that's exactly why I'm doing weekly updates from Reindeer Road. I don't trust Kayla McPherson and neither does Eden. I saw the way she was looking at you and Gabe. She's already made up her mind about you. So what we need is a high-profile publicity campaign that shows everyone what an incredible woman and mother you are. The press did a number on your reputation last summer, and it's going to take a concerted effort to rebuild it. Now, I thought we'd call the segments Love on Reindeer Road or Christmas on Reindeer Road. I'm leaning toward Love on Reindeer Road. What do you think?"

Mallory's heart pumped an extra beat. "That you

and Eden are worried I might actually lose custody of the boys."

"You have to stop focusing on losing the boys. Thoughts become things, you know. Stop focusing on the negative."

"How about the reality? First, Gabe is not going to let you put him and his sons on camera, and I don't blame him. Second, I don't want Oliver and Brooks on camera either. And third, Gabe and I aren't in a relationship and won't be, and I can't tell you why, but it's really important right now that not even a whisper that we might be gets out. I'm serious, Abby. This isn't me trying to shut down your matchmaking. For the next few weeks, we have to do whatever we can to protect Gabe's reputation."

"Okay, I know when you're serious, and you're definitely serious now. I'll do whatever I can to help Gabe. His reputation with the senior citizens in town could use a boost, so maybe you could help him there."

"I doubt it. After yesterday, I'm sure Dot and the seniors at her diner want me run out of town."

"Are you kidding me? You obviously haven't been online, Mal. They love you. In their eyes, you're a hero now. You saved Ruby."

"Really?" Her knees went weak with relief. She hadn't realized until that moment how nervous she was about facing the seniors Monday morning.

"Yes. Really. See for yourself." Abby nodded at a group of older women sitting together at one of the tables that were set up throughout the room. Each of the tables was draped in white linen and held a red poinsettia and a plate of baked goods. A couple of the women at the table waved, and the rest smiled warmly.

"Trust me," Abby continued. "We're going to milk that for all it's worth. I'll be here Monday to film your first day on the job. I'm so excited we're working together."

Along with being a famous YouTuber, Abby ran the Liz Findlay Foundation, a charitable organization named after her great-aunt. The foundation's main focus was helping homeless women get back on their feet, and Abby had begun actively looking for projects to invest in.

In a conversation a couple of weeks ago, when Abby brought up Gabe for what felt like the twentieth time in so many minutes, Mallory had suggested she turn her matchmaking sights on senior women. Not to find them a new love interest but to find them someone to share an apartment with. As Mallory had discovered over the past few months, many senior women could barely make ends meet after their husbands died. One thing led to another, and that was how Mallory found herself accepting the mayor's offer to coordinate the town's new senior initiatives.

"I'm excited to work together too. At least for the Golden Girls Project." They'd named the new initiative after the popular eighties television show about four widowed women living together in Miami. "I'm not sure about your new YouTube idea though," Mallory admitted.

"Trust me. I know what I'm doing." Abby chewed on her thumbnail. "We'll have to tweak my original idea though. If we can't tease my followers with a budding

romance, we'll have to go with the Christmas element.
Which should be almost as popular. Everyone loves the
holidays. So Christmas on Reindeer Road it is. We'll go
full-on Hallmark Christmas. The local holiday events,
the decorating, the cooking, the scenery. It'll be a great
way to showcase the home and life you're trying to
make for the boys and bring you guys closer together as
a family."

Mallory stared at Abby. This had to be a sign. "You're
right. It's perfect."

"Yay!" Abby hugged her. "I'm so glad you think so.
You had me worried for a minute."

"Hey, what are you guys celebrating without me?"
Sadie asked, joining in their group hug.

"Mallory is onboard with my plan. We're going live
with Christmas on Reindeer Road next week," Abby
told Sadie, who'd swapped out her Claire Fraser outfit
for jeans and a pretty cream sweater that accentuated
her baby bump. Sadie had pulled her long, dark hair
into a ponytail, her beautiful heart-shaped face shiny and
makeup free. A talented graphic designer, Sadie had a
full-time job at a company in Charlotte, and she worked
part time for Abby.

"I'm not sure live is a good idea, Abby. You might
want to film and then have Sadie edit and upload,"
Mallory suggested.

"The live posts are really popular. People love to interact in the moment so we'll try one and go from there."
Abby looked around and then her face lit up. "How
perfect is that? Oliver and Brooks are in line to visit
Santa. We'll get a couple shots for our teaser trailer."

"I don't think the boys will go for that, Abby. Oliver's almost sixteen, and Brooks is fourteen. And if you look closer, you'll see they're waiting off to the side while Teddy gives Santa his Christmas list." Mallory frowned. "Why's Teddy pointing at me?"

Abby grinned. "And would you look at that? Now he's pointing at his dad."

Mallory followed Teddy's finger to where Gabe leaned against the far wall near the refreshment table, talking to Kayla. His booted feet crossed at the ankle, he sipped on what looked to be a cup of coffee while keeping an eye on his boys. So Mallory had a pretty good idea why he'd just choked on his drink. Like her, he knew exactly what Teddy wanted for Christmas.

Apparently so did Abby. "If I had to take a guess," her best friend said, "he's just asked Santa to bring the Buchanans a new mom for Christmas, and you're it."

"Teddy told you at the Santa breakfast, didn't he?" Mallory said.

"Yes, and I nearly started blubbering right then and there. That kid is just the sweetest."

Sadie sniffed, then waved a hand in front of her face. "Ignore me. I'm emotional all the time now. Stupid baby hormones."

Abby and Mallory shared a glance. "Are you sure that's all it is, Sadie? Drew isn't giving you a hard time, is he?" Abby asked.

There wasn't anything Sadie had wanted more than a baby, and she'd been over the moon when she found out she was going to be a mom. She wasn't as enamored with the baby's daddy but she'd felt he at least deserved to know she was carrying his child. For the baby's sake, he'd insisted they try to make it work. Sadie had reluctantly agreed. Two months in, she knew it wouldn't work but Drew wasn't ready to concede or to let Sadie leave.

"Not any harder than usual. I know you guys are worried about me, but you don't have to be. Drew just needs some time to come to terms with the idea that we're not setting up the baby for failure just because we won't be living under the same roof."

"Did you talk to the lawyer Eden recommended?" Abby asked.

"Yes, and we're meeting next week."

"Good, and you're coming home for the holidays, right?"

Sadie nodded. "Drew's not happy I won't go to Boston to spend the holidays with him and his family but the last thing I want to do is ruin their Christmas. Besides, I'm looking forward to spending time with you guys."

"Yay! This is going to be the best Christmas ever. Now let's get your stepsons to pose with Santa before they take off, Mal."

"I have to head out, guys. Drew has a dinner thing, and I promised I'd be there."

"But you just got here," Abby complained.

"Not to mention that it's almost a four-hour drive back to Charlotte," Mallory added, concerned for her friend.

"Trust me, I know. I just don't want to make any more waves until everything's worked out with the lawyer."

After they said their goodbyes, they watched Sadie

make her way out of the room. "Do you really think she's okay?" Abby asked as some of Granny MacLeod's friends stopped Sadie to rub her baby bump.

Mallory nodded. "Yes, but I worry what will happen when she tells Drew it's over. He doesn't sound like a guy who takes no for an answer."

"That's what I'm afraid of. It'll be good to have her here over the holidays. We'll sit her down then and have a heart-to-heart." Sadie turned at the door, smiled, and waved. They waved back, and Abby said, "Okay, let's round up Oliver and Brooks."

"Honestly, don't waste your breath. There's no way they'll agree."

"Don't bet on it," Abby said while texting on her phone. She glanced up. "Great. Santa just bought us some time. Looks like he's headed to the little boys' room and his elves are free to socialize."

A woman, her hair long and dark, walked over with a smile. "Mallory, welcome home," Winter Johnson, the mayor, said and gave her a warm hug. Then she drew back to look at her. "I've heard that it was less than welcoming, and I want you to know I'm going to do what I can to intervene with social services on your behalf."

"Thank you. I appreciate the offer, but I'm sure it will work itself out." Mallory had a feeling that if the mayor tried to pull some strings on her behalf, Kayla would just make things harder for her.

"Did you also hear that she's a hero?" Abby asked.

"I did, and I was just going to thank her." The smile Winter offered Mallory was as warm as her hug. "I stopped by the hospital before the parade, and Ruby's prognosis is excellent. The doctor said it wouldn't have been had you not been at the station and intervened."

"I'm glad she's doing well. I thought I might drop by the hospital later today."

"I'm sure Ruby and her family would love to see you. And I look forward to seeing you at work Monday morning, but now I have to find our illustrious chief of police. Have either of you seen him?"

They pointed her in Gabe's direction. "Wish me luck. I have a special request to put to him, and I'm sure he's going to be less than thrilled."

"That's an understatement," Abby murmured, and from Gabe's expression when he noted the mayor coming his way, she was right.

"What's going on?" Mallory asked.

"Owen has offered to take over for Ruby until she can return to work. Actually, he didn't offer—he begged and pleaded—so I have a feeling that the mayor's going to insist Gabe agree."

"He didn't seem thrilled to see Owen at the station, but I thought it was because he knew our history."

"No, it had nothing to do with you. Owen can't seem to stay away. If he isn't telling Gabe how to do his job, he's trying to do it for him. There's even a petition started online to get Owen reinstated. If you ask me, Dot's behind it."

"That's horrible."

"Trust me, it gets worse. When I told you he could use some help rehabilitating his reputation, I was so not kidding." Abby's face lit up with a huge smile, and she lifted her hand. "Over here, honey."

Mallory glanced over her shoulder to see Hunter Mackenzie striding their way with Bella in his arms and Wolf at his side. The six-foot-four former soldier looked like this was the last place he wanted to be. Which was understandable given how much he disliked crowds. Before he'd met Abby, Hunter had lived a reclusive life on Honeysuckle Ridge.

"Hey," he said to Mallory, then thrust Bella at his fiancée. "You good? That's all you need?"

Abby's eyes sparkled as she tried not to laugh at her fiancé's grumpy demeanor. "How many people asked you to build their floats for next year?"

"Too damn many," he muttered before taking Abby's chin between his fingers and kissing her. "I'll see you at home."

Abby sighed as he walked away. "I swear, that man will make me swoon when I'm ninety." Then she spotted Santa heading back to his chair. "Boys! Oliver and Brooks, can you do me a big favor?" she asked as she hurried their way with Bella in her arms and Wolf loping after her. "I want to get a picture of our dogs with Santa, and I need some help. Would you guys mind?"

"No, that'd be cool. He looks like a real wolf." Oliver crouched to offer his hand for Wolf to sniff while Brooks adjusted Bella's reindeer ears with a big grin on his face. The dogs were a hit with the boys and, just as Abby had obviously expected, the perfect incentive to get them to pose with Santa. Although they did look a little leery when they were finally perched on either of Santa's knees. They looked even leerier when Abby had Mallory pose with them.

"I promise, guys. It won't take long at all," Mallory told them.

"Wait. We wanna be in the picture too," Teddy said, dragging his father over by the hand.

"Buddy, I think Abby just wants Mallory and her boys in the shot," Gabe said.

"But I want a picture of all of us together with Santa, Dad. Please, can we be in the picture too?"

"It's fine, Gabe," Mallory said, unable to resist Teddy's pleading puppy-dog eyes.

"The kid has your number," Gabe said under his breath as he came to stand beside her behind Santa's chair.

"Dylan! Cody!" Teddy waved over his brothers, who were loading cookies into napkins and stuffing them in their pockets. Only instead of stuffing a napkin into his pocket, Cody was unknowingly stuffing the tablecloth.

"Wait, don't run, Cody! You have the tablecloth... Oh, jeez." Gabe covered his eyes with a hand.

"It's okay. The mayor saved the day," Mallory said.

Gabe glanced over his shoulder as the twins settled in for the picture. "I wouldn't be so sure of that."

Mallory followed his gaze to see Kayla staring at them with her arms crossed. Santa *Ho ho ho*ed and then looked up at Mallory and winked. "You two kids have nothing to worry about. Santa's on the job."

Teddy grinned. "And he's going to make my Christmas wish come true. Yours too, Mallory."

"Okay, say Merry Christmas!" Abby instructed. "All right, how about we say *ho ho*—oh no."

Oliver and Brooks had pulled off Santa's beard, exposing him for the fraud that he was.

Chapter Twelve

Y ou might not believe in Santa, and you might not have been thrilled to pose for a picture with him, but that is absolutely no excuse for what you boys did today," Mallory said as she put the bags of groceries on the kitchen counter.

She had never been as angry with her stepsons as she was now. In the past, she'd let their behavior slide, made excuses for them, and walked on eggshells in order not to upset them. But she couldn't get Teddy's devastated little face out of her mind.

"I don't know why you're so bent. All we did was pull off the old man's beard. Everyone knows Santa isn't real," Oliver muttered, setting another bag of groceries beside hers.

"No, Oliver, some children, like Teddy, actually do believe in Santa. And now, thanks to you and your brother, he's not sure what to think."

"That's not my problem," Oliver said.

"Oh, yes it is. And you and Brooks are going to make it right."

"Brooks can make it right. I have things to do," he said and stormed off.

"Oliver, I'm not finished speaking with you. Oliver—" The bedroom door slammed.

"He's embarrassed. He feels bad he made Teddy cry. We both do. But the girls were laughing at us so he was just trying to be cool."

Mallory bowed her head. Oliver always seemed so self-assured that she sometimes forgot he was just a kid. Of course he'd be embarrassed. He was a teenage boy trying to make a good impression. She should've been firmer with Abby. Still, even though Mallory sympathized with the boys, there had to be consequences.

"Is that why you helped pull off Santa's... You didn't pull off his beard, did you?" she said, thinking back to that moment. "You just made it look that way so Oliver wouldn't have to shoulder all the blame."

Brooks shrugged. "I don't care what people think about me, but Ollie does. Is Teddy's dad mad at us? He won't blame you and put it in your file, will he?"

Her heart pinched. He was just like Teddy, carrying his family's worries on his shoulders. Only Brooks was more worried about being split up from his brother than he was worried about social services taking them from her.

"I'm sure Gabe isn't thrilled that Teddy was upset, and whether your brother wants to or not, he is going to make this right. But, Brooks, Gabe is trying to help us, not hurt us."

"Maybe, but the social services lady didn't look happy. I saw her watching us and writing something on her iPad."

As Mallory absorbed the worrisome news, her phone *ping*ed in her purse on the counter. She pulled it out. There was a text from Abby.

Just found out why Kayla McPherson has it in for you, and it's not only because our hunky chief of police obviously has the hots for you. She applied for your job! Because of what happened yesterday, the mayor didn't want to tell you. Call me when you have time to talk.

"What's wrong?" Brooks asked.

Mallory had been dancing around things with the boys long enough. "We need to have a family meeting." She pulled out the perishables from the grocery bags and put them away. She'd unload the rest of the food later. "Come on," she said to Brooks, her strides determined as she walked through the living room to the back hall.

Her determination wavered when they reached Oliver's bedroom. She gave herself a stern lecture and lifted her hand to knock. It was her job to parent the boys. Her job to carry the worry on her shoulders, not Brooks's. "Oliver, we're coming in," she said when there was no response to her knock.

He sat up on the twin bed and scrubbed his face. Then he scowled at her as if hoping to scare her away. It might've worked in the past but no longer. She saw through him now, and she wasn't about to let him push her away.

"I don't want to talk to—"

"Good, because all you have to do is listen." She pulled out the chair at the desk. Brooks went to sit beside his brother on the bed. "Oliver, your brother doesn't want social services to remove you guys from my care."

He shot Brooks a look.

"It's not because he likes me or wants to live with me. It's because he loves you, and he doesn't want you guys to be separated. So, what I need to know is whether you feel the same. What is it that would make you happy?"

"You really want to know?"

"Yes, I do. I really do. Because while you seem to think I'm the bad guy in all of this, I'm not. All I want is the best for you and Brooks."

"We want to go back to boarding school. All our mates are there. Our real mates. We don't fit in here."

"I know you miss England and your friends, and I wish there was something I could do. But I don't have the money to send you, Oliver. If I did, I would."

"Marsha does. You could ask her. She could take it out of our trust funds. It's our money."

"The money in your trust funds can't be withdrawn until you're twenty-one."

"But she's rich. She got everything."

"She is, but you know how set in his ways your father was. Marsha is the same. And the school fees are really high. It costs more than a hundred and thirty thousand dollars a year to send both of you to the school. And that doesn't include the extras."

He shrugged. "That's nothing to Marsha."

These boys seriously did not know the value of a dollar. "I can understand why you might feel that way, but Marsha doesn't. She made it clear to me she wouldn't pay for you to go back." She took in the defeated slump of their shoulders and sighed. "All right, I'll give it one more try, okay?"

"Thanks, Mallory," Oliver said, and he gave her a smile so much like his father's that she blinked.

She cleared the emotion from her throat and said, "I told you I'd ask, but that doesn't mean I think Marsha will change her mind. So please don't get your hopes up. I don't want you to be disappointed."

"We know. We just appreciate you asking."

They should. The last thing she wanted to do was ask Marsha for anything. "No matter what you think, I care about you and Brooks. I want you guys to be happy." She just wished they could be happy with her.

"I'm sorry about the Santa thing. But it's probably better that Teddy doesn't believe anyway. He'll just get teased."

"He's only five," Mallory said incredulously.

"Almost six," Brooks corrected her.

"Yeah, that's around the time Dad told us Santa wasn't real."

"I think I was four," Brooks said.

"That's horrible," Mallory said without thinking. She never criticized Harry to the boys. "I mean, believing in Santa adds to the magic of Christmas. It's what makes it so special."

"I guess," Oliver said, obviously humoring her.

"Okay, we can debate the merits of Christmas and Santa another time. Right now, we have another problem."

"I was right. The lady at the community center was making notes about us. She's going to try to take us away from you, isn't she? That's what the text was about," Brooks said.

"The text was about Ms. McPherson," Mallory confirmed. "But it wasn't about her trying to take you away." She weighed how much she should tell the boys and decided it was important, especially now, to be completely honest with them. "I got the feeling Ms. McPherson doesn't like me, and Abby—"

Oliver frowned. "Because Chief Buchanan does?"

"Chief Buchanan does what?"

"Likes you," Brooks said. "Like a girlfriend."

"Oh, no, he doesn't," Mallory said with a nervous laugh. "Chief Buchanan and I hardly know each other."

"Yeah, he does," Oliver said. "You should've seen the way he was looking at you at the parade." Oliver made a moony face, and his brother laughed.

"There's no way he looked at me like that. Anyway, it's not important. What is important is Abby texted me that Ms. McPherson had applied for the job I got."

"So you got the guy and the job she wanted."

"That's not good," Brooks said before Mallory could correct Oliver.

"No, it's not," she reluctantly agreed. "But I don't want you guys to worry about this. Leave that to me. However, it's more important than ever not to give Ms. McPherson any reason to doubt that you guys are happy and doing well."

"I thought it was Chief Buchanan who was keeping tabs on us," Oliver said.

"Yes, but I have a feeling Ms. McPherson will be looking over his shoulder now." Actually, after today, she was almost positive that would be the case. "So from here on out, let's think before we act, okay?"

"Brooks said she was taking notes at the community center. That was my fault, wasn't it?"

"No, it was mine. I shouldn't have put you in that position. But that's in the past now, and the three of us know what to do going forward."

"You're still calling Marsha though? About paying for us to go back to England," Oliver said.

"Yes, I'll call tonight." Her stomach turned at the thought. "But right now, you and Brooks are going to help me cook a fun supper to cheer up Teddy. And while we do, we're going to come up with a story to explain why Owen was pretending to be Santa." Mallory got up from the chair, surprised when both boys followed her from the room without complaining.

"What's in a fun supper?" Brooks asked as they walked into the kitchen.

"Pizza casserole for supper and snickerdoodles for dessert."

"Can we have some too? You didn't order pizza last night," Brooks said, then glanced at Oliver.

She'd offered, but after she'd come clean about the night their father died, they hadn't been interested in eating. "Sure. I'll make two batches." She went to unpack the groceries and stopped. She was doing it again. Staying silent in an effort not to upset the boys, but that hadn't worked in the past. "Did you guys have any more questions about the night your dad died?"

"No," Oliver said, and Mallory had the feeling she'd blown what progress they'd just made.

Brooks glanced at his brother. "I do."

"She told us all we needed to know yesterday, Brooks. Dad wanted to die. He didn't want her to save him. Marsha and Blair lied, and you and I both know why."

Mallory blinked, surprised. Oliver hadn't said anything after she'd relayed what had happened that night. She'd assumed his silence meant that Oliver still blamed her for not intervening and saving his father.

"I just wanted to know if he said anything about us before he died. Like did he say goodbye?"

"I'm sorry, Brooks. I thought I'd told you. Your dad's last words were *Tell the boys I love them*."

She kept her gaze averted from Oliver, afraid he'd see through her, but Brooks's smile made the lie worthwhile.

A loud cheer distracted her, and she glanced out the window. "Looks like the Buchanans are home. We better get cooking, boys. I'll let Gabe know we're bringing them dinner." She picked up her phone to text him while watching him play with his sons. She was afraid, if Oliver looked too close, this time he'd catch her making a moony face. Gabe was playing football with Dylan and Cody, showing off his physical prowess. He had the moves of a professional and the body of one.

"Ollie, look—they're playing rugby."

Mallory leaned over to look for Teddy and spotted him walking along the edge of the woods, probably looking for the reindeer he thought he saw this morning. "I think they're playing touch football."

"That's like rugby, right?" Brooks went up on his tiptoes to get a better look. "Do you think they'd let us play?"

"You want to play?" she asked, surprised. The only things they ever seemed to want to do were listen to music and play video games.

"Ah, yeah, Ollie was captain of the rugby team. He's the best."

"I'm sure Gabe—"

"No, it's okay. I don't feel like it anyway," Oliver said, then silently communicated something to his brother with his eyes.

"Ollie's right. They're probably mad at us."

"Come on." Mallory grabbed her jacket and theirs. "Let's get this over with." It took some cajoling but she finally got the boys into their winter jackets and out the door. Cody, Dylan, and Gabe stopped playing as she and the boys made their way up the driveway. Teddy hadn't noticed them.

"What are we supposed to say to the kid?" Oliver asked. "About Santa," he added when Mallory didn't respond right away.

"Maybe say you had a feeling it wasn't the real Santa and wanted to expose him," she said out of the side of her mouth while also trying to smile at Gabe and his sons.

"I don't think that's a good idea, Mallory," Brooks said.

"That's because you didn't let me finish. Then you apologize and say you didn't know that Santa had asked Owen to fill in for him because he has a cold and didn't want to give it to the kids."

"Good one," Brooks said.

"Okay, you tell him," Oliver told his brother.

"Why don't both of you do it?" Mallory suggested, and they walked reluctantly in Teddy's direction.

Gabe tossed Dylan the football and then walked over to where she stood. "So, what did you have to do to get them to apologize?"

"Promise to call Marsha and try to get her to pay for them to go back to boarding school," she said before adding, "That's not really true. I mean, I did promise to call Marsha, and I will, but the boys felt bad for upsetting Teddy. Oliver was embarrassed. Brooks says the girls were laughing at him." She told him the excuse they were giving Teddy. As far as she could tell, it was working.

"He'll buy it. Owen said something along the same lines." Gabe glanced at her. "So if they were going to apologize anyway, why did you feel like you had to bribe them?"

"It wasn't a bribe. Brooks saw Kayla writing down something after they pulled off Santa's beard, and then Abby texted that she found out why Kayla has it in for me. She'd applied for the director's position. So I just wanted the three of us to be on the same page and to work together. I asked what would make them happy, and it was like I thought. They miss England and their friends."

"What's the chance of Marsha ponying up for school?"

"Slim to none, which I told them. I think they just appreciate me making the effort."

"It's probably a good thing that you talked to them, got things out in the open," he said.

"Why? Did Kayla say something?"

Gabe rubbed the back of his neck and nodded. "Yeah. I thought I'd convinced her to leave things as they are, but after Teddy dragged us into the photo, she must've changed her mind. She came over after you guys left. Used the boys pulling off Santa's beard as an excuse and told me she'd handle the weekly meetings with you and the in-house visits."

"I never should've agreed to watch the parade with you guys. If I'd just stayed away none of—"

"And Teddy would've been devastated."

"I shouldn't have gone to the parade," she said.

"Yeah, but then you wouldn't have been able to put your Christmas plan into action with the boys."

Mallory narrowed her eyes at him. "You're making fun of me, aren't you?"

"Maybe a little. Oliver and Brooks seem a little too old and too cool to be won over by the Christmas spirit."

"Trust me, I know that now. The only thing that matters to them is moving back to England."

"How do you feel about that, honestly?"

She watched as Oliver and Brooks tossed the ball over Dylan's and Cody's heads, both of them laughing. "I want them to be happy. I'd hoped they could be happy with me but I'm beginning to think that's not possible."

"Trust me. It's not you, it's them, Mallory. They're at an age where their friends are more important than their parents. And in Brooks and Oliver's case, you probably can multiply that tenfold. Their friends were their family. But it sounds and looks to me like you've made some headway today."

She nodded. "I think we have. Only it came at a big price. I have to meet with Kayla instead of you."

"I don't think so. Not after what you just told me. If Abby's right and she did apply for the job, I can make a case that Kayla has a conflict of interest. I'm going to talk to her boss first thing Monday morning."

"But that might make it worse."

"Yeah, and that's why I didn't do it yesterday. But it's pretty obvious Kayla has a bias where you're concerned, and it's best to get her off your case. Just make sure the boys are on their best behavior for the next week or so, because this will probably bring some added attention your way."

"Come on, Dad! Oliver and Brooks want to play," Cody yelled.

"Why don't you guys play? I'm going to take Teddy inside. You wanna watch a movie with your old man, buddy?" Gabe called out, no doubt seeing the longing look in his youngest's face as he watched his brothers and Oliver and Brooks toss the ball.

"Can Mallory watch one with us?" Teddy asked as he put down a stick and brushed off his hands on his pants.

"I have a better idea. Oliver and Brooks were supposed to help me make a special fun dinner for you guys, and it looks like they'd rather chase after a ball. So would you like to help me, Teddy? As long as your dad doesn't mind."

"Can I, Dad? Can I?" Teddy asked.

"Sure, buddy."

"Are you sure, Gabe? This doesn't exactly work

with our plan to keep our distance. I should've thought before I said anything. I just felt so bad that Teddy was upset," Mallory said when the little boy ran over to tell the boys.

"We're neighbors who live in a small town, and as we discovered today, keeping our distance will be next to impossible. As long as we don't do anything to feed into Teddy's fantasy, we'll be fine. And you just saved me from a Mickey Mouse Christmas marathon so I'm definitely not going to complain. But what exactly is a fun dinner?"

"Pizza casserole and snickerdoodles. It was supposed to be the boys' make-up present for Teddy. But I'd just as soon have them play outside for a change."

Gabe nodded. "Oliver has a good arm. Great speed too."

"Brooks said he was the captain of his rugby team. He said he was the best. I thought he was just bragging. He idolizes his brother."

"Yeah, I don't think he was. If Oliver is interested, I'll get in touch with the football coach at the school."

"Rugby and football aren't the same though. Wouldn't he have a hard time transitioning?"

"No, not at all. And I can work with him on the weekends until he gets up to speed."

"You played?"

"College ball." He put out his hand and easily caught the football one of the twins had drilled in their direction.

"Nice catch," she said, wondering if there was anything this man wasn't good at.

"Yes, Dylan, I get the hint. Give me a minute, okay?" he said. Then to her, "Talk to Oliver and let me know. I think it would be good for him. Especially if the thing with Marsha falls through," he said before jogging over to the boys.

She smiled when he picked up Teddy like he was a football and ran around the yard with him before depositing him at her side. "All right, you two, you better go get our fun dinner in the oven. We're going to be starved after the big game."

Teddy smiled up at her and took her hand. "I guess Owen really is Santa's special helper. My Christmas wish is coming true. We're just like a real family now."

Chapter Thirteen

Do you want to explain to me how the seven of us eating at the same table played into Teddy's fantasy?" Gabe asked Mallory, who was washing the dishes while he dried. His boys and hers were downstairs playing foosball, as evidenced by the ten-decibel cheers that wound their way up the stairs every few minutes. "I mean your pizza casserole and the snickerdoodles were great, but we eat cookies and pizza all the time."

"But not cookies and a pizza casserole that Teddy helped make."

"True, and he made them with you so I can see that being slightly fantasy inducing."

"Huh, that's good to know," she said, fighting back a smile.

He nudged her with his hip. "You know what I mean. I thought, if I didn't touch you or kiss you—not that I would," he quickly amended. Unless she initiated it, because God knew he wanted to touch and kiss this woman. "It's just that I assumed, naively, it seems, if there was no PDA, we didn't have to worry about playing into Teddy's fantasy that you and I would get together."

"But indirectly I did. I made fun food. I didn't get upset when they made a mess or when they had a food fight in the middle of dinner."

"You're right. And worse than you not getting upset, or from Teddy's point of view the best, was you took part in the food fight. You've got some serious skills as a food fighter, by the way."

"I had lots of practice in foster care. You're not so bad yourself." She nudged him back with her hip.

"Four brothers." He turned to lean against the counter as he dried the casserole dish. He'd been hoping for leftovers but no such luck. "Yesterday, when Eden was talking to us after the meeting, she mentioned that my experience as a single parent with three sons would be beneficial because of your lack of siblings and experience with kids. But that's not true, is it? From what I saw today, you have plenty of experience with kids. You're great with them."

She shrugged. "I don't know if I'd go that far. But yes, I have years of experience dealing with children. Children who were lonely, abused, and terrified of what the future held in store for them. Children with behavioral and psychological issues and some of the sweetest kids you'll ever meet." She gave him a faraway smile. "I was older than most of the kids, so I took on the role of den mother in some ways."

And watched all those kids come and go while she stayed. "Why did you stay at the home? Did you not want to be adopted?"

"No one wanted me." She bent her head over the sink, giving the plate in her hand more attention than was warranted.

He cursed her father in his head. Boyd Carlisle had a lot to answer for. Gabe put down the casserole dish, then reached into the soapy water for her hands. "Their loss. They missed out." He gently dried her hands. "Teddy was right. You are perfect."

"We both know that's not true, Gabe. If I was, Oliver and Brooks wouldn't want to go back to England." She looked down at their joined hands, then raised her gaze to his. "And we both know that I'm far from perfect in your mother-in-law's eyes."

He'd answered his own question. Everything Mallory had said and done tonight had played into his son's hopes and dreams. She'd played the role so well that even Gabe had let himself be drawn into the fantasy and hadn't known it. But she was right—he wouldn't have a hope in hell of keeping custody of his boys if he was involved with her.

As if she read the acknowledgment on his face, she said, "It's probably best if I take the boys home now. And it would be best, I think, if we avoid joint family dinners from here on out."

"You're probably right." He knew she was because he was as disappointed as his youngest would be. "I'd still like to work with Oliver, though, and the boys seem to enjoy hanging out together so—"

"I don't want to take any of that away from them. And if you're okay with it, I'd still like to spend time with Teddy. Dylan and Cody, too, if they want. But I'm pretty sure they're not my number-one fans."

"Honestly, they were better with you than they'd be with any other woman horning in on what they see as their mother's territory." He smiled. "You won them over with your pizza casserole and food fighting skills."

She grinned. "Then they'd be very impressed with my cheeseburger cups and my burping skills."

He laughed. "No way you're a champion burper."

"I'm a little out of practice, but I used to be able to burp for almost a minute."

"This I have to hear. Come on, show me." He'd been teasing and was surprised when she took him up on the challenge. Almost as surprised as the five boys were when they came up to get a drink and heard the beautiful and sophisticated Mallory letting out the longest burp he'd ever heard. And from the looks on Dylan and Cody's faces, they fell a little in love with her in that moment. He wasn't the only one who noticed. Teddy looked at him with an I-told-you-so grin on his face.

"Okay, guys, we should probably get going," Mallory said with a nervous glance at his sons. She must've noticed the love-sick grins on their faces too.

"They can't go yet. We're in the middle of our game, and we're tied," Cody complained.

Gabe was going to suggest that the boys could stay and Mallory take some time for herself when his cell phone rang. He held up a finger for quiet, then answered. It was the mayor. "Hey, Winter, what's up?"

"I'm sorry to bother you, Gabe, but I didn't know who else to call."

"It's not a big deal. Tell me what's going on. You sound upset." He walked out of the kitchen. No matter how quiet the boys were trying to be, there were five of them.

"I am, Gabe. It's Owen."

Gabe barely managed to hold back a groan. "Look, Winter, I know he's bored. But I seriously can't—"

"It's not about the job, Gabe. It's about Boyd Carlisle, Mallory's father. I'm afraid Owen has gone up the mountain to confront him. Owen's never forgiven himself for removing Mallory from her home, and he's never forgiven Boyd for not going to get her. He always believed Boyd would bring her home. He didn't know... Anyway, I hate to ask this of you on a Saturday night after you worked through Thanksgiving, but I'm worried something might happen. There's a lot of bad blood between them that has festered for a very long time."

"I'll head out right now."

"Do you need someone to help with the boys? I could—"

"It's fine. Mallory's actually here, thanks," he reluctantly admitted.

"That's good, then—but, Gabe, don't say anything to her. The poor girl has enough on her plate."

"Yeah, she does. And I'd like to talk to you about that on Monday. But right now, I better take off." They said their goodbyes, and he disconnected.

Mallory was alone in the kitchen, wiping up the counter. She stopped and turned. "Is everything okay?"

"I have something I need to take care of. I shouldn't be long. Would you mind staying with the boys? It's no problem if you can't. I'll give Ainsley a call." Her family lived up the road. Gabe paid the teenager above the standard rate so she'd be willing to come at the last minute. If it was late and on a school night, her mother occasionally filled in for her.

"No, I'll stay. I'm sure the boys will be thrilled. You go and take care of what you need to."

* * *

Gabe drove along the rutted mountain road, the headlights cutting a swath through the barren trees. It was at least ten degrees colder up here, and a thick frost coated the forest floor. Black ice made the dirt road shine. Even in four-wheel drive he struggled to keep the SUV on the road. He should have put chains on the tires but the worry in Winter's voice suggested he didn't have time to waste. As long as he'd known her, she'd never shown a proclivity toward the dramatic. If anything, she tended to underplay a situation.

He glanced in the back to make sure he had his bulletproof vest. Some might say he was overreacting. A few years back, he might've said the same. Not anymore. His boys had only one parent. He'd be damned if he'd make them orphans because of some macho sense of pride.

Up ahead, tendrils of gray smoke floated up into the wide expanse of starlit sky. It looked like someone had shaken a container of silver sprinkles on black velvet.

"Keep your eyes on the road, dumbass," he muttered to himself when something lumbered through the brush on his left.

Boyd Carlisle and Owen Campbell weren't the only dangerous things in the woods tonight.

There'd been several black bear sightings in town earlier this month. They needed to pack on the pounds before hibernating for the winter. Gabe had his officers hang out at the area schools at drop-off and pick-up times just to be on the safe side.

There'd also been a Bigfoot sighting north of town, which he'd ignored. He was pretty sure it had been the seniors messing with him again. Although several of the locals swore Bigfoot existed. The next county over had a Bigfoot research group as well as a Bigfoot festival in the spring. Dylan and Cody were determined to go.

At the fork in the road, Gabe glanced at his GPS. Boyd Carlisle's place should be just up ahead. He'd heard it referred to as a shack in the woods, but the log cabin that came into view a few minutes later looked nothing like a shack. It looked like a home that had been well cared for.

As he pulled to a stop to the left of Owen's white truck, a rusted pink swing set got caught in his high beams, and it felt like a punch in the gut. Mallory had lived up here in the woods with her mother and father. No kids to play with. He rubbed his chest with the heel of his palm. She must've been lonely.

Gabe pushed the thought away and shrugged out of his winter jacket to put on the vest. Before he turned off the engine and climbed out of the truck, he checked his gun, praying as he did so that he didn't have to use it.

As soon as he opened the SUV's door, he heard the two men yelling at each other.

"Get the hell off my porch, Campbell. You've got no damn business being up here. You're not the law anymore," Boyd Carlisle growled through the screen door he held open with his foot, the light from inside the house shining on him. It was the first look Gabe had gotten at Mallory's father.

He appeared to be a youthful sixty with a head of wavy dark hair and a clean-shaven face. Around six-two with a wiry build, he wore jeans and a plaid shirt but it was the twelve-gauge shotgun in his hand that held Gabe's attention.

"I'm not going anywhere until we have it out. Your daughter's come home, and she needs a father. It's about time you did your damn duty, don't you think?" Owen's voice came from the other end of the porch. It was difficult to make him out. He stood in the shadows.

"You took away my chance to be her father seventeen years ago, Campbell."

"Mr. Carlisle, Owen's not the law but I am." Gabe moved his jacket aside so the man could see his badge and his gun. "I'd be obliged if you'd lower the shotgun, sir."

It was when the man turned his attention to Gabe that he saw his resemblance to his daughter. Mallory had gotten her blue eyes from her father. "And I'd be obliged if you'd get him off my property, son. If he's not outta here in two minutes, I'm going to shoot him in his sorry ass."

"Damn it, Boyd. You left me no choice. You were drunk off your head when Miriam died," Owen said, stepping from the shadows. "I thought you'd snap out of it. I thought you'd go get your daughter. I told you the home in the next county was full and that I'd found her a good place in Durham. Told the director at the home not to let anyone adopt her. Told them they'd see, you'd come and get her."

Gabe briefly closed his eyes. Mallory thought no one had wanted her, but that wasn't the case. He wondered if Owen knew what he'd done. From the tortured look on his face, he did.

"Are you telling me no one adopted my little girl because of you? Is that what you're telling me, Campbell?" Boyd took a menacing step toward Owen.

"It's not my fault! You left town a few weeks later for that job in Montana. Figured once you made yourself some money, you'd go collect Mallory."

"She deserved better than me. She deserved more than I could ever hope to give her. She needed a momma and a daddy that could give her everything me and Miriam never could. She took care of her momma all those years, and I wanted someone to take care of her. You stole that from her, you interfering no-good son of a bitch." Boyd stalked toward Owen, and his arm shot out, grabbing a fistful of the other man's jacket.

"Mr. Carlisle, I understand how you must feel but..." Gabe began as he cautiously closed the distance between him and the porch.

"You have no idea, son," he said. Then, releasing Owen's jacket, Boyd hauled off and punched him in the face.

Owen held up his hands. "You can beat me bloody, but I'm not leaving here until you agree to come down off this mountain and make amends to your daughter."

Boyd punched him again. "I'm not the one who has to make amends. You do! You ruined her chance for a good life."

"She's had a good life. She's a doctor. She married a rich man. But that don't mean she doesn't need her father," Owen said, and took a swing at Boyd.

"I heard all about who she married last summer when she came to town. A rich old man who died and left everything to his first wife. And now I know why. It's because of you she did. You made sure she never got that family I wanted for her."

They were going in circles, ducking and throwing punches.

"Would you two just listen to yourselves for a minute?" Gabe said as he stepped onto the porch. "It's obvious you both made mistakes, big mistakes that hurt Mallory. But what's just as obvious is that you care about her. So instead of beating each other bloody, why don't you figure out what you can do to help her? Because from where I'm standing, she could use some help."

From the way they continued dancing and ducking with the shotgun between them, they either didn't hear him or didn't give a damn what he said. The mayor was right. This fight had been coming for a long time. And if Gabe wasn't mistaken, one of these men would die tonight if he didn't intervene.

He took a step toward them. "Stop it right now or I'm going to drag your sorry asses into the station."

"Good," Owen said as he attempted to put Boyd in a headlock. "That's where the stubborn son of a bitch belongs."

"I said asses, Owen. You'll be in the cell right along with him."

"That's exactly where he belongs for what he did to my daughter," Boyd said as he broke free of Owen's grip, only the momentum caused him to lose his balance, and he tripped. Gabe stepped forward to break his fall, and a shotgun blast ripped through the cold late November night.

Chapter Fourteen

Mallory glanced at the time on her cell phone when Gabe's front door opened. It was after midnight, and she'd fallen asleep reading. She sat up on the couch and finger-combed her hair. Then she straightened the throw she'd pulled around herself earlier. The night had grown cold. She would've started a fire in the stacked stone fireplace but didn't feel it was her place.

She frowned and came to her feet, worried when Gabe didn't immediately walk into the living room. Maybe it wasn't him. "Gabe," she called softly as she walked toward the entryway. "Is that you?"

"Yeah." His smile seemed strained. "Boys give you any trouble?"

"No, not at all. Teddy went to sleep around eight, and once I sent Oliver and Brooks home, Dylan and Cody went down around ten."

"I won't keep you, then. Thanks for stepping in. I appreciate it. I imagine we'll see you around tomorrow." He went to open the door.

She put out her hand to hold it shut. "What's going on? Something's wrong." He wouldn't look at her.

"It's nothing. Like I said, I appreciate you helping out. Now I'd just as soon—" He bowed his head when she didn't move. "Mallory, I'm tired, and I want to go to bed."

He was keeping something from her. She was sure of it. She searched his face but now he held her gaze and raised an eyebrow as if she were keeping him from his bed. "Okay, it's none of my business. I'll go now, but if you don't mind, I need my jacket."

"Right. Sorry." He took a step away from the coatrack behind him, wincing as he did so.

She looked down and gasped. "Gabe, you're bleeding."

He glanced down the hall. "Would you keep it down? The last thing I need is for the boys to wake up."

"I'm sorry, but you're dripping blood through your fingers so excuse me for overreacting. What happened? Where are you hurt?"

"It's nothing, Mallory. I can take care of it myself, okay?"

"No, it's not okay. I'm not leaving until you tell me exactly what it is you're taking care of."

"I got shot." He put up his hands at what must've been her horrified expression. "Relax."

"That's a little difficult to do when you just told me you were shot, and you're standing here and not at the hospital. I'm going to call Oliver and Brooks to come over and watch the boys. I'll drive you to the—"

He took her phone from her. "You're not calling the boys, and I'm not going to the hospital. It's a flesh wound."

"Why don't you let me be the judge of that? And even if it were just a flesh wound, you could go into shock, get sepsis or lead poisoning, or develop post-traumatic stress."

"Fine. I stand corrected, Doc. Now that we've got that cleared up and you've listed everything I need to watch for, can you leave so I can clean myself up?"

"I'm not going anywhere until I've examined you, and then you're going to tell me why you won't go to the hospital."

"If I went to the hospital, I'd have to arrest the person—persons—who shot me, and it was an accident."

While he was talking, she looked him over. From what she could see, he'd been shot on the left-hand side just below his bulletproof vest. "All right, let's get your jacket and vest off you for starters."

"I give up. You're obviously not going anywhere until you get your way." He went to shrug off his jacket.

"You're an extremely stubborn man, Gabriel Buchanan," she said at his grimace.

He snorted. "I could say the same thing about you, Mallory Maitland."

She rolled her eyes and reached up to help him. "Let me do it. You've already lost enough blood. You'll have to take this to a dry cleaner." She laid the jacket across the bench against the wall, then went to help him out of the vest but first his gun and holster had to be removed. "You didn't shoot anyone tonight, did you?" she asked, letting him remove the gun and holster himself.

"No, but I was severely tempted to."

"Have you ever shot anyone before?"

"I was a big-city cop, Mallory. What do you think?"

"Have you been shot before?"

"I've been shot *at* a few times. This is the first time I've been hit. I've lost my edge working here."

"You'd rather be in New York, wouldn't you?"

"If it was just me to think about, yeah, I'd be back in New York in a heartbeat. But the boys are happy here."

She nodded. Funnily enough, if not for the memories and her father, she preferred the pace of Highland Falls to Atlanta, and she loved the natural beauty here. She had a feeling if Oliver and Brooks gave the town half a chance, they'd come to feel the same way.

"Sorry," she said as she struggled to release the Velcro. "You'll have to take off your vest. While you do that, I'll run home and get my bag."

She didn't give him a chance to argue. She slipped on her boots and ran out the door without her jacket. After hurrying across the Buchanans' front lawn and up her driveway to her side door, she took a second to gather herself in case Oliver and Brooks were up. Her hand trembled as she turned the doorknob. The sight of Gabe standing there bleeding had shaken her.

She'd come to care about him, a man she barely knew. Only that wasn't completely true. She felt like she'd known him forever. Maybe because she'd been fantasizing about him for so long. But every moment she spent in his company, those feelings intensified. Tonight's joint family dinner had just made it worse. It had given her a glimpse of what life could be like. Of a life she'd fantasized about as a little girl.

Gabe was everything a father was supposed to be: strong, loving, and protective. There was no doubt he loved his boys just as there was no doubt they loved him. Her heart had broken a little for Oliver and Brooks as they'd watched Gabe play touch football and interact with his sons at dinner. She'd seen the way they'd reacted to his stories about college ball. How they'd responded to his attention by sitting a little taller, mimicking some of his movements and mannerisms.

She'd never allowed herself to think about it before—it felt disloyal to Harry—but her stepsons had missed out on a normal relationship with their father, and a normal relationship with their mother. Mallory worried what that would mean for them in later years. Her relationship with her parents hadn't been normal either, and look what had happened to her.

As she hurried through the living room to her bedroom to grab her leather satchel, she noticed the thump of the bass making the hardwood reverberate beneath her feet. The boys were still up. She was torn between running back to Gabe and checking on them. She hooked the purse over her shoulder and fast-walked to Oliver's room.

Of course they didn't hear her knock so she yelled, "I'm coming in, boys."

Just as she thought, they were sitting on the floor, propped against the bed with their headphones on. She turned off the speaker. "You guys will be deaf before you're eighteen. Come on, time for bed. You need to be up at nine for church in the morning." It had been

Abby's idea. Mallory had gotten back to her about Kayla while she and Teddy waited for the cookies and casserole to bake.

"Ah, come on, Mal," both boys groaned at almost the same time.

"Church is a social event in Highland Falls. You'll get a chance to meet some of the kids from your school. And it'll make a good impression on Ms. McPherson." There was also a Christmas craft sale after the service that Mallory wanted to check out. Since Marsha had inherited the holiday decorations along with the mansion, Mallory had nothing to decorate the house on Reindeer Road.

"Hey, what happened to your hand? You're bleeding," Brooks said, his gaze shooting to hers.

"It's not my blood. It's Gabe's." Oh crap, she probably wasn't supposed to say anything.

"Is he okay?" Oliver asked.

"Yes, but it's important you don't say anything about this, okay? The boys would be upset, and the person who accidently shot Gabe would get in trouble."

Their eyes practically bugged out of their heads. "He got shot?"

"I know. But it sounds worse than it is." At least according to Gabe. "I have to get back there. I shouldn't be long. I'll lock the door. You guys go to bed."

"Did you call Marsha?" Oliver asked as she walked from the room.

Mallory briefly closed her eyes. She'd hoped they'd forgotten about it or that maybe hanging out with Gabe and the boys tonight would've made them reconsider staying here with her. Obviously wishful thinking on her part. "It was late by the time Teddy, Dylan, and Cody went to bed. I'll call after church."

By the time she'd made it back to Gabe's, he was no longer in the entryway, kitchen, or living room, from what she could see. "Gabe?" she called out softly and slipped off her boots.

"Back here." His low and deep voice came from down the hall. At least he didn't sound faint from blood loss. If anything, he sounded frustrated and annoyed. He looked it, too, when she found him in his bedroom. Only he was shirtless, the top button of his jeans open, and a bloody white cloth pressed to his side so her eyes didn't stay long on his face.

She forced her gaze from his six pack and put her bag on the bed. It was a masculine room done in gray and camel. "Has the bleeding stopped?" she asked as she walked into the master's en suite to wash her hands.

He lifted the cloth from his side, then raised his eyes to meet hers in the mirror. "Yeah. I told you. I can take care of it on my own."

"Humor me, please." She dried her hands as she walked back into the bedroom to get her first aid kit out of her bag.

"You haven't left me much choice."

Definitely annoyed and frustrated with her. "Yes, I have. I'll take you to the hospital right now if you'd prefer."

"Very funny, Doc. Where do you want me?"

"If you lie down on your right side, that should work." She picked up the towel and spread it on the side of the bed closest to her. Then she put out a hand to help him stretch out on the bed.

"I'm not an invalid, you know."

"Oh, I know. You're a superhero who feels no pain." He had the muscles of a superhero, that's for sure, and he was putting on a very good act of being pain free. From what she could see of his wound, he was right; it had been a peripheral hit and hadn't penetrated the abdomen so there was no damage to any internal organs. He'd been very lucky. Still, infection was an issue.

His lips quirked. "I wouldn't go that far. Dammit," he swore through clenched teeth as he stretched out on the bed.

She gave his arm a comforting squeeze. His skin was smooth and warm. Too warm? she wondered, and gently placed the back of her hand against his beard-roughened cheek. Her hands were cold so it was difficult to tell.

"I don't have a fever, Doc," he said when she moved her hand to his forehead.

"I'd like to make sure." She went to get the digital thermometer from her purse.

"You're like Mary Poppins with her magic carpet bag. What else do you have in that thing?"

"If you're good and stop complaining, I'll give you a spoonful of sugar."

He snorted. "That might work with Teddy."

"I don't know. You ate twice as many snickerdoodles as he did."

"And I'm at least five times his size."

"Mm-hmm, yes, you are." He turned his head to look at her. *Son of a nutcracker*, she'd hummed out loud.

She stuck the thermometer in his ear. Seconds later it beeped. "Normal," she said. This time in a completely professional manner. "That's very good."

"I'm glad you're pleased. Now do you think you could check my wound?"

"I'm going to clean it thoroughly, and I have an anesthetic spray as well as some acetaminophen with codeine that will help with the pain." They were left over from when she'd strained her back lifting Harry. "But you need to go to your doctor and get a prescription."

She went to the bathroom and filled a small tray from her first aid kit with warm water, then returned to pull on a pair of disposable gloves. "I'll be as gentle as possible but it might sting a bit," she warned him and then got to work. He flinched a couple of times but otherwise stayed quiet.

She refilled the tray three times with warm water before she was completely satisfied the wound was thoroughly cleaned. Gently patting it dry, she checked again for signs of inflammation. Once she was satisfied, she sprayed the area with the antiseptic spray. "I'm going to let that dry, and then I'll dress the wound."

"Thanks," he said, and went to get up.

She put her hand on his arm to keep him in place. "I know you don't think it's a big deal, but you were shot. Physically, it's traumatic, so I'd feel better if you took it easy."

"I don't want the boys to wake up and see any signs I've been hurt."

"They won't, Gabe. I'll take care of it." She returned with a glass and two pain pills. "Here, take these." She handed them to him and waited to take the glass and return it to the nightstand. "I can help you take off your jeans and socks, and then you can put on a pair of sleep pants or whatever it is you're most comfortable to sleep in."

He looked at her, and the way he did, she got the distinct impression that he slept in all his naked glory. He truly was an incredible specimen of a man. And for one brief and glorious moment, she let herself fantasize about what it would be like to lie down beside him, to be held in his arms, to be kissed by him, to be . . .

"Okay, then," she said as heat rushed to her cheeks. "I'll help you take off your jeans, then dress your wound."

"Uh, as much as I appreciate the offer, I'm pretty sure I can manage to get changed on my own."

"Just be careful. I'll go wipe up in the entryway while you're getting changed. Let me know when you're ready."

It took her ten minutes to clean up any sign that Gabe had been injured. She'd take his jacket home with her and try to get the blood out on her own. She spent another ten minutes tidying the living room and kitchen while waiting for him to call her. Worried that something had happened to him, she went to his bedroom and lightly tapped on the door. "Gabe, are you okay?"

"Yeah, I'm good," he said, and she walked in to find him standing barefoot in a pair of black sweatpants dressing his own wound.

"I'll say it again, Gabe: you are a very stubborn man." She went over and moved his hand to finish dressing the wound. The dressing was stark white against his golden-bronze skin. Her fingers rested against his firm, muscled abdomen as she taped the dressing in place. She tried to stay focused on the bandage instead of the dark happy trail that disappeared below the waistband of his sweatpants.

"There, you're all set," she said, and for some unknown reason patted his stomach as if he were a five-year-old who hadn't cried when he'd gotten his shot instead of a man with an upper body so beautiful it could make a twenty-nine-year-old woman weep in sexual frustration.

He tipped her chin up with his finger and smiled down at her. "Thanks for everything, Doc. I didn't deserve it. I acted like a jerk."

"Under the circumstances, you're forgiven. You weren't all that jerky anyway."

"I was mad at myself, not at you, if that helps. I should've intervened sooner. The mayor warned me. I just figured Owen..." He grimaced as though angry at himself for saying too much.

But why would mentioning Owen... "This has something to do with my father, doesn't it? Did he shoot you? Did my father do this to you?"

He placed his hands on her shoulders. "Doc, relax, okay? Your father had asked Owen to leave. He didn't, and they got into it. Boyd had a shotgun. It got out of hand. Like I said, I should've intervened sooner."

"You should've arrested him. You should've thrown him in jail."

"It was an accident. The way it went down, I honestly can't say which of them is responsible."

"So what? They get to shoot you without consequences?"

"Trust me, there's consequences, and neither one of them is happy about it. The two of them have to do a hundred hours of community service at the senior center. Winter thought it was a good idea."

"I'm sorry. I must've heard you wrong. You didn't just say that, because Owen and my father were fighting and you can't be sure which of them shot you, you've sentenced them to community service with *me* instead of throwing them both in jail?"

He winced.

"So I'm not wrong. Well, that's just wonderful. Now maybe you can explain to me why I'm being punished."

"Come on, Doc. It's not a punishment. I just thought—"

"Trust me, anyone with a heart would see this exactly for what it is. You're punishing me, Gabe, not them. Owen Campbell took me from the only home I'd ever known days after my mother's funeral, and my father left me there. He left me there for six years." She brushed a tear from her cheek, and he took her face between his hands.

"Listen to me. I understand why you might feel like I'm trying to punish you, but, Doc, that's the last thing I want to do. There are things you don't know, things you need to know."

"No, I don't. I don't need to know anything. The past is in the past, and I want to leave it there. Please, Gabe, make them serve their time with somebody else."

"The reason your father and Owen were fighting was because of you. They care about you."

"Do you really expect me to believe that? They left me in foster care, Gabe. You don't do that to someone you care about."

"You do if you're trying to protect them. Owen took you in hopes of snapping your father out of his grief. He was so positive that Boyd would go get you that he made the director promise not to let anyone adopt you."

She stared at him. Because of Owen, she'd lived all those years with the belief that there was something wrong with her. That she was unlovable. Why else would everyone always pass her by? And those feelings of inadequacy, of never being enough, had plagued her into adulthood. Every person, every situation, she viewed through those defective lenses.

The story she'd told herself made her believe that Harry had never really loved her. He'd just wanted a nurse with a purse. And she'd walked away from everything without a fight.

"Weeks later, your dad left Highland Falls. Owen had assumed it was to get you."

"He made a lot of wrong assumptions, didn't he?" It didn't matter that she now had an explanation as to why no one had wanted to adopt her no matter how good she'd tried to be. The one person who should've wanted her hadn't.

"Owen did, and he needs to answer for them, and so does your father. But you need to know Boyd believed you deserved more than he could ever give you. He wanted you to have the best of everything, and he seemed honestly devastated to learn that, because of Owen, no one had adopted you."

"What am I supposed to do with this, Gabe? What do you want from me?"

"You don't have to do anything other than give them eight hours of work to do every day."

"No. I might not have known you for long, but the one thing I do know is there's more to this than you're letting on." She searched his face. "You think I need this, don't you? You think I need to forgive them so that I can move on."

He carefully drew her into his arms. Less than twenty minutes ago, she'd fantasized about being held by him. Being kissed by him, she thought when his lips brushed the top of her head. But right now she was furious he'd put her in this position.

"Maybe I do. But even more than you, Mal, they need to make amends."

She eased out of his arms. "And I'm supposed to care about that why?"

"Because you're you." He tucked her hair behind her ear.

"If I refuse?"

"I'll charge them, and they'll probably each get two years."

Chapter Fifteen

Aw, come on, Dad. Do we really have to? Let's go to the diner instead. Teddy loves Dot's pancakes," Dylan said as Gabe parked just down from the butter-cream-clapboard church on Main Street.

Gabe could've told Dylan to save his breath. It wasn't going to work. Teddy was determined to go to church this morning, and his youngest was the stubbornest of his sons. He'd also done an excellent job of guilting Gabe.

"It's the first Sunday of Advent. We have to go," Teddy said as he undid his seat belt.

"Why? We haven't been to church since...we left New York."

Gabe glanced at Dylan in the rearview mirror. They hadn't been to church since Lauren's funeral.

"Santa isn't the only one who's watching, Dylan. So is Jesus, and he's the reason for the season."

"Aw, Dad, do we have to? Church is lame," Cody said.

Teddy ignored him and kept talking.

"Advent. A. D. V. E. N. T. That's my word for the

day. Dad, hurry up. We can't be late." Teddy tried to open the door. "We don't want to miss the lighting of the pink candle. It means hope. H. O. P. E. I *hope* Mallory and Oliver and Brooks are here too." He grinned, pleased with himself.

How had Gabe missed that? He should've known Mallory was behind Teddy's newfound desire to go to church. Now Gabe really didn't want to be here. It was bad enough his side was sore and the thought of sitting in a hard pew for an hour gave him a bad case of indigestion. Not to mention the church on Main was a senior magnet. But worse than being on the receiving end of the seniors' angry glares was being on the receiving end of Mallory's. She'd do her best not to let Teddy know she was angry at him, but his son was smart. The last thing Gabe wanted today was to answer questions about why Mallory hated him.

"Yay, she's here," Teddy cheered, pointing at the black Jag four cars over from them.

"You're so annoying," Cody said to his baby brother.

"I bet Gabriella is here," Teddy said, knowing full well his brother had a crush on one of the girls from the neighborhood.

"All right, let's get going, boys," Gabe said. "We'll be here an hour max."

"Can we go to the diner after?" Dylan asked.

"Nope, we have to go to the Christmas bazaar in the church hall after the service. Don't worry, they're going to have even more treats than after the parade. You can buy some, too, Dad. Did you bring your wallet?" Teddy asked.

This day was going from bad to worse. "Yes, I brought my wallet," he said, unable to stifle a pained groan as he got out of the SUV.

"You okay, Dad?" Teddy asked, looking worried.

Gabe ruffled his hair. "I'm good, honey. Overdid it playing touch football yesterday, that's all." His hand felt sticky, and he looked from his palm to Teddy's hair. "Did you put gel in your hair?"

"Yeah." He touched his head. "Did you mess it up?"

Gabe fought back a grin. "Nope, you're styling, honey."

He took Gabe's hand, looking him up and down as they crossed the road. "You're not, Dad. You should've dressed up. Look." Teddy lifted his chin at a well-dressed couple walking up the cement stairs to the front doors. The church sat on the top of a hill framed by the blue mountains behind and towering pines on either side.

"No one will notice what I have on. They'll all be looking at you and your brothers." He hoped, because Teddy was right. Gabe wore a pair of black leisure pants that in his mind passed for dress pants if no one looked too closely and a black V-neck sweater that concealed the bulky bandage on his left side. Both had been easy to put on and were comfortable, which had been all Gabe cared about. He should've given his outerwear more thought. The brown leather bomber jacket he wore rubbed against his side if he moved in a certain way.

He stifled a groan as he began the long climb up the cement stairs.

"Dad, you're walking like an old man." Dylan mimicked him stiff-walking up the stairs.

"No, Dyl, he's walking like this," Cody said, walking like a bowlegged cowboy.

"It's okay, Dad. I'll help you." Teddy guided Gabe up the stairs like he was ninety.

A dark-haired man in his early thirties stood greeting the parishioners wearing a purple robe and a white stole around his neck. He did a double take when he saw Gabe and the boys.

"Chief Buchanan, this is a nice surprise. Boys," Pastor James greeted Gabe's sons with a smile and shook Gabe's hand. "Are you looking for someone in particular?" he asked Teddy, who'd gone up on his tiptoes to search the pews.

"Mallory. She's our neighbor, and she's really pretty with shiny gold hair and blue eyes that sparkle."

The pastor's eyes twinkled. "She really is pretty, isn't she?"

Teddy's eyes narrowed on Pastor James and so did Gabe's.

"And she's as smart as she is pretty," Pastor James added. "I went to grade school with Mallory." His face clouded. "Shame what happened to her and her family. It's good to have her home."

"She's my dad's girlfriend," Teddy said, and Gabe, Dylan, and Cody turned to stare at him.

"Is that so?"

Gabe couldn't tell whether the pastor was disappointed or amused. "No, it's not so," Gabe said. "Someone has a vivid imagination."

Teddy opened his mouth, but something caught his attention, and he said bye to the pastor as he dragged

Gabe into the sanctuary. Gabe was thinking he got off lucky until he saw where Teddy was headed. A pew on the left, four from the back, where Mallory and her stepsons sat.

Gabe tugged on Teddy's hand to get him to stop. "We'll sit here, buddy." He was just about to nod at the pew on his right when Teddy let go of his hand and took off to Mallory's side.

Teddy waved him over. "Mallory saved us a seat," he said loud enough that everyone in the church turned. Including Mallory, who very clearly had not saved them a seat.

But no matter how she felt about Gabe at that moment, she smiled at Teddy and held out her hand. Except instead of his son sliding into the pew beside Mallory as she had intended, he gave Gabe a push that he hadn't been prepared for, a push that caused him to jar his side so hard that he actually cursed, in church. Mallory's sons and his thought it was hilarious. The seniors who sat in the surrounding pews did not. He got loudly *tsk*ed.

"Sorry," he murmured and took the seat beside Mallory. She reached in her bag, shook out a pill, and passed it to him without looking at him. "Thanks," he said and dry-swallowed it.

Teddy leaned around him to smile at Mallory. "You look really pretty today," he said.

He was right, she did. Her hair cascaded down the shoulders and back of her purple winter coat.

"And you look very handsome." She smiled at his son.

"I put gel in my hair." He opened his jacket. "I'm wearing a tie too."

Gabe frowned. "Is that my tie?"

Beside him, Mallory's shoulders shook as she struggled to hold back her laughter. But when Gabe glanced at her to share a smile, she wiped the amusement from her face and stared straight ahead. He leaned in to whisper in her ear. "I'm sorry. I—"

She and the two older women in the pew in front of him *shush*ed him. He sighed; it was going to be a long morning. Except not nearly as long as he'd anticipated. He'd fallen asleep, and he knew he had when Mallory nudged him on one side and Teddy did on the other.

"Gabe, you're snoring," she whispered.

"Wake up, Dad. You sound like a bear, and the old ladies in the pew in front of us are getting mad," Teddy said in a voice that everyone around them heard.

"So are the old ladies in the pew behind you," said a familiar voice from behind. "A fine example you're setting for your children, Chief. Falling asleep in the Lord's house."

"At least he brought them to church," Mallory said to Dot. "He was up half the night keeping the residents of Highland Falls safe."

Gabe raised an eyebrow at her.

She shrugged, clearly still angry at him but angrier at the diner's owner for taking him to task in front of his sons.

"Yeah, and he got shot doing it," Oliver said, then his eyes went wide. "I mean stabbed. I mean, hit. Beaten up. Hurt, he got hurt."

It took ten minutes to get his sons calmed down, and nearly the same amount of time to get out of the pew because of the crowd that had gathered around them, anxious to hear about the shooting.

As Gabe made his way out of the pew, Mallory apologized, explaining why she'd told the boys. Oliver apologized too. Gabe was just glad she hadn't told her stepsons who'd accidentally shot him.

He managed to keep the identity from Dot and her merry band of seniors, although he heard them speculating as they walked ahead of them. Gabe had hoped that he'd garnered enough sympathy from his sons to earn himself a reprieve from the church bazaar. No such luck. The twins had spotted friends from school, and Teddy had heard his two favorite words: *Christmas* and *crafts*.

Gabe was about to ask Mallory if she'd consider forgoing the church bazaar in hopes he could convince the boys to leave when he spotted Abby at the doors to the hall. "Hey, guys. Hey, Gabe."

"My dad got shot. He's a hero. You should interview him for your show," Teddy said to Abby, who stared at Gabe.

"Seriously? Someone in Highland Falls shot you?" She took him by the arm and gently led him into the crowded hall. "Here, sit down." She pulled out a chair from a table and then turned on her friend. "Mal, you're a doctor. What is this man doing out of bed?"

"He's fine, Abby. It's barely a flesh wound."

"That's not what you said last night," he grumbled, because she made him sound like he was being a baby.

"Hmm, I sense a story here. Who's going to share?" She looked from him to Mallory and sighed. "You're no fun. Okay, well, no time to waste. You're going to die when you see the crafts, Mal. I saw at least ten pillows and blankets that would look amazing in your living room. And the cutest reindeer decorations. I thought maybe, for our first episode of Christmas on Reindeer Road, we'd do a segment of you decorating the house for the holidays, and then maybe we could do a couple crafts that you could incorporate into the segment."

"I love crafts. Can I help too?" Teddy asked. "Maybe we can decorate our house?"

"For sure. As long as your dad is okay with it. You good, Gabe?" Abby asked.

"Yeah," he said, because how was he supposed to say no? Two hours later, he decided he should've said no and dragged his youngest out of the hall. Gabe had escaped the senior contingent by trailing after Abby, Mallory, and Teddy, and if he had to listen to them *ooh* and *aah* over one more holiday decoration, he was going to throw himself on the mercy of the seniors manning the table.

"You've gotta be kidding me. This is the third time you've watched the wreath-making demonstration." He held up his hands when the three of them gave him pursed-lipped looks. It was a little scary that his son had the expression down pat. "Hey, Teddy, your friends from school are at the baked goods table." Gabe dug his wallet from his pocket and pulled out a five-dollar bill. "Get yourself a cookie and hot chocolate."

"Dad, can't you see I'm busy? We have to figure out how to make the wreath before we do our video."

Mallory pressed her lips together, clearly trying not to laugh.

"Fine. I'll get a cookie and a coffee." He looked for the twins as he walked away. The last time he'd seen them, they'd been playing charades with a bunch of kids from school. Pastor James had kicked them into the room off the hall when the game got too loud and rowdy. Oliver and Brooks were playing it cool, sitting at a table just down from the one Ainsley and her girl-friends occupied. The girls were making holiday cards with the younger kids.

Gabe ducked into the other room to check on the twins, then found a quiet corner to drink his coffee and eat his cookie undisturbed. Mallory walked by with her arms loaded down.

"You need a hand?" he asked as he tossed his empty cup in a recycle bin.

"I'm good, thank you," she said.

"You're still mad at me, aren't you?"

"Yes, Gabe, I am. And you know why I am so don't look surprised." She backtracked and lowered her voice. "I know what you're doing. You're foisting Owen off on me so you don't have to deal with him at the station."

Now that she mentioned it, it was an added benefit. "No, I—"

"Please, give me some credit."

"Maybe you should do the same. You and your dad—"

"I'm not having this conversation with you."

"Damn, you're stubborn."

"I—" Mallory began, only to be cut off by Teddy.

"Why are you and my dad mad at each other?" Gabe hadn't even noticed him standing there. The poor kid looked crushed.

"We're not mad at each other, sweetie." Mallory forced a smile, but even Teddy would be able to tell it was fake.

His youngest looked from him to Mallory. "I'll be right back," he said and ran off.

"Listen, if it doesn't work out with Owen and Boyd, I'll talk to Winter and we'll come up with something else. I just think you should give it a chance. I have no idea why, but the seniors love Owen. Clearly, as today proved, it's going to take more than you saving Ruby to win over Dot and her gang. I'm betting Owen can help you out with that." Gabe frowned when Teddy dragged over a chair.

He stood up on it and held out a sprig of mistletoe. "Okay, kiss and make up."

"Teddy, your dad and I aren't fighting," Mallory said, her color high.

"Are too," his son said with a familiar glint in his eye.

Gabe sighed. "He's as stubborn as you are."

"I'm not kissing you in the middle of the church hall, Gabriel Buchanan," she whispered, shooting a panicked glance around her.

"Fine. I'll kiss you." He bent his head and touched his mouth to hers. Her lips were soft and sweet, and in that moment, he knew he'd made a fatal mistake. And it wasn't because his son was watching with a big smile on his face or that, out of the corner of his eye, Gabe saw Abby filming them or that Dot and her friends looked shocked and horrified. It was because Gabe wasn't thinking that he'd betrayed his wife. All he was thinking about was Mallory and how much he wanted her in his life.

* * *

"Teddy, what are you..." Gabe began as he walked into the kitchen a few hours later. His youngest had been too quiet, and now he knew why.

"Hey, Mom and Dad," Gabe said to the couple smiling at him from the computer screen. His parents were in their late sixties and could easily pass for a couple in their late forties. And they were as in love now as they had been when he and his brothers were growing up.

Like most kids, they hadn't realized what a gift it had been living in a home with two loving adults. Thanks to their dad's proclivity for PDA, they had been grossed out plenty of times. Still, Gabe had hoped to have a marriage just like theirs, and, for the most part, he had. Only it had ended far too soon.

"Hi, honey," his parents said at almost the same time. The amusement in their eyes and knowing smiles made him nervous but he supposed it was better than panic or concern. His son had obviously not shared about the shooting.

"Teddy tells us he finally found you a match, and he didn't need one of those dating apps to do it. Santa helped him."

"Teddy," Gabe grumbled, "you know better than to talk to Nana and Pop Pop about your old man's dating life."

"A dating life, now is it?" his dad said. "Good job, Teddy. We should've thought to ask for Santa's help before."

"I'm going to ask for Jesus's help too," Teddy said.

"We don't have a lot of time, and Dad says Mallory's stubborn."

That'd teach him not to speak before looking around. "I didn't say Mallory was—"

"Yes you did, Dad." He leaned forward on the chair. "They were fighting but I got them to kiss and make up."

"Really?" his mother said, giving Gabe an intrigued look that promised he'd be getting a phone call later. Probably a conference call with his entire family on the line.

"No, not really," Gabe said.

"Dad, I need your cell phone."

"Why?"

Teddy dug in Gabe's pocket and pulled out his phone. "I'm going to send Nana and Pop Pop the link to *Abby Does Highland Falls*. That's my friend. She's famous, and she put up the pictures of our family and Mallory's with Santa on her YouTube channel last night. She might even have the video she shot at the church this morning up, and you can see Dad kissing Mallory," he said as he typed on Gabe's phone, better and faster than Gabe did. At the sound of a *swoosh*, Teddy told Gabe's parents to check out the link.

"Which one of us did you send it to, honey?" Gabe's mother asked as she checked her cell phone.

His dad did the same. "I didn't get it either, Teddy Bear."

Teddy frowned and swiped through the screen. Then his eyes went wide, and he looked up at Gabe. "Uh-oh, I sent the link to the wrong grandma."

Chapter Sixteen

Bright and early Monday morning, Mallory sat in her parked car in the driveway with Brooks, waiting for Oliver to grace them with his presence. It was the first day of school for the boys, and the first day of work for her.

"Brooks, do me a favor and text your brother. We're going to be late," Mallory said, applying her pink peppermint lip gloss in the rearview mirror. As she did, she found herself thinking about Gabe's kiss. In the middle of the church hall with everyone looking on, including her best friend, who had her smartphone in hand.

Mallory didn't know what he'd been thinking. The last thing either of them needed was the town gossiping about them. They had enough problems without Kayla or Gabe's mother-in-law hearing about the kiss. And Mallory had enough to deal with today without worrying about how that brief and completely unromantic lip-lock had made her feel. She shouldn't have felt anything, but she did. And it wasn't just anger.

She tossed the lip gloss in her bag. If Oliver was as nervous for his first day at school as she was for her first day at the senior center, he might need some added support. "Never mind. I'll go check on him myself," she told Brooks.

"He's okay, Mal. He's just changing his shirt again. He does that when he gets nervous."

"You're not nervous?" she asked him.

"No, I'm kinda looking forward to it. The kids we met yesterday at church seemed nice."

"Did Oliver like them too?"

"He likes Ainsley, but she has a boyfriend. He's the captain of the football team and a real wanker."

Mallory held back a smile. She imagined, with his cute accent and good looks, Brooks would be a popular new addition at school. He was easier going than his brother and didn't give off the arrogant vibe. But as Mallory was beginning to discover, Oliver was the more sensitive of the two and used the attitude to protect himself.

"Maybe Oliver will meet someone else who's just as nice as Ainsley."

"Let's hope so. Otherwise, he won't be much fun to live with when he finds out Marsha gave boarding school the thumbs-down."

Mallory turned to stare at Brooks in the backseat. "You heard me on the phone with Marsha last night. I wish you would've told me. We could've talked about it. I don't like to think of you going to bed upset."

"I wasn't upset. Ollie's the one who wants to go back to England. I kinda like it here." He glanced at her from under his lashes, a flush causing his cinnamon freckles to join together. "With you."

"Oh, Brooks, I can't tell you how happy I am to hear that. I just wish Oliver felt the same."

"Sometimes I think he does but he's afraid to admit it." He looked out the window. "When we found out our dad died and we were going to live with Marsha, Ollie contacted our mother."

Mallory's mouth dropped. "I didn't think you guys had any contact with her."

"We didn't. We don't. But Ollie found her on the Internet. He asked if we could come live with her or if she'd pay for our school. We thought she had lots of money, but Ollie says she's broke now. Anyway, she didn't want us either."

"I want you, Brooks. I want both of you."

He smiled. "I know." Then he glanced out the window again. "Here comes Ollie. Don't tell him what I told you. He'd be embarrassed. And maybe wait a couple days to tell him Marsha said no. Gabe's going to talk to the football coach, and Ollie was pretty excited about it. Even if he doesn't act like it, he was."

"Okay. You can tell me when would be a good time to let him know." She smiled when Oliver got in the backseat. "You all set?" she asked him.

He gave her a clipped nod. In the past, it would've bothered her, but now she knew he was just nervous. She wished she could take away his worries like his brother had taken away hers. Okay, she thought when her stomach dipped, maybe she was still a little nervous at the idea of seeing her father for the first time in seventeen years. Her father who had shot Gabe, she thought as she started the car and went to back out of the driveway.

"Mallory!"

She slammed on the brakes. "What?"

Oliver looked at her with wide eyes. "You nearly hit Gabe's SUV."

She glanced in the rearview mirror. He was right. Gabe had parked at the end of their driveway, and she'd nearly backed into him.

He got out of the SUV. He was wearing his uniform, and her mind inconveniently reminded her what was underneath his navy uniform shirt. Her cheeks warmed, and she fought the urge to fan herself. He tapped on the driver's-side window.

"Rough morning?" he asked when she powered it down.

"Sorry. I was worried we were going to be late and didn't check behind me."

He raised an eyebrow, then reached inside his jacket, pulling out three envelopes with their names printed in big block letters. "From Teddy for your first day on the new job and for the boys' first day at Highland Falls High."

"Aww, he is just the sweetest." She reached back to hand the boys their cards.

"He is," Gabe said but she couldn't help but notice he was staring at her lips. He drew his gaze from her mouth to look at the boys. "Have a good day, guys. I'll give the coach a call, Oliver."

"Thanks, Gabe, and I'm sorry again about blurting

that you got shot in front of the kids. Mallory warned us to keep it to ourselves," Oliver said.

"Hey, you were defending me. Besides, I should've told the boys." He patted the car. "See you guys later."

"Thank Teddy for our cards," Mallory said and powered up the window. She ended up following Gabe to the school. He beeped his horn as she pulled into the high school parking lot and he continued on to the elementary school next door.

Oliver groaned when she took off her seat belt. "Mal, you don't have to come in with us."

"Sorry. I know it's not cool, but I have paperwork to fill out. I promise I won't embarrass you," she said as she walked to the entrance doors with them. "I used to go to school here, you know."

The boys shared a look. Someone must've told them she'd been put in foster care. "I thought you left Highland Falls when you were twelve," Oliver said.

"I did, but I'd skipped a couple of grades." She'd lived up on the mountain and didn't have friends nearby to distract her. The teachers had tried to get her to join the after-school clubs, but her mother had needed her. "They used to have lots of extracurricular activities and clubs, and the sports teams always did really well in the surrounding counties. If you guys want to join anything, I don't mind picking you up later or dropping you off earlier, so don't let the fact that we're a little out of the way stop you from joining."

An older woman looked up from the group of teenagers she'd been speaking to. "Mallory Carlisle, is that you?"

"Mrs. Jones?"

The older woman nodded with a wide smile creasing her lined face. "I'd heard you were moving back to town, and I'd hoped you'd stop by." She came over and hugged Mallory. "Are these your boys?"

She nodded. "My stepsons, Oliver and Brooks. I'm registering them today."

"How wonderful. Welcome to Highland Falls High, boys." She shook their hands. "Let's go to my office and get you registered. I'm the principal now. Your stepmother was my favorite student," she told Oliver and Brooks while patting Mallory's arm. "I just wish we would've had her here longer. We heard all about you saving Ruby. None of us who taught you were surprised. We always knew you'd do great things."

"I wouldn't go that far. I'm a medical doctor, but I didn't finish my residency. I haven't practiced medicine since then, and that was years ago now."

"You kinda did, Mal. You took care of Dad," Brooks said.

"Did she? Well, your father was a very lucky man, then," Mrs. Jones said at the boys' nods. "Mallory won't tell you this, but she looked after her mother from the time she was barely this high." She held a hand to her hip. "She cared for her right up until the day she died. How is your father doing? I heard he came back to Highland Falls about six years ago, but I never see him. Is he still living up on the mountain?" Mrs. Jones asked, ushering them into her office.

Oliver and Brooks looked surprised. They must've assumed her father had died. "As far as I know, he does.

We lost contact after I went into foster care." She smiled, ready to end this part of the conversation. "I probably should get the paperwork done. I'm starting work at the senior center this morning."

"Someone mentioned that they thought Winter had hired you for the position. I have no doubt you can help turn this crisis around. It's a shame how some of our seniors are living. And it's only going to get worse." She hunted around on her desk. "Here we go," she said, placing the papers in front of her.

Mallory glanced at the boys. She had to tell Mrs. Jones about social services. "Would it be possible for Oliver and Brooks to go to their homerooms? I don't want them to be late on their first day."

"Certainly. I'll take them myself." She rested a pair of glasses on the bridge of her nose and looked at her computer screen. "I see you took care of the preregistration. Oliver, I have you in eleventh grade, and Brooks, you're in ninth. Off we go, now. Don't you worry about them. I'll take good care of your sons, Mallory."

"I know you will, Mrs. Jones. Thank you." She hesitated and then stood, giving each of the boys a quick hug. Oliver held himself stiff, and Brooks awkwardly patted her back. "I'll see you guys after school. Text if you need me."

* * *

Mallory pulled into the recreation center's parking lot with twenty minutes to spare. She turned off the engine and leaned her head against the headrest. She needed a few minutes before facing her father and Owen. Her stomach flip-flopped with nerves. It probably didn't help that she'd been worried about telling Mrs. Jones about Kayla McPherson. Her former teacher had been offended on Mallory's behalf. As Mallory was leaving, she'd actually been on the phone with social services. Mallory appreciated her support, but she doubted it would be enough to change Kayla's mind.

She leaned over to take out Teddy's card from her bag. She opened the envelope and nearly cried. He'd drawn a picture of her walking into the recreation center with what looked to be Gabe and the boys, hers and his, cheering her on. He'd included several seniors with big smiles on their faces welcoming her inside.

Someone knocked on the passenger-side window, and she hurriedly wiped at her eyes. It was Gabe. She unlocked the door, and he opened it to slide into the passenger seat beside her. He looked from the card to her. "He made you cry."

"No. Yes," she admitted. "But they're appreciative tears."

"Unlike his father, who makes you cry sad tears." He wiped her cheek with his thumb.

"Angry tears," she said, unable to contain a shiver. And her reaction just then had nothing to do with anger. She held up her hand when he went to apologize. "I'm still not happy about what you did, but your intentions were good. I don't want to talk about it anymore. I'll just deal with it."

He opened his mouth then closed it and nodded. "How did it go at the school?"

She told him about Mrs. Jones calling social services.

"Okay, that it explains it, then."

"Explains what?"

"I got a call from Kayla. She said you're trying to ruin her good name. I probably didn't help matters. I went over her head and talked to her boss about the conflict of interest. She didn't know Kayla had applied for the job so that didn't go over well. And I gather Winter had called her too."

"So now Kayla's really out to get me, isn't she?"

"Let's just say you and the boys should be on your best behaviors for the next week or so. I gather she also heard from Marsha Maitland."

Mallory shook her head. "I don't believe it. Marsha told her I asked her to pay for the boys to go to boarding school, didn't she?"

"She did. Kayla said it was because she was concerned about the boys. But you gotta wonder what is Marsha's endgame. It's not like she wants Oliver and Brooks."

"No, it's not. She was more than clear about that last night. Just like I was equally clear I would prefer the boys stay with me but I wanted them to be happy." She told him what Brooks had said that morning.

"That's great." He glanced to his right and groaned. "Winter didn't tell me Dot and her friends were coming."

"Well, they are seniors." She frowned. "You're not coming in with me today, are you?" she asked, feeling a little like the boys must have.

"Winter put me on the senior committee. She's hoping it will help improve my relationship with Highland Falls' seniors. I gather she got several complaints about my swearing and snoring in church yesterday." He narrowed his eyes when a small laugh escaped from her.

"Sorry, but at one point you were snoring so loud we couldn't hear Pastor James's sermon. You're just lucky Winter didn't hear that you kissed me in the middle of the church hall."

"I'm pretty sure she did hear about it. She just chose not to say anything to me."

She groaned. "Honestly, could this day get much worse?"

"I'm afraid so."

"Really?"

He told her about Teddy sending the link to Abby's YouTube channel to Diane instead of his mother.

"Did you explain that I was mad at... No, I guess you wouldn't explain that, would you? But she must've been able to tell it wasn't a real kiss."

"She didn't actually say much about the kiss. She had more of a problem with who I was kissing."

"She watched the other videos, didn't she?"

"Yep, and she knows that I arrested you last summer."

"Thank goodness she doesn't know that my father shot you."

"Yeah, that's definitely something we should keep on the downlow."

Chapter Seventeen

Gabe glanced at Mallory as they walked into the recreation center together. She had her hand raised to her ear, twisting her pearl earring. "Don't be nervous. It'll be fine," he reassured her.

If he hadn't felt guilty about forcing the reunion between father and daughter before, he did now. It had seemed like a no-brainer at the time but maybe the loss of blood had affected his thinking. Or maybe it was because of his own relationship with his parents. There was something special about knowing they'd always be there for him no matter how badly he'd screwed up. They'd always love him.

He wanted to give his boys the same. He wanted them to know that they were the most amazing little humans on the planet in his eyes. It killed him that this sweet, loving, and generous woman beside him had felt unloved and unwanted for even five minutes. If things were different, if they'd met under different circumstances, he'd spend a lifetime proving to her that she was loved and wanted.

He drew her hand from her ear and gave her fingers a gentle squeeze. "I've got your back."

"Thanks." She freed her hand from his with a strained smile. "As much as I appreciate your support, we should probably forgo the hand holding and kissing. The last thing either of us needs is people gossiping about us."

He hadn't meant to keep holding her hand. He'd fully intended to let it go after giving her fingers a brief, reassuring squeeze. Obviously, his brain hadn't gotten the memo. Or was it his heart? *Brain, definitely your brain.* "I couldn't agree with you more, and I probably should've apologized for kissing you yesterday. You knew why I did, right?"

She raised an eyebrow. "The magic of mistletoe?"

"You felt it too?" he asked, relieved that it wasn't only him. Then he realized she was probably teasing and winked at her as if he'd been doing the same.

To think there'd actually been a time when he'd been good at this sort of stuff. Now his sons were probably better at playing the flirting game than he was. Okay, maybe not the twins, but Teddy definitely.

"Of course I knew you'd only kissed me because Teddy was upset that we were fighting."

"We weren't really fighting though."

"You're right, we weren't. I was just mad at you, and Teddy is a sensitive little boy who picked up on my feelings. I'll be more careful from now on."

"Me too. And trust me, that's the last time I try my hand at a family intervention."

She hesitated at the open double doors and scanned the room. Rows of blue chairs had been set up for

the meeting, and the majority of them were filled. The
Christmas trees had been moved to the side of the hall
near where a refreshment table now stood.

Santa's chair was gone, although fake Santa was in
the audience. Owen sat at one end of the front row,
and Boyd sat at the opposite end. The mayor sat at the
center of a long table facing the audience with three
chairs on either side of her. The three chairs on her right
were empty, while out of the three on her left, two were
occupied. Elsa Mackenzie, the owner of Three Wise
Women Bookstore and Owen's best friend, sat beside
the mayor, and then there was Mallory's favorite social
worker, Kayla McPherson, occupying the chair beside
Elsa. Gabe figured Winter had offered Kayla a place on
the committee as a peace offering. Besides that, social
services dealt with many of the seniors Mallory would
be trying to help.

He wasn't sure if Mallory's soft groan was because
she'd spotted her father or Kayla. As they walked into
the room, people turned to look at them.

Mallory glanced at him. "You know how you said
Owen could help me win over the seniors of Highland
Falls?"

"Yeah," he said, pretty sure he knew where this was
going, considering the animosity in the seniors' gazes
was aimed at him, not her.

"I think you could use his help more than me." She
hefted her Mary Poppins magic carpet bag over her
shoulder.

"Except he's the reason they hate me," he said under
his breath as they walked toward the table. "And the

only way to change their minds would be for me to give him back his job."

"Or to find him another one." With her eyes focused on Winter, Mallory walked straight to the table without sparing her father a passing glance. Gabe didn't say anything, but he didn't think ignoring the elephant in the room was going to make this any easier on her.

They both said hello to the committee members, and Kayla gestured for Gabe to take the chair beside hers. Since he didn't want to make an already difficult situation worse, he took the seat. He didn't miss the smug smile Kayla gave to Mallory or that Mallory rolled her eyes before moving to the other end of the table.

"Sorry I'm late," Abby called out as she hurried down the aisle with her Yorkie in her bag and Wolf loping after her.

"Abby, slow down before you—" Mallory began, then gasped when it looked like her best friend was about to take a header into the table. An older woman on the inside aisle reached for Abby, but Wolf was quicker. He latched on to the back of Abby's jacket, saving her from falling on her face.

Gabe wouldn't be surprised if Hunter had trained his dog to protect his fiancée from falls. Abby was an accident waiting to happen, and it wasn't because she did everything at full speed or was a klutz. It was because she'd suffered a stroke and traumatic brain injury when she was twelve and to this day had issues with her balance when she was tired or stressed.

"Isn't he just the smartest?" she said to everyone while turning to love on the white dog. "Did anyone happen to get that on video? No?" She tapped her finger on her lips.

"No, you're not reenacting it for your channel. Come sit down," said Mallory, who obviously knew how her best friend's mind worked. She patted the chair beside hers.

"Did I miss something?" Pastor James, who was dressed in jeans and a heavy gray sweater with a plaid scarf around his neck, walked up the aisle behind Abby.

"Just me being me." Abby smiled at the pastor, then something to her left caught her attention, and she gasped, "Oh my goodness, is that you, Mr. Carlisle?"

Mallory's dad looked about as uncomfortable with the attention as his daughter. "Yes, ma'am." He cast a nervous glance in Mallory's direction.

Abby hurried over and offered her hand. "I'm Hunter Mackenzie's fiancée, Abby, and your daughter's best friend." She flashed Mallory an apologetic smile over her shoulder as if just realizing this might be a little awkward for her best friend. But of course that didn't stop her from saying, "I'd love to interview you, Mr. Carlisle. I heard about the boys you rescued last winter, which I'm sure would make a great story. But what I'd really like to feature is your mouth-blown, hand-painted glass ornaments."

Mallory frowned. Apparently she didn't know her father was an artist.

"Mayor, perhaps Ms. Everhart could do this later. Some of us have to get to work." Kayla made the point by holding up her phone. She shrugged when Abby gave her a look. Then she turned to Gabe and whispered,

"I was under the impression that Mallory had nothing to do with her father. If that's not the case, it changes everything."

"How so?"

"Come on, Gabriel. The man runs an illegal still in the mountains and sells moonshine. The last thing the Maitland boys need is someone like that in their lives."

"Used to run an illegal still and sell moonshine. As far as I know, that's no longer the case. And it sounds to me like he was a hero. I guess you missed that part. Not that it matters because your boss reviewed Mallory's case and found no legal basis for mandatory supervision."

"That may be true, but as far as I'm concerned, the case hasn't been permanently closed. It's my sworn duty to protect the children in our community, and I take that very seriously. So while Mallory is no longer subject to random at-home visits or weekly meetings, I have my eye on her."

And from where he was sitting, so did Pastor James. The pastor and Mallory shared a smile when the mayor called the meeting to order. Gabe crossed his arms. That'd teach him to try smoothing over a situation for Mallory. He'd made it worse for himself. Because the last thing he wanted to sit through was Pastor James flirting with Mallory and doing a much better job of it than Gabe could ever hope to.

The mayor came to her feet. "Welcome to our first meeting of the Highland Falls Senior Initiative. We're very excited to implement some of Mallory's ideas. Although today is her first official day on the job, she has reached out to many of you over the past ten days with a survey to establish what programs you feel are needed. Thanks to all of you who responded, I believe you'll be as happy as I am with what Mallory has come up with."

She gave Mallory a warm smile before continuing. "Now, for those of you who don't know her, Mallory comes to us with years of experience dealing with issues that affect seniors."

"Like being married to a man more than twice her age qualifies her to be director of senior programming," Kayla said under her breath.

Elsa Mackenzie gave her a quelling glance, and Kayla had the good sense to look chastened. While Granny MacLeod believed herself to be the matriarch of Highland Falls, Elsa Mackenzie held sway over the town. In fact, Gabe wouldn't have been surprised if Elsa also gave Kayla's boss a call on Mallory's behalf. Abby hadn't been Elsa's favorite person when she'd first moved to town, but now the two would work together to ensure Mallory kept her job.

"For five years, Mallory served on the board of Emory University Hospital as well as the board of the Atlanta Women's Foundation, and until recently she volunteered several days a week with Meals on Wheels."

Elsa raised an eyebrow at Kayla as if to say *You see?* The caseworker shrugged in response.

"And if that's not impressive enough, Mallory also has a medical degree, and just the other day used her expertise to save one of Highland Falls' favorite people, Ruby Lee. So please join me in giving a warm welcome to one of Highland Falls' own, our esteemed director of senior programming, Mallory Carlisle Maitland." Winter clapped, smiling her encouragement for others to do the same.

Abby made up for Mallory's lukewarm reception from the audience. She was loud enough and enthusiastic enough for fifty people, and Owen picked up where she left off. Which meant some of the less enthusiastic seniors became much more enthusiastic.

Mallory rose from her chair, acknowledging the applause with a smile. "Thank you very much for the kind words, Mayor Johnson. And to all of you for the warm welcome. I'm looking forward to working with you to make Highland Falls Senior Initiative a model for other communities. I'd also like to thank the members of the committee for offering their expertise and volunteering their time," she said, introducing each of them in turn.

Dot, who was sitting in the front row, put up her hand. Gabe could've sworn Mallory bit back a groan as she pretended not to see the older woman's hand waving in the air.

"Yes, Dot," Winter said grudgingly. She knew better than to think Dot would give up.

"Nothing against Chief Buchanan, but don't you think Chief Campbell would be a better choice for a committee member? After all, the current chief of police barely knows us, him being an outsider and all. But Owen kept us safe for a good forty years. Don't recall him ever getting shot either," she said under her breath.

If she'd glanced to her right and then to her left, she would've noticed both Owen and Boyd sinking down on their chairs. Winter noticed and looked from the men to

Gabe, an eyebrow raised. He'd left out the part that he'd been shot when he spoke to her last night.

"Mayor Johnson, if you don't mind, I'll answer Dot's question," Mallory said sweetly, but there was nothing sweet about the look she gave the owner of the diner.

Gabe appreciated Mallory being angry on his behalf, but he didn't want her making enemies because of him. He tried to catch her eye to silently share that with her, but she'd already begun to speak.

"I was going to save this announcement for later, but you provided the perfect segue, Dot. So thank you for that, and thank you to everyone who took the time to answer the survey. A lot of you were looking for ways to earn extra money and feel like productive members of society again, and there are a couple of programs we'll be putting in place for you to do that. But thanks to the former chief of police volunteering his time to our senior initiative, and for volunteering his friend"—she cleared her throat—"my father, Boyd Carlisle, we have an opportunity that I'm super excited about, and I think any of you who love the holidays and want to earn a little extra money will be too."

Boyd and Owen were looking at her with their mouths hanging open, and it was all Gabe could do to hold back a laugh. It looked like Mallory had come up with a way around his mandated community service for her father and Owen, while maybe taking care of his Owen problem as well.

"As some of you might know, there's been a Christmas tree shortage for a couple years. Both climate change and retiring farmers have played roles. However,

Chief Campbell's Blue Ridge Tree Farm is still up and running. But I think even he'd admit, there are many money-making opportunities that he's not taking advantage of."

Owen gave Gabe a *What the hell is going on?* look.

Gabe shrugged but he had a feeling they were about to find out when Mallory walked to the easel and uncapped a marker. "All right, let's call this—"

Abby waved her hand. "Highland Falls Does Christmas." She wrinkled her nose. "A Blue Ridge Tree Farm Christmas. That works better, doesn't it?" She clapped, and Bella yipped from where she sat in Abby's lap wearing red booties and a white sweater that matched her owner's. "I'm excited. Are you excited, Owen? This is exactly what Aunt Liz wanted you to do: diversify. You have that gorgeous red barn going to waste. Oh my gosh, oh my gosh, I have the perfect idea. All of our seniors who were selling their crafts at the church bazaar could sell them at your place. We could do a Christmas Market."

"We could sell our wreaths," someone yelled.

"What about sleigh rides?" a woman at the back called out.

"We could sell baked goods and hot chocolate."

"Hey, Boyd, you could sell cider. The one without a kick." An older man laughed.

"We could sell holly and mistletoe."

As fast as Mallory wrote, the ideas kept coming. When she had five pages of suggestions, she said, "Okay, if we want to be up and running by this weekend, I think it's time we get organized."

Owen stared at her. "This weekend?"

"Yes. This weekend." She smiled, and Gabe could've sworn she was fighting back a laugh. But he had a feeling she was as excited about the response to her idea as she was about getting rid of Boyd and Owen. Aside from the two men, the majority of seniors in the room had fully embraced the idea. So did the other committee members. Well, all the committee members except for Kayla.

"Excuse me, but am I the only one wondering how this little project of yours is supposed to benefit our seniors?" Kayla asked. "You've lived the majority of your life in Atlanta, enjoying what some might call a Cinderella lifestyle, so I suppose you could be forgiven for not understanding the seriousness of the issues we are dealing with here. But we have seniors who can no longer afford to keep their homes or apartments. They're having trouble paying their bills. And the number of our seniors at risk for developing Alzheimer's and dementia has quadrupled."

"Seriously, Kayla, what is your problem? Mallory—" Gabe began, only to have Mallory cut him off.

"Thank you, Chief Buchanan." She gave him a tight smile. He wasn't sure why until he glanced around the room. His quick defense of her had drawn several raised eyebrows as well as a grateful smile from her father.

"I'm well aware of the issues facing our senior citizens, Ms. McPherson," Mallory said to the woman, who was shaking her head at Gabe. It looked like he could cancel his coffee date with Kayla.

"And I'm aware not because of the committees I've served on," Mallory continued, "but because I've asked the very people we're supposed to be helping what it is they want. What is it they feel they need." She reached into her bag and pulled out a sheaf of papers. "I'd planned on handing these out once we'd organized a committee for the Christmas Market at Blue Ridge Tree Farm, but we can go over the programs I hope to put into place over the next six months. As you'll see, your concerns, but more importantly, the concerns of our seniors, have been addressed. And thanks to Abby and the Liz Findlay Foundation, we will be able to address one of the most pressing needs right away. Abby." She smiled and nodded at her best friend to take her place at the easel.

"Mallory is giving me too much credit. The idea was all hers. It all came about when I was trying to play matchmaker—"

"We're a little tight on time, Abs, so maybe you can tell them about the program," Mallory said, her face flushed.

"Oh right," Abby said with a laugh, then glanced at Gabe. "Probably not a good idea to go there today."

So now he knew his suspicions had been right after all. Abby had been trying to set him up with Mallory. And like him, Mallory had done her best to dissuade her best friend. But as Abby outlined what they were calling the Golden Girls Project, explaining that the Liz Findlay Foundation had purchased two four-bedroom homes in Highland Falls and would be renting each home at reasonable rates to in-need senior women from the community, Gabe had a feeling that the foundation had also purchased Mallory's home on Reindeer Road.

Just like he had a feeling Mallory had no idea who her landlord was.

Mallory stood as Abby wrapped up her presentation. "Thank you, Abby. This is a beautiful way to honor your aunt's memory and the town that she loved."

"Hear, hear," Elsa Mackenzie said. "You've done Liz proud, Abby. She's smiling down on you from heaven. On both you and Mallory. On you, too, Owen. It's about time you fulfilled your promise to Liz and made something of the farm. It'll be good for the town."

"Don't forget Hunter," Abby said. "He sold his property on Mirror Lake and donated the proceeds to the foundation so we could buy the houses for the Golden Girls Project."

Elsa pressed her hands to her heart. "That boy."

Mallory smiled. "I'm glad you approve of the plans, Elsa. From the feedback on the surveys and from talking to Abby, I've identified a couple of women who I think should be given first chance at participating in the Golden Girls Project, but I'm hoping you, Pastor James, Chief Buchanan, and Ms. McPherson will give us some input too."

Just as Gabe expected, Dot's hand shot up. This time she didn't wait to be called on. "Probably best if you ask Owen. Chief Buchanan hasn't been on the job long—"

This time he cut off his nemesis. "I'd be happy to give you some input, Mallory. We've been providing emergency shelter to a couple of seniors off and on. But you should probably talk to Ruby. She coordinated most of our efforts, and I'm sure she'd be more than happy to advise you."

Elsa nodded. "I agree with the chief. Ruby's who you want to talk to. Plus, it'll give her something to do while she's off."

"That's a great suggestion, thank you. Now, I'll pass these around"—Mallory held up the papers—"and if you have any suggestions or questions, I'll take them after we've had a short break for refreshments. You can also sign up to volunteer at the tree farm and let us know if you have a craft or product that you'd like to sell. We also need someone to manage the advertising and social media."

Abby raised her hand. "I can head up the marketing committee."

"Perfect. So it looks like we're all set. Please help yourself to the refreshments." Mallory smiled and began handing out her proposal. A group of seniors congregated around her. The majority wanted to congratulate her on the position and to let her know how pleased they were with what they'd heard so far. Like Kayla, Dot and her friends found several things to complain about but were taking a wait-and-see approach for the most part.

Gabe grabbed a cup of coffee for himself and one for Mallory. He knew from their joint family dinner that she liked double cream and double sugar. He was waylaid by the mayor on his way back to the table.

"You better get over there and run interference for Mallory. Boyd and Owen are in line to speak to her." She glanced over her shoulder, then gave Gabe a knowing smile. "I'm sure you're more than pleased with her suggestion for the tree farm." She sighed when Dot waved her over to the refreshment table. "Hopefully with him busy and away from the station, his old friends will stop trying to get you fired because, Chief, the other members of the town council are making noises."

Okay, this wasn't a joke anymore. His job might actually be on the line.

As he approached the committee's table, Gabe noticed Owen and Boyd standing off to the side. From their downtrodden expressions, they'd already spoken with Mallory, and it hadn't gone well.

"I know you're not happy about working with me," Gabe overheard Owen say to Boyd. "I'm not exactly thrilled to be working with you either, but it's what Mallory wants us to do, so that's what we do. We've both got a lot to make up to her, Boyd. You even more than me."

Gabe moved closer in case he needed to intervene. He was afraid Boyd was going to knock Owen on his ass for the remark. But instead the other man shoved his hands in the pockets of his jeans and cast a wistful glance over his shoulder at his daughter. "She doesn't want anything to do with me, Owen. Nothing I say or do will make it up to her anyway."

"Don't go all doom and gloom on me. I told you exactly what we're going to do. You and me are playing the Maitlands' and Buchanans' secret Santas. Little Teddy wants a mom, and Gabriel might not admit it, but he needs a wife. And Mallory and her boys need a family. What better way to give them all a Christmas to remember than to bring the two families together?"

Boyd nodded. "The two of them seem to like each

other. I saw them holding hands when they came in. They're quick to defend each other too."

"Chief can't take his eyes off her."

Gabe stared at the two men. They couldn't be serious.

He took a step in their direction to set them straight but stopped midstride. It wasn't like their secret Santa project would work. Besides, with Mallory's and Abby's plans for A Blue Ridge Tree Farm Christmas, they wouldn't have any time to spare.

Chapter Eighteen

Please don't be the school, Mallory thought at the ringing of her cell phone in her purse. They'd almost made it through the first week with no incidents. She'd made reservations for a celebratory dinner with the boys tonight. Her first week on the job had also gone better than she'd expected.

"Sorry, Mrs. Beckett. I have to take this," she said to the older woman who was making tea and toast in the recreation center's kitchen.

Mallory had completed the four assessments for memory impairment and functional abilities she'd scheduled for the day, but Mrs. Beckett's daughter had called the center this morning, concerned about some memory issues her mother was having, and begged Mallory to fit her in. Mrs. Beckett's children lived out of state and didn't get to see their mother as often as they wanted.

"No problem, dear. I'll fix you a cuppa while you're on the phone."

"Thank you." She smiled at Mrs. Beckett and went to retrieve her phone. It was Gabe. Mallory hadn't seen him since Monday. He'd texted her a couple times during the week to check on them, and she'd done the same, but seeing his name on her screen now, she realized she'd missed their daily interactions. Although the number of times she'd tried to catch a glimpse of him through the kitchen window probably should've clued her in that she missed seeing him.

"Hi, is everything all right?" She rolled her eyes at herself. She'd meant to sound a little less happy to hear from him.

"Hey, Doc. You got a minute?"

"This isn't just a hey-how-are-you-doing call, is it?" She pulled out a chair at the table.

"Afraid not. There's been a problem at the sch—"

"Are the boys okay? Is it my boys or yours? Who's in trouble, Gabe? No one got hurt, did they?"

"Okay, take a breath. It's nothing to get overly upset about. We got called out to the high school on a false alarm. Supposedly it was Oliver who did it."

She shouldn't have told him that Marsha had said no to boarding school. She should've waited for the weekend. But yesterday he'd asked her outright, and she hadn't wanted to lie to him. She had dangled the hope that she'd try again, anything to wipe the disappointment from his face.

"What does Mrs. Jones think?" she asked, forcing a smile for Mrs. Beckett, who was buttering the toast with her tea.

The older woman winked at her. "Don't tell my

daughter. She thinks I'm daft but she dunks her toast in tea and the soggy bits drop in." She shuddered.

That at least was a relief. Gabe's response wasn't. "Oliver's having problems with a couple of the twelfth-grade students, and Mrs. Jones thinks they pulled the alarm and blamed him."

"He never said anything to me. Neither did Brooks. I thought they were doing well and fitting in." She bowed her head, rubbing her forehead. A cup of tea appeared in front of her, and Mrs. Beckett gave her shoulder a comforting squeeze.

"Take it from me, dear. You're always the last to know what's going on with your children, no matter how good a mother you are."

"Thanks, Mrs. Beckett."

"Sounds like Mrs. Beckett knows what she's talking about. I'm sure the boys didn't want to worry you, Doc. Oliver's not admitting to anything, but he's not denying pulling the alarm, so there's not much I can do. Mrs. Jones's hands are tied too."

"I appreciate you being there for him, Gabe. Would you mind telling Mrs. Jones that I'll be—"

"I'll take Oliver home with me, spend some time with him, and see if I can get him to talk. I'm pretty sure I know who's giving him a hard time. I'll have a word with Sully—that's the football coach—before we take off."

"Are you sure? Don't you have to get back to the station?"

"I work tomorrow so I had a short shift today. I'd planned to work on my car when I got home. Oliver can give me a hand. Unless you'd rather he do his homework. I don't want to overstep."

"Feel free to overstep. It's obvious I'm failing pretty badly dealing with the boys on my own."

"Come on, give yourself a break."

"Gabe, I had no idea this was going on. I'd planned to take them out to dinner to celebrate. That's how clueless I am."

"Doc, I have to go. We'll talk later, okay? I'm going to pass you to Mrs. Jones to give her the okay for me to take Oliver."

"Thanks, Gabe. You have no idea how much I appreciate this."

* * *

Mallory smiled as she walked into the heated garage. It smelled like motor oil and pine trees. Bruce Springsteen's "Glory Days" was playing on the car's speakers, and Gabe was singing along as he worked under the hood.

As though he sensed her presence, he straightened, wiping his hands on a rag. "I heard you picked up dinner for us at Zia Maria's Pizzeria."

"Dessert too. It's the least I could do." She leaned back to look at the car. "I hear this is your pride and joy."

"And you haven't got a clue what make it is, have you?"

She tapped a finger on her lips. "A 'ninety-six Corvette with a six-speed tranny and three-thirty horsepower."

He laughed. "The boys told you, didn't they?"

"It was all Oliver could talk about." She peeked

through the window at the pristine white leather seats. "He really enjoyed spending some one-on-one time with you, Gabe. As far as I know, he never really had that with Harry. Neither did Brooks, but I get the feeling it's something Oliver feels he's missed out on."

"I think you're right." He opened the driver's-side door and lifted his chin at the passenger side. "You let me sit in your car—seems only fair I return the favor."

"Except you got to sit in the driver's seat," she said even while she walked around the car to the other side.

"Yes, because I actually have a deep appreciation for cars. You, on the other hand, don't. Oliver does. I'd be surprised if he didn't have you waiting outside the DMV on the morning of his birthday."

"I've already been warned. Something else to be terrified about," she said as she slid in beside him. "It's a cute car."

"Doc, there is nothing cute about my car."

She laughed at his offended expression. "I'm sorry. It's a hot car, sexy too." He didn't have to know she was referring to him. He looked both hot and sexy in his long-sleeve black Henley and well-worn jeans.

"I feel the same way about your car." There was something about his sidelong glance that made her wonder whether he was referring to her or her car.

Most likely her car, she decided, thinking there was nothing hot or sexy about her black pants and puffy blue winter jacket. Her hair was also a windblown mess and whatever makeup she'd put on this morning had worn off.

She self-consciously smoothed her hair. "I'll let you take the Jag out for a drive before I sell it."

"Are you kidding me? You're selling the Jag?"

She shrugged. "It's not like I want Oliver driving it. Marsha let him drive with her in her nineteen-sixties Cadillac, but it's like a boat and hasn't got much get-up-and-go left. It's not like I can afford two cars so I thought I'd buy a nice, practical van. From your expression, I don't have to ask what you think."

"A van." He shuddered. "I told my wife we had to stop at three kids. No way was I driving around in a van. Then she showed me an SUV, and I was willing to be persuaded."

He looked deep in thought, and she didn't want to remind him of what he'd lost by asking if they'd tried to have more children so instead she said, "Isn't an SUV a van?"

"Seriously, Doc, we have to educate you. Don't buy anything unless you let me check it out first, and definitely don't accept any offers for the Jag without running them by me. Did you want to trade it in before or after Oliver's birthday?"

"His birthday's next weekend so that would be a little fast. He can't drive on his own anyway, so maybe I'll wait until spring."

"Probably a good idea. I don't mind taking him out once in a while."

"If you're sure you don't mind, I'd really appreciate it. I have a feeling I might make him nervous."

"Maybe in exchange you can help me out with Teddy's birthday party. It's on the twentieth. He wants a Christmas theme."

"Why am I not surprised." Mallory laughed. "I'd love to help. Um, will Diane and Karl be there?"

"No, not at the kids' party. They're coming for dinner

the next night. They'll probably do their Christmas exchange with the boys. They're planning to go to Florida for the holidays."

"Do the boys mind?"

"No, not at all. We lost Lauren ten days before Christmas, and Diane has a hard time with the holidays. We all do, really. All except Teddy, I guess."

"That makes sense. He was very young when Lauren died."

"Yeah, but it's not fair to him. I'm going to try harder this year. Get the twins onboard too."

"I don't know if this is something that would help, but instead of putting the emphasis on the anniversary of Lauren's death, what about doing something special on her birthday to celebrate and honor her life? When was her birthday?"

He smiled. "December twenty-first."

"That's perfect. You can celebrate her birthday and then celebrate Christmas."

"You think you'd be able to help me out with that too? I'm not really good with this party-planning stuff."

"Well, you're in luck. I love party planning, and I'd be honored to help you plan a celebration of Lauren's life. I'm thinking of doing the same next spring for Harry. There's so much that Oliver and Brooks don't know about their father, so much they missed out on, and I want to try and fill those voids. Hopefully I can get Marsha onboard."

"Have you spoken to her again? Oliver told me you said you would."

"I know I should just let it go and tell him it's a

definite no so we can move forward. But he was so disappointed that the words were coming out of my mouth before I could stop them."

"You know you're a pushover, don't you?"

She buried her face in her hands and groaned. "Is that what Oliver and Brooks think?"

He gently tweaked her hair. "Probably, but in a good way. You're a sweet, loving, thoughtful woman who has more empathy in her baby finger than most people have in their entire bodies. Oliver and Brooks are lucky to have you, and trust me, they know they are. But they're teenage boys, and if you give them an inch, they'll definitely take a mile."

"So we probably should get in there and make sure everything's under control."

"I'm paying Oliver and Brooks to look after the boys." He held up his phone and pulled up an app. The boys appeared on the screen. The five of them were sprawled on the brown leather sectional eating pizza and watching the big-screen TV.

"Who's the pushover now? They're eating pizza on your couch with their feet up and watching a movie about"—she leaned in to get a look at the television screen—"robots."

"My guys are introducing your guys to *Lost in Space*. Think the Swiss Family Robinson goes to space," he said at what must've been her blank look.

"We don't watch a lot of TV. The boys play their music and play video games."

"And you read your romance novels," he said, fighting a smile.

"Yes, I do. And you play with your car."

He laughed, then narrowed his eyes on the screen. "They're going to eat all the pizza if I don't get in there and grab a few slices."

"Go, go. I'm sorry for keeping you." She went to open the door.

"I didn't mean for you to leave. I thought I'd grab us a couple slices and a couple bottles of beer if you're up for it. No worries if you're not."

"You want us to eat here? In your car?"

"Yeah, as long as you promise not to spill anything on the upholstery." He winked at her and got out of the car. "I'll be right back."

He lived up to his promise. She'd just settled back into her seat after changing the radio station when he appeared at the driver's-side door. She leaned across to open his door for him. "Are you sure you got enough?"

He had a pizza box, two beers, paper plates, and napkins.

He groaned when he settled in beside her, handing her the pizza box. "I leave you for two minutes, and you change the Boss for...who is that?"

"Keith Urban."

"The country guy?"

"Yeah, the country guy who is singing 'I'll Be Your Santa Tonight.'"

He grinned. "Does bringing you beer and pizza count?"

"Definitely." She clinked her beer bottle to his and then put it between her legs to open the box of pizza and hand him a slice.

"Thanks, and just so we get our stories straight:

You're not here. I told Teddy you needed some time on your own so you were taking your pizza and beer home. Otherwise, he would've been out here with us. And I don't know about you, but by the end of the week I'm ready for an hour of alone time, or, in this case, adult time."

She once again clinked her beer bottle to his. "Completely agree. I usually get mine in the bathtub with my book, but this is..." She sighed when he choked on his beer. "I'm never going to mention my book or bathtub in the same sentence with you again."

"I have very fond memories of...Pretend I didn't say that." He lifted his chin. "Eat your pizza."

They ate in companionable silence—or it was entirely possible the silence was due to them both thinking about that night, which she was not about to mention. Instead, she listened to the Christmas carols playing on the radio and focused on thinking only companionable thoughts where Gabe was concerned. She found that difficult. She imagined any woman would when sitting in the close confines of a car with him. Even if that car was in a heated garage.

Mallory decided that what she needed to curb her romantic fantasies was a dose of reality. "So, did you have any luck getting Oliver to admit who pulled the alarm?"

"No, but I honestly didn't expect to. Things haven't changed much since we were in school. No one wants to be labeled a rat."

"Did you talk to the football coach? Does he know who's giving Oliver a hard time?"

"Oh yeah, he knows exactly who it is. Ainsley's boyfriend and captain of the football team, Dirk McFee, and a couple of his buddies."

"Why does that name sound familiar?"

"Dot's his grandmother."

"Oh no, this could get really bad, couldn't it? Gabe, you absolutely can't get involved. Dot is already out to get you."

"I know. I thought it would eventually blow over, but I was fooling myself." He told her what the mayor said at the meeting.

"Okay, we can't just sit around hoping that Dot will back off now that Owen is busy with the farm. We have to...I've got it. You can help me with my in-home visits. While I check on how the seniors are managing at home, you can check for safety issues. It'll give you the opportunity for some one-on-one time."

"Sure. Sounds good."

"You can also volunteer a couple times a week delivering hot lunches to our homebound residents. It's another nice way for you to get to know them better."

"Okay, I can probably do that too."

"Great. And maybe we can do cops take a senior for lunch and a holiday shop. That would be fun, wouldn't it? Do you have any money in your budget for holiday events with the community?"

"I don't know. I'd have to check. But I think I'll be busy enough with the in-home visits and meals-on-wheels thing."

"We'll see how it goes. You should also consider doing a team building event with your staff. A holiday party would be good. Dot wouldn't be able to stir the pot if your staff was on your side. Maybe I'll talk to Ruby about it. She'll know exactly who to target."

He gave her a raised-eyebrow look. "I was enjoying our pizza date until you brought up work, you know."

"Sorry. I...Are we on a date? I thought we agreed it wasn't a good idea—"

"Slip of the tongue. We're just enjoying an adult— Oh, crap, get down." He shoved her head into his lap.

"Gabe, what's going—"

"Shh, stop talking, and if you can stop breathing, too, that'd be great."

She didn't understand why he...Okay, as she felt something grow very large and very hard beneath her face, she no longer had to wonder what he meant.

"Hey, honey, what do you need?" she heard him ask and realized why she was face-first in his lap.

"The boys aren't letting me have a turn picking what we watch on TV," Teddy said from somewhere in the vicinity of the door leading from the house into the garage.

"Okay, I just have to take care of a few things, and I'll be right in."

"Dad, you sound funny, and your face is kinda red."

"I'm okay. Everything's good. You don't have to come check on me. Careful there, buddy, there's some grease on the floor."

"I don't see any grease," Teddy said, sounding closer than before, which caused Mallory to give a muffled squeak of alarm and burrow deeper in Gabe's lap.

He stifled a groan.

"Sorry," she whispered, but he'd turned up the radio.

"Why are you grinning at me, buddy?" Gabe asked, sounding nervous.

"My plan is working, Dad. You're listening to Christmas carols." There was a pitter-patter of little feet and then the squeak of the door between the house and garage opening. "Hey, guys, guess what? Dad—" Whatever else Teddy was about to say was lost as he walked back inside the house.

"Okay, that was embarrassing. I'm sorry, Mallory. I—"

"It's not your fault, Gabe. I understand that random erections are normal," she said, trying to sound as clinically detached as possible, but then she ruined everything by laughing.

"I'm glad you think it's funny, but do you think you could sit up now?"

"Sorry," she said, and went to push herself upright. "Ouch. I can't."

"What do you mean, you can't?"

"My hair is caught on something. I think it's wrapped around the button of your jeans. Just give me a minute," she said, moving her head up and down as she tried to free her hair.

"Oh, jeez, I think Teddy's bringing reinforcements. Hurry, and maybe stop doing that," he said.

"Okay, okay," she said, imagining what it would look like if the boys walked in. She moved her hand to the button of his jeans. "I just need a minute." She worked his button and then her hair was free and not a moment too soon. As she sat up, still half in Gabe's lap, the door between the house and the garage opened.

"See, I told you. Dad loves . . . Mallory?"

Chapter Nineteen

Mallory tossed back the covers and stumbled from her bedroom. She'd spent another almost sleepless night. She'd woken up at three again. She was coming to think of it as the witching hour.

Reading her latest romance novel hadn't lulled her back to sleep, possibly because Gabe had once again taken on the role of the hero in her mind. This time he was a big-city homicide detective instead of a small-town sheriff.

The bath she'd taken before bed hadn't helped relax her either. Not really a surprise when her explanations to the boys for why she'd practically been in Gabe's lap hadn't been warmly received. There was a decided chill in the air when she'd made her way home last night, and it had nothing to do with the weather.

If this kept going, her worry journal would be filled by next week. Not that the journal was helping with her insomnia as it was supposed to. Neither was the extra exercise she was getting in at the senior center. Every day she ran a chair exercise program in the morning and a dance class in the afternoon. Last week it had been jazz. This coming week was Zumba.

She turned on the light over the stove—six in the morning. Yawning, she picked up the kettle from the back burner and turned to fill it in the sink, blinking at the sight that greeted her. "It's snowing!"

She looked around for someone to share the exciting news with, then remembered she was the only one up. Although Oliver and Brooks would probably be too cool to make a fuss anyway.

They'd rarely had snow for Christmas in Atlanta, and it was the one thing she missed about Highland Falls. Seeing it now made her feel like a kid again, and her eyes went to her boots on the mat and her winter jacket hanging by the door. She couldn't believe she was actually thinking about going outside.

You're sleep deprived, she told herself with a laugh when she put the kettle on the back burner and went to slip on her boots and coat. But even the thought that she'd look like a fool didn't stop her from opening the door and stepping outside. She breathed in the cold, crisp air—the smell of wood smoke and pine. Then she walked to the edge of the backyard, tilting her face up to catch the fat flakes on the tip of her tongue.

Snow fell fast and furious from the pink-tinged navy sky, coating her hair and her face. She put out her arms and slowly began to spin like she used to when she was a little girl up on the ridge. And suddenly, for no reason she could think of, tears mingled with the snowflakes on her face.

They weren't sad tears, they weren't happy tears, they weren't tears for long-lost memories of her years in Highland Falls. They were healing tears, cleansing and rejuvenating. As if Mother Nature was telling her it was time to let go of the burdens and the shame, the hurt and the pain that she'd been carrying with her for so long. It was time for her to reclaim the girl she might've become had she, her mother, and her father lived up on the mountain together instead of death and the law separating them.

"You look like an angel out here dancing in the snow," Gabe said from behind her.

She wiped the tears from her cheeks and turned to face him with a sheepish grin. "You caught me. I should've known you'd be up."

Snow coated his hair and his leather jacket. He had two steaming mugs in his hands and offered her one. "Nothing like the first snowfall," he said. "I was standing at the back window having my coffee when you appeared." He cocked his head, searching her face. "You okay?"

"I'm good." She moved to stand at his side and look into the woods. "It's beautiful, isn't it? Almost magical with the way the snow's coating the branches and everything's so quiet and peaceful."

"Makes it worth getting up early." He took a sip of his coffee then glanced at her. "You're up early every morning though. You don't like sleeping in even on the weekend?"

"I wish I could sleep in. I have insomnia. Every night I wake up at three in the morning, and that's it. I can't go back to sleep no matter what I do. And I've tried everything. Everything except medication."

He frowned. "That can't be healthy."

"It's not, which is probably why I'll try medication if something doesn't give soon."

"How long has this been going on?"

"Almost two years. Harry basically needed around-the-clock care that last year, and he didn't want anyone else looking after him but me." She shrugged. "I guess my body got used to the schedule and decided it liked it even if I don't."

"I'm sure the stress you've been dealing with over the past year hasn't helped. Maybe once you and the boys settle in here you'll start sleeping through the night."

"That was my hope, but I can't seem to escape the stress even here."

He put his arm around her shoulders and tucked her against him. "Give it a chance, and for now, just enjoy the peace and quiet."

She smiled up at him. He was solid and strong and smelled as wonderful as the nearby woods, and she relaxed against him. "This is nice. Thank you for the coffee and for letting me lean on you."

"Anytime, and I mean that, Doc." He gave her shoulder a gentle squeeze.

"I know you do, and I appreciate it. The same goes for you, though, Gabe. If you need someone to look after the boys today, I'm happy to. Unless, um, you don't think that's a good idea after last night."

"Yeah, about that. I'm sorry for how the twins reacted. I don't know what got into them."

They'd yelled at Mallory to get off their dad, and Teddy had burst into tears while Oliver and Brooks looked disgusted. "I don't think any of them believed I was checking your wound."

"They might have if you didn't look like you'd just been—" He cleared his throat.

She winced at the memory of her flushed face, puffy lips abraded by denim, and hair that looked like she'd been having a very good time in bed. "Poor Teddy. He was so excited to show his brothers that he'd converted you from a holiday hater into a holiday lover, and instead he gets us, looking like we were making out in your car."

"Yeah, about, uh—"

"It's okay. We don't have to talk about it. We're both adults."

"And one of us adults had a good laugh at the other's expense."

"Trust me, you have absolutely nothing to be embarrassed about." *So nothing to be embarrassed about,* she thought with a long, inward sigh. "It was a nervous laugh, not an amused one." She glanced up at him. His silver-gray eyes were almost black, and she had a fairly good idea the emotion darkening his eyes had nothing to do with embarrassment or nerves; it was heat. Want and need. And she knew this because she felt the same. "Maybe we should just enjoy the peace and quiet together."

At the sound of the door opening, they both turned to look at Gabe's back deck.

"Should've known it wouldn't last for long." Gabe smiled when Teddy let out a shriek of delight, and then he stepped back from her, letting his arm drop to his side.

Funny, she hadn't realized until just then that she was cold.

* * *

Six hours after she'd offered to take Gabe's boys for the day, Mallory wanted to take the offer back, but it was too late. "Where are Dylan and Cody?" she asked Teddy, who was kneeling at the coffee table carefully threading the popcorn and cranberries onto the thin strand of red wool with a dull needle.

"They went to cut you down a birch tree for the candleholders." He smiled up at her. "You know, for the candles in the picture you showed us."

Her first thought was gratitude at the sign that they must've forgiven her for what they'd assumed was her making out with their father. Followed immediately after by the thought that Teddy must've misunderstood them. Surely they couldn't be cutting down a tree. They were probably looking for birch bark on the ground or pulling it off the trees. So much for what she'd thought was her brilliant idea to keep them occupied until six this evening: decorate the house for tomorrow's appearance on Abby's YouTube channel.

"Yes, but I told you guys I was going to buy the birch-tree candleholders." She hurried to the window to look outside.

"But Oliver and Brooks said you're broke." A frown creased his forehead, making him look like a miniature version of his father. "Maybe you should write a letter to Santa and tell him you need money."

"It's okay, sweetie. I have money. I just don't like to waste it." Which is why she'd decided to go with a rustic decorating theme. "I can't see your brothers anywhere. We better get dressed and go find them. Oliver and Brooks!" she shouted. They'd helped her place the plaid pillows on the couch and chairs, draped a couple of blankets over the backs of them, and considered their job done.

"They can't hear you. They have their headphones on," Teddy said as he got up from the floor. "I'll go get them."

Her cell phone rang as she was sliding her feet into her boots. Seeing the name, she answered, "Abs, I can't talk right now. I've lost Cody and Dylan."

"How did you lose two ten-year-olds?"

"Trust me, easily. I saw a couple of old lanterns in the basement the other day and thought I'd spray-paint them and put them on the mantel. I swear I was down there five minutes and then they were gone."

"I'd come but I'm taking pictures of the Christmas Market to upload on social media. Do you want me to send Hunter?"

Her heart dropped to her feet. "Do you think I need him?" she asked just as Oliver, Brooks, and Teddy appeared. "I'm good. I've got the other three boys. We'll go look."

"If you don't find them in the next five minutes, call. You back onto the forest and Hunter's seen signs the bears haven't gone into hibernation yet."

Fighting back a panic attack, Mallory opened the door and was greeted with one of the twins yelling, "Timber!"

"I hear them," she said, running out the door to follow the sounds of a tree crashing to the ground in the forest.

"Bloody brilliant—they cut down a tree," Oliver said, pulling on his winter jacket as he ran behind her.

"There's nothing brilliant about it, and don't you make them feel that there is. They look up to you and your brother." She glanced over her shoulder to see Brooks running with Teddy's hand in his and breathed a sigh of relief. If not for her stepson, she might've forgotten him. Oh my gosh, what was she doing? She'd almost forgotten Abby's warning. "Guys, you stay out of the woods. Hunter said there've been bear sightings."

"Cool," Oliver said.

"Trust me, it's far from cool. It's terrifying."

"Have you seen one up close before?"

She nodded. "I lived the first twelve years of my life in a cabin in the mountains. We saw plenty of wildlife."

"Did you see Bigfoot? Cody and Dylan did," Teddy said.

She left the boys arguing about Bigfoot's existence while she went in search of the twins. "Dylan! Cody! Where are you?" she called out, making plenty of noise. Most bears didn't want to run into you as much as you didn't want to run into them.

The twins didn't respond but she heard them squabbling about the best way to move the tree. At one of them suggesting they'd cut off the rest of the branches, she ran in the direction of their voices. She arrived in time to see Dylan raise an ax.

"Stop!" she yelled, holding up her hands as she ran toward him.

Frowning, Dylan lowered the ax. "What's wrong?"

"You're ten, and you have an ax in your hands." She looked at the tree on the ground. "And you chopped down a tree." While she was supposed to be looking after them. Gabe was going to kill her. He'd never trust her to look after his children again. Okay, that might be a positive.

"I chopped down the tree," Cody said proudly. Despite them being identical twins, Mallory could tell them apart. Cody's hair was more copper and Dylan's more auburn, and Dylan had his father's cleft in his chin. "You wanna help us carry it out? Then we can cut it in pieces for your candleholders. We got a big tree so we can have some too. They'll look cool in our bedrooms."

No doubt they'd burn the house down was her immediate thought, quickly followed by affection for them. They might be mischievous, but they were also sweet and thoughtful, which was why, instead of lecturing them, she called for Oliver and Brooks to help them carry out the tree. After she took the ax, of course.

The weight of it felt familiar in her hand. Her father had taught her to chop wood at the same age as the boys. He'd taught her to do a lot of things that most parents wouldn't teach their children. But it was because she often found herself alone with her mother up in the mountains with no neighbor close by, and her mother was confined to a wheelchair. She had been for as long as Mallory could remember. Her mother had been diagnosed with MS just before Mallory had been born.

Once the tree was lying at the edge of the backyard, Mallory had the boys step back and went about chopping the tree into varying lengths for their rustic candleholders. When she'd finished, she looked up to see the five of them staring at her open-mouthed. Their awe didn't last long. Not two minutes later, they were engaged in a snowball fight.

"No snowballs above the shoulders!" she called out, trying to protect their eyes. Only to get a snowball to the back of her head seconds later. She turned to see Dylan smirking and was tempted to retaliate but Oliver took care of it for her. Cody, who was as protective of Dylan as Oliver was of Brooks, charged Oliver.

"Okay, that's enough. No more snowball—Brooks, do not scrub Cody's face with snow. Or put it down his back! Teddy, come over here. They're being...No, Teddy, don't kick snow at Dylan. Dylan, do not—Boys, stop that right now!"

They completely ignored her as the snowball fight turned into a free-for-all. She'd run back to the house to lean the ax against the garbage bin and was turning to race back to break up the fight when a loud whistle rent the air.

"Oh, thank goodness," she said at the sight of Gabe, looking all big, hot, and authoritative in his uniform.

He grinned. "Having second thoughts about volunteering to babysit, Doc?"

Chapter Twenty

Y ou've got some mustard"—Gabe wiped the corner of Mallory's mouth with his thumb—"right there."

"Thanks." She took another bite of her sausage on a bun as she looked around the red barn. They'd set up the vendors selling food and homemade goods inside. "For not having a lot of time, the place looks great," she said after she'd swallowed, looking up at the white lights draped from the beams.

"So, am I forgiven for suggesting you come here with the boys?" With Boyd putting in his time at Blue Ridge Tree Farm, Gabe knew it was the last place she wanted to be but, considering what he'd come home to at lunch, he'd figured a change of scenery would be good for all of them, especially because he'd assigned himself to work the event. Due to Abby's ability to get the crowds out through her social media accounts, the Christmas Market ran the risk of being a victim of its own success. Parking had already become an issue. Owen was ferrying people from the main road with his tractor and wagon.

"You were right. It was a good idea." She looked around and frowned. "Where are the boys?"

"Oliver and Brooks asked if they could go watch Hunter carving a wooden reindeer, and I didn't think you'd mind." She'd been in line getting them something to eat and had gotten sidetracked by a group of seniors. Her week as director of the senior center had obviously been a success given her popularity at today's event.

"Dylan and Cody are with Owen." The former chief of police might be a pain in his ass, but he was great with the twins and didn't seem to mind them hanging out with him. Gabe also wasn't worried about Owen convincing Dylan and Cody to play Santa's little helpers. The boys had a love-hate relationship with Mallory. As long as they didn't think he was interested in her romantically, they thought she was great. But the smallest hint that they might be more than friendly neighbors, and she was on their hit list.

"Teddy thinks he's Abby's producer," Gabe said, then sighed. "Here they come."

"It might be better if he were behind the scenes instead of in front of the camera. Are you sure you don't mind Abby filming him?"

"As long as it doesn't become a regular thing, and I don't get dragged into the action. Abby covers his face with an elf emoji." He stepped out of Abby's line of sight but Teddy grabbed his hand and pulled Gabe beside him, and then he grabbed Mallory by the hand. He stood between them swinging their hands and smiling.

"What's up, buddy?" Gabe asked.

"We're doing a promo video for tomorrow." Teddy

moved his head in time with Abby counting down from three with her fingers.

"Well, if it isn't our favorite chief of police and director of senior services and my official little helper, Teddy. So how's it going, guys? Are you ready for our visit tomorrow?"

"Yep, this morning we helped Mallory decorate for Christmas," said Teddy. "It looks really good. I made popcorn and cranberries on a string. I'll show you how to do it tomorrow. The twins wanted to make candles. Mallory thought she lost them but they were in the woods chopping down a tree with an—"

Gabe was relieved when Abby cut him off.

"Oh wow, okay," she said. "What other exciting stuff has been happening on Reindeer Road?"

"My dad got shot. But he's okay. Mallory fixed him up. She's a doctor. They were playing doctor in my dad's—"

Both he and Mallory put their hands over Teddy's mouth. Gabe wondered if his cheeks were as red as Mallory's. He felt pretty flushed.

Teddy pulled their hands from his mouth. "I can't breathe."

"Abby, erase that," Mallory said.

"Sorry, we're live. And it sounds like our favorite couple...I mean neighbors"—Abby turned the camera to herself and winked—"are having some exciting times on Reindeer Road. Tomorrow you guys can vote as to whether those exciting times are Christmassy or romantic."

"Christmassy," Teddy said, and Gabe nodded. "Definitely Christmassy."

"Totally Christmassy," Mallory said, looking at Gabe like she wanted to hide behind the bales of hay in the corner.

"I don't know. There's an old saying you guys might know: I think they doth protest too much. What do you think? Do you agree? Let me know as we take another walk around our fabulous Christmas Market. And if you're in the area, you should totally drop by. You never know who you'll meet. Look over at the Highland Brew booth. Is it just me or does that look like Jamie Fraser?" She started to walk toward the booth, then looked back. "Teddy, are you coming?"

"No, we're going to roast s'mores over the fire," Gabe said. He had to come up with something good or Teddy would put up a fuss. And there was no way he was letting Abby within ten feet of his youngest again. "Come on, let's see if the twins are back. Maybe Oliver and Brooks will want to have s'mores with us."

"Aw, do you hear that, guys? The Maitlands and Buchanans are having a nice family outing today. By the way, Chief, my followers shared a clip from our interview, and you're trending as hashtag HighlandFallsHotCop on social media."

"That's great. Thanks a lot," he muttered, but Abby must've missed the sarcasm because she shared his thanks with her followers.

"Aren't you glad you suggested we come?" Mallory said as they walked outside with Teddy between them. Unlike Abby, he picked up on the sarcasm in Mallory's voice.

As they approached Hunter, who'd drawn a crowd

with his wood carving, Gabe said, "Any chance you can hide your wife's phone?"

Hunter smiled. "You're not the first one who's asked me that today." He glanced at Mallory. "So did your dad."

Teddy's eyes went wide. "You have a dad?"

She nodded. "Yes, I do."

"Her dad's right over there." Hunter lifted his chin at a booth across the way. "He makes glass ornaments. You should check them out. They're pretty cool. Oliver and Brooks just headed over there."

"Come on, Mallory. Let's go."

"Okay," she said, reluctantly letting Teddy lead her away. He had a feeling if Oliver and Brooks weren't already deep in conversation with her father, she would've done whatever she had to to distract Teddy. Even if it meant tracking down Abby.

Gabe hung back as Hunter talked to some potential customers and someone he'd served with in Afghanistan. Hunter glanced at him when the others had moved away. "You planning on giving me hell?"

"No, just wondering what that was all about. You gotta know it's not easy for her being around her old man."

"Yeah, and you know as well as I do that the two of them have to talk or you wouldn't have ordered Boyd and Owen to do community service at the senior center. Mallory outmaneuvered you on that one, didn't she?" He laughed, brushing wood shavings off the carving before looking up at Gabe. "Boyd's hurting, and so is she. He's a good man, Gabe. He hasn't touched a drop of moonshine since Mallory came to town last summer. Hasn't made any either. Got back to him that he was being used to embarrass her."

"You know, that's the most I think I've ever heard you say at one time," Gabe said.

"Yeah, well, you can blame Abby."

"Blame me for what?" She appeared at Gabe's side. "Hey, where's Wolf and Bella?"

"Mallory's stepsons have them," Hunter said.

"Cute. Where are they?" She looked around, and her mouth dropped. "Mal's talking to her dad. Oh my gosh."

Her phone went up, and Gabe covered her hand with his and pulled it down. "No. If you want to go over and be supportive, fine. But your phone stays in your pocket."

She smiled and cocked her head. "I was right, wasn't I? You are totally falling for my best friend." She patted his arm. "Don't worry, she's head over heels for you, even if she doesn't know it yet."

She headed for the booth but turned back. "I put the family of three deer on hold for you. They'll look perfect in Mallory's front yard." At what must've been his blank look, she shook her head. "For her appearance on my channel tomorrow. I know the case social services had against her is technically closed, but I don't trust Kayla McPherson as far as I could throw her. I mean, you saw how she was at Monday's meeting. Anyway, it's a good cause so buy my best friend the deer. She'll love them, and if you could put up some Christmas lights, that would be awesome."

Gabe stared after her, then gave his head a slight shake. "How much for the deer?"

"No charge. Just don't tell anyone else. I've got thirty orders for these things already." He watched Abby with a smile on his face. Then he said to Gabe, "You know, she's doing this to boost Mallory's popularity, but from where I'm sitting, the person whose reputation could use a boost is yours. What did you do to Dot and her friends?"

"It's got nothing to do with me. It's your buddy Owen who's the problem. He's at the station so often they think I pushed him out."

"Yeah, he hasn't really taken to retirement. But this should keep him busy until the—" Hunter got up from the stool he'd been sitting on. "Okay, so Mallory's reputation might need some rehabilitation after all."

Gabe was just about to ask him what he was talking about when he heard a woman yelling and turned to see Mallory standing between Oliver and another kid. The woman who was yelling was none other than Dot McFee. Gabe didn't recognize the broad-shouldered teenager with the buzz cut, but from Dot's reaction, it had to be her grandson Dirk. There were a couple guys behind him wearing football jerseys that seemed to validate Gabe's hunch.

"You need a hand?" Hunter asked.

"Appreciate the offer, but I think I can handle it. If I can't, I should hand in my badge. I'll be back for the deer, and I'll make a donation to the Liz Findlay Foundation," he said, then jogged over to where the standoff continued.

"Your grandson pushed my son, Dot. I got in the middle of them to de-escalate the situation. I put up my hands, and Dirk walked into them. I didn't touch him or shove him on purpose."

"We'll see about that. Here comes the chief now."

Oh great. Dot was probably going to try to get him to arrest Mallory again. Except she was looking past him. He glanced over his shoulder to see she'd been talking about the former chief of police.

"What's going on here?" Owen said, moseying on over with the twins in tow.

Gabe decided to keep his mouth shut and see where this went. He had a feeling it might actually go his way for a change. Owen had appointed himself and Boyd as Mallory's secret Santas, so it's not like he'd take Dot's side against hers. Gabe tried to share that with Mallory in a silent eye exchange, but she was staring at Dot.

"You can't seriously be standing within a couple feet of Gabe—you know, the actual police chief—and think you can have Owen intervene," Mallory said.

Gabe's hopes of the situation de-escalating just went out the window. He didn't realize exactly how far out the window they'd gone until Mallory added, "The man who you've spent the last several months deriding and campaigning to get rid of—he's not just some small-town cop with no experience, you know. He was a big-city homicide detective, and he gave up the job that he loved and a job that he was incredibly good at for his sons. Maybe you should think about his boys when you—"

"Doc, it's okay. I appreciate what—"

"I am not finished. She has no idea that she's putting your boys at risk. None at all. Except from what I've seen, she probably wouldn't care. All she cares about is putting

Owen back in office. Well, have I got news for you. Your precious Owen, who you think can do no wrong, he—"

Gabe moved in and took Mallory by the arm in hopes of leading her away before she made everything a whole lot worse. "Doc, you don't want to go—"

She shook off his hand without looking at him. "Owen shot Gabe. That's right, he shot the chief of police, and Gabe's been protecting him all along."

Owen took off his cowboy hat and rubbed his head. "Now wait a minute. You're making it sound like I shot him on purpose."

"You shot my dad?" Dylan and Cody said at almost the same time, their eyes narrowed and their hands balled at their sides.

Worried what they might do, Gabe said, "Boys, come—" he began, and then felt a small hand slip into his. "Why did he shoot you? I thought he was one of the good guys," Teddy said, his bottom lip trembling.

Mallory gasped and met his gaze. Putting a hand over her mouth, she closed her eyes and shook her head as though just realizing what she'd done in the heat of the moment.

Boyd came out from his booth. "It wasn't Owen who shot your dad, boys. It was me. And I'm very sorry. I never meant to hurt him. Me and Owen were fighting, and the gun went off. You know I never intended to hurt you, Chief Buchanan, but my daughter is right." He put his hands together and raised them to chest level. "You should arrest me."

"Probably drunk on his moonshine," Dot scoffed, crossing her arms.

"Put your damn hands down, Boyd. I was as much responsible for shooting Gabe as you. We were behaving like a pair of old fools, fighting with a loaded shotgun between us. We're just lucky no one got killed." Owen turned to Dot. "You keep your yap closed. No call for casting aspersions against Boyd. He's been off the juice for months now."

Owen glanced at Gabe, rubbing the side of his face as he looked around at the crowd of people. "And stop petitioning the mayor to get rid of him, Dot. I don't want the job, and he'd be damn fine at it if you'd give him half a chance." He waved his cowboy hat at the crowd, shooing them away. "What are you all doing standing around? Show's over. Go enjoy yourself. That goes for you, too, boys. And I don't wanna hear that you and your friends have been giving Oliver here a hard time, Dirk. The Maitland boys are new to town. Highland Falls prides itself on making strangers feel like they've come home. Isn't that right, Dot?"

She sniffed and lifted her chin. "Sounds to me like you've been drinking Boyd's shine, chi—Owen Campbell. Come on, boys. There's a tree farm in the next county." She raised her voice. "Trees are much nicer at Evergreen Tree Farm." She flounced off with her grandson and his friends following behind.

Owen watched her walk away, turning the brim of his hat between his fingers. "Sorry, Gabe. I didn't realize how bad it had gotten with Dot. I'll go by tomorrow, smooth things over with her. She won't give you any more trouble. You have my word."

"Thank you. I appreciate that, Owen." Gabe glanced at Mallory as she came to stand beside him.

"I…" She bit her bottom lip, her eyes shimmering with unshed tears. "I'm sorry. I'm so sorry. I don't know what got into me. I was just so mad that boy was bullying Oliver, and I hadn't known about it, and then when Dot started bullying you, Gabe, something inside me just snapped. I was worried you were going to lose your job, and your mother-in-law would have an excuse to take the boys. I—" She looked around and bowed her head at the shocked expressions on their audience's faces. "What's wrong with me?"

"You're exhausted, for one." He rubbed her shoulder. "It's okay, Doc. Can't say I'm a fan of airing my dirty laundry in front of a crowd. But in the end, you probably did me a favor."

Her father approached with a box in his hand and crouched in front of Teddy and the twins, who'd moved to stand beside Gabe. "Dylan, Cody, and Teddy, I'm really sorry that I hurt your daddy." He opened the box. It was a beautiful handblown Christmas ornament. "I don't have much, but I thought you might like this for your tree. If you can think of something I can do to make this right between us, I'd appreciate you telling me."

Owen came to stand beside Boyd, reaching down to give his once-best-friend's shoulder a squeeze. "Same goes for me. Boyd's taking all the blame, but I'm as much at fault as him. So, if there's anything we can do for you kids to make it better, you let us know—you hear?"

"We'll think about it," Cody and Dylan said at almost the same time, then looked up at Gabe.

He nudged his head at the two older men and the twins offered their hands. Boyd and Owen looked relieved at their offer of forgiveness. Teddy surprised him by staying silent. His little peacemaker didn't seem quite ready to forgive and forget as he cradled the gift box to his chest.

All of them watched as Teddy's gaze moved from Boyd to Owen. "Okay, we'll forgive you for hurting my dad. But you have to promise not to hurt him again and not to let anyone else hurt him."

The two older men nodded solemnly. "You got a deal, son," Boyd said.

"I'm not done," Teddy said, and Boyd and Owen shared a look. "You gotta put up Christmas lights at Mallory's house and you have to make it look really special because she's going to be on Abby's YouTube channel, and we want everyone to like her and to see how good a mom she is."

"We can do that," Owen said slowly, glancing at Mallory as though doubtful she'd let them on her property.

Teddy nodded and then turned his attention to Boyd. "And you need to promise to be a good dad to Mallory and a good Pop Pop to Oliver and Brooks, cuz they don't have any family, and they need one."

"I haven't been a good daddy to Mallory, son. But if she'd let me, I'd like to try and change that. And I'll do my best to be a good Pop Pop to Oliver and Brooks. Because you're right, Teddy: everyone needs a family." He turned to Owen and held out his hand. "And everyone needs a friend who has their back, even if they didn't see it at the time."

Chapter Twenty-One

Mallory sat cross-legged on the middle of her bed, tapping under her eyes with her fingers. After her embarrassing outburst at the tree farm today, she was desperate to find a solution for her insomnia. She'd been on the Internet for over an hour when she came across a forum for insomniacs. Several women swore that they'd tapped their insomnia away, and several others said CBT—cognitive behavioral therapy—had worked for them.

At this point, Mallory was up for anything. But there were no CBT practitioners in the area, and the more she looked into EFT, emotional freedom techniques, or tapping, as it was more commonly known, she understood from a scientific standpoint how it might work. The technique was based on several different alternative therapies—acupuncture, neurolinguistic programming, and energy medicine.

She'd downloaded the app on her phone and was now trying to tap her cortisol levels to a manageable quantity. While tapping on the acupuncture points, she gave voice to her fears and emotional triggers as the woman on the app had instructed.

Words like *guilt, shame, unwanted,* and *unloved* kept coming out of her mouth. She thought the guilt and shame came from not being able to save Harry, although the shame probably went hand in hand with the feelings of being unloved and unwanted.

Except right now, as she tapped those feelings out, she saw her father's face when he apologized to Gabe's boys, when he promised to be a better father to her and a Pop Pop to Oliver and Brooks. Time had stood still for a moment, and the little girl she'd remembered that morning as she twirled in the freshly falling snow had turned to look at her. *Listen,* she'd said. *Do you hear him?* she'd asked. *You were wrong; he loved you.*

"Mallory, hurry! It's Teddy." Brooks pounded on her bedroom door.

She scrubbed her damp cheeks, grabbed her phone, and jumped off the bed. She opened the door to Brooks, Dylan, and Cody standing in the hall, clearly panicked. "What's wrong?"

"Dad said to come get you. Teddy can't breathe. Hurry." Cody grabbed her hand. "We have to hurry."

"Okay, calm down," she said, even though her heart had begun to race. Bringing her phone to her ear, she ran back into her bedroom to grab her bag. "Gabe."

"Doc, you gotta get over here. He's bad."

"I'm coming. I just need to grab a few things. Have you used his rescue inhaler?"

"Yes, but it expired last week." He swore. "How could I not—"

"It's okay. They may lose some of their strength over time but they can be used for up to a year after they've expired. Do you use a spacer with his inhaler? It makes a difference."

"I don't know where it is."

"I've got one. Get Teddy in—" She broke off, hearing Oliver tell Gabe that he'd started the shower. He must've run over there as soon as Cody and Dylan came to the door. "That's good, the steam should help. I'm coming now," she said, sliding on her boots. "Do you have a humidifier?"

"I think so. It's okay, honey. Yes, Mallory's coming. She's coming right now."

"Brooks, sweetie, go get the humidifier from under the bathroom sink and bring it over, okay?" she said, her voice tight from holding back a swell of emotion that came from Teddy asking for her.

Brooks nodded. "Is he going to be okay, Mal?"

"He's going to be just fine." She prayed it wasn't a lie as she ran out the door and raced across the snow-covered driveway to Gabe's. The fact that Teddy could speak, even though he was struggling to breathe, brought some relief. She couldn't bring herself to ask Gabe if Teddy's lips or fingernails were pale or, God forbid, had turned blue. A cursory examination would give her the answer. If she didn't like what she saw, she'd call 911 immediately.

Dylan held open the door for her as he fought back tears. Cody had already raced inside. She gave Dylan a quick hug. "He's going to be okay, sweetie," she said, then ran down the hall to the steam-filled bathroom right behind Cody.

She patted Oliver's back, proud of him for racing to Teddy and Gabe's aid. Her eyes went to Gabe, who sat on the floor with Teddy. The little boy was wearing a pair of red fleece pajamas and was sitting between Gabe's legs with his head resting on Gabe's chest.

She knelt down in front of them and smiled as she took out her stethoscope, putting it around her neck. "Did you know your daddy thinks this is my magic carpet bag? Just like the one that Mary Poppins has?"

"No," Teddy said.

Even from where she knelt, she could hear the crackle and wheeze in his chest. "Well, he does. And you know what?" she said, taking Teddy's wrist between her fingers to check his pulse, pleased to see that his nail beds were a healthy pink. "He's right. I have a special machine that's going to help you breathe right away. But first, let's loosen your pajama top. Maybe just take it off, Gabe." She'd been avoiding looking at him directly, knowing what she'd see. A father desperately worried about his baby boy. A man who'd already lost the mother of that child.

"I've got this," she told him, putting as much confidence as she possessed into the words. And she was confident in her abilities. She'd loved medicine. She'd never wanted to be anything other than a doctor. She'd wanted to do exactly what she was doing right now—relieve a father's fear and help a little boy to feel better.

"Okay, sweetie. I'm just going to warm this up and then I'm going to listen to your chest." She held the drum in her hands for a few seconds and then gently placed it on his narrow chest, smiling as she moved it around. Both father's and son's eyes were glued to her face, watching for a reaction.

"Can you breathe in and out for me, Teddy? Take as deep a breath as you can. Excellent. You're doing really, really well. Almost done. I just want to listen to your back now." She moved the drum to his back and listened to his lungs. "The good news is, no pneumonia. I think that deserves a high five, don't you?" She held up her hand and got a small smile and a high five in return.

And with that, just as she'd intended, Gabe and the boys relaxed, which in turn would help Teddy relax. He'd been feeding off his father's and brothers' panic, and that just made his symptoms worse. "Are you ready? Here comes the magic now," she said, pulling the nebulizer from her bag. "This is going to make you feel so much better."

"It really is a magic carpet bag, isn't it?" Gabe said with a half smile.

"It is," she said as she came to her feet. She put the bag over her shoulder.

"You're not leaving," Gabe said at the same time Teddy said, "Don't leave." Both of them looking equally panicked.

"I'm not going anywhere. But how about we move this party out of the bathroom? We'll get you all tucked into bed with the super-duper magical breathing machine." She was about to help Teddy off Gabe's lap but thought of something. "Teddy, were you playing in the hay at the barn?"

He nodded. "Is that okay?"

"Yes, but I think you might've been coming down

with a cold, and there's lots of dust and stuff in the hay that could've triggered your asthma attack." She rubbed his head, then looked at Gabe. "Did he have a bath when you came back from the tree farm?"

Gabe shoved his fingers through his hair and blew out a breath as he shook his head. "No, he didn't feel like it, and I didn't want to push."

"Okay, here's the deal. Your dad's going to give you a shower and wash your hair, and I'm going to make your room all nice and cozy. I'll even make you a special hot drink with honey. Sound good?"

Teddy looked from his dad to her. "Are you going to stay for a little while?"

She took in the four older boys' worried faces. "How about we have a sleepover?"

"Yes!" came the immediate response from all five boys, as well as a muttered, "Thank God," from Gabe.

She had the twins show her Teddy's room and spotted several issues right away. For starters, the drapes had to come down and the carpet had to come out and the stuffed animals had to go.

"You know what? I think I'll put Teddy in with your dad tonight." If she'd remembered correctly, the master bedroom had a hardwood floor and blinds.

Brooks handed her the humidifier. "Thanks, sweetie. Why don't you guys go home and get your pajamas and video games. Maybe grab the sleeping bags too. The four of you can crash in the living room. Sound good?"

"Sounds great," they said and took off.

"Don't forget to lock up," she called after them, then smiled at Cody and Dylan, who were standing in front of her, shifting from one foot to the other. "Teddy is going to be just fine. We're going to set up a protocol for your dad to follow if this should ever happen again, but we're also going to figure out what's triggering Teddy's asthma. Okay?"

"Yeah." Cody glanced at Dylan and then moved close to Mallory, putting his arms around her waist. Dylan did the same. "Thanks, Mallory. Thanks for saving our little brother."

Blinking back tears, she put down the humidifier and then hugged them tight. "You're welcome. But Teddy was never in any danger. It just looks scary when someone is having an asthma attack, especially when that someone is your baby brother. And it makes it even scarier when you feel helpless and don't know what to do."

"Yeah, it does," Dylan agreed, still hanging on.

"Okay, well, how about instead of putting together an action plan with your dad, I do it with all of you, so you guys can be part of it too?"

"Sounds like an excellent plan to me," Gabe said, walking toward them with Teddy wrapped in a towel in his arms. "I think we could all use a Buchanan family hug." He put out his arm, and the boys let her go to wrap theirs around their father.

She smiled and went to walk away to give them time alone, but Gabe pulled her in, lowering his head to nuzzle her ear. "I don't know what we would've done without you, Doc."

* * *

Mallory didn't need a clock to tell her it was three in the morning. She opened her eyes, smiling at the little boy who lay beside her. She reached out and gently brushed his hair back from his forehead, relieved that he was cool and his breathing was even. She felt the weight of someone's gaze and looked over to see Gabe watching her with a tender smile on his face.

At Teddy's request, they'd lain down on either side of him in the king-sized bed and had promptly fallen asleep in their clothes. Although she'd had Gabe shower and change before he lay down in case he had any residue from the barn.

"So, looks like your tapping experiment was a bust," he said.

"It probably deserves a second chance. I was only five minutes in when the boys arrived at my bedroom door."

"Maybe I can help you out. Come here." He patted the mattress beside him.

"What about Teddy?"

"Scooch him over a bit, and we'll put a couple of pillows on the other side of him."

She did as Gabe suggested and then crawled in beside him. Lying flat on her back, she looked up at him. He had his chin propped in his palm, and he was looking down at her.

The moonlight shining through the open slats of the wooden blind illuminated his face and those steady gray eyes. She thought better of asking *Now what?* because she had a feeling she knew what he wanted, and she wanted it too. But not here, not now. Maybe at another time, years from now, when the boys were grown up and he no longer had to worry about his mother-in-law's threat, they could explore whatever this was between them.

Their eyes locked, and they stared at each other like they had the first day they'd met. He removed his hand from his chin, and she wondered if he would kiss her. Her heart began to race in anticipation.

He lowered his mouth to the side of her face, his spearmint-scented breath warming her ear. "Turn on your side," he said, his voice low and gruff.

She turned to face him, and he smiled. "There's only so much temptation I can withstand, Doc. Other side."

She rolled onto her other side, wincing as her behind brushed against something very large, and very hard. "Sorry," she whispered.

"No sorrier than I am," he said as he gathered her hair to move it off her face and her shoulder. Then he lightly trailed his fingers up and down her arm before moving them to her neck. Gently, his strong fingers stroked and kneaded, melting away her tension.

At one point she moaned, and he leaned in to nip at her earlobe. "Shh."

"I might have a magic carpet bag, but you have magic hands," she said, and he smiled against her ear.

"Go to sleep," he said, and he began to hum. The rumble of his deep voice in his chest against her back was as soothing as his touch.

"What are you humming?" she whispered.

"'Danny Boy.' My wife used to sing it to the boys when she'd put them to sleep. It got to be that, as soon as she'd begin to sing, their eyes would close."

Her eyes did the same, drifting closed as she melted into him and the mattress.

When next she awoke, the room was filled with sunlight, and Teddy was gone. Sometime in the night, she'd turned to face Gabe and was now snuggled up against him.

"Morning," said a gravelly voice, and she lifted her gaze to Gabe's face. He inched up, looked around, and then lay back down beside her, giving her hip a squeeze. "Looks like we're alone."

"Yes, it does, and it sounds like the boys are busy in the kitchen."

He moved his hand from her hip to wrap his arm around her, drawing her even closer. "I like waking up with you in my bed, Doc."

She smiled. "I can tell."

He laughed, then sobered. "There's only one problem."

"What's that?" She ran her fingers through his hair, smoothing it from his face like he'd done to her in the middle of the night.

"We have too many clothes on."

She moved her hand from his hair to his chest, playing with the button of his shirt. "You and I both know we have more problems than that."

"How about, for one minute, we pretend that's the only problem we have?" He slowly began to lower his head. "Make that five minutes," he said as his lips touched hers.

"Ten, let's make it ten," she said, as he moved his mouth to the underside of her jaw, trailing hot kisses down her neck and back to her mouth.

She framed his face with her hands; his stubble-shadowed jaw made him look rough and disreputable, every inch a romance hero. Only he was real, and for ten minutes, or for all the time they had in this bed, he was hers. All the passion she'd kept bottled up inside of her came out in her kiss.

He pulled away to stare down at her. "Forever isn't long enough for me," he said, then proceeded to ravage her mouth with a kiss that had her panting for breath.

"Surprise!" The door opened, and there were the boys, all five of them with a breakfast tray between them. Their sweet smiles of surprise turned to shock. Except Teddy, who looked like he thought Santa had come early.

Chapter Twenty-Two

I've got it covered, Miss Mallory. Your two in-home visits canceled so you're free for the afternoon. Go pick up your boy's birthday cake. You ask me, you're a saint inviting your late husband's first wife to the party. Don't you think she's a saint, Chief?" Ruby Lee asked as she helped Mallory roll up the blue exercise mats.

The older woman cast him a knowing glance over her shoulder when he didn't respond right away. Gabe had walked in on Mallory leading a seniors yoga class in a pair of purple leggings and a tight, long-sleeved T-shirt. Right now, she was bent at the waist rolling up the mat, giving him a view of her backside.

A backside that he'd very much enjoyed having pressed snug against him five mornings ago. He'd also had his hand on that backside later that same morning, ensuring that every fantasy he'd had of Mallory Maitland felt like it might come true for a brief moment in time. Until five boys had stood on the threshold of his bedroom and destroyed his hopes and dreams. She was back on the twins' hit list.

"I used to think she was a saint until I found out she was stealing you out from under my nose, Ruby."

"It wasn't me," Mallory protested, straightening to turn with the mat in her hands. He wasn't disappointed. The view from the front was equally delectable, and tempting. She grinned. "Although, if I'm being completely honest, I would've tried to steal her from you if I had to."

"Oh, don't you go blaming Miss Mallory, Chief. I needed a change of scenery. My job at the station was bad for my waistline, and my heart. Like the rest of the seniors in town, I'm eating right, getting my exercise, and socializing, too, thanks to Miss Mallory. Tell you the truth, I'd work here for free."

"I don't think a lack of socializing has ever been your problem, Ruby. But I've got a big one now. Who am I supposed to get to take your place?"

"I sent you a long list of candidates, Chief. But if you want my advice, I'd go with Dot's daughter-in-law. She's a nice gal, and it would go a ways in mending fences with Dot. She's blaming you for her being on the outs with Owen."

He shoved his fingers through his hair. "I seriously cannot win with that woman."

"You can if you'd listen to me," Ruby said as she followed behind Mallory to put the mats away. "The chief's just like you, Miss Mallory. He needs a break. I remember what it's like raising young uns on your own. Didn't always have Charlie in my life, you know. It's not easy being a single parent. You two go have some fun. Get some of your Christmas shopping done."

He waited at the entrance while Mallory took care of a last-minute phone call, and he checked in at the station. He'd worked two double shifts earlier in the week so he decided he could afford to take an extra-long lunch.

Having Oliver and Brooks living next door had come in handy. Ainsley hadn't been able to babysit, and Mallory's boys had pitched in. Mallory had offered, but after catching them kissing in his bed Sunday morning, Dylan and Cody had vetoed that option.

They'd quickly forgotten about her saving their baby brother. It didn't help that said baby brother was busy planning Gabe and Mallory's wedding.

Gabe leaned against the wall, watching her hurry toward him. The twins might not be her number-one fans, but he was. He'd never forget how she'd made him feel that night. She'd taken away his worries and fears with her confidence, reassuring smile, and three little words: *I've got this.*

Over the past few years, he'd gotten used to doing things on his own. He hadn't realized how much he'd missed having a partner, someone to share the bad times, the scary times, and the good times with, until that night.

"Hey, what's going on? Why do you look so serious all of a sudden?" she asked.

He looked around, then reached for her, looping his arms around her waist. "I missed you this week. I hardly got to see you."

"I missed you too," she said, leaning into him, her

palm on his chest. "But we did do three in-home visits together."

"We did, but I didn't have you to myself. I had to share you with three old guys who made no bones about wanting me gone."

She laughed. "You usually have to share me with five not-so-old guys. Two, sometimes four, who want me gone."

He grimaced. "I'm sorry Dylan and Cody have been such jerks this week."

"It's okay. I know where it's coming from. Oliver and Brooks weren't much better, although it had nothing to do with you and me. They got over their disgust that we were making out pretty quick. I've been told I've made things worse between Oliver and Dirk with how I acted at the tree farm." She wrinkled her nose. "Sometimes I feel like I can't do anything right."

"Welcome to the club." He opened the door for her. "So what will it be: Christmas shopping or do you want to grab a coffee at the bakery?"

She inhaled deeply of the crisp mountain air and smiled, tilting her face up to the sun. She looked relaxed and happy. She was finally sleeping through the night. She credited tapping for breaking the cycle, while he credited his magic hands.

"The benefit of working right off Main Street is I've gotten a good start on my shopping. I just need to pick up Oliver's birthday cake. Then, if you're up for it, I'd love to go for a walk. It's a beautiful day."

He glanced around the parking lot before leaning in to kiss her. Anytime he was around her, he wanted his hands or his mouth on her. He didn't remember being this way with Lauren, but he was older now, he'd experienced unimaginable loss, and he knew how fleeting and precious these moments could be. "You're beautiful," he said against her lips.

"So are you." She smiled and playfully nipped his bottom lip as he went to pull away.

Something came over him in that moment, and he took her by the hand. Later, he'd wish he'd taken the time to think it through. But right then, all he wanted was to be as close as humanly possible to this woman. He needed her like he needed air. "I've got an even better way for us to spend the afternoon."

"Really? What?"

"A picnic."

She laughed. "Okay, it's a beautiful day, but it's also cold and there's still snow on the ground."

"Who said we're having our picnic outside?"

"Oh, I like it. We're going to have a picnic in your cute car." She grinned up at him and beeped the lock on her keys.

He laughed and opened the driver's-side door for her. "No, we're going to have a picnic in bed. The only thing you have to decide is which bed, yours or mine. I'll stop by Sweet Basil and grab our lunch and a bottle of wine while you're picking up Oliver's cake."

Her flushed cheeks and dilated pupils indicated she wanted him as much as he wanted her. And then he noticed her fingers go to her ear.

He smiled, taking her hand in his. "It doesn't have to be anything more than a picnic. We can have it in my cute car or we can have it at a picnic table down by the rapids or we can have it by the fire in my living room. I'm just happy to spend time with you, Doc. Anywhere. Anytime."

"I liked your first suggestion. And we've slept together in your bed, so why don't we try mine?"

"Yeah?"

"Yeah." She moved the zipper on his jacket up and down, staring at her hand as she did. "I just don't want you to get your expectations up. It's been a long time."

"Same. But that kiss we shared Sunday morning, it exceeded all of my expectations, Doc. So I'm not too worried about it. And I don't want you to worry either. Let's just have fun, enjoy our time together, alone and in a bed, without worrying that our kids are going to bust down the door."

* * *

Hours later, Mallory reached for the Sweet Basil takeaway bag on the nightstand in her bedroom. "I hope you didn't get anything that needs reheating because I don't think I can make it to the kitchen."

"Good thing I got us sandwiches and salads, then." He frowned. "Where did my phone go?"

"I don't know. You put it on the nightstand, didn't you?"

"Yeah, right beside…" He got out of bed and looked behind the nightstand, moving the drapes to see if it had fallen behind them. It had. He bent over and grabbed his phone, staring at what looked to be twenty messages on the screen.

Only moments ago, he'd been thinking this was it, one of the best afternoons of his life, a memory he'd cherish. Now, staring at his screen, his worst fear had come to life. He'd been thinking with his dick, and he'd put his boys at risk. He'd let his feelings for Mallory cloud his judgment. His desire for her made him selfish. He'd promised himself his kids would always come first, and because he'd broken that vow and put his own wants and needs before theirs, he was going to lose them.

"What is it?" She searched his face. "Gabe, you're scaring me."

"The school called. Three times. Volume's messed up on my phone. Dylan got in a fight and needed stitches. When they couldn't reach me, they called Karl and Diane. They're my emergency contacts."

"Oh, Gabe, no." She covered her mouth.

"It gets better," he said as he grabbed his pants off the floor. "They're at my place. Have been for ten minutes. They've figured out where I am."

"They don't have to know you're here. You can say you were having problems with your SUV, and that you're using another car from the station. You can sneak out, and I'll meet you down the road and drive you to work."

"According to Diane's latest text, they've called the station, and they've called the senior center. Ruby told them we'd left hours ago to get some Christmas shopping done."

"So we'll say that's where we were. That we just got

back, and you were helping me unload my parcels." She leaned over the bed to search for her clothes.

He didn't want to hurt her, but she had to know how messed up this was. How they never should've let what they felt for each other put everything else on the line. The kids were going to be hurt by this. Hers and his.

He sat on the edge of the bed, and unable to resist touching her one last time, he smoothed his hand down her hair and her back. Then he leaned in and kissed her shoulder. The kids weren't the only ones who were going to be hurt. "Doc, the reason Dylan got in a fight was because the kids were teasing him about us getting married."

She sat up, holding the comforter to her chest. "What? I don't understand."

"After the boys caught us kissing in bed Sunday morning, Teddy started planning our wedding. He asked me if I wanted to wear a black tux or a white one." He laughed, then shook his head. "I know. Leave it to Teddy. Anyway, I thought I'd nipped it in the bud. But apparently I didn't do a very good job."

He took her hand and looked her in the eyes, needing to do a better job of making her understand than he had Teddy. "Doc, this isn't going to work. As much as I wish it could, it isn't."

She gave him a tight smile and nodded. "I know. I just wish there was something I could do. I feel responsible. I'd die if you lose the boys because of this. It's not fair. It's not fair that you don't get to have a life." She shook her head. "Diane probably wouldn't mind if you had a life with anyone else but me. This is all my fault."

"Stop. This isn't on you. I honestly don't know what I would've done without you these past couple of weeks. But I was kidding myself. We both were." He stood up and put on his shirt. "I really hate to do this, Doc. But the kids won't be able to come to Oliver's birthday party tonight. There's no way I'll get rid of Diane and Karl now, and I can't rock the boat until I've talked to someone about my rights." He'd gotten busy and put off looking for a lawyer.

"But, Gabe, he's turning sixteen. He wants the boys to come. I don't have anyone else to invite. The few friends he's made won't come for fear of upsetting Dirk."

"You're right. Don't worry. I'll figure something out. I won't be able to come. I wish I could but it'll just give Diane more ammunition, and Dylan is more likely to come if I don't. I'll make it up to Oliver. If it's okay with you, I'll pick him up early one day next week, and we can work on the car. Maybe we'll take it out on the road."

"He'd absolutely love that. Thank you." She looked out the window that faced onto the snow-covered backyard. "We went from making love in the middle of the afternoon to this. I can't believe it."

He crouched in front of her, taking her hands in his. "You have to know that, if it was just me, if I didn't have the boys to think about, I'd want to be with you. That might not sound like a very big deal but, after I lost Lauren, I didn't think I'd ever want to be with another woman. I didn't think I could, and then you came along. I wish..." He looked away.

She placed her hand on the side of his face, stroking

his cheek with her thumb. "I know. Me too." Someone pounded on her front door, and she let her hand drop to her side. "You better go."

He straightened, leaning in to brush his lips across the top of her head. "Bye, Doc," he said, then headed for the door. Ready to give whoever was on the other side of it hell. Diane had probably sent Karl over to drag him from Mallory's bed. The thought didn't ease his anger, and he nearly took off his officer's head.

She grimaced. "Sorry, Chief, but we've been trying to reach you for the past half hour. Mrs. Rollins said we'd find you here."

He glanced at his place to see Diane standing on his front porch with her arms crossed. There was lots he wanted to say to her, none of it good, but instead he focused on his officer. "What's up?"

"We got a call from Kayla McPherson. She says she has reason to believe Mrs. Maitland"—she glanced into the house—"the first one, I mean. She's been kidnapped."

Chapter Twenty-Three

Mallory's legs felt like they were boneless when she walked into the Highland Falls Police Station after dropping off the boys at home. And it wasn't from spending the afternoon making love with the chief of police. As fantasy-fulfilling as the experience had been, learning that Gabe had missed being there for Dylan and now was in danger of losing his boys because they'd been making love had immediately snapped her body out of its blissed-out state.

But it was when Gabe called her to come to the station that she'd turned into a weak-kneed nervous wreck. Marsha Maitland was missing, and Mallory had a feeling she was the prime suspect.

"Mallory Maitland. I'm here to see Chief Buchanan," she said as she approached the desk.

The officer gave her a clipped nod. "He's expecting you." She gestured to Gabe's closed office door.

Mallory felt the curious stares of the officers at their

desks as she made her way to the back of the station. She knocked on Gabe's door.

"Come in," he said, his voice cool and professional. So unlike the voice that had been whispering in her ear only hours before.

The same voice that had ended things before they'd really gotten started. Even if it felt like they'd gotten started the moment their eyes first met. She hadn't put up a fight though. How could she, in the face of him losing his sons? She didn't blame him. She just wished it had ended differently. No, in all honesty, she wished it hadn't ended at all.

But since it had, she thought she'd been punished enough for one day. But as she opened the door, she realized she hadn't been. Kayla McPherson sat in the chair in front of Gabe, turning to look at Mallory as she walked into the office.

Mallory's gaze shot to Gabe. Surely he could've warned her. She hadn't thought he blamed her for missing the calls from the school, but maybe once he was out of her bed and out of her house, he'd had time to think.

"Sorry, I didn't know you were busy." She turned to walk out. She wasn't doing this, not today.

"Mallory, would you come in and sit down, please."

She briefly closed her eyes and then turned to face him, lifting her chin. "I'll stand." She shut the door, perhaps harder than was necessary, and leaned against it.

"Someone's got attitude today, don't they?"

"Kayla, that's not helpful. Mallory, Kayla was speaking to Marsha around two this afternoon. While they were talking, Marsha indicated she was almost in Highland

Falls, then she said a truck was broken down on the side of the road and a man was flagging her down. No one's heard from her since."

She raised an eyebrow. "And...?"

He cocked his head to look at her. She didn't care if he thought she was being bitchy. She knew what this was. She knew exactly what Kayla was trying to accuse her of, and she resented Gabe putting her in a position to have to defend herself. No way would she make this easy for him. Not after... She bowed her head. She hadn't realized until that moment how angry and hurt she was that he'd dumped her.

"And where were you at two o'clock this afternoon?" Kayla said.

Mallory held Gabe's gaze. "Having a picnic in my bed with an incredibly hot cop." Gabe looked like he'd swallowed his tongue. She would've laughed if she didn't know why. "His name is Aidan Gallagher. He's the hero in *Sugarplum Way*. The book that I'm reading." She didn't know if it was better or worse but now, thanks to her afternoon with Gabe, she had plenty of fodder to fuel her book fantasies.

"When was the last time you spoke to Marsha?" Gabe asked.

"When I invited her to Oliver's birthday party Sunday night. She'd planned to be here at four."

"You know, maybe it's just me, but I don't understand why you'd invite Marsha in the first place. She took you to court, destroyed your reputation, and then got everything that had been left to you," Kayla said.

Mallory shrugged. "I'm a saint."

Gabe's lips twitched. Like her, he was no doubt remembering their conversation with Ruby only hours before. It was true what they said: things change in an instant. And in her case, not for the better.

"Do something, Chief. She's not taking this seriously," Kayla whined.

"What would you like him to do? Put me in handcuffs?" She gave Gabe a challenging stare. She'd enjoyed when he'd handcuffed her to her bed this afternoon but she certainly wouldn't enjoy him handcuffing her under these circumstances.

He leaned back in his chair, moving it from side to side. "Kayla, would you mind giving me a minute alone with Mallory?"

"Every minute we waste puts the chances of you finding Marsha alive at risk, Gabriel," Kayla said. "You know this. You know the statistics."

"You know what I'd like to know?" asked Mallory. "What exactly is your relationship with Marsha, Kayla? You seem awfully chummy with someone you supposedly talked to for a few minutes on the day I arrived in town."

"Classic. You don't answer any of our questions, and then you turn it around on me."

"Like you just did?" Mallory blew out a breath, frustrated with herself as much as with Kayla. As much as she didn't want to admit it, it did seem odd that Marsha hadn't arrived yet. And if Kayla's conversation with Marsha had played out like she said—and Mallory had no reason to doubt that it had—then she had to put her anger aside and stop being so defensive.

"Not that it's any of your business, but I asked Marsha to come for Oliver's birthday because, other than me, she's all the family the boys have. Lately I've begun to worry that Oliver and Brooks would have no one to turn to if something happened to me." She lowered her eyes. She didn't want to look at Gabe. Because while everything she said was true, over the past week, she'd begun to think they'd have Gabe and his sons.

"I don't know many women who would do the same in your shoes, but it's a good thing that you're doing for the boys. I just hope Marsha is all right." Kayla must've noticed that both she and Gabe were looking at her, because she sighed. "You already know, don't you?" she said to Gabe.

"I do. Your concern and the number of times you've been in contact with Marsha gave you away." He turned to Mallory. "Kayla is on Marsha's payroll. When Marsha learned you were taking the job in Highland Falls, she started looking into social services for someone who would keep an eye on you and the boys."

"Keep an eye on us? She tried to have the boys removed from my care."

"No... Well, yes, that might've been in the back of *my* mind," Kayla admitted. "But only because I was concerned for the boys' well-being. Marsha, on the other hand, only seemed to want updates. Not that she wasn't concerned about Oliver and Brooks— she was."

"All right, so now that we've cleared that up, can you remember if Marsha mentioned the color or make of the truck or what the man looked like?" Gabe asked Kayla.

"No, I don't think so. She seemed annoyed that the man was flagging her down when there was another man sitting in the cab. Oh wait—she said the man was flagging her down with a cowboy hat."

Gabe looked at Mallory and raised an eyebrow.

"No. There's no way. It can't be," she said.

Kayla's eyes went wide. "What? Do you know who it is?"

"I have a pretty good idea," Gabe said and picked up his cell phone. "Owen, you have ten minutes to bring Marsha Maitland to the station before I head out to your place and haul your and Boyd's asses into jail."

* * *

"You and Mallory could pass for mother and daughter," Owen said to Harry's first wife, who sat between him and Boyd in Gabe's office. Mallory and Kayla were sharing the couch in the back corner.

"It's true, you know. It's uncanny how much you look alike," Kayla whispered, then grinned when Mallory gave her the evil eye. No doubt reminiscent of the one Marsha had just given to Owen.

Owen laughed and patted Marsha's thigh. "Let me tell you, Gabe. This gal's a corker. Reminds me a lot of Lizzie. You never knew her, but Boyd did, and he says the same thing. Marsha's a spitfire."

"Are you quite finished, Mr. Campbell?" Marsha said, brushing off her winter-white pants with a gloved hand. She looked elegant in a fake-fur-trimmed, winter-white, ankle-length coat. Although, since she'd been hanging out at the cabin in the woods for the past couple of hours, her coat and pants would need to be dry-cleaned.

"I am," Owen said with a laugh, like she was just the cutest thing.

Marsha pinched the bridge of her nose and then addressed Gabe. "Chief Buchanan, this is nothing more than a misunderstanding. I have no intention of pressing charges."

"See, I told you, Gabe. We just wanted to have ourselves a little chat with Marsha."

"Okay, so let me get this straight. You flagged her down, pretended you'd blown a tire, and then tied her up and tossed her in your truck and drove off. Has all the hallmarks of a kidnapping, if you ask me. And just so we're straight, Marsha, as the victim, for your own protection, you don't get a vote on whether it's a crime or not. As an example, you could have Stockholm syndrome or fear retaliation."

"Please, it was like being kidnapped by Laurel and Hardy." She glanced over her shoulder. "Remember how much Harry loved those two, Mallory?"

"Uhm." She gave her a tight smile. It had been torture sitting through hours of Laurel and Hardy.

"Laurel and Hardy?" Kayla made a face.

"He was addicted to Pink Panther movies too," Mallory said.

"You really are a saint," Kayla said, and Mallory looked over to see Gabe struggling not to laugh.

He cleared his throat. "Boyd, do you have anything to say?"

"We heard Marsha was coming to town, and we were

worried she was going to take the boys from Mallory. So we staged an intervention."

"That's what we did, Gabe. We staged an intervention. We brought Marsha up to Boyd's place to show her where Mallory grew up. Showed her Mallory's room and her diaries and her yearbooks and all those prizes she won. And we told Marsha what a mess we've made of Mallory's life."

"Told her what a mess she'd made of things for my daughter too." Boyd twisted in his chair to look at Mallory. "She doesn't want to take the boys from you, honey. It was a test. All along she's been testing you. The court case, everything. It was one big test to see if you were—"

"I think I can share my reasoning for doing what I have done with your daughter, Boyd." Marsha half rose from her chair to move it enough that she could comfortably look at Mallory. "I realize, given the negative publicity that you endured throughout the court case, that you may have a difficult time understanding or sympathizing with my rationale for doing what I have done."

"Don't like to speak ill of the dead, but—" Owen began.

"And you will not speak ill of Harry in my presence or in Mallory's or the boys'. Is that understood, Mr. Campbell?"

Owen chuckled. "See what I mean? She's a corker. All I was going to say was that Marsha was more than Harry's partner in their marriage. She was the brains behind his business while he was the face. She's the one who invested their profits in Microsoft and made Harry his fortune. Then he left her for some two-bit floozy who—" He glanced at Marsha. "Did you want to take it from here?"

"No, go ahead. You're so much more eloquent than me."

He patted her thigh again. She slapped his hand with her glove, which only made him grin. "You're my kind of gal, Marsha. Anyway, where was I?"

"The two-bit floozy," Marsha said.

"Right." He went to pat her thigh and caught himself in time. "Anyway, Mrs. Maitland the Second decided she didn't want to be a mother or wife, and Harry, without discussing it with Marsha, gave away more than half their fortune to get rid of her."

"Thank you. I'll take it from here, Owen."

He waggled his eyebrows at Marsha using his first name, and she rolled her eyes. "Harry returned to Atlanta with the boys, and everything went back to the way it used to be. I assumed, to my detriment, that things would continue that way but then Harry became restless again, and the next thing I knew, he was dating you and introducing you as the future Mrs. Maitland the Third. Then he sent the boys away, and he shut me out of his life and the company. So when he left everything to you, I was furious. It was more my fortune, my home, than it ever was his."

"You never stopped loving him, did you?" Mallory said.

"No, I didn't. As they say, there's nothing as foolish as an old fool. And I was that."

"I wish you would've told me, Marsha."

"I was angry and humiliated. Blair took advantage of

that. She led me to believe that, as a doctor, you knew all along Harry was dying and that you were just biding your time. I should've seen through her, but jealousy and grief are powerful emotions. And I wasn't about to let you burn through the fortune that I had worked so hard to build like the boys' mother did."

"My taking custody of the boys was my test, wasn't it?"

"It was. I'd begun to believe that you didn't care about Harry's—my—fortune after all. You agreeing to take custody of Oliver and Brooks without seeking any financial remuneration seemed to validate that. But I had to be sure."

"I didn't care about Harry's fortune. I was trying to honor his wishes and protect his reputation."

She nodded. "I saw that. And I talked to some of your clients at Aging Awesomely, which, by the way, is a ridiculous name. Growing old is far from awesome."

Mallory bit back a smile. "It can be."

"We'll talk about that at another time. Your champions here"—she nodded at Owen and Boyd—"did a good job of convincing me—"

"Her secret Santas," Owen said with a wink.

Marsha sighed. "Your secret Santas, then. They showed me how unfairly life, and they, had treated you. I'm sorry that I ever made you feel unworthy of Harry's love. I would say he was unworthy of yours."

"Damn straight," her father said.

"I would also say the proverb 'People who live in glass houses shouldn't throw stones' applies in this case, Mr. Carlisle."

"She got you there, Boyd."

"Be quiet, Owen."

"Seeing that Mallory passed your tests, does that mean you're going to give her back the fortune and the mansion?" Owen asked.

"No. I don't want Marsha's fortune or the mansion. What I want is to get home to celebrate Oliver's birthday. Boyd, Owen, you're welcome to join us. Unless Gabe plans to arrest you." She frowned; the color had drained from his face. "Gabe, what's wrong?"

He held up his phone. "Diane and Karl took the kids to Atlanta for the weekend."

"You didn't know they were taking them?"

"No. Diane was giving me a hard time about Dylan, and then I had to come into work, and she gave me a hard time about that. But I didn't think she'd pull this. Teddy..." He swore under his breath and dragged a hand down his face.

"Is there anything I can do, Gabe?" Kayla asked.

"No. Thanks for the offer but—"

Mallory interrupted him. "Yes, Kayla, you can. Gabe's mother-in-law is threatening to go after custody of his boys. He is one of the best fathers I've ever known, and his sons absolutely adore him." She shared with Kayla what she'd seen and heard over the past couple weeks. "I'm sorry, Gabe. I know you're a private person but sometimes you have to let other people in to help you, and this is one of those times."

"Mallory is right, Gabe. And if it makes you feel better, grandparents are rarely awarded custody over the parents. Or parent, in this case," Kayla said.

"Maybe, but my in-laws have both money and influence, and I don't."

"Marsha does," Mallory said, and then added for the older woman's benefit, "Gabe was married to Diane and Karl Rollins's daughter, Lauren."

"I see. My condolences on the loss of your wife, Chief Buchanan. I remember her well. She was a lovely young woman. Your mother-in-law, on the other hand, was not my favorite person. If you'll excuse me for a moment." She pulled her phone from her purse and walked away.

Mallory walked over to Gabe and gave him a hug. "I know we can't have a relationship, but I still care about you and the boys," she whispered before stepping back. "You need to go to Atlanta tonight, Gabe. You can't let her get away with this. Have you heard from the boys?"

"Yeah, they've been texting nonstop. I gave them a cell phone in case they needed me when they were with their grandparents. I didn't trust that Diane would let them call me if they asked," he told Kayla.

"Okay, I agree with Mallory that for a myriad of reasons, you need to go to Atlanta. Tonight. I can walk you through the best way to handle it so this doesn't escalate and the boys aren't upset more than they no doubt are. I noticed that, when you were talking, you kept referring to your mother-in-law. Is your father-in-law supportive of her going after custody or is he perhaps an ally?"

"Karl Rollins is a wimp. He won't go against his wife. She wears the pants in the family," Marsha said as she went to hand Gabe a card. "This is the number for my lawyer's partner. He's one of the best family law attorneys in Atlanta, and he's expecting your call. He's

prepared to meet you at your in-laws' house this evening
with the chief of police, who I'll be calling next. She's
a friend of mine and owes me a favor. As does the
governor." She pulled the card back. "In return, I'd appreciate it if we pretend Boyd, Owen, and I staged a fake
kidnapping for our amusement and have been severely
reprimanded for our behavior."

"Sounds a little kinky, but I like it," Owen said
with a grin.

"Please don't make me regret providing you with an
alibi," she said, then once again handed the card to Gabe.

"Thank you. I appreciate you making the call on my
behalf, but I have a feeling your lawyer will be out of
my price range," he said, looking at the gold-embossed
business card.

"Let's take it one step at a time, shall we? You may
find calling Diane's bluff is enough. I hope that it is for
your sake and your children's," Marsha said.

"And don't rule Karl out. He may surprise you and
step up," Mallory said and rubbed his arm. "Please text
and let me know what's going on."

"I will, and thanks, Doc. I wouldn't have said anything, and then where would I be." He glanced at Owen
and Boyd. "Go on, get outta here, and no more playing
Mallory's secret Santas. Tell Oliver we'll celebrate with
him next week."

When they left Gabe's office, he was laying everything out for Kayla. He looked a little less devastated
now, which made it easier for Mallory to leave.

"So, you and the chief of police?" Marsha smirked as
they left the station.

Chapter Twenty-Four

Joy. J. O. Y. That's today's Advent theme," Teddy said.

He'd slid into the pew beside Mallory despite his grandparents and father whisper-shouting for him to sit with them. Instead, Gabe, his in-laws, and the twins moved to the pew behind where Mallory and the boys were sitting, and she swore she could feel their eyes drilling holes in the back of her skull.

Gabe had gone to Atlanta buoyed by his support from Marsha and Kayla, but in the end, he'd caved to pressure from his father-in-law and didn't play the lawyer card. He'd been worried about the drama leaving a lasting effect on his sons. He'd arrived home yesterday afternoon with the boys—and his in-laws.

He'd been avoiding Mallory since he'd gotten home. So had the twins. But it was possible it hadn't been their choice. Diane had tried to stop Teddy from delivering Oliver's birthday present with the excuse that they had things to do. Like just a few moments ago, Teddy wouldn't be deterred.

"Good job." She patted his hand, then lifted hers to look at it when it practically stuck to his. He smiled and smoothed his hair back. "I couldn't find any gel so I used Vaseline."

She bit her lip to keep from laughing. "It looks wonderful." She didn't envy Gabe trying to get it out. Beside her, Oliver and Brooks weren't successful holding back their laughter and were loudly shushed from the rows behind and in front of them.

"Battle-ax. B. A. T. T. L. E.-A. X," Teddy said, and Mallory heard a choking sound that she suspected was coming from Gabe, behind her. This time Oliver and Brooks did a better job containing their laughter, although the bench shook with their silent mirth. Mallory had to work not to join in.

Perhaps emboldened by the boys' amusement, Teddy looked over his shoulder at his grandmother and father. "Grinch. G. R. I. N. C. H. Sad. S. A. D. Those are my words of the day."

Mallory glanced at Gabe. He avoided meeting her eyes, looking instead at his hands in his lap. She followed his gaze, blinking at the sight of the gold band on his wedding finger. This was the first time she'd seen him wear his wedding ring. He couldn't have made it clearer to her where they stood if he'd said the words out loud. Which he had, she reminded herself.

"I think I'd stick with *joy*, sweetie." She didn't know how she got the words past the emotion clogging her throat.

He leaned his head against her arm. "I want to but

my house is sad like my dad." He gestured for her to bend her head. She did, and he whispered, "When Dad came to get us after Grandma scolded us, she told him it was his fault our mom died. She said he loved his job more than he loved our mom and didn't have time for us."

Mallory wasn't a vengeful or violent person, but at that moment, she wanted to shake the bitter woman in the pew behind her. She now had a better understanding as to why Gabe had backed down and why he now wore his ring. Diane had known exactly what to say to him.

Lifting her arm to tuck Teddy close, she kissed the top of his greasy head. "Your mommy died in an accident, sweetie. It was no one's fault. Least of all your daddy's. He loves you and your brothers to the moon and back."

He grinned up at her. "To infinity and beyond."

"Indubitably."

"I like that word. How do you spell it?"

"I'll tell you after church. Let's listen to Pastor James's sermon now."

Behind her, Diane said in a fierce whisper, "I expect you to put a stop to this, Gabriel."

Mallory turned to look at the older woman, holding Diane's gaze until she lowered hers. Gabe caught Mallory's eye and gave his head a slight shake as if telling her not to make a scene. As if she would in front of the children and in church. But that didn't mean she was letting this go.

As soon as church was over and people started to

file out of the pews, she said to Gabe, "I need to speak to you."

"Gabriel, we'll meet you in the car. Come on, boys. Theodore, that means you too."

"Diane, Marsha says hello."

Gabe's mother-in-law turned, frowning at her. "Harry's Marsha?"

"Yes. It was a shame you decided to…take off with the boys. She was hoping to see you. She came for Oliver's birthday."

"I didn't know you and Marsha spoke after—"

Mallory cut her off before she said anything embarrassing in front of the boys. "Yes, we're dear friends now." Mallory thought she heard Oliver snort behind her but ignored him. Now was when she'd give Diane a message she hoped Gabe's mother-in-law would understand. "Marsha had a lovely visit with Gabe before he was forced to leave. He made quite an impression. She said if he ever needed anything from her, anything at all, all he had to do was—"

"Karl, Diane, we better get going. The diner fills up fast after church. I'll meet you out there." Gabe took Mallory by the arm and steered her into a quiet corner at the back of the sanctuary.

Mallory mouthed *It's okay* to a concerned-looking Oliver and Brooks, who nodded and followed Teddy and the twins out of the church.

"Okay, look. I know what you're doing, and I know why you're doing it."

"I don't think you do." She crossed her arms. "Teddy told me what Diane said to you."

"I don't know what you're talking about."

She repeated what Teddy had said, and Gabe cursed under his breath. "I thought he was asleep."

"Well, he wasn't." She touched his arm. "Gabe, don't you see what she's doing? By making you feel guilty for something that was absolutely not your fault, she ensures that she'll get her way."

"You're wrong. It was my fault. Lauren had asked me a few days before the accident to have snow tires put on her car. I had a big case and it slipped my mind. She was a social worker. She was on the road after visiting with a client when the snowstorm blew up."

"Were there more cars involved in the accident than hers?"

"Yeah, why?"

"Did they have snow tires on? Did they check the weather before they went out? Did they lose control of their car first or did Lauren? Don't you see, Gabe? No one can predict these kinds of things. It was horrible, and it was unfair, but it was not your fault. And while I didn't know your wife, I'm almost a hundred percent positive that the last thing she'd want is for you to blame yourself."

"I appreciate what you're trying to do but—"

"I'm not doing it for you. I'm doing it for Teddy. Dylan and Cody, too, but mostly Teddy. You promised, Gabe. You promised that you weren't going to let the anniversary of Lauren's death get in the way of you celebrating Christmas."

"You don't understand."

She raised an eyebrow.

"Come on, Doc. It's not the same. You don't have kids. You didn't love Harry like I loved—"

"Wow. I didn't expect that." Hurt, she turned to walk away.

He reached for her. "Wait. I'm sorry. I shouldn't have said—"

"No, you shouldn't have, but I don't know why I'm surprised. Not after what you said to me last summer when you were interrogating me. Enjoy your brunch."

"Don't do this. Don't walk away angry. I'm sorry. I didn't mean to hurt you. I'm taking my frustration at the situation with Diane out on you, and that's not fair. Yesterday was the anniversary of Lauren's death." He held up a hand. "I know what you said about celebrating her life instead, but it's Diane. They'll be here for a few more days and then they'll be gone and we'll get into the Christmas spirit for Teddy."

"Maybe you should try getting into the spirit for yourself instead of faking it for Teddy. He's pretty smart, you know. He can see through you."

"Yeah, he is. I'll talk to him."

Cody stuck his head in the sanctuary. "Dad, Grandma says to hurry up."

"Okay, I'll be right there. Thank you for what you tried to do, Doc. It probably doesn't seem like it, but I do appreciate it."

"You're welcome. I hope you guys have a better week. We'll see you on Friday for Teddy's birthday. I ordered his cake, and I picked up..." She searched his face, stunned, and really, really hurt. "You don't want us to come."

"It's not that I don't want you there but I'm not sure when Diane and Karl are leaving or if they'll be coming back for Teddy's birthday. They're being vague."

"Then maybe you should just ask them or maybe you should tell them, seeing as it is your house, and they are your sons."

"You don't understand."

"I think I do. Better than you, actually. And I'm sorry, but I promised Teddy I'd be at his party and so did the boys, and we don't intend to miss it."

* * *

When Mallory pulled into her driveway after church, Abby was waiting for her. "Would someone like to explain this to me?" Abby waved her hand around. "I've never been on a less Christmassy or more depressing street than this. What the heck has happened to Christmas on Reindeer Road?"

"The Buchanans have leached it out of us. And the Rollinses. Not Teddy though." Then, thinking of him in church, Mallory stared at Abby and slapped the hood of the car. "What am I saying? They've leached the Christmas spirit out of him too."

Abby sighed. "We're supposed to be filming our outdoor segment today, and the way it's looking, that's not going to happen."

Thinking of Teddy made Mallory realize that she'd dropped the ball on her Christmas plan. Things might be better with Oliver and Brooks. She didn't have to worry about anyone taking them away from her anymore, and they certainly didn't hate her like they used to. But thanks to Dirk and his football buddies—and to Gabe's boys not being around as much as they used to because of Diane—Mallory's stepsons had seemed down in the dumps lately. It was past time she reinstated the Christmas plan.

"We'll make it happen, won't we, boys? And I know who to call for reinforcements: Boyd and Owen." She glanced at her watch. "We have to hurry though. The Buchanans will be back soon from brunch."

"I heard Gabe tell Teddy they were going to the tree farm to cut down their Christmas tree. But the grandma didn't look happy about it so maybe she'll kibosh the plan."

"When did you hear Gabe tell Teddy?" Mallory asked Oliver.

"Right after you guys finished talking."

Mallory smiled, pleased at the thought that she may have gotten through to him. "I don't think Gabe will let her kibosh the plan this time." Later in the week, maybe. But she thought they were safe for today.

Abby held up her phone. "Boyd and Owen are on their way. They've got a ton of volunteers at the tree farm, and they've told everyone to stall Gabe and his family. They'd planned to get your lights done Friday but Marsha sidetracked them so they already have everything they need. Supposedly they have enough lights to light up the entire town. So we should have enough to do the Buchanans' too."

They had more than enough. What they didn't have

enough of was time. "Abs, help me get Gabe's porch finished while Boyd, Owen, and the boys put the last of the lights on the shrubs and trees."

Mallory had thrown a red-and-black-plaid blanket over the swing at the end of Gabe's porch, added a pillow, and right now she was wrapping a swag of evergreen around a pair of old, red cross-country skis and leaning them in a corner. All she had left to do was get the evergreen wreath on the door and put a red lantern on the table.

"Look." Abby walked across the yard with a wooden deer in her arms. It was identical to the ones Hunter had been carving at the tree farm last weekend. "Hunter just reminded me I had them in the truck. Gabe bought you a family of three, but you have those cute reindeer lights leaping across your yard, so I think these would be overkill. We'll use them in Gabe's yard instead."

"He bought them for me on his own or did you suggest he buy them for me?"

"Well…" Abby grinned. "It doesn't matter whose suggestion it was. He bought them or, in this case, donated to Aunt Liz's foundation. And he bought them for *you*."

"They'll look great right there," she said as Abby placed the deer near the evergreen in the front yard. Mallory wasn't about to get sucked into a conversation about her nonexistent relationship with Gabe. Or so she thought until she blurted "He's wearing his wedding ring" when her best friend joined her on the porch.

"It's the anniversary of his wife's death this week, isn't it? I'm sure that's all it is, sweetie."

"I don't know why I said anything or why I let it bother me. He made it pretty clear there's no future for us."

"But you want there to be, don't you?" Abby said, holding the wreath while Mallory centered the nail on the doorframe just above the frosted-glass windowpane and lifted the hammer.

"Yes. No. I don't know. I'm just going to focus on making this the best Christmas the—"

"Mallory, don't hammer—" Owen began.

She looked over her shoulder as she hit the nail with the hammer, and the frosted windowpane shattered into a million pieces. "It's not like a mirror, is it? I won't have seven years of bad luck?"

"I'd say your luck is pretty bad, honey. Gabe's just turned onto Reindeer Road," Boyd informed her. Then he jogged across the lawn and onto the porch to remove the hammer from her hand. "I'll take the rap."

Chapter Twenty-Five

Mallory leaned against the kitchen counter watching the snow fall as she sipped her coffee. She wasn't as excited as she had been last weekend to see the snow. Then again, she didn't know if she could work up excitement for much these days. Diane Rollins had sucked the joy right out of her.

Since Sunday, she wouldn't allow Mallory or the boys within ten feet of the Buchanans. Other than when Gabe took Brooks and Oliver out of school Monday afternoon to make up for missing Oliver's birthday. She had a feeling Diane had no idea what had transpired or she would've found a way to put a stop to their outing. It didn't look like the woman planned on leaving anytime soon either. Mallory wondered what that meant for Teddy's birthday.

Despite what she'd said to Gabe at church, she and the boys wouldn't go where they weren't wanted. It would just upset Teddy on his special day. If worse came to worst, she'd come up with an excuse and do something special with Teddy on his own. If Gabe would let her, she thought, with a soul-deep sigh. This certainly wasn't how she expected to be feeling with Christmas only eight days away.

So far, her plan to put both the Buchanans and her sons in the holiday spirit was a bust. Every night she looked out to see if Gabe had turned on the Christmas lights, and every night she was as disappointed as the last. So were Oliver and Brooks. Even though they tried to hide it from her, she could tell.

She took another sip of coffee and looked out the window to see Gabe putting out his garbage. She choked on an excited breath, spewing coffee down the front of her. "Son of a nutcracker!" Grabbing a wet cloth to wipe at her long-sleeved white pajama top with DEAR SANTA, I TRIED imprinted on the front in red, she glanced out the window.

Gabe was seconds away from reaching the end of his driveway. She dropped the cloth and ran out the door in her pajamas and slippers. Her red snowflake-covered pajama bottoms were fleece and her fuzzy red slippers were warm so she wasn't worried about hypothermia. She was more worried about missing the opportunity to speak to Gabe face-to-face.

Except she didn't want to look desperate so she ran to the garbage bin and pulled out an overstuffed green garbage bag. The bag was heavy, too heavy to carry, so she dragged it after her and called out a casual "Good morning" to Gabe. Hopefully he didn't notice the breathless quality to her voice. She smiled and waved when he looked her way.

He did a double take and then a slow grin creased his ridiculously handsome face. "Doc, by the time you reach the end of the driveway, you won't have anything left in your bag."

She looked over her shoulder to see that she'd left a trail of garbage behind her. "Son of a nutcracker!"

He laughed as he put his garbage bag down at the end of his driveway and then walked across the lawn toward her. "Get another garbage bag, and I'll give you a hand."

"No, you're ready for work. You'll get your uniform dirty. As you can see, I'm already a mess." She looked down and realized it was probably not a good idea to draw attention to her top. It was cold out, and she was braless. She let go of the garbage bag to cross her arms over her chest.

"So what did you try?" he asked, his voice huskier than seconds ago.

"A damp cloth but it didn't work."

"No. Your top says 'Dear Santa, I tried.' I was asking what you'd tried."

"Everything, but it's not working." She wondered if he understood what she meant.

He nodded, looking back at his house before bringing his gaze to hers. "You probably missed the light show the other night. I'd turn them on, and Diane would turn them off. She felt it was disrespectful to Lauren's memory to have the house lit up like the Fourth of July. And yes, I know it's our house, not hers. But the twins seem to feel the same way she does. Teddy's just happy the yard is decorated and the tree is up. He enjoyed your cookies and the dancing snowman." He raised an eyebrow. "I'm not wrong, am I? You are our secret Santa?"

She nodded. "I'm glad he enjoyed them. I was worried Diane would throw them out if she found them on your front porch."

"I'm sorry. I don't know what's gotten into her this year. She's worse than she's ever been."

Mallory had a fairly good idea she was the reason Diane was worse. Maybe she should back off. Maybe then Diane wouldn't feel so threatened and would go home. "Are they planning to stay through the holidays?"

"Her church group has a Christmas tea Friday afternoon, so they'll be heading home for that. Karl's going to try to convince her to go to Florida for the holidays like they'd planned. But I can tell he thinks it's a lost cause."

She didn't realize her teeth were chattering until Gabe shrugged out of his jacket and put it over her shoulders. "You're freezing. Let's go. I'll just grab a garbage bag from you and take care of this. No arguing. It's the least I can do after everything you've done for us."

She snuggled into his jacket, breathing in his warm, woodsy scent. "You took Oliver out driving, which we both appreciated. A lot. So did Brooks, by the way."

He smiled. "He told you I let him take a turn behind the wheel, did he? It was on a back road. There was no danger to anyone."

"I was just teasing. I trust you with the boys, Gabe."

"Thank you. And it wasn't a big deal. I felt bad we weren't here for Oliver's birthday. Turning sixteen is a big deal. I wanted to make it up to him."

"You did and then some," she said as he held open the door for her.

He looked around the kitchen. "You've been busy."

She'd put a red glitter snowflake on each of the cupboard doors, placed garland lit with white lights and decorated with red bows above the cupboards and around the window, and hung a ball of mistletoe from the door frame. He either hadn't seen it or was pretending that he hadn't.

"Abby's coming over tonight to help make cookies for the seniors' cookie exchange. And you know Abby, she has to put it on her channel so she ordered up a Christmassy-looking kitchen."

"Yeah, Teddy told me. I'm sure he'll be tuning in."

"He can come over and help. We'll start as soon as I get home from work if you're worried it's too late for a school night."

"It's probably best if he didn't, Doc. Diane already thinks he has an unhealthy fixation on Christmas."

"You've got to be kidding me. You don't buy that, do you?" At his shrug, she stared at him. "Gabe, he's five years old."

"Six in two days. The twins were never as obsessed with the holidays as he is. From what Oliver and Brooks said, neither were they. The only person I know who is as fanatical about Christmas as Teddy is you."

"Fanatical? We're hardly fanatical."

"Really? So the other night when it was freezing cold, what were you doing with your windows wide open playing Christmas carols loud enough that I had to turn up the sound on the television?"

"I like to clean listening to music, and I was airing out the house." She shrugged at his skeptical look. "Teddy liked it."

"You've proved my point."

"And you've proved Teddy right. You and the twins are as grinchy as your mother-in-law. So you might want to take a good long look at her and see if that's who you want to be." She took off his jacket and handed it to him. "And just so you know, it's been scientifically proven that people who believe in the magic of the holidays are happier than those who don't."

"Are you happy, Doc? Because from where I'm standing, you look like you're wearing yourself out getting into the Christmas spirit."

"Well, maybe if you, Dylan, Cody, Oliver, and Brooks would get onboard, I wouldn't have to try so hard."

"Is that what all this is about? You're trying to put us in the Christmas spirit?" He searched her face.

"I don't know why you seem so surprised, Gabe. I told you about my Christmas plan at the Santa Claus parade."

"You told me you were trying to get Oliver and Brooks in the Christmas spirit, not me and my boys."

"I know, but poor Teddy can't do it all on his own. Not when he's up against your mother-in-law." She crossed her arms. "Are you canceling our invitation to Teddy's birthday or not? I need to know. It's only two days away, and if we're not allowed to come, I have to get everything organized for you."

"What do you mean, get everything organized?"

"Teddy's party. You'll have to set up the gingerbread house station, the hot chocolate station, and the pizza-making station. Then there's the games and the scavenger hunt."

"Just listening to you is making me tired—and nervous."

"He's going to be six. Surely you've had birthday parties for him before."

"Not the year Lauren died, and my mom and my brothers' wives took care of his fourth and fifth birthday parties. We went to the Brooklyn Children's Museum for one and the New York Hall of Science for the other one." He sighed. "You sure you don't mind doing this?"

"No, I'm more than happy to. But I don't think Diane will be happy to have me there, and I don't want to ruin Teddy's special day."

"You gotta know that, for Teddy, his birthday would be ruined if you weren't there. So of course you guys are coming."

She released a heartfelt sigh, and her shoulders sagged. "Thank you."

"No, thank you, Doc. For everything. Even if you are going overboard on the Christmas thing, I appreciate what you're trying to do."

* * *

Later that same night, he wasn't so appreciative of her efforts. "Doc, this is insane. I could've shot you," he said, the beam from his flashlight nearly blinding her.

"You coming out here with your gun drawn is insane,

Gabe. All I was doing was putting out blocks of salted sunflower seeds, corn, and molasses for the deer."

"How was I supposed to know what you were doing? All I saw was someone wearing a black knitted hat, black hoodie, and dark jeans creeping around in the woods behind my house."

"I didn't want Teddy to see me."

"It's midnight, Doc. He's in bed." He lowered his flashlight from her face and shone it around the forest floor. "I know I'm going to regret this, but I have to ask. Why are you putting out food for the deer?"

"I was hoping that they might come visit for his birthday." She explained to him what Teddy had said to her the morning after she'd moved in.

"Did you know it's illegal to bait deer in a wildlife management area at any time of the year?"

"No, I didn't. But I'm not baiting them to hunt them. I'm trying to attract them to give Teddy a special birthday surprise."

"What you really mean is that you want him to think Santa paid him a visit on his birthday, right?"

She narrowed her eyes at him. "You were watching Abby's YouTube channel, weren't you?"

"I was." He stepped closer to her.

So close that she had to tip her head back to look up at him. "Abby said it, not me."

"But you didn't deny that you wanted me for Christmas, did you?"

"I'm pretty sure that I did, but one of Abby's paid advertisements popped up in the middle of my answer and drowned it out. I knew Teddy was watching. I wouldn't want to get his hopes up. I mean, if he still had hopes of us getting together. He might not anymore."

"Trust me, he does. He's just smarter about hiding his wedding planner notebooks. Doc, I—"

"Gabriel, are you all right? Did you find the intruder? Should I send out Karl to help you look?" A beam of light moved back and forth through the woods.

Gabe moved to shield Mallory from Diane's view. "No, it's fine. Probably just a deer."

"It looked awfully tall for a deer."

He grinned down at her. "Maybe it was Bigfoot."

Chapter Twenty-Six

Gabe walked across his front lawn to give Mallory a hand. She was loaded down with boxes and bags. She'd left work early and so had he. Today was Teddy's birthday. His friends were arriving right after school.

"Here, let me grab the boxes," Gabe offered.

"I've got them, thanks. But if you don't mind, there are a couple more bags in the kitchen, and the cake is on the counter." She rested her chin on top of the boxes. "On second thought, leave the cake. I'll get it."

"I won't drop the cake, Doc. But you do know there are only six kids coming, right? You look like you've bought enough for a hundred. And whether you want me to or not, I'm paying, so let me know what this set you back."

"I told you before, this is my gift to Teddy. Besides, it just looks like a lot because of the stuff for the games."

"Sure it does," he said as he walked to her place, pulling his wallet from his back pocket.

She wasn't hurting financially, but he knew she didn't

have a lot left over after she paid her bills. He'd watched a couple of episodes of Christmas on Reindeer Road on Abby's channel, and Mallory always had tips to share on how to save money on decorating and gift giving. The woman was downright frugal, and from Abby's followers' feedback, Mallory's tips were almost as popular as Bella in her latest Christmas fashions. Granted, Gabe hadn't been watching because of Mallory's tips. He'd been watching because he couldn't get enough of her. He missed her.

As he opened the door into her kitchen, he looked up at the ball of mistletoe. It had taken everything he had not to use the mistletoe as an excuse to take her in his arms earlier in the week and kiss her. He'd wanted to do more than kiss her when she stood shivering in the cold in her pajamas. Same as when he'd discovered her in the woods later that same night.

He might have, if not for Diane calling out to him, reminding him what happened when he followed his heart. He didn't even bother correcting himself. Deep down, he'd known it was his heart, not his dick, that had gotten him into trouble the day Dylan got hurt at school.

Gabe shut the door and took off his boots. The house smelled like Christmas. Looked like it, too, he thought, as he walked through the living room to get to Mallory's bedroom. He'd leave the money on her dresser. But as he walked into her room, the memories of that day came back to him, and he sat on the end of her bed to look around. It was just a room: pretty, feminine, and tidy. Nothing special, but it had felt special that afternoon. It had felt almost magical.

For years, he'd been on autopilot, but in those couple of hours with Mallory, something inside of him had shifted. He'd felt alive again. He'd felt like he could move mountains, take on any challenge life threw at him. Even turn around the situation with the Highland Falls seniors. His future had suddenly looked brighter, and that was because she was in it. And then he'd looked at his phone and his hopes and dreams had been snuffed out.

It wasn't until this morning when the taillights of Diane and Karl's SUV faded from view that the depressing weight that had suffocated him for the past week started to lift. Dylan, Cody, and Teddy felt it too. Their smiles were bigger and brighter, and it wasn't just because of Teddy's party or that Mallory and the boys were coming over. Just as it had for him, the heavy weight of Diane's sadness had cast a pall over the entire household.

And that was when he knew he couldn't allow Diane to manipulate him with guilt any longer. No matter how afraid he was of taking the next steps and possibly losing his sons, he knew the time had come to face his fears. Thanks to Mallory, his guilt over Lauren's accident had lessened, loosening Diane's hold on him. The fear was harder to shake. Still, he'd taken the first step and set up a call for Monday morning with Marsha Maitland's high-priced attorney.

Gabe stood, his eyes falling on the mountain of pillows on Mallory's bed. He smiled at the memory of them tangled in the sheets. What he wouldn't give to be in this bed with her again. He couldn't think about that now though. He couldn't give Diane anything to use against him.

"Gabe, where are you?" Mallory called out.

He grabbed the money off the dresser and headed out of her room. The last thing he'd need was to be alone with her in her bedroom. That was a temptation he didn't think he could withstand.

"You caught me. I was going to leave you money, but I didn't know where to hide it. Then I was afraid you wouldn't find it," Gabe said as he walked through the living room. He rolled his eyes at himself. He really had no game where this woman was concerned.

"I'm not taking your money. I ... Why are you looking at me like that?"

"Ah, what are you wearing?" She had on a green sweater with ropes of gold tinsel on the front and miniature Christmas balls hanging off it.

"I'm a Christmas tree." She bent over to dig in a bag and then straightened with a lime-green sweater in her hands. "And you're the Grinch."

"You can't be serious. I'm not wearing that."

"Yes, you are." She pushed the sweater against his chest and then handed him the bags from the floor. "And please tell me you have your decorations hidden somewhere in your house because we can't have a Christmas-themed party with it looking the way that it does now."

He rubbed the back of his neck. "We have a Christmas tree."

"No, what you have is a naked evergreen sitting in your living room."

"We could just stand you up in the corner, add a strand of lights, and we'd be good," he teased.

She didn't laugh.

Two hours later, Gabe lay down on the couch in his living room. "You're a slave driver, Doc. I'm exhausted."

"Sorry, no rest for the wicked." She reached for his hand to pull him up.

Instead, he pulled her down on top of him. His eyes locked with hers, and he couldn't look away. He hadn't meant to do that. It was like his hand had a mind of its own. So did other parts of his anatomy. He didn't want to tell her why they couldn't be more than friends and neighbors. He'd told her before. It didn't matter how much he cared about her or wanted her in his life—it never came out right. "I called Marsha's lawyer today."

"That's good. You can't go on like this. It's not healthy for you or the boys. It'll be okay, Gabe. No one is going to take them from you."

Her smile didn't quite reach her eyes. She was a smart woman. She knew what he was trying to say without him coming out and saying it.

She didn't look at him as she went to stand. "It's time for you to pick up the boys."

* * *

Gabe was ready for the kids to leave or at the very least for the games to be over.

The kids weren't. "This is the best party, Teddy. We really like your mom. She's fun."

Teddy beamed and didn't correct his friend. The little boy wasn't the first one to mistake Mallory for Teddy's mom.

Squeals came from across the room, and Gabe glanced to where the twins were being wrapped in toilet paper by Team Two and Team Three. Teddy's team had already turned Brooks into a snowman using toilet paper, black construction-paper buttons, a pipe, a carrot nose, a scarf, and a hat.

The twins were distracted by something in the kitchen and hadn't heard what Teddy's friend had said. Gabe figured that was a good thing. Because as much as they were Mallory's number-one fans for throwing their baby brother the best birthday party ever, he knew from experience that could change in a heartbeat.

They hadn't even minded that their house looked like Santa's elves were color-blind and hyped up on candy canes when they decorated. Still, as much as it gave Gabe a headache, he'd never forget Teddy's face when he'd walked into the house. His youngest had looked like he'd died and gone to heaven and Mallory was his angel. Gabe didn't blame him. He just wished that he didn't feel the same way.

"Gabe," Mallory whisper-shouted his name, waving him over to the dining room table, where she was placing the miniature gingerbread houses the kids had decorated in their personalized Christmas bags.

"What's up?" he asked.

"Oliver and Ainsley. Get in there and break them up before Cody does." She nodded at the two teenagers standing in the kitchen feeding each other birthday cake.

"What do Oliver and Ainsley have to do with Cody?" he asked. Then he realized the couple were in the twins' line of sight. He frowned. "Am I missing something? Why would Cody care about Ainsley and Oliver?"

Ainsley's arrival had been a surprise. Teddy had invited their babysitter on his own. He'd invited Owen and Boyd too. At the moment, the two older men were cleaning up the hot chocolate station and pizza-making station for Mallory.

"You're not serious, are you? You didn't realize Dylan has a crush on Ainsley?"

"No. Jeezus, Doc, he's ten, and she's sixteen."

"As if you weren't attracted to older girls at that age." She glanced into the kitchen. "But as much as I don't want Dylan's feelings hurt, I'm more concerned that my son is hitting on Dirk McFee's girlfriend."

"No worries there," Abby said from where she sat on the floor with Bella, who was entertaining Teddy and his team. Unbeknownst to Gabe, Teddy had also extended an invite to Abby. "I heard through the grapevine that Ainsley broke up with Dirk last week."

Mallory gasped. "I knew Oliver wasn't telling me the truth about his black eye. He said he got it during football practice, and I bet I know exactly who gave it to him." She looked at Gabe. "You knew, didn't you?"

"About where he got the black eye? Yeah, but he handled it, Doc. He's…Oh, hell," he said as Cody ran toward the kitchen with the toilet paper unraveling and the members of Team Three yelling at him.

Gabe sprinted for the kitchen but he was two seconds

too late. Cody had launched himself at Oliver. "Okay, that's enough. Break it up, boys."

Oliver did as he asked, dropping his hands to his sides. Which gave Cody the perfect opportunity to punch Oliver in the nose. Gabe suspected that his son was angry not only on his brother's behalf. Lately, the twins, especially Cody, had been griping about how much time Gabe spent with Mallory's sons. Of course Diane had latched on to their jealousy and stirred the pot.

"You little brat—you broke my nose!" Oliver said, looking at Gabe as if he'd betrayed him.

All hell broke loose then. Little girls were crying at the sight of blood, Teddy was crying because his brother had hurt Oliver and ruined his party, and Ainsley was crying and saying how it was all her fault. When Oliver went to comfort her, Dylan launched himself across the kitchen in full snowman gear, although he lost the pipe and carrot nose along the way.

"My brother is not a little brat. You're a big butthead!" Dylan cried as he charged Oliver.

With an arm around Cody's chest, Gabe made a grab for Dylan and got a fistful of toilet paper instead. "Owen, Boyd, I could use a hand here."

Boyd stepped between Oliver and Dylan and got a fist in the eye for his troubles. And Owen, who'd grabbed Brooks as he ran by to join in the fray, slipped in a puddle of hot chocolate on the floor and lost his balance, bringing down Brooks, who reached out at the last second and brought down Dylan.

It took an hour to calm everyone down and to clean up the mess. Mallory had put Oliver's nose back into place, and he was sitting on the couch with an ice pack on his face and Ainsley beside him holding his hand. The twins apologized, but it was clear from their sullen expressions that they hadn't forgiven Oliver for poaching Dylan's girlfriend. And it was just as clear from the way Brooks cracked his knuckles every few minutes that he hadn't forgiven Gabe's boys. On the other side of Oliver, Boyd sat with an ice pack on his eye and Owen sat with one on his butt.

Beside Gabe, Mallory said, "Don't say a word."

"I was just going to say you throw an entertaining party." He looked around. "Where's Teddy?"

She frowned. "I don't know. I thought he went to play with his presents after he said goodbye to Abby and Bella."

Gabe leaned back. Half the presents were gone. "He probably took them to his room." He rubbed her shoulder. "Don't worry, he'll be fine. He's used to his brothers fighting."

"Not at his birthday party, Gabe." She wiped up the kitchen counter. "I wanted it to be special for him."

"Trust me, it was." She gave him a look. "It was, and one day he'll look back on this and laugh."

But not right now, he thought, when he walked into Teddy's room. "Hey, buddy." He went to sit on the bed. "I'm sorry your brothers ruined your party."

His youngest lifted his tear-stained face. "Were they mad because everyone was having fun?"

"No, honey." He cursed Diane in his head. "I think they're jealous of Oliver and Brooks."

Anytime the boys had laughed or were roughhousing

or having a good time this week, his mother-in-law had looked mortally wounded. In case they hadn't made the connection between her offended expression and her week of mourning for their mother, she'd share with them a memory. He wouldn't have minded her sharing memories of Lauren. In fact, he would've encouraged it. But Diane couldn't share a memory without crying or bemoaning Lauren's death. Worse, she'd use it as a way to guilt the boys into being good. *Your mother would expect… Your mother wouldn't like…*

Teddy nodded, playing with the Lego set Gabe had bought him. "Dylan and Cody are buttheads."

"Yeah, but they're your brothers, and they love you. It's still your birthday, you know. What could they do to make it up to you?"

"Can I ask for anything?"

"Within reason, buddy. What would make you feel better?"

"Is you marrying Mallory within reason?" he asked with a mischievous grin.

Gabe tickled him. "Good try. I asked what do your brothers have to do to make it up to you, not me. I was on my best behavior today and didn't hit anyone."

"You yelled at them though. Mallory didn't. She made my friends feel better, and she fixed Oliver's nose. Did you see her do it, Dad? It was so cool."

"I did, and it was pretty cool." So was she. She didn't overreact. She took control of the situation and was able to have Teddy's friends laughing about it before they left. He imagined she'd handled similar situations playing den mother to a bunch of unruly kids in foster care. "So, have you decided what your brothers' punishment is?"

"Yeah. I want Mallory, Oliver, Brooks, Owen, and Boyd to stay and help us decorate the tree, and I want to play Christmas carols really loud like Mallory does, and I want to have a Christmas movie marathon." His blue eyes twinkled. "And I want you to kiss Mallory under the mistletoe again."

"Yes to everything but the last one. Mallory and I aren't mad at each other, so I don't have to make it up to her with a mistletoe kiss." Sometimes, he really had to be more careful with what he said.

A little while later, the Buchanans and Maitlands had pulled together to make Teddy's birthday wish come true. Christmas carols played in the background while a Mickey Christmas movie played on the big screen, and the colored lights were up and twinkling on the tree. Better yet, the four boys no longer looked like they wanted to kill each other. And to their credit, because they were obviously not into hanging ornaments on the tree; they were playing along for Teddy's sake.

"Brooks, careful," Oliver said as his brother reached past him, knocking the ornament he held from his fingers. It fell to the floor, and the twins gasped.

It was the Christmas ball Lauren had made with the twins just days before she'd died, and it now lay in a million pieces on the floor. Gabe's heart broke a little in that moment, too, for himself and for his sons. Everything he'd carefully locked away, the emotions and the memories, came back to haunt him. As if it was happening right then, he saw himself arriving at the scene of the accident on his way home from work, having no idea it was his wife who lay dead on the side of the road. Hours later, kneeling in front of his little boys, gathering them in his arms as he told them that Mommy wouldn't be home for Christmas.

And just like that, the memories flipped a switch, releasing the anger he'd kept under lock and key. "What the hell were you thinking? I told you guys to be careful. I told you no horsing around. But did you listen? Do you even care that you broke the last gift my wife gave to my sons?" he yelled at Oliver.

"Gabe, it was an accident. He didn't mean—" Mallory began.

Gabe looked up from where he knelt on the floor, furious with her. He'd forgotten, and she was the reason that he had. "That's all you've got to say? You don't tell the kid to apologize. You don't—"

"I understand you're upset. But you don't get to yell at my son, and you don't get to yell at me." She ushered her boys from the room. Then she turned. "Dylan, Cody, and Teddy, I'm very sorry about the ornament."

Chapter Twenty-Seven

Mallory arrived home from the seniors' cookie exchange with takeout from Zia Maria's Pizzeria and a new video game. She hoped one or the other would cheer up Oliver and Brooks. If it didn't, she'd go get something else. She couldn't stand to see them so sad. She glanced at the Buchanans' house as she balanced the pizza box, soft drinks, dessert, and video game in her arms.

Christmas lights lit up their house on the outside and inside while hers was in complete and utter darkness. She was happy that Teddy, Dylan, and Cody seemed to have recovered from last night's ordeal, but she was angry at Gabe for what he'd done to her boys. She still couldn't believe he'd yelled at them like that or that he'd yelled at her. He'd made everything so much worse than it had to be.

She hip-checked the door to her car closed and walked to the house. It took her a minute to get the kitchen door opened, but as soon as she did, she called out to Oliver and Brooks. She was anxious to see how they were doing. She'd gotten muted responses last night and this morning when she'd tried to make conversation.

"We're in here," Oliver called out from the living room.

She looked up to see them both sitting on the couch, and every muscle in her body contracted. She wasn't exactly sure why, but there was something about their familiar silent exchange that put her on alert. "I've got pizza from Zia Maria's. Come and get a slice," she said, pushing aside her worries.

"We have something we'd like to talk to you about first," Oliver said.

This sounded bad, but the sympathetic look Brooks gave her said it was so much worse. She left her coat on and walked into the living room to sit on the edge of the chair across from them. "What is it?"

"I called Marsha. She'll pay for me and Brooks to go back to boarding school, but only if you give the okay. You won't have to pay for anything. She said she'll cover everything. Can we go, Mal?"

Tears welled in her eyes, and she turned to look at the tree, blinking her eyes in an effort not to cry. "Do you want to go?" she asked, her voice so low she wondered if they heard her.

"Yeah, we just mess everything up here anyway."

"No. No you don't. You don't mess up anything. What happened last night wasn't your fault, Gabe shouldn't have yelled at you."

"He shouldn't have yelled at *you*," Oliver said, his expression hard. "All you've ever done is try to make things nice for his kids."

She'd thought she'd made things nice for them too. "Brooks, do you want to go?"

He nodded without meeting her eyes. "Yeah. We don't fit in here."

"I thought things were getting better," she said, her brain scrambling for something to change their minds.

"No, it's just getting worse."

"Maybe after the Christmas break things will get better. Maybe you—"

"I know it's hard for you to understand, but our mates are there, Mal. They miss us. We miss them."

But what about me? she wanted to ask. "I see. You're sure this is what you want? This is what you both want?"

They looked at each other and then nodded. "You can come visit, and we can come here and visit too," Brooks said.

"Yes, of course." She forced a smile. "When will you leave?"

"The twenty-eighth." Oliver searched her face. "You'll let us go, then? We can tell Marsha you said okay?"

"Yes. If you're sure this is what you want."

"Brilliant. Thanks, Mal. Thanks so much," Oliver said, and came over to give her a quick hug. It took everything she had to let him go. To let them both go.

"I guess we should celebrate," she said, pushing off the chair. She surreptitiously wiped away tears as she hurried to the kitchen. "I just remembered," she called to them. "Abby invited me to a special event tonight. Would you guys mind if I went?"

"No, go ahead. We're going to FaceTime with our mates and let them know the good news."

* * *

Mallory walked through the woods with Abby.

"I'm glad you changed your mind," Abby said. She'd left Wolf and Bella at the farm with Hunter. "This will be good for you. It feels kind of serendipitous."

"Why do you say that?"

"Winter Solstice is sometimes referred to as the dark night of the soul. Or the inner world reflecting our outer world."

"Dark night of the soul. It pretty much sums up how I feel."

Abby took her hand. "Just remember, you're not alone. You have me, and you have Sadie, and you have your dad and Owen. And then there's all the seniors at the center. You have so many people who love you, Mal."

Other than Abby and Sadie, it didn't feel that way. "I know, and I'm very grateful." Up ahead, she heard the women's voices, and she hung back. "Are you sure they don't mind you bringing a guest?"

"You're not a guest. You're being invited to join. We voted on it last week. I can't tell you how hard it's been keeping it a secret."

"I don't understand. Why am I being allowed to join?" Abby was accepted into the Sisterhood when she'd started the foundation in her aunt's honor. Liz Findlay had been one of the founding members of the Sisterhood.

"Are you kidding me? Look what you've done in only a matter of weeks for the seniors in town. I would've nominated you but Winter, Elsa, and Ruby did." She grinned. "They said they like how, when most millennials are telling seniors to move over, you value them and their opinion."

"Maybe I should've asked them what to do about Oliver and Brooks." She looked around as they walked deeper into the woods, their flashlight beams bouncing off the snow-covered ground. "Aren't we going to the standing stones?"

Deep in the woods to the right of Honeysuckle Farm, there was a circle of seven standing stones. The stone circle had been the inspiration behind Abby's *Outlander* tourist attraction. They looked just like the monolithic groupings Claire Fraser was reputed to have used to travel back in time. Several were over seven feet tall, with a couple standing four feet high and just as wide. The standing stones were the meeting place of the Sisterhood, or so she'd thought.

"No. Tonight we're meeting at the hot springs. Why else did you think I told you to bring your bathing suit?"

"I thought they danced among the stones naked but that guests were allowed to wear bathing suits."

Abby was still laughing when they reached the hot springs. Several women were already in the water. Ice lanterns circled the springs, casting the area in an eerie glow, made eerier by the steam rising from the women sitting in the water.

The older women called out their hellos as Mallory and Abby piled their clothes with the others on the tarp. Shivering, Mallory climbed carefully into the water, smiling her thanks at Granny MacLeod but avoiding her outstretched hand. She knew better than to let the older woman touch her with her bare hand. The last thing Mallory wanted to know was what her future had in store for her. She didn't think she could take more bad news. Both Abby and Sadie had been the recipients of Granny MacLeod's *gift*.

"We're so glad you came tonight, Mallory," the mayor said. "Abby has probably already told you, but we'd be honored if you would join the Sisterhood."

"I'm honored that you want me." She smiled at the women smiling at her. "Is there some kind of initiation ceremony?"

"She thought you were going to make her dance naked under the moonlight and pledge her fealty to Mother Earth," Abby said.

The other women laughed and then Winter explained, "We're a group of women who are trying to reconnect with Mother Earth and the old ways. It's time as women that we raise each other up rather than bring each other down. Like my ancestors, the Cherokee and the Scots, we need to respect the elderly and not push them aside. We no longer value their opinion and that's a mistake. We can learn from those who've walked the path before us. That's what you do, Mallory. And that's why we want you to join us."

"You're a healer, Mallory Carlisle. You always were." Granny MacLeod said, and everyone turned to look at her.

"She's not touching your hand, is she?" Elsa Mackenzie asked.

"Trust me, you know when Granny MacLeod is

prophesying. She gets a weird look on her face, and her voice drops to a creepy monotone," Abby said. "No offense, Granny MacLeod."

"None taken, dear."

"Granny! Granny, where are you?" A voice called from somewhere in the woods, a beam of light shining through the bare trees.

"Sadie, is that you?" Abby called out.

"Yes, it's me. Where are you guys? I thought you were supposed to be at the standing stones."

"We're at the hot springs."

There was some cursing and branches snapping before Sadie stepped into the clearing.

"What are you doing here? I thought you weren't coming home until Christmas Eve," Abby said, pulling a worried face at Mallory.

"She left the bairn's father," Granny MacLeod said.

"About time, if you ask me," said Elsa Mackenzie.

A couple of the other women, including Abby, agreed. Mallory did, too, but she kept her opinion to herself. She didn't think Sadie needed everyone piling on.

"Join us in the springs," Winter suggested.

Sadie demurred. "I didn't bring a bathing suit."

"It's probably better for you and the baby if you don't, Sadie," Mallory said.

"We should get out anyway. It's about time we light the yule log," Elsa Mackenzie said. Then she explained that each of them, Mallory and Sadie, too, should write whatever they wanted to get rid of on scraps of paper and burn it in the yule fire. Then they'd write their hopes and dreams for the future to fill the void. Some of the women would spend the night at the stones waiting for the sun to come up.

"I'm sorry, but you're not sleeping under the stars tonight," Sadie told her grandmother, who slipped as she was coming out of the water. Sadie reached for her, grabbing her by the hand.

A gasp went up from some of the women when Granny MacLeod began to speak in what could only be described as a creepy monotone. "On the day of hearts, you will experience both an all-consuming pain and an all-consuming love. A man will come from the shadows and deliver you from the pain. But be warned, he will bring you more. He isn't who he says he is. You'll be forced to make a choice. Follow your heart or risk that which is most dear to you. This I see, so it shall be."

Sadie sighed. "Wonderful, Granny. Thank you so much. You just made my night."

"I didn't see you getting arrested for kidnapping again, did I?"

"No, Granny," Sadie said, pulling a sweatshirt over her grandmother's head.

"That you were carrying a bairn?"

"I don't think it's physically possible to get pregnant when you already are."

"Well, that's good, then. What did I say?"

"Nothing good, Granny. Nothing good."

"It wasn't that bad," Abby said to Sadie later when they sat around the fire writing down what they wanted to let go of in the coming year.

"So says the eternal optimist. How is unimaginable pain, a man who isn't who he said he is and is going to bring me more pain, plus a chance I'm going to lose everything I hold dear, not that bad?"

"It sounds kinda like last summer. You get a little bad mixed in with a whole lot of good." Abby smiled and patted Sadie's baby bump.

"I suppose, but right now, this whole lot of good comes with a daddy who—" Her eyes went wide when a man called, "Sadie! Sadie, where are you?"

"I can't believe it. It's Drew. He must've followed me," she whispered, looking panicked.

Mallory glanced at Abby. This couldn't be good. Abby nodded and pulled out her phone. "I'm calling Hunter."

Mallory knew how frightened Sadie must be when she didn't argue. "Sadie, go stand with your grandmother, Elsa, and Winter behind the stones."

"What are you going to do?"

"Hold off Drew until Hunter arrives," Mallory said, picking up her flashlight and a big stick. She'd stood between abusive parents and scared little kids. She'd stood between abused women and abusive men. She wasn't afraid to stand between Drew and her best friend.

Abby stared at her as she disconnected from Hunter. "Don't do anything crazy, okay? Hunter's calling—"

Drew crashed through the trees. "Where is she? Where's Sadie?"

"We thought she was with you in Charlotte. What happened?" Mallory said as she walked toward him. He looked beyond her, sweeping his flashlight over the bonfire and standing stones.

Mallory shone her flashlight in his eyes. "Drew, answer me. Why did Sadie leave you?"

"Get that thing out of my eyes." He took a step toward her. "Why do you think Sadie left me? What did she say?"

"She didn't say anything, but she didn't have to. You're here, and she's not." She narrowed her eyes at him. "Have you been drinking?"

"None of your damn business. Get out of my way." He shoved her hard, and she stumbled.

Abby stepped in front of him. "You're trespassing, Drew. Get off my property."

"Piss off." He went to shove Abby but Mallory got between them and pushed him back. He stumbled, his arms pinwheeling as the momentum took him backward. He fell, grunting and groaning as he rolled down the steep incline to crash into a tree. Hunter ran into the clearing with Wolf at his side, glancing over his shoulder at the sound of approaching sirens.

"I see you didn't need me after all." He smiled at Abby, wrapping his arm around her shoulders. He looked around. "Everyone okay?"

"All good. Mallory took care of it," Elsa said.

But that story changed when Gabe arrived moments later. He crossed his arms when each of the women swore that Drew was drunk and had tripped over his own feet.

That might've worked had Drew not been crawling up the incline yelling, "Arrest her! She tried to kill me." Apart from being covered in snow, dirt, and leaves, he seemed perfectly fine to her.

Gabe looked at Mallory with an eyebrow raised. "I didn't try to kill him. He was going to push Abby, and I stepped between them."

His lips quirked in the glow of the firelight. "And he ran into your hands?" he said, repeating what she'd said happened with Dirk McFee that day at the tree farm.

"Yes. Yes, he did. Do I need to call my lawyer, Chief Buchanan?"

"She's already here," Eden said, stepping out from among the trees. She was a member of the Sisterhood too. Mallory had heard someone say she was running late.

"You don't need a lawyer, Doc. Even if he wanted to press charges, he couldn't. He's got too many witnesses willing to testify against him. Besides that, I believe you. I can smell the alcohol off the guy from here so he has his own legal issues to worry about." He sighed when Owen appeared. "Owen, you mind taking him to my car? I want a word with Mallory."

"Maybe Mallory doesn't want a word with you," she said, despite being relieved that he believed her.

"I understand why you wouldn't. I'm sorry about last night. I crossed the line. I stopped by to apologize to you and the boys and to try to explain what happened. They said you were out. They were at my place when the call came in. I hope you don't mind that they're staying with the boys."

"If they wanted to, it's fine with me."

"They told me, Doc. They told me Marsha's agreed to pay for boarding school and that they're leaving after the holidays."

She looked away, fighting back tears at the sympathy

in his voice. He, more than anyone, would know how she felt.

He took her in his arms. "I'm sorry. I wish things could be different."

He was apologizing for more than just last night and for Oliver and Brooks leaving; he was apologizing for what could never be.

Chapter Twenty-Eight

It was Christmas Eve Day, and Mallory wasn't feeling the least bit Christmassy. The boys were more excited about packing for boarding school than they were for Santa's arrival. She'd made one last desperate attempt at her Christmas plan. But they hadn't been interested in joining her to deliver gift baskets to the housebound seniors.

Beside her on the passenger seat sat one last basket. She pulled up the list on her phone. All the seniors had been checked off and accounted for. As she pulled out of the apartment complex, her car headed for Mountain Road as though of its own accord. It was inevitable that she would find herself on this road. She just hadn't expected it to be today.

Boyd had been trying to make things right since the night he'd shot Gabe. She'd thought she'd forgiven him but at Winter Solstice, as she sat in front of the fire writing the list of everything she wanted to let go of, she realized she hadn't.

It shouldn't have come as a surprise. Not after all those years of feeling unloved and unwanted. It didn't help that Oliver and Brooks had chosen boarding school over her. It served to magnify those feelings. And then there was Gabe. But she didn't blame him for not fighting for her. He had another more important battle to win.

Her car bumped along the rutted road, causing her to second-guess herself at nearly every turn. And then the memories came, and she couldn't turn back if she wanted to.

Ten minutes later, she found herself pulling in beside her father's truck. The cabin looked the same as she remembered. She sat in the car, watching the tendrils of wood smoke rise up to the purple sky. The setting sun was almost invisible as it slid behind a blue mountain shrouded in clouds. She didn't have time to waste. She'd promised Teddy that she and the boys would be at church. Teddy was a shepherd in tonight's nativity play. Yesterday she'd helped him with his costume.

As she got out of the car, she spotted the rusted pink swing set. She had a distant memory of her father setting it up on her sixth birthday. She left the basket on the front porch and went to sit on the swing. She didn't know how long she'd sat there or how long her father had been watching her.

"I've got the tea on. You wanna cup?" he asked, leaning against the porch rail.

She nodded. "Yes, please. It's for you," she said when he looked down at the basket.

He smiled. "Thank you." He was still a handsome man with his bright blue eyes and dark hair. He only

had a touch of gray at his temples. "I have something
for you and the boys. I was going to give it to you after
the service."

"I have your present at the house. I thought you'd join
us for Christmas dinner. I'd like you to come," she said
when he hesitated. "Owen is welcome to come too."

"I think he has other plans. But I'll be there, thank you."

"It looks the same as I remember," she said as she
followed him inside.

"Hasn't changed much. Your room's the same; so is
your mother's. You can have a look around if you want.
It's still your home."

She'd forgotten he and her mother hadn't shared a
room. Her mother had needed a special bed. She remembered him taking on two more jobs to be able to pay for
it. He'd been a hard worker. She remembered that too.

She stood in the threshold of her mother's room, and
the memories flooded back.

"I should probably donate the bed. Her wheelchair
too. I'm sure someone could use them," her father said
from behind her.

"If you'd like, I could look into it for you."

He nodded and then walked into her mother's room.
He went to the window and stared outside. Her mother
had the best view. He'd made sure that she did.

His shoulders bowed. "I killed her. That's why I didn't
fight Owen when he took you away. I kept waiting for
him to figure it out and arrest me. Then I started drinking
to dull the guilt and the pain." He turned to look at her,
his face stricken. "Even if I'd known that Owen had told
them I was coming and that you stayed in foster care

instead of being adopted, I wouldn't have come for you. You were better off without me. You deserved so much more than I could give you. I left you there because I loved you, not because I didn't." He turned back to look out the window.

She slowly lowered herself onto the rocking chair in the corner. She used to sit on it and read to her mother for hours. She'd liked romance novels too.

"You couldn't have killed her. You wouldn't have. You loved her." The only memories she'd had of him were of a good father and a good husband. It was what made it so hard to understand how he could just let her go.

"She begged me. She was in constant pain. She didn't want to live anymore." He turned to look at her, his blue eyes burning bright. "She said if I didn't do it, she'd get you to. I couldn't let her do that to you."

Mallory stood up and went to the dresser, picking up a photo of her parents on their wedding day. So young, so beautiful, so hopeful. "How did you do it?"

"It took awhile. I stockpiled her pain medication. Not so much that the doctor noticed. Then I mixed her up a cocktail and left it on her nightstand. I didn't give it to her. I couldn't. I kept praying she'd change her mind."

"You were there though. You held her until she died. I remember. I remember coming home. Owen was here, and so were the paramedics."

"I waited until she was gone to call them."

"I did the same."

He frowned. "What do you mean?"

She told him about Harry. "I wish I had done for him what you'd done for Mom, but I couldn't. He asked."

"I'm glad you didn't. No one should put someone they love in that position. I understand why they do though. We wouldn't let an animal suffer."

She went to stand beside him at the window. "Thank you for helping her, and thank you for protecting me. Back then, I would've done whatever she asked. I don't know if I would've been able to live with myself after."

"You were my world. I would've done anything to protect you."

"I know you thought you were protecting me when you let me go. I have a better understanding of why you did now. I...I just..."

The gates she'd kept closed on all her emotions for all those years opened. Her father took her in his arms and rocked her as she cried. He was crying too. The room was dark by the time they stopped.

"Come on, let's get you that cup of tea. Then I'll drive you down the mountain myself. It's starting to snow, and the winds are picking up." He guided her into the kitchen and pulled out a chair for her. He handed her a piece of paper towel to wipe her eyes and blow her nose.

"I'll need to wear sunglasses to church," she said.

He smiled, and then, changing to what he probably thought was a happier subject, he asked about the boys and what they wanted for Christmas.

"To leave me, and they got their wish." She told him about Marsha paying for Oliver and Brooks to go back to boarding school.

"Owen and Teddy mentioned that you were looking for a way to make the boys want to stay. So I'm surprised you're letting them go."

"I had a Christmas plan." She told him about her plan and how she'd come up with it.

He smiled. "Do you remember what your mother used to say about Christmas? Jesus is the reason for the season."

"That's what Teddy said."

"He's a smart little boy." He handed her a cup of tea. "And your friend Abby is a smart woman. Jesus is the reason for the season, and Jesus is love. Love is always the answer, honey. Have you told Brooks and Oliver that you love them? Have you told them that's why you don't want them to leave?"

"I...No, I never have. I told them I wanted them to stay with me, but I never told them I loved them. I'm not sure I realized I did until now."

"Maybe that's something they need to hear."

"Maybe it is. Thank you, Dad." She smiled, feeling hopeful for the first time in days.

"And while you're at it, you might want to tell Gabe you're in love with him too." Her father stood up and went to the counter. Then he returned with a box.

"I can't tell Gabe how I feel about him." She told him about Gabe's upcoming battle with Diane.

"Did you forget I was there that day? Seems to me you're good at standing up for the people that you love. But when it comes to fighting for what you want, you back down. You deserve to be happy. You were a special little girl, and you've turned into a special woman. You're even more beautiful on the inside than you are on the outside. You always were."

He reached for her hand. "I love you, Mallory. Always have and always will, and I'll spend the rest of my life making it up to you. I hope one day you'll be able to forgive me."

"I forgive you, and I love you too."

He gave her a watery smile and wiped at his eyes. Then he opened the box. "The night the boys broke the ornament, I shooed Gabe off to take care of his sons and me and Owen swept up all the broken pieces. I put it together as best as I could."

She stared at the ornament, reaching out to stroke it. "This must've taken days."

"Pretty much. But it was worth it just to see your face." He smiled. "I thought maybe Oliver and Brooks would like to give it to Gabe and his boys."

"It should be from you too."

"If that's what you want." Outside the wind howled, rattling the shutters, and he said, "I'd better get you home before we're snowed in."

"You should stay with us tonight. I have room."

"I'd like that. I'll just go pack a bag."

As they drove down the mountain, they sang along with the carols playing on the radio, and Mallory was filled with the spirit of Christmas. She also had a plan. Her father was right. It was time for her to fight for what she wanted. And along with wanting Oliver and Brooks to stay with her in Highland Falls, she wanted a Maitland and Buchanan Christmas.

"What on earth is going on?" she said as they pulled onto Reindeer Road. Emergency vehicles lined the side of the road, their flashing lights illuminating the street and the stricken faces of Gabe, his in-laws, the twins, and Oliver and Brooks.

Chapter Twenty-Nine

Her heart in her throat, Mallory jumped from the car and ran to where Gabe stood speaking into his radio. "What's wrong? Where's Teddy?"

Gabe handed her a piece of paper. "He's gone to find Santa."

"I don't understand. What—"

"It's our fault, Mal," Oliver said, his face pale and tear-stained. "Me and Brooks were babysitting. We should've kept a closer eye on him. We thought he was playing in his room."

Gabe put a hand on Oliver's shoulder. "The important thing is you did the right thing as soon as you realized he was gone, son. You all did," he said, then explained to her that the four boys had split up and searched the house and the neighborhood before calling Gabe.

"It didn't help that it started snowing, and with the winds, we can't follow his tracks. Hunter's coordinating with search-and-rescue, and he's on his way with Wolf. He asked us to wait until he gets here."

"Can't we go talk to the neighbors? Or search Main Street? Granny MacLeod had Santa visiting her store this afternoon. Maybe he went there. We have to do something, Gabe. We can't just stand here."

"Trust me, I know how you feel."

"I'm so sorry." She hugged him. Feeling self-conscious with his in-laws looking on, she stepped back. "Of course you do."

"We put out an Amber Alert right away, half of my officers are doing door-to-door canvassing, and the other half are spread out downtown. Abby's got social media covered." He pulled her close and stroked her hair. "We'll find him, Doc."

Standing huddled with her husband, Diane turned, trembling with rage. She stabbed a gloved finger at Mallory. "If something happens to him, it's your fault. You filled his head with Santa Claus and wishes coming true. I warned you, Gabriel. I warned you that she was no good for you and the boys, and I was—"

Noting Oliver and Brooks balling their hands into fists at their sides, Mallory moved between them, taking their hands in hers. "It's okay. Everyone's upset and saying things they don't mean."

"Enough," Gabe said to his mother-in-law, his voice icy cold. Even though he sounded calm, it was obvious he was fighting to keep his anger under control. "You don't get to speak about Mallory—"

"She is so good for us. She's better for us than you," Dylan yelled at his grandmother. "She doesn't get mad at us or make us sad. You're the reason Teddy went to find Santa. It's all your fault. He opened the letter your lawyer sent our dad." Dylan flung his arms around his father, sobbing. "I don't want to live with her, Dad. I won't go."

"Me neither. I hate you. I hate you!" Cody yelled at his grandmother.

"Okay, okay, calm down. No one is going anywhere." Gabe gathered his sobbing sons in his arms.

"Don't you see what you're doing to them, Diane? Stop this. You can end this right now," Mallory implored.

"Why? So you can swoop in and take my daughter's place? I don't think so."

"Karl, please. Look at what this is doing to your grandsons," Mallory begged the older man.

He lifted a hand as though imploring her to understand.

She shook her head, disgusted. "You won't win. You won't win custody, and you'll have alienated Gabe and your grandsons."

"I have money and influence. You out of anyone should know how that turns out. I will—" Diane began.

"Lose," said a familiar voice from behind Mallory. "Surprised to see me?" Marsha asked Mallory as she moved to stand beside Brooks. "Owen invited me to spend Christmas."

"So did I," Mallory reminded her.

"We're planning to join you for dinner. So, have you told the boys? Your father called Owen, and he told me the news," Marsha said at Mallory's blank look. "In case you're wondering, it's the outcome I'd been hoping for all along. But I suggest you tell the boys before I say what I have to to Diane."

"I don't think this is the time—"

"It's the perfect time. Would you like me to do it for you?" she offered.

"What's Marsha talking about?" Oliver asked.

"I don't want you and Brooks to go away to school. I love you. I love you both, and I want us to be a family. I want us to put down roots here, in Highland Falls."

The twins pulled away from their father and wiped their eyes. "We don't want you to go either. Neither does Teddy. He wants us to be a family. That's why he went to find Santa. He thought Owen forgot to tell him his Christmas wish because everything was messed up. Grandma was trying to take us away, you guys were leaving, and Dad and Mallory are mad at each other."

Mallory met Gabe's gaze. "I'm not mad at your dad. I love him. I love him very much, and I want us to be a family too."

Gabe blinked, then cocked his head. "Are you proposing to me?"

"I guess I am. But there's a very important member of your family who is missing, so I think I better wait until we find him."

"Are you guys staying?" Dylan asked Brooks and Oliver while Gabe continued to stare at her.

"Yeah, we can't be a family without us, now can we?" Oliver grinned.

Cody shared a look with Dylan and nodded. "Then that must mean Teddy delivered his wish to Santa, because everything's coming true."

"Just a minute now. We have to make one more part of Teddy's wish come true," Marsha said, and stepped forward. "Diane, if you could stop crying over your grandchildren getting a family for Christmas, I'd like to give you a word of advice."

The other woman lifted her head from her husband's chest. "And what would that be, Marsha?"

"I'd suggest, instead of fighting a battle you can't possibly win, you should try to rebuild a relationship with your daughter's family. Lauren was a lovely woman, and I'm sure that's what she'd want. You know it's true, Karl. So perhaps it's time for you to grow a pair and rein your wife in."

"What did I tell you, Boyd? She's a corker." Owen chuckled from somewhere behind them.

"How dare you?" Diane snapped.

"How dare you do this to these children, and at Christmas, no less? This is your last chance to do the right thing, Diane. If you don't, I will have no choice but to use my considerable wealth and influence to ruin you." She smiled at Oliver and Brooks. "Your new brothers can consider it a gift from you to them. Now that you've decided to remain in Highland Falls, I'll give the small fortune I would be sending to the boarding school to Chief Buchanan to fund his fight for his family. A fight he will ultimately win." She looked around. "Are we allowed to search for Teddy now? It seems to me the whole town has come out."

They all turned. The road was filled with people, young and old, carrying flashlights and lanterns. "Wow," Dylan breathed.

Gabe looked even more amazed than his son. Mallory reached for Gabe's hand and gave it a gentle squeeze. "One of the benefits of living in a small town is that, while they might drive you crazy at times, they'll always be there for you when you need them."

"I'm beginning to see that, Doc." He drew her close and kissed the top of her head. "You and I have a few things we need to talk about, but right now, it's time to find our boy."

As though he sensed she was unsure where she stood, he kissed her again. "Don't ever doubt that I love you. I've loved you from the moment I first saw you, and that hasn't changed the more time I spend with you. If anything, I love you more." He gave her hand a light tug. "Come on. Hunter's coordinating search parties. He wants to go in first, though, with Wolf."

* * *

They'd been searching the woods for more than an hour, and there was still no sign of Teddy. Balls of light bounced through the forest, voices calling out his name echoing in the cold, dark night, and the snow crunching underfoot. It began snowing harder, making it more difficult to see, making it harder, she imagined, for Wolf to pick up Teddy's scent.

She swallowed a sob, her throat tight from keeping her emotions in check. She had to believe they'd find him. She thought of him in church on Sunday, the final Sunday of Advent, spelling *love*, his face filled with hope as he looked from her to his father. And every day that followed stole a little bit more of his hope.

She brushed a tear from her cheek and clung to her hope and faith as hard as Teddy had. Gabe was talking into his radio, checking in. "Wolf just found his backpack." Hunter's voice came over the radio. Gabe reached for her hand. "What about Teddy? Any sign of him?"

They could barely make out Hunter's *no* over the crackling sound.

Gabe squeezed her hand as he continued walking. "We'll find him."

"I know we..." She trailed off. "Gabe, do you hear that?"

He stopped. "Hear what?"

"A woman. It sounds like she's singing."

"It's just someone calling Teddy's name."

"No. No it's not. Gabe, she's singing 'Danny Boy.'" Mallory turned in circles, trying to figure out where it was coming from. "Tell everyone to stop calling Teddy's name."

He looked skeptical but did as she asked.

"There." She pointed to a place several yards back and to their right. It was no longer a woman singing that drew her attention; it was an amber light.

"Doc, I don't see anything."

As Mallory ran toward the light, there was no doubt in her mind that Teddy was there. Just as there was absolutely no doubt in her mind who'd led her to him.

But as she approached the spot where she could've sworn the light had been, she didn't see him and the disappointment nearly brought her to her knees. "I thought," she began, pushing the words past her tear-clogged throat.

"There!" Gabe shot past her, running toward a

towering evergreen. Tucked underneath, like the most precious of presents, was Teddy.

* * *

"I need to go home. It's Christmas Eve, and Santa's going to be here soon," Teddy said to the doctor the moment she walked into the room. He lay propped on his pillows in the hospital bed, looking a little pale but otherwise healthy.

"I thought you told me all your Christmas wishes came true," the doctor said as she sat at the edge of his bed with his CT scan in her hand. Mallory leaned to her right to get a look. The doctor handed it to her with a smile. "You really should think about my offer. You could continue your residency here. We'd love to have you."

"I'll drop by after the holidays, and we can talk about it then. And unless I've forgotten how to read a scan, I think somebody is good to go."

"He is, especially because he has a doctor at home." She patted Teddy's leg. "You're a very lucky little boy. I'm still shocked he didn't have hypothermia given the length of time he was out there," she said to Mallory.

"My mom kept me warm," Teddy said matter-of-factly. The boys and Gabe didn't react. Teddy had been talking about Lauren since he woke up. "My first mom. Mallory's going to be my second mom. She proposed to my dad, and he said yes. Do you want to come to the wedding?"

"Of course." The doctor laughed. "I wouldn't miss

it." There was a light knock on the door, and she looked around the room. "Mr. and Mrs. Rollins have been waiting for a while. Can I let them in now?"

Gabe, the twins, Oliver, and Brooks responded with a definite "No." While Mallory and Teddy said, "Yes."

"It's Christmas Eve," Mallory added, giving the doctor a nod.

"It's okay, Dad. I have something I need to tell Grandma and Grandpa. It'll make my last wish come true."

Mallory had a feeling she knew what he was up to.

And five minutes later, while Gabe and the four boys leaned against the stark white wall with their arms crossed, Teddy said, "Yep, that's what she looked like." He pointed at the woman in the picture on Diane's phone. "Only her hair was shorter, and she had on a red lace dress with long sleeves."

They hadn't heard this before, and Gabe stared at his son.

"What is it?" Mallory whispered.

"Lauren was buried in a red lace dress with long sleeves," he whispered back. "There's no way Teddy would know that."

Mallory smiled. She'd known all along that Lauren had been looking out for her son tonight, and now they had proof.

"My mom gave me a message for you," Teddy said. "She wants you to know she's happy. She's having a good time in heaven, but lately, not so much. You're making her sad, Grandma. She wants you to stop trying to steal us from our dad. And she really, really likes

Mallory. She said Mallory's her Christmas present to us." He grinned at Mallory, and she knew he was making it up.

She looked at Gabe, who was shaking his head. Then he leaned in to whisper in her ear. "You sure you're up for this? He's only six—think what he'll be like at sixteen."

"We'll have to keep him busy. Very, very busy."

In the end, Teddy was right. He'd made his last Christmas wish come true, with a little help from his mother. Diane apologized to Gabe and the boys and left the room sobbing.

"I'm sorry. I shouldn't have let it go this far. Marsha was right." Karl looked at his grandsons. "I'm going to get your grandma some help, boys. I should've done it long before now. What she did was wrong, just as much as me standing by and doing nothing was wrong, but we love you boys, and we always will."

Gabe turned to Teddy as soon as Karl left the room. "So, buddy, any of that true?"

"Mom didn't talk to me. She just smiled." He touched his forehead. "I think she kissed me too. But I could tell she was happy. She wouldn't want Grandma to break up her family, and I know she'd pick Mallory for your other wife and our other mother because she led Mallory to me. That was her sign."

"Like her stamp of approval?" Gabe asked.

"Yep. Now can we go home? I'm starved."

He wasn't the only one. All five boys' stomachs were growling by the time they finally got them all loaded in the SUV twenty minutes later. As they came out the other side of the covered bridge, Gabe said, "You have got to be kidding me" at the sight that greeted them.

Under the white lights that lit up the canopy of tree branches, they watched as a line of deer walked along the side of the road. They turned off onto Reindeer Road and then walked up Mallory's driveway to head into the woods.

Chapter Thirty

Since Teddy had been positive that the reindeer congregating in the woods behind the house was a sign that Santa had already come, Christmas came early to the house on Reindeer Road with a little help from Owen, Boyd, and Marsha. Which meant that they didn't have to get up at the butt-crack of dawn on Christmas morning.

Teddy stood at the threshold of Gabe's bedroom staring longingly at Mallory. Gabe patted his butt to get him out of the way and then quietly closed the door. "We'll let her sleep another hour, honey. Why don't you go help the boys set up the racetrack in the basement?"

"No. We got too much to do. Everyone's coming for Christmas dinner, and we've gotta plan our proposal before they get here. It has to be really special, Dad."

"Mallory proposed to me last night."

He rolled his eyes. "That doesn't count. I wasn't there, and I want to propose to her too. Should we propose to Oliver and Brooks or would they think it's weird?"

Gabe worked to hold back a laugh. "Maybe you could make them a card."

"Good idea."

"Thanks. Anything else?"

Teddy's eyes went wide, and he looked like he might cry. "A ring. You need a ring, and all the stores are closed."

He crouched in front of him. "I got her a ring, buddy. Last night when you were having the scan, I called up the jewelry store. They brought some for me to look at." Like Mallory said, there were perks to living in a small town. He'd discovered the most important ones yesterday. The town had been there for him and his family, and he'd never forget it.

"Did Mallory see?"

"Nope, we were sneaky. You would've been proud of me. We met in the cafeteria behind a potted plant."

Teddy gave Gabe a high five. "Okay, now what about a present?"

"You saw what I bought her last night."

"Yeah, the kissing books, the sweater, and chocolates were all nice but not special enough. You're not very romantic, Dad."

He grinned. His son was in for a surprise. "What would you suggest?"

"Hmm, how about a dog?"

"Okay, that sounds more like a present for you guys than one for Mallory."

"We'll get her a girl dog. A little one like Abby has. She can dress it up. She needs a girl, Dad. It's six against one."

"I see. So we're doing this to even the odds." He picked up his phone. "Have you ever heard the saying *Great minds think alike*?"

"No. Why?"

"Because this little one is on her way over to us right now." He showed him a picture of a white ball of fur he'd bought from none other than Dot McFee.

Dot had dropped by the station on the twenty-second, the same day Gabe had finally taken Ruby's advice and hired Dot's daughter-in-law, Dirk's mother. Dot had suggested the dog would be a good way to make amends to Mallory. Somehow, she'd heard what had happened the night of Teddy's birthday. It felt a bit like kismet because, after seeing Mallory at the standing stones the night before, Gabe knew he had to keep her in his life no matter what the risk.

Although it was possible that the dog had been Dot's way of making amends to Mallory. The older woman explained to Gabe why she'd reacted the way that she had with Mallory. Her own son, Dirk's father, had been abusing her grandsons and her daughter-in-law. Dot hadn't known until Dirk had ended up in the hospital with a broken arm.

It also went a way toward explaining why Dirk had become a bully. Gabe hoped to use the knowledge to find a solution to Oliver's problem with Dirk. Oliver was a good kid, kind and empathetic. Gabe figured it would help him to know Dirk's history.

"Hey, where are you going?" Gabe asked when Teddy took off like a shot.

"To tell the boys," he said, then yelled all four of

their names at the top of his lungs. So much for Mallory getting to sleep in, Gabe thought, at the same time the doorbell rang. He went to answer the door but the five boys bolted past him, nearly spinning him around in their wake.

They answered the door. The five of them were staring at whoever was on the other side with their mouths hanging open. Gabe realized why when he approached the door. "Hey, Dot. Dirk. As you can see, the boys are pretty excited about Mallory's surprise."

Dirk handed Gabe the dog crate with the puppy inside. "We kept the other puppies, and we have her mom. You can bring her over to visit if you want."

"Sure. Thanks," Oliver said, then smiled. "You can bring the puppies and her mom here, too, if you want. We got a new racetrack."

Dirk nodded. "Cool."

Dot smiled and chucked Teddy under the chin. "Good to see you're all right. No more sneaking off, you hear? Just about gave everyone in town a heart attack." She offered Gabe a brown paper bag. "Know how much you all like my pancakes."

"Wow!" Teddy beamed. "Thank you. They're my favorite."

"Welcome. You all have a merry Christmas and enjoy the pup."

"Wait!" Teddy said, and ran into the living room. A few minutes later, he ran back with a Christmas bag that looked suspiciously like the one Gabe had given Mallory. He leaned over to peek inside. Sure enough, it was. Along with the expensive box of chocolates he'd given her, there were also treats that Santa had left for all five boys.

"Merry Christmas!" Teddy said, and handed Dot the bag. "There's some stuff for you and your brother," he told Dirk.

They'd just gotten the front door closed when Gabe's bedroom door started to open. "No," Teddy cried, running to pull it shut. "You can't come out. Go back to bed."

Gabe thought of offering to keep Mallory company, but knowing his youngest, that wouldn't be allowed until he'd—they'd—proposed.

Teddy explained the morning's agenda to the boys. The proposal now included breakfast in bed for Mallory, with Dot's pancakes as the main course. Hot chocolate with a cinnamon stir stick, oranges, and toast were also on the menu. Teddy wasn't impressed that Gabe hadn't thought to get flowers and reluctantly agreed that a poinsettia plant would do.

"Can I come out now?" Mallory called from behind the closed door.

"No!" the boys yelled back, mostly because they were stressed. They were trying to make bows and put them in the puppy's hair, and she wasn't cooperating.

"What's that? It sounds like a dog."

"It's not a dog. It's me," Teddy said, and started barking. The puppy barked back at him, and the boys rolled on the floor laughing.

"It doesn't seem fair that you guys are having all the fun, and I'm in here all alone."

"Buddy, trust me, nothing is ever going to be perfect in

this family so you might as well get used to it. I promise, Mallory will love our proposal just the way it is."

"Okay, but we need to put the dog in a box and wrap it," Teddy said.

"How about we put her in her crate and wrap that up instead?" While the boys took care of that, Gabe took care of Mallory's breakfast. "Are we all set?" he asked as he placed the mug of hot chocolate on the tray.

"Yep," the five boys agreed, and Brooks held up the wrapped crate.

"You got the song ready to go?" Gabe asked Oliver.

Oliver nodded and held up his phone. "Yeah, but do we really have to sing?"

"I think she'd like it, but it's up to you guys," he said as he reached his bedroom door.

The twins and Oliver sighed, and Brooks and Teddy grinned. It had been their suggestion. As Mariah Carey's "All I Want for Christmas Is You" began to play, Gabe opened the door and the five boys went in ahead of him, singing along. Only they changed *I* to *we*.

"I thought you said she'd love it," Teddy said to Gabe when they ended their song by holding up a sign asking Mallory to be their mom.

"She does love it, silly. These are happy tears. The happiest of tears," Mallory said, wiping her eyes. "You've made my Christmas wish come true. All five of you. And if you haven't already guessed, my answer is yes. I'd be honored to be your mom."

"How about my wife?" Gabe asked as he put the breakfast tray on the dresser and then moved to the side of the bed.

"You already know the answer to that question." She smiled up at him, looking surprised when he went down on one knee and took her hand in his.

"Yeah, but our boys weren't satisfied with that." He held up the rose-gold diamond engagement ring. "They wanted you to have a sign of my love and commitment to you, and to them." He slid the ring onto her finger and held her tear-filled gaze. "I didn't think Christmas would ever be special again or that I'd find someone I wanted to spend the rest of my life with again until you came along and managed to do both. I love you, more than you probably know, Doc. But I plan to spend the next sixty years showing you just how much."

"You couldn't possibly love me more than I love you, Gabe. But I'm happy to have you show me every day for the next sixty years, and I'll do the same." She held up her hand to admire her ring. Then she leaned over to kiss him. "It's the most beautiful ring I've ever seen. Thank you."

"Merry Christmas, Mrs. Soon-to-Be Buchanan."

"Merry Christmas, my soon-to-be—" The dog started to bark, and Mallory turned to look at Teddy. "That's not you."

The five boys grinned and placed the wrapped crate on the bed. "It's from Dad and us," Teddy said as he began opening the present for her.

"It's okay." Mallory laughed when the twins yelled at him to stop. "Oh, look at you. Aren't you the sweetest," she said when the dog came into view.

"Do you like her?" Teddy asked when Gabe opened

the crate to put the puppy in Mallory's arms. "Dad got you a girl dog cuz we're all boys."

"That was an excellent idea, and I love her. Thank you," she said and kissed Gabe.

"Hey, what about us?" Teddy said.

Mallory laughed and put the dog down to pull Teddy into her arms, showering his face with kisses. "You four get over here too." The twins, Oliver, and Brooks pretended they were too cool for kisses, but it was obvious from the smiles and laughter that they weren't too grown-up for motherly affection.

The dog jumped on the boys, nipping at them and barking.

"What are you going to call her?" Dylan asked.

"I don't know. What do you guys think?" Mallory asked, reaching over to pick up the puppy.

"Holly, Mistletoe, Fluffy, Snowflake!" The five boys called out the names almost at the same time.

"What do you think, puppy?" she asked, holding her up. Then she looked at Gabe. "The puppy isn't a girl—she's a he."

"No way," Gabe said, then looked. "Oh, wow, you're really outnumbered now, babe." He laughed as the boys voted to name the puppy Snowball.

Teddy patted Mallory. "It's okay, you're not too old to have babies. You can ask the stork to bring you a girl. Maybe it would bring you three or four. I think five girls would be too many, don't you?"

Teddy didn't give them a chance to answer, which, in the end, Gabe figured was a good thing. He didn't relish the idea of a birds-and-bees conversation right before their company arrived.

"Dad, can you sit behind Mallory on the bed and snuggle her?"

"Happy to." He grinned, moving in behind her and wrapping his arms around her. He nuzzled her neck to gagging sounds from the twins, Oliver, and Brooks.

Teddy interrupted his brothers, directing them to join Mallory and Gabe on the bed for a group hug.

"Okay now. Mallory, show your ring. Good." Teddy said when she did as he asked.

Then he raised the phone and held up his fingers, silently counting down just like Abby did.

"This is what love looks like on Reindeer Road," Teddy said, zooming in on them before turning the phone to face the screen. "Merry Christmas from me, Teddy Buchanan, and my family."

About the Author

Debbie Mason is the *USA Today* bestselling author of the Highland Falls, Harmony Harbor, and Christmas, Colorado series. The first book in her Christmas, Colorado series, *The Trouble with Christmas*, was the inspiration for the Hallmark movie *Welcome to Christmas*. Her books have been praised by *RT Book Reviews* for their "likable characters, clever dialogue, and juicy plots." When Debbie isn't writing, she enjoys spending time with her family in Ottawa, Canada.

You can learn more at:
AuthorDebbieMason.com
Twitter @AuthorDebMason
Facebook.com/DebbieMasonBooks
Instagram @AuthorDebMason

Fall in love with these charming contemporary romances!

A VERY MERRY MATCH
by Melinda Curtis

Mary Margaret Sneed usually spends her holiday baking and caroling with her students. But this year, she's swapped shortbread and sleigh bells to take a second job—one she can never admit to when the town mayor starts courting her. Only the town's meddling matchmakers have determined there's nothing a little mistletoe can't fix...and if the Widows Club has its way, Mary Margaret and the mayor may just get the best Christmas gift of all this year. Includes a bonus story by Hope Ramsay!

THE TWELVE DOGS OF CHRISTMAS
by Lizzie Shane

Ally Gilmore has only four weeks to find homes for a dozen dogs in her family's rescue shelter. But when she confronts the Scroogey councilman who pulled their funding, Ally finds he's far more reasonable—and handsome—than she ever expected...especially after he promises to help her. As they spend more time together, the Pine Hollow gossip mill is convinced that the Grinch might show Ally that Pine Hollow is her home for more than just the holidays.

Find more great reads on Instagram with
@ReadForeverPub

CHRISTMAS ON REINDEER ROAD
by Debbie Mason

After his wife died, Gabriel Buchanan left his job as a New York City homicide detective to focus on raising his three sons. But back in Highland Falls, he doesn't have to go looking for trouble. It finds him—in the form of Mallory Maitland, a beautiful neighbor struggling to raise her misbehaving stepsons. When they must work together to give their boys the Christmas their hearts desire, they may find that the best gift they can give them is a family together.

SEASON OF JOY
by Annie Rains

For single father Granger Fields, Christmas is his busiest—and most profitable—time of the year. But when a fire devastates his tree farm, Granger convinces free spirit Joy Benson to care for his daughters while he focuses on saving his business. Soon Joy's festive ideas and merrymaking convince Granger he needs a business partner. As crowds return to the farm, life with Joy begins to feel like home. Can Granger convince Joy that this is where she belongs? Includes a bonus story by Melinda Curtis!

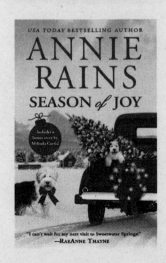

HER AMISH WEDDING QUILT
by Winnie Griggs

When the man she thought she would wed chooses another woman, Greta Eicher pours her energy into crafting beautiful quilts at her shop and helping widower Noah Stoll care for his adorable young children. But when her feelings for Noah grow into something even deeper, will she be able to convince him to have enough faith to give love another chance?

THE AMISH MIDWIFE'S HOPE
by Barbara Cameron

Widow Rebecca Zook adores her work, but the young midwife secretly wonders if she'll ever find love again or have a family of her own. When she meets handsome newcomer Samuel Miller, her connection with the single father is immediate—Rebecca even bonds with his sweet little girl. It feels like a perfect match, and Rebecca is ready to embrace the future...if only Samuel can open his heart once more.

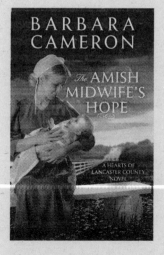

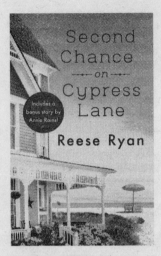

SECOND CHANCE ON CYPRESS LANE
by Reese Ryan

Rising-star reporter Dakota Jones is used to breaking the news, not making it. When a scandal costs her her job, there's only one place she can go to regroup. But her small South Carolina hometown comes with a major catch: Dexter Roberts. The first man to break Dakota's heart is suddenly back in her life. She won't give him another chance to hurt her, but she can't help wondering what might have been. Includes a bonus story by Annie Rains!

FOREVER WITH YOU
by Barb Curtis

Leyna Milan knows family legacies come with strings attached, but she's determined to prove that she can run her family's restaurant. Of course, Leyna never expected that honoring her grandfather's wishes meant opening a second location on her ex's winery—or having to ignore Jay's sexy grin and guard the heart he shattered years before. But as they work closely together, she begins to discover that maybe first love deserves a second chance...